AMBROSJA'S THORNS:
ASHBOUND

written and illustrated by Alisbeth Vale

CONTENT WARNING

This book contains intense themes, including graphic violence, gore, profanity, and explicit sexual content (all consensual). It also depicts death—human and animal alike—presented as part of the narrative, not for shock value.

979-8-9947821-0-1

Library of Congress Control Number:

2026909012

Table of Contents

THE MAP OF VAESTORIA

GREYMIRE
ALARION
MARROWIND
Bleakrun
Driftmere
Briarhold
Shadcreed
Greymire
Mirewatch
Nettlewharf
Toad's Hollow
Mossmere
Larkfen
Mire's End
Thornmere
Gloamhollow
Selvaran
Fenrest
Harthwillow
Ornaverre
Duskrend
Alarion
Goldrest
Thornbridge
Gildmere
Rosevale
Cresthollow
Emberloch
Dovewatch
Caelthorne
Stillmere
Tallowmere
Veilmere
Graysward
Dustreach
Rowanthorpe
Kestrel Ford
arkvale
Marrowind
Redharrow
Dunrow
Hayholt
aymoor
w

PROLOGUE

THE VOW

The raven stared back at her, wings outstretched, carved into the bow like it was watching her leave. She pressed her palm to the wood, breath misting in the cold air. A sharp gust whipped her ash-blonde hair as she crouched, piling snow and brush until the little boat vanished beneath it. The pine groaned under her touch, reluctant to be buried.

The Elder, joined by a few at his side, watched the pale-haired woman shove the last bit of snow onto her little boat. When she stood up from her crouch, the Elder stepped forward.

"Empress?" His voice was warm and gentle from the years of a life long-lived. "Shall we have dinner now and discuss why you're here?"

The pale-haired woman — the Empress — turned to look at him. She dipped her head once to the older man. "Yes, that would be lovely." Her accent was thick, her R's were rougher, nothing like the calm and clean way the Elder spoke. "I appreciate your willingness to hear me before spearing me out of fear," she admitted as she took a few steps forward — but stopped as she felt something tap her side.

The Empress looked down. A little girl with chestnut-brown hair was holding a carrot up to her side.

"Would you like a bite?" She was smiling brightly, missing a tooth, cheeks rosy from the chilled air.

"Mora—" the Elder spoke gently but firmly, "did you take that from the neighbors again?"

Mora took a bite of her carrot, innocent and unashamed. "No… Not *this* one." Then she giggled, running off with her sack of carrots while her small feet moved across the snow with great effort.

The Elder looked back at the woman before him, "Forgive her, Empress, she… loves carrots. Too much."

The Empress smiled, wide and genuine. "Worry not, I love carrots, too." She approached again, tugging the white-fur cloak around her shoulders, and lifting the black skirts of her battle dress higher so she could walk through the snow.

The Elder returned her smile. He approached the woman, "I am surprised you arrived with no envoy, but I trust whatever reason brings you *here*, is a good one." The old man gestured towards the hamlet just past the trees, "Shall we, Empress?"

She nodded, still smiling. "Please, call me Ambrosja."

The hall rose like a long wooden spine, its rafters lost in the shadowed haze of smoke drifting from the central hearth. Three tables shaped the heart of the room: a broad, shorter one at the far end where the Elder held his place, a high-backed chair, carved armrests, the Empress beside him as his guest. The hearth burned between the two longer tables, a living river of orange light running down the center of the hall. Sparks drifted upward to vanish in the smoke hole cut into the high roof.

Laughter was heard around the room. Food shared and drinks served. The Empress smiled as she took in the scene; the children running around, Mora still had a carrot in her hand, but this time she was wielding it as a sword and not a snack. Ambrosja laughed softly into her cup.

"Well, Empress Ambrosja," the Elder spoke, taking Ambrosja out of her thoughts. "What do you think of Vaestoria so far? It's not like your cold country of Nordorn, but… the people here are good. They take care of each other."

Ambrosja nodded with a kind smile. She leaned in closer to the Elder, "I meant it when I said you could call me Ambrosja, you do not need to say Empress every time," she placed a hand on his shoulder and gave a reassuring squeeze. Then she leaned back in her chair. "It is… nice. Though I have only seen a portion of Vaestoria for the first time, this little portion is a nice first impression…"

The Elder nodded, his hand adjusting his beard. "Right, Ambros-

ja," he said awkwardly, as if he couldn't quite keep her title from his mind. "Well — I'm glad our little portion is the first thing you see of Vaestoria… Though…" His gaze settled sharply on her. "I cannot help but wonder what exactly you are doing here, in the hamlet of Wintersong. Your country is not friends with Vaestoria's… or any country, for that matter.

"That is not entirely true," she said with a smile, "Nordorn is allied with Mercinari."

The old man laughed at that. "Everyone is allied with Mercinari."

Ambrosja had a small smile, but her gaze was fixed on her drink. She took a deep breath, nodding slowly once. "Yes, you are right, Elder, Nordorn is — mostly — enemy to all… But…" she looked at him again, her golden eyes settled on his calming brown gaze. "The people of Wintersong were once Nordorners."

Those surrounding them quieted a bit as they heard this. Those further down the tables hadn't heard. They were too busy reveling in the evening festivities, but those closest had tensed slightly.

"And I would like you all to be Nordorners once more," Ambrosja said, keeping a steady gaze on the Elder. "I have come to bring the children of the north back home, Elder. I promise you," she leaned forward a bit, her gaze was steady, but her words sounded more urgent, "Nordorn is not what it used to be. It has not been the brute force it was known for before the Fracture. Come back with me, Elder, please. Be a part of my people once more."

The Elder was silent. A quiet concern laced in his lowered brows. Then he shook his head. "Empress — Ambrosja…" he sighed. "We are Vaestorians now. We have been since those before us ran from Nordorn. We don't even know your language or your customs! We would be fish out of water if we left."

Ambrosja reached out, her hands desperately holding onto the Elder's. "You will not, I will guide you, protect you! I can protect you! I promise!"

The old man's eyes glanced down at Ambrosja's hands. He saw how they shook — he *felt* how they shook. "I cannot do that, I cannot speak for these people. They've named me Elder because I am wise, I am steady. I am *here*." He shook his head again at her. "I am sorry, but I will not ask these people to leave."

"Elder…" Ambrosja whispered, her voice laced with desperation. "… Please… My people need to know that I am not the soft gem that they call me… They need to know that when I set out to do something, I can do it."

The Elder pulled his hand away then. "This is what it's about, child?"

his voice had gone colder now, edged with something close to disappointment. "It's not about us returning — it's about *worth*." He raised his hand, pointing his finger, his brows furrowed low, his smile gone. He looked ready to scold. To point toward the grand door of the hall and send her away. But he *really* looked at her. The stuttering of her eyes, the fear of disappointment that only the young really held in their bones. He sighed heavily. "Let me tell you something, Ambrosja, not everyone's worth is proven by what they can do. Sometimes… it is proven in how you do things. And there is nothing wrong with you walking away from us, accepting our answer, with *grace*. You tried. But we are who we are. And our home is here."

He placed his hand on her shoulder, then, returning that reassuring squeeze she had given earlier. The Elder continued to say, "Trust me, there are better ways to prove one's worth." He saw her eyes glistening. "Don't cry, girl," he smiled. "Trust me, if the people have to judge you based on how well you can convince a hamlet to join a country… They must have some very low standards. And I am *certain* you can do better."

Ambrosja released the smallest laugh at that. She wiped her eyes before any tears could fall. Then a slight *umph* left her lips as she felt a weight upon her lap. She looked down — and there sat Mora, chewing on a carrot that was once her sword.

"Hi," Mora said sweetly. "Why are you crying?"

"I am not," Ambrosja remained stoic but smiling. "It's the ash from the hearth. Got caught in my eyes."

"Well — okay," Mora said, leaning into Ambrosja now. "I like you. You're really pale, like snow. And I love snow." She looked up at the Empress, tilting her head back to meet her eyes. She whispered, like she was asking for a secret, "Are you made of snow?"

Ambrosja laughed. She leaned forward, dropping her voice to whisper back, "Promise to keep a secret?" Mora nodded very happily. "I am the *Empress* of snow!"

Mora's lips parted, shocked, surprised, and joyful. She looked to the Elder, whispering a little too loudly, "She's the Empress of snow, Grandpa!"

Ambrosja's head fell backwards at how happily the little girl spilled her secret. Her arms simply came around Mora's frame, hugging her while she laughed.

Ambrosja's hair snapped behind her as she ran; the dark powder around her eyes had smeared with sweat and tears. Mora was crying in her arms, screaming for her grandfather, her hands outstretched back towards the burning hamlet.

The Empress set Mora down, "Stay here!" her voice cracked with urgency. "Stay hidden!"

Ambrosja couldn't spare another glance. After placing the girl behind the tree, the Empress made her way back to the hamlet. Her free hands now pulled her sword out as she rushed into the middle of the burning homes. Riders upon black horses tossed torches onto everything they saw. Ambrosja spotted another child crying in the center, face red with anguish and tears streaming down. Ambrosja's heart ached, but her feet acted fast as she saw a rider approaching with a sword.

The Empress's hand reached the child, pulling him out of the way as her other hand came up to parry the attacker's swing.

"To the trees!" Ambrosja shouted to the child.

Smoke was thick. The scent of blood was thicker. Ambrosja fought and pushed. Until darkness took hold.

Ash fell onto her face—she jolted awake.

Ambrosja rose in the middle of the ruins of Wintersong, ashes clinging to her skin. A sting pulsed across her body as she stirred in the snow, breath catching in her throat. Moonlit strands of hair fanned around her. Her golden eyes blinked, slow shapes shifting from shadow into sharp, cruel clarity. Snowflakes drifted down, kissing the pale, freckled skin of her cheeks.

She groaned, the sound resonant in the still air, and forced herself upright. A wince escaped her as she felt a sharp sting across her jaw. Her fingertips touched the spot and felt the mix of drying blood and torn flesh. Ambrosja pressed harder against the wound, her other hand gripping at nothing but snow as her lips parted to release labored breaths, while her eyes glowed and the gash along her jaw began to shift. Threads of skin found each other and closed the wound.

Around her, the hamlet lay in ruin—blackened timbers, collapsed rooftops, and smoke curling upward in thin, bitter ribbons. A few fires still burned, their embers glowing weakly against the snow. Her sword lay nearby. She grasped it with trembling fingers, rising unsteadily as the armor bit into raw skin. Ash smeared across her cheek as she wiped at her face, eyes

scanning the desolation. There were bodies—some friends, some foes. But the people? Perished. The villagers—men, women, children—their bodies buried beneath snow and ash. Even little Mora, always stealing carrots from her neighbors' sills.

She dragged her boots across brittle cobblestones, uneven beneath the ash. Her shivering legs carried her toward Mora. She fell to her knees beside the little girl's fallen form, a small carrot hidden in her pocket, her hair matted with soot, her fingers cold, and not just from the snow.

Ambrosja choked on her cry, her tears fell — a droplet fell onto the little girl's cheek.

"I — I am —" she choked again. "I am so sorry!" Her trembling hands slowly closed the distance to the little girl. One hand moved to brace her small head, the other looped around the underside of her legs. She brought the girl close, crying into the matted hair.

The Empress stood then. Knees shaking. And her steps were more uneven than before. She felt as if she could collapse into the snow and never come out. A part of her wanted to.

As some of the dark plumes parted before her, she spotted someone. A sharp breath escaped her. Ambrosja winced as she began to dart forward, sore feet uneasy as she thudded through the ruins and snow. She coughed as the lingering smoke brushed past her face. She held Mora close, not once losing grip on the little girl.

Ambrosja tumbled forward as she bent her knees the best she could to reach the figure. But when the smoke parted? That person was long gone like the others. Ambrosja fell to her knees, keeping one hand on Mora's body, the other reaching over the form and turning them so she could see their face beneath the bloodied hood.

Recognition hit her fast. It was the Elder of Wintersong. The man she had first greeted when she arrived. When she promised that her home had changed, that she *could* take care of them. Ambrosja's eyes welled up with tears once more; her form was curled and hunched over the Elder while she held his granddaughter. A shaky hand reached to his eyes as she gently closed them for him.

"I am sorry…" she whispered. "I said I could protect you—all of you… Yet—I failed…"

Ambrosja gently set the Elder in place, crossing his arms over Mora, keeping the two close. The sound of ravens croaked not too far from her. She followed the sound to the center of the hamlet… And there it stood—the only thing left untouched: the statue. A woman carved in

stone, tall and unyielding. A veil over her face where only her lips could be seen, one hand gripped a spear raised to the heavens, the other held a broad shield to her chest. Her face bore no smile, no sorrow—only that steadfast look of quiet resolve. And the ravens, each one perched on a shoulder, stared at Ambrosja.

The Empress screamed—her cry rising like thunder, shattering the silence that followed the slaughter. The blood that had splattered her armor now steamed against the cold, and tears carved harsh valleys through the ash upon her face. She raised her blade high, then brought it down with a raw, breaking cry, driving it deep into the frozen earth.

When the steel met the cold and sank in… Flashes of red painted her memory. Her skull ached as her mind brought her back to what may have been hours ago, how she charged through lines of black armor and burning hands, how she fought to grab and carry every child she could to safety. How she urged every living soul she had promised to bring back home, promising to protect them from this force. Only for her vision to go black and awaken to a world that was torn and quiet.

"Let it be carved into the bones of the world — I will not rest until justice bleeds for this."

She wrenched the blade free. Her breath was wild. Her gaze was burning. One last glance at the statue and then she turned—eyes locked on the trails left behind: the mark of heavy boots, the indent of hooves, and the scorched path where the guilty fled.

And so, she gave chase.

Allies in Smoke

She did not know how long she'd walked. Only that the numbness in her toes had long since spread, and the silent ache in her muscles throbbed like old wounds reopened. But her heart, heavy and hollow within the cage of her ribs, cared little for bruises or blood; pain clung to her like a second skin. Her feet were ruined—split, bloodied, screaming with every step—but she kept moving. She had to. The steady thud of her heartbeat beat louder than reason, like war drums in her ears, pushing her forward when everything else begged her to stop.

Time had slipped somewhere behind her, and distance felt like something she no longer had a grasp on. She couldn't remember how far she'd come, or how many days had passed since she first started walking. It had all blurred together, one step bleeding into the next until everything before now felt out of reach. The dark plate dragged on her frame like guilt, its weight biting through the leather beneath as if reopening wounds that never healed. If only she could cast it off. If only guilt came off as easily as armor. But she was bound to both. With no direction left to follow, only the fading trails of ash in the air and the faint impressions of war-hooves and wheels carved into the snow like ill-portents.

And now… smoke. It kissed the inside of her freezing nose like fire-stoked iron pressed hot against a wound.

Ambrosja had snapped from her mindless and bloodied

march. She lifted her gaze. Beyond the skeletal trees and snow-laden branches, a thin trail of blackness crested the horizon. Far enough that she hadn't been seen—close enough to reach. She adjusted her armor, lips parting in a soundless cry as she felt straps dig into her frosted flesh. She hunched over, hands meeting her knees as her breathing deepened, trying her best to fight back the groans of pain that, for now, she had to silence. She stepped carefully but painfully, battered feet within boots sinking into the softest patches of snow, praying that silence could carry her forward while she ached to scream. Ambrosja moved from tree to tree, seeking to approach the source.

A clearing opened.

Three figures sat around a low fire. No tents. No mounts. Only leather packs and weapons slung at their hips. Their silhouettes were distinct in the firelight—one slender and feminine, the other two male, both broad-shouldered, though one was shorter than the other. None of them bothered to whisper.

Ambrosja inched closer; every step was measured.

The tallest man spoke first, his voice deep and rough like stone dragged over gravel. "They moved fast. I reckon they're heading for the other hamlets along the northern border."

The woman responded between bites of dried meat. Her voice was raspy, sharp. "Probably. Bastards are clearing out the places with the least resistance."

The shorter man didn't raise his head. His voice came low—unbothered, but not unsure, "We should head for Greenfield. Maybe catch a cart southwest to Stonehaven."

"Stonehaven?" The woman scoffed, kicking a patch of snow as she let out a sharp laugh. "What the fuck for? You think those pompous bastards are gonna lift a finger for the borderlands? Half the hamlets aren't even *on* Vaestoria's godsdamned map."

"Yeah, we know that, Cinder," the shorter man replied, his tone still calm but more firm now. "But we saw what they did to Wintersong."

Wintersong... she whispered it—like an ache in her throat.

Silence fell around the fire for a brief moment.

Then the tall man grunted. "Johann's right, Cinder," he said, tilting his head toward the shorter man. "We saw the aftermath. It's our duty to help however we can."

The woman clicked her tongue, arms crossing, jerky still in hand. "I still say it's fucking pointless. But if you two relics wanna march to Stonehaven, then I guess it's two against one, huh?" Her eyes cut to the tallest man.

"Ain't that right, Gunnar?"

The man crossed his arms and leaned forward slightly. "Now, lass… You know we wouldn't make you go anywhere you don't want to. And we wouldn't leave you alone, not after what we've been through. So, if you don't want to go, we don't go. Simple as that."

The woman didn't answer right away. But after a breath, she gave a small dip of her chin, reluctant but real.

Ambrosja crept forward—unaware of where her foot landed. She didn't see the patch of snow that gave way beneath her. Her boot slammed against a buried rock, and though the armor held, the jolt tore through her foot like fire. She stumbled, hands catching against the rough bark of the tree beside her, a sharp cry catching in her throat. A breath of pain, bitter and whispered, slipped past her lips.

Three heads snapped toward the sound in perfect unison. But it was the woman who moved first—fast. Her hands snapped to her bow, arrow drawn and held, ready to fire.

The tall man stood up in one fluid motion, his hand already on the axe at his hip. "Easy, Cinder," he said, voice deep but steady, eyes scanning the trees. "Right… how about we make this easy and you just step out, huh? Whoever you are."

"Slow," she added sharply. "I'd hate to send this arrow into your fucking eye 'cause you twitched wrong."

"Cinder…" The shorter man's voice was calm but careful, like someone trying to keep his hot-headed friend from starting a tavern brawl. Soft, but not uncertain.

Ambrosja exhaled, *I'm in no condition to run, I'm too tired to fight… But they know something…* She then stepped from behind the tree, raising her hands slowly but keeping them near her shoulders — not too high and not too low. Her voice carried easily—smoky, low, and unmistakably feminine, and once more, her accent was nothing like theirs. "I heard you speak of Wintersong… What do you know about it?"

She walked with caution, golden eyes darting between them, always drawn back to the string on the woman's bow. Now, up close, she saw them clearly.

The woman was younger than she sounded—mid-twenties, maybe. A burn scar crept from the center of her chest, up the side of her neck, curling around her jawline. She was lean, built for speed, with chestnut hair styled in a shaggy bob and sharp brown eyes. The taller man looked like he'd been carved out of a glacier. Easily six-foot-five, with a square, scarred and bearded face and a broad frame wrapped in thick northern furs. His bald head gleamed in the firelight, and even standing still, he looked like a man built to break siege lines. The other man was short—even when standing— but thick with muscle. His dark hair curled beneath a fur-lined hood, warm robes wrapped around his form, though it was clear he could hold his own in a fight.

The tall man's grip eased slightly on the axe, his posture shifting. Not a surrender, just a signal. "What do *you* know of Wintersong?"

"I asked first," Ambrosja replied, taking a step to the side—not to encircle, but to shift the angle. From here, the woman wouldn't be able to shoot without risking one of her own.

But the woman noticed. She mirrored the movement instantly. "Don't think you've got much of a choice, Blondie."

"Ambrosja," she spoke, scowling at the stranger. "My name is Ambrosja."

The tall man gave her a long look, then nodded. His massive hand reached out gently toward the woman. "Alright, lass. Don't think she's gonna say much if you keep aiming for her eye."

Her jaw clenched. She held the pose for a few more tense seconds— then finally lowered the bow. "Ambrosja," she repeated, testing the name. "Fancy northern name, yeah? You from Wintersong?"

Ambrosja lowered her hands, drawing a breath. "...I was there."

The shorter man tilted his head, eyes narrowing. "You were there?" He looked between his friends—a curious or uncertain look—before settling back on Ambrosja. "Are you sure about that?" he asked, voice low in possible disbelief. "We walked through Wintersong. Found only death."

Ambrosja's jaw tightened, holding back a bitter scoff, "Then you did not look hard enough."

The tall man gave a grim nod. "You'd be right. Place looked fucked. Burned straight through. It was too quiet… The only sound left was the fire still crackling." He stepped forward and gestured toward the fire. "Come, sit with us." He was already settling back onto the log. "You look tired, sore, and frozen half to hell. Bet your toes are ready to fall off."

Ambrosja didn't move at first. Her hand hovered near the hilt of her sword. Her eyes remained on the woman's, even though the bow was lowered. Just because it wasn't aimed didn't mean it couldn't be again.

The fire crackled. Snow drifted softly between them. Even the wind had gone still—as if the world waited on her decision.

Finally, she exhaled through her nose. "They might be. I haven't

checked." Her hand slid from her blade, not to unsheath, but to rest atop her hip. She nodded once. "I cannot afford to." And this time—she stepped forward. She sat down with a soft clank of metal, stretching her legs toward the fire until her boots nearly kissed the edge. "Thank you."

The woman scoffed, but sat beside the tall man and tossed a pack of jerky toward Ambrosja, who caught it without much effort. The woman eyed her. "So. You're geared for war, but you talk like royalty with a pine brush up your ass. So what are you? Some rich girl who decided to play soldier? Garrisoned at Wintersong? Or just committing to the brooding act?"

*Rich girl who decided to play soldier…*Ambrosja had twitched, barely noticeable, too exhausted to bite back. She glanced at the jerky, then up at the woman. "That is… an unfortunate comparison. But… You could say that."

The woman simply stared, unimpressed and annoyed, brows lowering while she was quiet for a moment—until finally "…You could say that…" she echoed, "…to *which fucking part?*"

The tall man smirked, clearly amused, but held back a chuckle.

She kicked snow at him. "Oi. Don't start, you overgrown snow beast." She turned back to Ambrosja. "So what, *all* of the above, Blondie?"

Ambrosja nodded as she chewed. "Sure," she said calmly. "All of the above."

The shorter man gave a slow breath, then offered a small smile. "Well…" he gestured to himself, "I'm Johann," he then moved his hand towards the woman, "that spitfire there is Cinder," then finally he gestured to the tall man, "Big guy is Gunnar."

Ambrosja's eyes met each new face. Gunnar, *He looks like a threat, not a man you want to face up close…*Then her eyes settled on Cinder, *Bow and arrow. Long legs, slender. She could chase me down, but she would shoot me first…* Then she looked at Johann last. *He's far more calm than the others, not particularly tall, but he could throw a punch judging by the size of him… Hard to read him…* Finally, she spoke once more, "Ambrosja, but you already knew that."

Johann cleared his throat, speaking again, "If you survived Wintersong, you're welcome to travel with us, Ambrosja. We're heading toward Greenfield—weather's clearer there, barely any snow left. From there, we'll take a cart south to Stonehaven. You in?"

Ambrosja's brows rose slightly. "Stonehaven?"

Johann nodded. "The closest major city—and the reigning regency over this stretch of the northwest. Best chance at finding allies. Hopefully."

"Hah," Cinder leaned back, sprawling along the log with her elbows braced behind her. "Didn't realize we *voted* on that already. These two old bas-

tards seem to think Stonehaven gives half a shit about the northern hamlets. I think they're dreaming."

"Why?" Ambrosja asked, already trying to understand the land she was on.

Cinder sat up again, elbows resting on her knees. "Because Stonehaven's filled with rich fucks more worried about getting their tea on time than sending soldiers past their walls. You know who ends up guarding the farmlands, the outer villages, the nobodies?" She paused. "It's the kids. The ones barely old enough to drink. Barely strong enough to swing a sword straight."

Ambrosja held Cinder's gaze—a flicker of understanding passing between them. She nodded. Ambrosja looked down at the jerky and took another bite. "The figureheads. Lords. Ladies. They do not care for anyone beyond the walls of Stonehaven. Because those who live beyond them… simply are not important, are they?" She added bitterly, "The only ones they value are the farmers. And even then, when a farmer dies? They just get another. It is not the people they care about—it is the land."

Cinder nodded. "Yeah. You get it."

"I do." Ambrosja glanced at the three of them. "Yes, I will join you. Besides, at the very least, we can warn Greenfield. About this force… whatever it is that tore through—" A tremble in her voice, "—through Wintersong."

"Exactly," Johann said gently, his eyes full of quiet concern. "Eventually, they'll go after something bigger."

Gunnar pulled open his pack as he spoke. "That's how you do it, if you're smart about war. Take the hamlets. Scavenge their resources. Rebuild, refuel. Then move to the villages. Then the towns. Rinse and repeat until you've got enough strength to hit the cities."

Cinder gave a humorless smirk. "Yeah, bet once they get close to a city, that's when Stonehaven'll finally shit itself."

Gunnar stood and pulled out a thick fur blanket. "That's enough talk. We've got a long road ahead. Best to sleep while we've still got firelight." He spread the blanket over the snow, then lowered himself onto it with a heavy stretch. One large hand patted the empty space beside him.

Ambrosja squinted. "…Are you calling us to bed like we are hounds?"

Gunnar barked a laugh, low and hearty. "Not like hounds. Though, Cinder *can* be a bitch."

Cinder kicked snow into his face. "Watch it, old man. I'll shoot you in the fucking ass."

Johann laid down a few feet away from Gunnar, pulling his cloak tighter. Gunnar noticed, "Heyyy, what's this? Not in the mood to cuddle?" He grinned. "You break my heart, Johann."

Johann sighed. "Gods, no. Last time I slept near you, you rolled over, hugged me like a lover, and snored in my ear. Called me Penelope. Whoever that is."

Ambrosja's lips twitched—almost a smile. Something soft stirred behind her stern expression. Like a crack in the armor. A flicker of warmth.

Gunnar grinned and looked her way. "You're a stranger, sure, but I know you understand winter. We sleep close, for heat. If that makes you uncomfortable, I get it. But you don't look great…" He gestured to the space beside him. "I don't bite. I might hug in my sleep, though."

Cinder stretched out beside them, lying between Johann and Gunnar. "He'll probably roll over and crush your ribcage," she muttered. "But don't worry—we care more about sleep than invading your personal space."

Ambrosja didn't answer right away. They were strangers. But it was true. She needed the heat. Her body ached in ways she couldn't yet inspect—not without removing armor she couldn't risk unfastening.

She stood weakly but tried her best to hide her pain. Her injuries. Her vulnerabilities. "Very well." She walked forward, then eased herself beside Gunnar, all while biting back a wince. She pressed her back against his side.

For a moment, silence blanketed the clearing.

"…If I feel *anything* poking me," she murmured, "I *will* cut it off."

Gunnar laughed loudly, hands up in mock surrender. "Fear not. Besides my axe, that's my favorite weapon."

"Ew," Cinder muttered. "You're disgusting, Gunnar."

"And yet, you still travel with me," he said, grinning widely. "Get some rest. We've got two days ahead before Greenfield."

Their eyes closed one by one. Except for Ambrosja. She lay still, her gaze drifting over the snow-speckled earth, then up to the stars. Her hand lingered close to her sword, no matter what. Her breath rose slowly and softly. Then she sank into the warmth of the furs, but not before gripping the hilt tightly as her mind fought to remember yet forget every scream she heard at Wintersong…

…And the small form of Mora.

From the journal of Guinylda Thorn
Snjorhald, 32, 997

WINTERSONG

Once the coldest hamlet in all of Vaestoria, Wintersong was a whisper beneath the snow, known for its fine furs and cured leathers. Nestled beyond the Bramble and claimed by the regency of Stonehaven, it clung to the northern western region—just beneath the mountains of Nordorn, where snowflakes drifted like fallen memories.

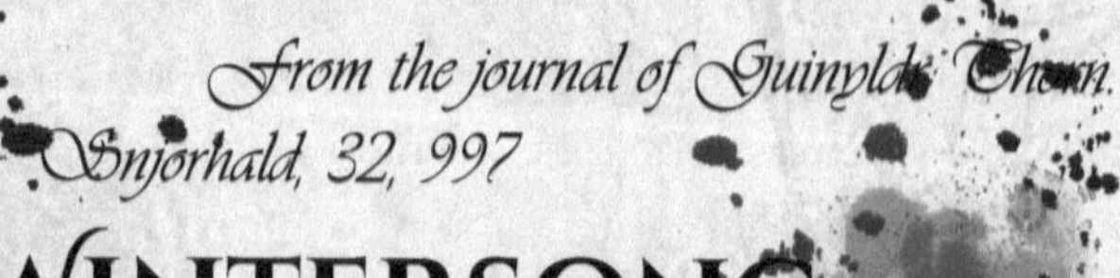

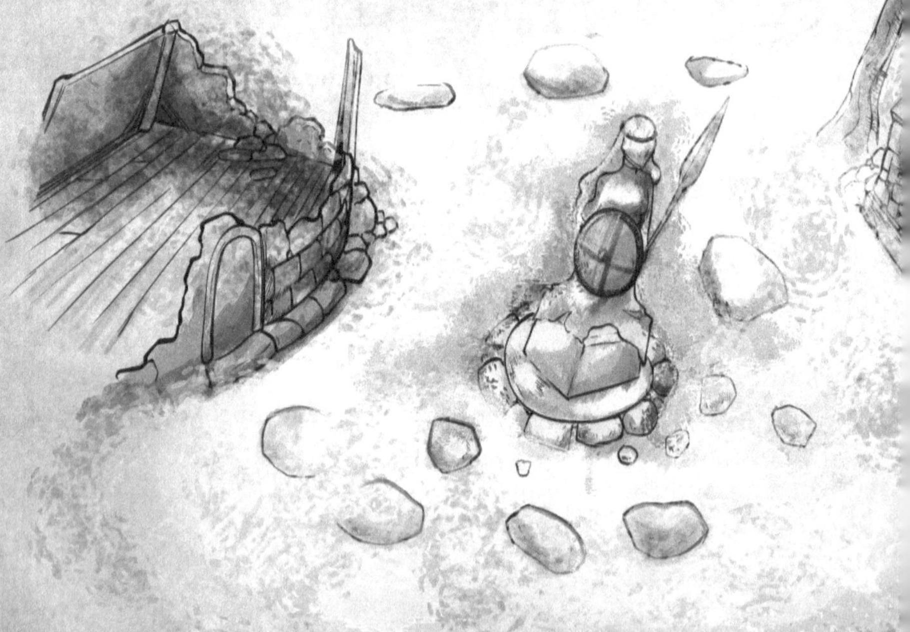

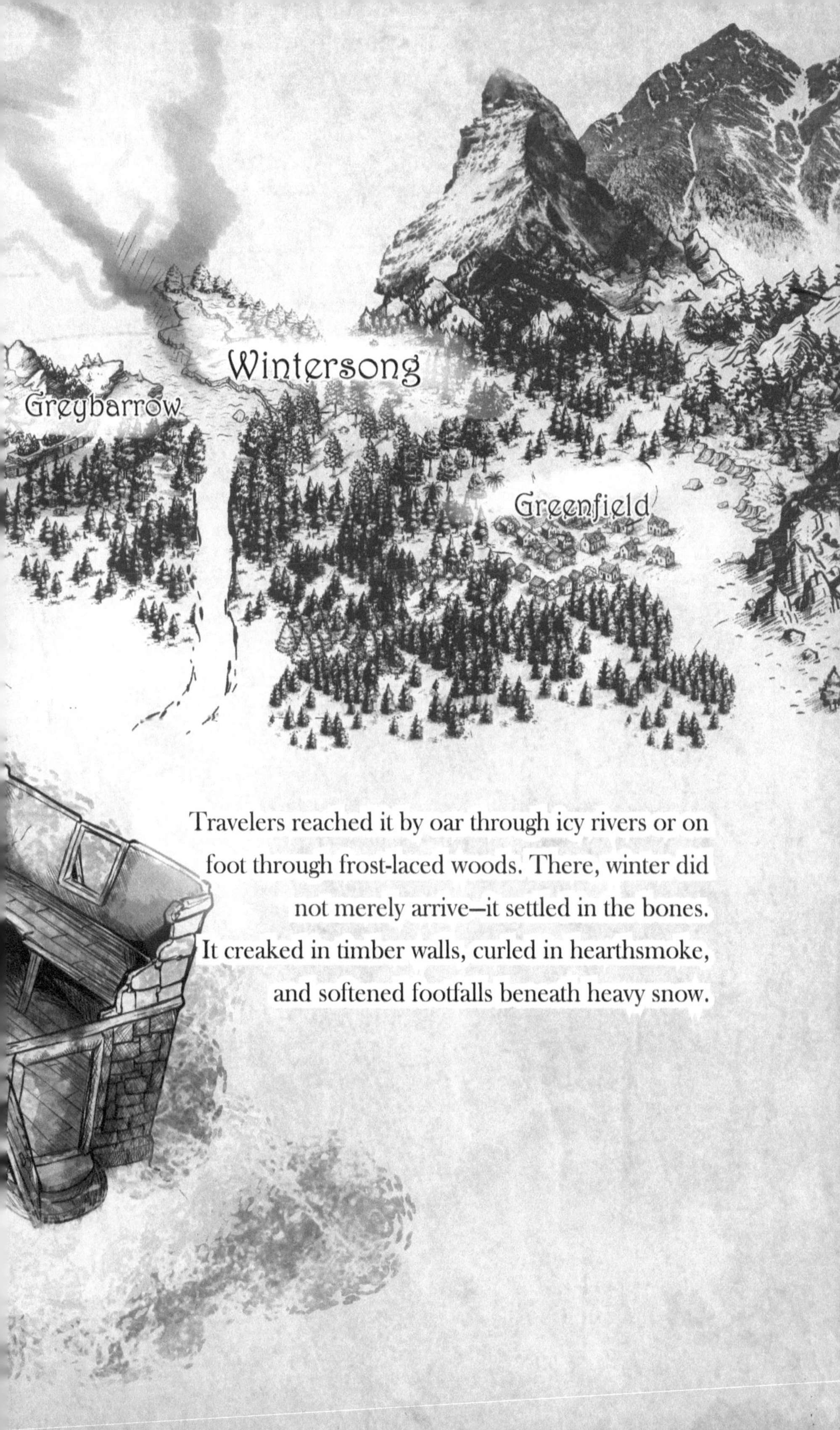

Travelers reached it by oar through icy rivers or on foot through frost-laced woods. There, winter did not merely arrive—it settled in the bones. It creaked in timber walls, curled in hearthsmoke, and softened footfalls beneath heavy snow.

SNOW & SILENCE

Four sets of boots pressed through the snow—some more grace-fully than others. Gunnar moved through the drifts like he was born of them—the snow clung to him, and if he were any other man, he might have slowed, but Gunnar did not falter. Cinder followed just behind him, using his broad frame to carve a path through the deeper patches. It made her pace easier, though she'd never admit it.

Ambrosja kept her head down, but her ears remained alert. Or they tried to. The night hadn't been kind to her — the memories of Wintersong tormented her. Mora, the Elder, the little boy crying in the middle of the hamlet. It all was so clear — yet a blur. The amount of blood that covered the snow was what haunted her. She squeezed her eyes shut. Trying to drown out the cries, the screams, and the ab-solute helplessness she felt.

"You never did say if you're from Wintersong, lass," Gunnar called back over his shoulder. "And judging by your accent… I'd say you're not Vaestorian. Sounds more like Nordorn." Ambrosja's step faltered at that, but she tried to mask it with a misstep in the snow. Gunnar looked ahead again. "But if you're here in Vaestoria, that's near suicide. Folk don't take kindly to Nordorners, you know? Nor-dorn's brutal and rough ways of life don't exactly complement the fancy and proper folk of this dragon land."

Ambrosja didn't answer right away; her thoughts pulled at her, *What do I do here? What answer do I give? Must I answer? He's right, after all… Just avoid it.* Her gaze flicked to him briefly, then forward.

"…Do *you* take kindly to Nordorners?" She kept her voice a calm wall of neutrality.

Gunnar glanced back once. "Do I?" he echoed. "Lass, I've been alive too long to care about where someone comes from. But if you are from Nordorn, you're in enemy territory, and you know this."

Cinder looked at Ambrosja. "So, are you from Nordorn or not?"

"I am from up north."

"You keep dodging the question."

"You keep prying."

"Prying?!" Cinder snapped, and Gunnar turned at that. Cinder moved to close the distance between her and Ambrosja. "Of course I'm prying! Nordorners are raging brutes, and I'm not quite sure how comfortable I am traveling with a brute *and* a liar." Cinder's bow shifted as her hand reached for it.

Ambrosja took a step back, already grasping at the hilt of her sword.

"Raging brutes?!" Ambrosja snapped back. "You've never even met one, if you had, I doubt you'd be standing! Do *not* speak of people that you've never met! You clearly don't understand them, their struggles, or their reason for doing what they do!"

Cinder's hand moved, already pulling an arrow. Ambrosja's golden gaze blazed with magic when she gripped the hilt of her sword tighter. But Johann rushed over. His hand urgently came over Cinder's, forcing her to lower the arrow. "Let's not turn this into a fight we don't need. We're all on the same side, and that's enough. Ambrosja doesn't owe us answers—just like we don't owe her ours."

Cinder growled under her breath, then scoffed and looked away. "Fine. Keep your secrets."

Silence returned as the snow thickened underfoot. Whatever trail of destruction the mysterious force had left behind, it was gone now. No more scorched ruins, no signs of fire. Whatever it was… it had moved elsewhere.

The day continued with an awkward tension, as if at any moment a fight would break out from someone breathing too loudly. No one spoke. But the silence didn't stop Cinder from shooting glares in Ambrosja's direction, and even holding her stare as she tapped the fletches of her arrows. And Ambrosja returned it. She stomped harder through the snow, glaring right back while her hand remained firm on the grip of her sword.

When they finally stopped, it was another night of the usual routine. Of Cinder and Gunnar gathering dry sticks, or as dry as they could find

them in the snow, and preparing to start a fire. Of Johann setting down the thick blankets they carried in their heavy packs and bringing out their rations of dried meat. While Ambrosja, uncertain of her place with these strangers, scouted around to ensure the area was safe.

When Ambrosja returned, she broke the silence, "Do any of you know who they were?"

Cinder was chewing on another dried piece of meat when she answered, not bothering to swallow. "What—the bastards who torched Wintersong?" Ambrosja gave a single nod. "No clue. But that wasn't their first."

Gunnar added, "We've heard of three other hamlets that had been struck; none were torched down like Wintersong."

Ambrosja went quiet. Her fingers twitched once.

Johann leaned forward, elbows on knees. His eyes narrowed slightly. "You look uneasy. Do you know them?"

She didn't answer at first. Her eyes tracked each speckle of snow that glittered from the firelight. Her memories came like a wave crashing against the shore. Abrupt and moving in manners that bore down with force. She recalled flashes of fire, a roof caving in, a pillar toppling over—causing a wall to tumble down. A little girl crying for her mother as a neighbor swept her up. Steel against steel, blood staining the white snow. All she could gather was that they wore black entirely and used fire. *Fire…* She thought to herself as she remembered a burst of flames coming towards her and her need to turn away—then nothing.

Ambrosja sighed. "Not a clue. I do not even remember if they had any insignia, just… dark armor."

The night was kinder than the last. They'd moved south, just far enough for the air to soften. The difference was small—but it mattered. The air no longer claimed their lungs, and the flesh of the travelers wasn't as pink from the touches of frost gracing their skin. The snow had lessened just enough that Cinder didn't need to follow Gunnar's footsteps to get through it. But the silence was still there in the morning, and no words were wasted when they packed their things and continued south. This was the final stretch before Greenfield.

Greenfield…

"What is Greenfield like?" Ambrosja broke the silence, walking beside Gunnar.

"It's a village," he replied, thinking as his stride remained the same. "They trade services and artifacts more than coin. Simple folk, but they've got an inn, food, warm water... or were you asking about the people?"

Ambrosja shrugged—a small, nearly invisible lift of her shoulders. "Either or."

Gunnar nodded. "The people are kind. Keep to themselves. Stay busy. They're no threat, if that's your concern."

"Maybe drop the accent," Cinder chimed in, eyeing Ambrosja like she was still ready for a fight. "Right now, you sound like the enemy. But hey—so long as you don't go cutting folks down with that sword, I'm sure you'll be fine."

Ambrosja's gaze settled on her—cool and sharp. Her hand drifted to the hilt of her blade.

"No one shall be cut down. Not by me. Not unless they *ask* for it."

Johann cleared his throat. "Perhaps we could try resolving conflict with words instead of blades?"

Cinder barked a laugh. "Please, old man." Her gaze never left Ambrosja, now settled just shy of a challenge. "I solve my problems with poison and arrowheads."

Gunnar smirked over his shoulder. "Johann, I think you've gotta give up on pacifism near Cinder. That girl will drag you into a fight and say you started it. Remember two years back? At the inn in Emberloch?" Gunnar chuckled, but Cinder groaned. He continued, now looking between Ambrosja and Johann. "She challenged this heavy-set man to a drinking match. Lass thought she'd be clever to wedge her dagger in the bottom, just enough where the drink would flow out—but she forgot to cover the hole when she tilted her head back to drink. Oh—ho!" Gunnar had stopped walking now, hands reaching his knees as he barked out a laugh. "That man was pissed! Cinder pointed at Johann, saying he told her to do it. Never seen the two of them run so fast before!"

Johann shared a pointed glance towards Cinder that she avoided. Instead, she retorted, "Hey! It made sense! I played the young and stupid card!"

"And you nearly got me killed by an enraged drunk miner," Johann added dryly.

Ambrosja smiled despite the tension that carried from the day before. She let it be set aside. "How long have the three of you been traveling together?" Ambrosja asked, still keeping pace beside Gunnar. "You remind me of soldiers who bonded during war."

Gunnar didn't slow, but his expression turned thoughtful. He rubbed

the back of his neck. "Eh, what—maybe a decade? At least with her," He gestured over at Cinder. "Met her when she was about fifteen, right?" Cinder gave a short nod. "As for him?" Gunnar tilted his head towards Johann. "He's always been with me."

Johann gave a deadpan stare. "He abducted me."

Cinder chuckled. Ambrosja blinked, then cocked a brow. She was looking from Johann to Gunnar, then back again. "Abducted?"

"Yeah." Johann's voice was flat. "Back in my youth, I was a traveling clergyman. One day, this barbaric behemoth—" he gestured at Gunnar with a glare that carried no real venom "—barrels through the inn I was staying at. A sword wedged in his shoulder. Arrows in his ribs. Bleeding everywhere."

He sighed. "So, being the fool I am, I tended to him. The next day, when I was preparing to continue my journey, he walks out of that inn, grabs me by the collar of my cloak, drags me like an unruly child, and throws me onto the back of his wagon."

Ambrosja released the smallest of chuckles, her smile growing wider. "And you *let* him?"

"I was in disbelief," Johann muttered. "The sheer disrespect this man had for my cloak."

Gunnar laughed, loud and unrestrained, shoulders shaking as he walked. "In my defense, I wasn't good with words. I needed a healer."

Johann scoffed. "A simple *please assist me in my travels* would've sufficed."

Gunnar shrugged. "Eh. That would've meant waiting for you to give the right answer."

Ambrosja looked between them. "So, you have been traveling together for what, twenty, thirty years?"

Gunnar nodded. "I'd say so. Maybe twenty-five? Johann was a damn little shrimp when I found him." He paused, grinning, then clapped a heavy hand on Johann's shoulder. "Now look at him. Built like an overgrown rabbit!"

Johann choked. "O-overgrown *rabbit*?!"

Cinder had to stop, hands finding her ribs as she cackled, "You *are*! You're an overgrown rabbit. Just don't hop."

"The absolute *disrespect* of this group!" Johann shouted, storming ahead of them down the snowy path. "I should've let that man *bleed out*! I really should have!"

He muttered furiously to himself, pushing ahead while the others laughed in his wake.

They stepped from the tree line onto the outskirts of Greenfield. Finally, there was no silence. They heard the lively sounds of family and work: the tumbling of wagon wheels, the chatter of adults, the delighted shrieks of children. Gunnar smiled widely and marched forward with renewed energy. Cinder let out a loud sigh of relief, jogging to catch up with him. Johann murmured a prayer and pressed a kiss to his holy symbol—its design, Ambrosja just realized, resembled the head of a dragon—as he thanked whatever god he believed in for civilization.

Ambrosja lingered last, her eyes scanning the edge of the village. Snow thinned here, melted away where warmth clung to stone and soil. Children in woolen coats balanced on low stone walls while nearby mothers gossiped, a chorus of gentle voices and laughter—a sisterhood in the cold.

As they drew closer, villagers paused mid-task. One child, previously balanced like a little acrobat, lost his footing and tumbled into a bush. Gunnar winked at a group of women. They blushed, giggled, and nudged one another with their elbows like it was a game. Cinder rolled her eyes. Johann pinched the bridge of his nose. Ambrosja said nothing—but her lips twitched, just barely, as if that sort of behavior was all too familiar for her.

They walked along the dirt path, passing families on strolls, wagons hauling lumber and stone, and small farms where hounds rounded up scattered cattle. One of the hounds even had a baby goat perched calmly on its back. The air was alive with conversation, grunts from labor, and the clinks of metal tools.

Sections of low, stone walls encircled Greenfield, creating a crumbled barrier between the snow-frosted forests and the roads that led to other places. But these short, crumbling stone walls kept the vibrant families of Greenfield. The houses were of wood and stone, most of them small, built close together, windows sharing clothes-line with a red ribbon in the middle to clearly tell who owned which side of the line. The larger homes were few and scattered about, not grand, but with enough space for the smallest of gardens or sheds for tools. Businesses shared spaces, a bakery nestled next to a working man's market of needs—a perfect blend of a place where a traveler might purchase equipment and pick up rations right after.

"Poor asses have no idea…" Cinder muttered under her breath, eyes on a young couple walking hand in hand. "Absolutely no clue that four days north, a hamlet turned to ash."

"Keep your voice down," Johann murmured. "Last thing we need is to cause a panic."

Gunnar nodded, still smiling as he scanned the peaceful faces. "Right as rain, old friend. We eat. We drink. Take a warm bath. Then we speak to the Captain of the Guard." He glanced back over his shoulder. "Deal?"

All nodded. Already moving down the road until they found the village inn—*The Goose's Nest*, likely the only one in Greenfield.

Without ceremony, Gunnar shoved the doors wide—not to show off, just too big to bother with subtlety. He marched inside, weaving through smaller folk like a bull among sheep, and plopped himself down at a corner table near the back. The room quieted for a moment. Not crowded, but busy—traveling merchants, laborers on lunch, a few families sharing meals.

Cinder followed and flopped into the seat beside him, throwing her legs up onto an empty chair. Johann took a seat across from them, settling with far more grace but an equally tired expression. Ambrosja chose a spot with her back to the wall.

No surprises, she thought.

A young woman approached—long black curls, olive-green eyes, skin sun-warmed like honey. An apron was tied snugly around her waist, and her dress clung just right. Gunnar, predictably, stared without shame.

Cinder didn't even look at him. "Close your mouth, you buffoon. You're drooling."

"Drooling?" Gunnar echoed, still gazing. "No, lass. I'm admiring the fine work of the gods."

"Oh?" The barmaid raised an eyebrow. "That is cute. But listen, *grandpa*, unless you're paying my wages today, maybe admire the mead instead."

Gunnar chuckled low, leaning forward so his shoulders flexed under the fur. "Oh, I certainly admire a woman who's not afraid of a little sass. Makes things exciting."

Johann sighed like a man who had aged five years in ten seconds. But Ambrosja's attention had shifted. She noticed a man step in, a black cloak clinging to his frame, the faintest of snow coating his shoulders. The cloak in itself wasn't strange — but the light from the hearth caught his jawline when he moved to the empty table at the center. *Ash…* Ambrosja thought to herself as she noted the smearing marks of it across his barely visible jawline. Ambrosja didn't speak. She simply nudged Cinder's boot with her own. Cinder looked up and followed her gaze. Saw him. Said nothing. Just nodded.

"What'll it be?" the barmaid asked.

"Your name," Gunnar purred.

Johann facepalmed with such force that it was a surprise he hadn't broken his own nose. "My gods, just order a drink so the poor woman can do her job."

Gunnar waved him off. "The man has no appreciation for the art of courtship." He sat upright. "Something sweet to drink. A plate of meat—fatty, tender. The kind I can tear with my hands and teeth."

The barmaid raised a brow, then turned to the others. "Same," Cinder and Ambrosja said together. They exchanged a brief glance, then nodded once at each other, as if their taste in food had settled whatever hostility they had.

Johann, with the resigned expression of a man losing a war he never wanted to fight, simply said, "Me too."

The barmaid smiled, grateful for the easy order. "I'll be back with your drinks." She moved, dress swaying as she returned to the bar.

Cinder leaned into Gunnar and whispered, "Man in the black cloak. He's got snow on him… Yet it's not snowing, not here."

"And ash on his jawline," Ambrosja added in a hushed tone.

Gunnar didn't move his head—just shifted his eyes toward the man, then away. "Think he's one of them?"

"If he is…" Cinder frowned. "Why is he *here*?"

Johann tilted his head, "He's positioned quite close, a lone wolf? You'd think he'd sit by the bar, not at a table. Not this close. Maybe he followed us, but why?"

Ambrosja's expression remained unreadable. "We should find out. We eat, drink, then move. See if he follows. If he does—we grab him."

Gunnar gave a short nod. "Fine plan."

Cinder looked at Ambrosja; her eyes were still gleaming with a hint of challenge, but her tone held no bite. "Makes sense, no reason to shove my arrow up his ass. Yet."

The barmaid returned, carrying a wooden tray stacked with mugs of mead. She handed one to each of them. "Food's coming. Enjoy." But she paused, her eyes lingered on Gunnar. "Ordering all that meat, I sure hope you can handle it when a proper feast is displayed before you." Her hand moved across the broad expanse of his shoulders as she walked off.

"Looks like I'm not sleeping alone tonight," Gunnar smirked, a slight blush creeping across his cheek, not bashfulness, oh no, this was *heat*. He didn't wait. He lifted his mug, "Cheers," and tilted it back—draining half the drink in one long, unbroken gulp.

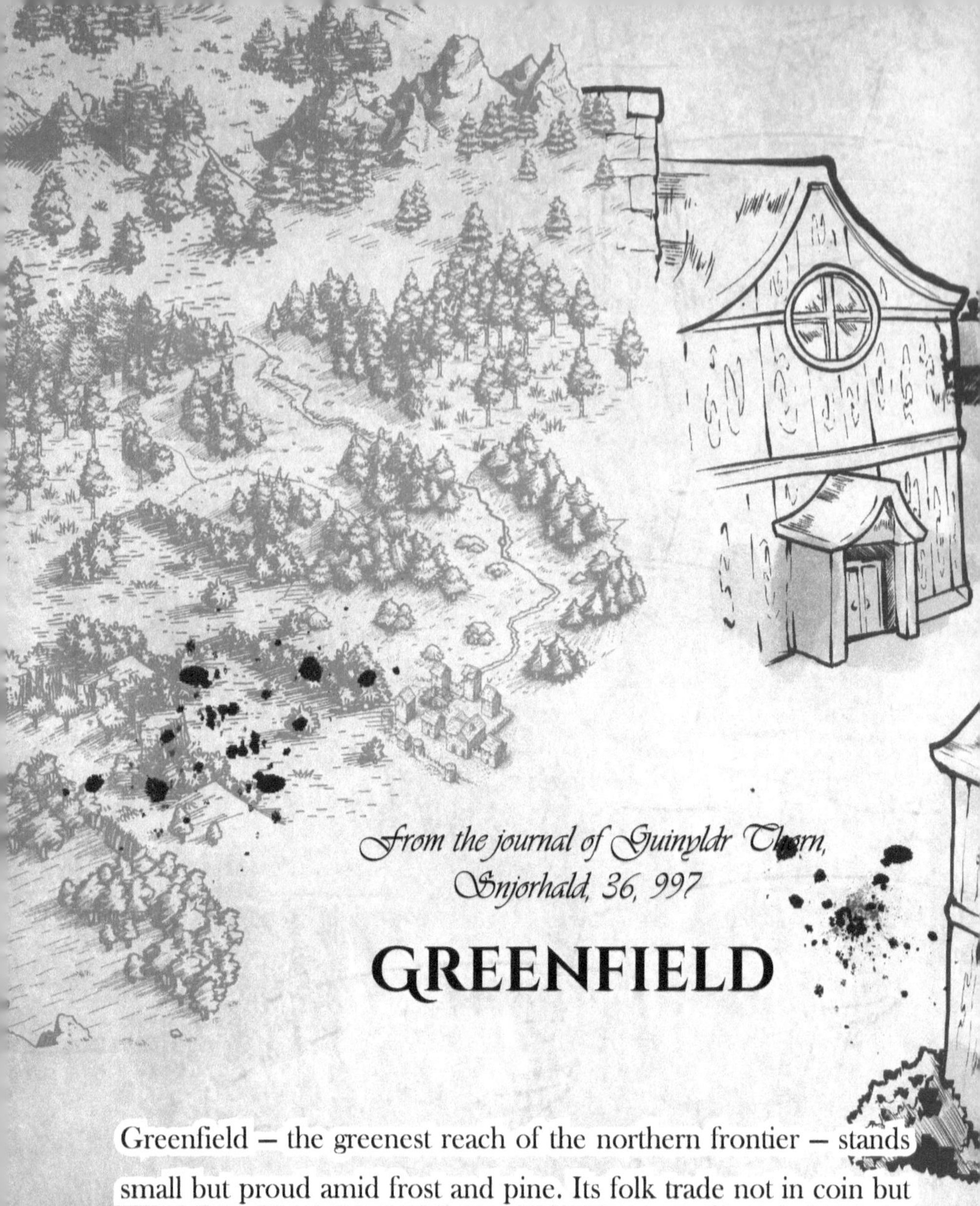

GREENFIELD

Greenfield — the greenest reach of the northern frontier — stands small but proud amid frost and pine. Its folk trade not in coin but in craft, bartering wood, ore, and kill to see each other through lean seasons. Lumber from its woods builds the hearths of neighboring towns, and from its hardy youth come the wanderers and hunters who chase fortune beyond the Frostmarch.

CHAPTER THREE
BENEATH THE CLOAK

Empty plates remained on the table, just like the drained mugs—left with a pouch of coins to cover the debt.

Gunnar, as always, took the lead. Cinder and Johann flanked him. Ambrosja walked behind. They had no specific destination in mind—only the goal of walking long enough, and far enough, to see if the man in the dark cloak would follow. If he made the same turns, if he arrived wherever they stopped, then they'd know.

They talked. Not of anything meaningful—just enough to keep things natural. Gunnar kept his body angled so he could glance over his shoulder mid-conversation, keeping an eye out without drawing attention.

The air was crisp, touched with the faint drift of snowflakes from the northern mountains. They didn't stick—just floated like ash before dissolving. Hooves clomped steadily over damp earth as workhorses pulled carts. Children ran beside them, giggling, reaching up to pet their sides.

Gunnar looked back again—his gaze briefly landing on Ambrosja, possibly studying her, then scanning elsewhere—before he spoke, voice loud enough for anyone nearby. "Greenfield's nice, sure, but I've always preferred the outskirts," he said, trying to appear as casual as he could. "Access to the woods, let the kids run wild. Pretend you're camping—make it a little vacation, yeah?" He gestured with one broad hand, waving them onward. "Come on, let me show you something."

He turned, weaving through the foot traffic and stepping into the edge of the woods. That was the signal. The man was following. The others followed without hesitation. Their boots hit dry leaves and loose soil, stones kicking aside beneath their feet. Branches snapped quietly underfoot. They kept talking. They had to. It had to stay natural. For Cinder, that came a little *too* easily.

"What kids, Gunnar?" she smirked. "Can you even *get it up* at your age?"

Gunnar scoffed, wounded pride in every syllable. "Can I even get it up?!" he echoed, aghast. "Guess we'll find out tonight with that barmaid, eh?" He elbowed her—hard.

Cinder actually stumbled, glaring as she rubbed her arm. "Gross."

Ambrosja glanced between them. "Do either of you have families?"

Gunnar tilted his head. "I mean…" He scratched his chin in thought. "I might have a few brats running around. Not exactly easy to keep track when you move from place to place."

Johann answered next. "Family in the clergy. I write to them now and then. No children, though."

Cinder hesitated before speaking. "…I had a family. Lost them in the fire." Her voice dipped lower. "Raid hit my village in the southeast of Vaestoria. Bastards torched everything that wasn't stone." She looked to Ambrosja. "The regency that looked after my village didn't send aid. Said it wasn't worth the effort. Too far. Too *dead*."

Ambrosja's gaze lingered on her. She nodded once. "My condolences."

Gunnar glanced back. "And you, Ambrosja? Any bastards running around? Heartbroken men? Maybe disappointed fathers, hm?"

She didn't lift her eyes. "Lost my mother when I was five." Her voice was quieter than before. "Lost my father in battle when I was seventeen." No one pressed further. They just nodded—and kept walking.

They were deep into the woods now. Trees thickened around them, muffling the wind. Gunnar led them into a small clearing and swept an arm around.

"See?" he said. "Could hook a swing from that tree, or drape a cloth over this branch here…" He reached up and tugged the limb. "Instant tent for the night. Makes the kids feel like they're on an adventure."

Cinder crossed her arms. "Hell, if we don't want to pay for rooms tonight, we could just camp here ourselves."

Ambrosja nodded. "That is an excellent idea... I shall gather wood for a campfire."

She turned, slipping between the trees with deliberate ease. Her eyes scanned the dark line of the forest—searching. She had a plan. To circle the man. Catch him from behind. And leave him no room to escape.

Ambrosja moved through the trees with practiced grace. Her steps were quiet, deliberate—always seeking firmer ground, never too soft or wet where her boots might sink. She avoided dry twigs and hidden stones. Her golden eyes scanned the underbrush. But she didn't see him. What she didn't account for, however, was how easily her pale, ashen-blonde curls stood out among the deep greens and browns of the forest.

Then a voice—soft but firm, "Be still." It didn't belong to the others. It was *him*. "One wrong move, and I'll set your pretty locks ablaze."

Ambrosja calmly stilled. She felt it now—*heat*, blooming behind her spine.

Not close enough to burn… No smell of charred bark… Magical, she thought. *Definitely magical.*

Slowly, her hands lifted in surrender. She turned, eyes meeting him for the first time. He was young. No older than twenty. Ash and soot dusted his face. His skin was tanned, clothes all black, stitched with embroidery of red, gold, and orange. His hazel eyes burned with orange light—the same as the flickering flame that danced across his palms. His hood was drawn, but she could see his hair—wavy brown hair that clung to his scalp.

"You're the one..." he whispered. His voice shook. "...the one who got away." He swallowed hard. His hands trembled, fire still alive. "I'm really sorry... but we don't leave witnesses. Not unless they can serve."

Ambrosja saw the boy hesitate, but she didn't. She charged. A hard stomp of her boot to the ground pushed her to tackle him. Sparks flew from his fingers, catching onto wet wood that didn't hold a light. The sound of sharp air leaving lungs echoed loudly enough. Ambrosja wrapped herself around the boy and spun, rolling them over until her forearm pressed hard against his throat. His eyes widened, but they also blazed with a glow as his free hands came up to grab at Ambrosja's face—a sharp cry left her as fumes drifted from the contact of their skin.

Gunnar, Johann, and Cinder whipped around at the cry. Already rushing in the direction of the source without faltering. "Ambrosja?!" Gunnar shouted from somewhere behind the trees.

When they came to the spot where Ambrosja and the young man were, they saw the steam rising in his hands. Cinder immediately reached for her quiver, but Johann stopped her, giving caution, "You might hit her!" Ambrosja kept her forearm against his throat, releasing her other arm so her own hand could pull his away—but that only made him grasp her face with his other hand. Ambrosja was forced to release his throat—and that's when he rolled out of her grasp, standing to his feet and lighting his hands ablaze.

The boy didn't stand for long when the barreling form of Gunnar rushed forward and slammed into him, sending the cloaked stranger into a tree—hard—and forcing him to drop onto the cold ground.

Ambrosja scrambled up, her golden eyes blazing as her chest heaved, the steam on her face lingered with the burn marks of the young man's hands. Her skin healed over, cutting the steam short. She touched the skin that once held his handprints. Her brows furrowed dangerously low. Anger rising in her veins. She didn't wait. Ambrosja moved like lightning. One boot came hard into his ribs, kicking him against the tree. A groaning cry left his lips. Before he could blink, she moved. Swift, practiced—her sword was unsheathed. Like the weapon was an extension of her will. The darkened blade with a deep groove of dark blue at the center of it, from hilt to tip, pressed to his throat.

Her voice dropped into a growl, "Talk." The young man's chest heaved beneath the pressure of the blade. A beat of silence passed. Then Ambrosja pressed her sword in—just enough to kiss the skin. "*Talk!* Who are you with? Where did you come from? Are you with the ones who ruined Wintersong?! Who are you?!" His hands started to flicker with flames like a threat, Ambrosja noticed, but she didn't back away, "I said *talk* or I shall take your hands!"

Johann stepped forward instantly. "Ambrosja, please! He's just a boy!"

"A boy who aided in burning down my hamlet—*my people!*"

Cinder lowered her bow, her voice cool. "Sorry, Johann. But I'm with Blondie on this one."

Johann turned, desperation in his eyes. "Gunnar, do something—*before she spills blood she can't wash from her hands!*"

Gunnar exhaled sharply, dragging a hand down his face. He met Ambrosja's eyes. "If he dies… we lose answers. Valuable ones. And we may never know why your hamlet burned." He stepped forward, slow and steady. "Don't let vengeance blind you before truth has a chance to speak."

Ambrosja said nothing. Her jaw clenched, nostrils flared. Then—after a long, frozen moment—she exhaled, closed her eyes, and withdrew her blade. The boy, now breathing freely, collapsed slightly, catching himself on trembling hands that were steaming. He sat up, slow, cautious.

"I don't know how much help I'll be," he whispered with a tremble

still clinging to his throat. "I don't know why they're doing all this… not really."

"And who *are* they, lad?" Gunnar crouched beside him. "And who are *you*?"

"Donathan," he whispered. "My name's Donathan. And the people you're after… they call themselves the *Black Hand*."

Cinder scoffed. "Donathan? What, parents didn't like the way the 'J' looked?"

Ambrosja's eyes, still unkind, remained on him; the tension hadn't left her. "And where do you fit into all of this?"

Donathan's voice wavered, but he didn't look away. "My hamlet was burned too. Same as yours. They take magic users. Take resources—linens, grain, blades, armor… anything." He swallowed hard. "It was *join them or die*." He paused for a moment. "I wanted to live long enough to get better at magic. Strong enough to escape. But now that I've told you this? I'm dead anyway. Either by your hand—or *theirs*. Doesn't really matter."

Cinder took a slow step closer, arms still crossed, "How long have you been following us?"

He sighed. "I wasn't following *you three*… just her." He nodded subtly toward Ambrosja. "I was left behind to make sure no one survived. To confirm the kill. And if everyone was dead? Catch up to the main force. I didn't even know she was alive until I heard her cry." He glanced at his hands, resting in front of him. "I had a plan. Wait 'til she was weak. Kill her fast. But then she found *you three*… and, well… things went downhill from there."

Ambrosja crossed her arms, her stance wide and unyielding. She looked down at him like judgment itself. "Why even bother?" she asked. "You're far from them now. Days away. You could leave."

Donathan let out a bitter, barked laugh. "*Leave?*" he echoed. The sound died quickly. His face soured. "That's not how it works." He pushed his cloak aside and pulled down part of his tunic, exposing the skin of his shoulder. There, seared into flesh, was a black mark—a twisted hand, human in shape, monstrous in detail. "They've branded me." He looked up at them. "They can track me. That's why I've been dealing with this and waiting. Trying to get stronger. Trying to find a way to lift the curse."

Cinder froze. "They can *track you?!*" She stepped forward, eyes blazing. "You fucker—you *led them to us!*"

Donathan scrambled back across the leaf-littered ground. "They're *not* going to send an army! If anything, just a few! Maybe one or two!"

Johann rubbed his chin slowly. Gunnar saw it—the quiet way his old friend was starting to turn an idea. "What is it?" Gunnar asked.

Johann looked up. "I think we just found our bait." He pointed to Donathan. "Think about it. If they *do* send someone to retrieve him, it won't be another expendable grunt. It'll be someone stronger. Someone closer to the top. If we grab that person, we might get real answers."

Ambrosja tilted her head slightly, her brows furrowed with suspicion. "You really think they would send someone up the chain for *him?*"

"Why not?" Johann shrugged. "Sending someone on his level would just invite a fight. Magic-user to magic-user. They know Donathan could resist. But send someone stronger? He wouldn't stand a chance. He'd *have* to return."

Donathan pushed himself upright, nerves clearly rattled. "Listen, there's no guarantee any of that happens. What—you want me to just *tag along* and hope they come for me?" He scoffed. "I'm a *nobody.*"

Cinder snorted. "Yeah. We noticed." Johann shot her a warning look.

But Gunnar just rubbed his beard, thoughtful. "I say we try it. Worst case? It's someone like Donathan. We take that one too."

Ambrosja kicked a stone, her arms still folded tight. "You are speaking as if you plan to collect them."

Gunnar grinned. "Hey… that's how armies *start*, isn't it?"

Johann stared at him, deadpan with a twitch of annoyance. "That's a joke. Right?"

Donathan shifted, nerves twisting through his face. His eyes flicked between Johann and Gunnar. "O-okay. Listen…" he stammered, "…I *heard* the Black Hand has a hideout somewhere in these woods. I think it's a mining camp." All heads snapped toward him. He swallowed hard. "That's what I heard. I've never been there myself," he explained quickly, raising his hands. "But apparently… There are a few of them across Vaestoria. Outposts, camps… Places they operate from, I hear they put up a front, like an inn, or something. You know, hiding in plain sight."

Ambrosja turned to Gunnar. "If they have bases scattered across the country—"

"—then they're bigger than we thought," Gunnar finished.

Cinder stepped forward, arms tense at her sides. "Right. And what's the *point* of telling us that now? Trying to buy our trust? Not happening."

Donathan hesitated, clearly weighing his words. "…What if," he said slowly, "instead of waiting for someone to find *me*, one of you pretends to be my prisoner? I bring you into the hideout. You get inside, poke around, maybe find out what they're planning."

Cinder's brows dropped like a storm cloud. "Oh, *that's* real fucking convenient, Donny-Boy," she snapped, waving a hand wildly. "Let's just let the *guy* who tried to *light Blondie on fire*—" she thumbed toward Ambrosja "—*escort us into enemy territory* like he's suddenly our tour guide!"

"I like it," Ambrosja said plainly.

Every head turned toward her. "What?!" they shouted in unison.

Ambrosja took a deep breath once, eyes closing once with a nod, "It is risky," she agreed, "but it might be the only plan we have that does not involve sitting on our asses waiting for someone to hunt Donathan. I am willing to go." A pause. "…And I shall act as if I desire to serve them. I have magical potential."

Donathan's jaw slackened in genuine surprise. "…You do?" he asked. "You have magic?"

"Do you see your damned hand prints on my skin?" Ambrosja glared at Donathan. He shook his head, so she continued. "Healed. I have healing magic."

His expression changed, a bit of hope peeking through the soot. "Healing magic? That would make it far easier; everyone is always in need of a healer."

Johann shook his head sharply. "That's lunacy, Ambrosja."

Gunnar frowned deeply, arms crossed, brow furrowed, "You sure about this, lass?" he asked. "It's a bloody gamble."

Ambrosja met his gaze. "I am, perhaps if they hear my accent… they might think I am from Wintersong, maybe that could work to our advantage."

"Maybe, but your accent is still thicker than even our own Northern-most people. But let's try it." Gunnar gave a long sigh, then nodded once. "We'll head back to the inn, get rooms, rest up. Tomorrow—" his eyes fell on Donathan "—we search for this hideout of yours. And *then* we make a decision, make a plan. And we'll be keeping our eyes on you."

Donathan dipped his head. "I hope it's there, Sir. Truly."

They fell into a tight formation as they returned to *The Goose's Nest*, flanking Donathan from all sides. The night would be long. But the morning promised something darker—a path straight into the shadows of the Black Hand.

In a room at the Goose's Nest, Ambrosja had finally stripped down to her sleeping garments. Her form was hunched over a piece of parchment that

she was pressing down onto the wardrobe trunk between the two beds. She glanced over at Cinder, who was sleeping, but her hand never let go of her bow, and her other hand held tight to an arrow.

A low sigh escaped the Empress. Her eyes glanced back down at the parchment.

Ambrosja,

You were meant to write upon your arrival to Wintersong. You haven't. You haven't perished because the ravens don't cry and the mountain doesn't tremble. Where are you, woman? If you do not reply within three days… I will come into Vaestoria and grab you myself.

Hådvard

Ambrosja picked up the quill, dipping it into ink once, and began to write.

My Beloved,

Wintersong has fallen. I'm well — but all of the hamlet has fallen into ruin. I seek to find the culprits of this attack. I will write when I can. Be well.

Ambrosja

She handed the letter to the raven on the sill. Its long beak clamped around the parchment and turned its gaze toward the night sky. Leaping away and turning into smoke and dust.

From the journal of Guinyldr Thorn,
Bjarnvakt, 04, 997

THE GOOSE'S NEST

When one speaks of Greenfield's beginnings, one must inevitably speak of the Goose's Nest. Founded by Gideon Oakwood when the village was little more than a scattering of cottages, the inn became both beacon and hearth for the weary traveler. Oakwood's simple vision—to offer food, fire, and fellowship—sparked a quiet transformation.

Travelers lingered, merchants stayed, and soon new roofs rose where fields once lay. Around its great hearth, tales were traded that wove the first threads of Greenfield's lore, inspiring generations who would later call the town home.

typical room
all bedrooms at the Goose's Nest has two beds and one trunk for items.

the kitchen
used from dawn to dusk for preparing meals, storing provisions.

common area
here guests dine, rest by the hearth, and exchange tales over ale and stew

Cinder rose with a groan, rubbing sleep from her eyes as she stretched in the doorway of her rented room at The Goose's Nest. Her shaggy brown hair was even messier, a towel slung over one shoulder, tunic halfway laced, and the smug satisfaction of a night in a real bed worn clear across her face.

The door across from her opened just as she stepped out. Out walked the barmaid from the day prior—the one with the sun-kissed skin and dark curls that bounced down her back. She looked… tousled. But not in the sleepy kind of way. Her apron was missing. One sleeve slipped low over her arm. The bodice of her dress was only half-tied, exposing the flush on her collarbone. She looked up. Paused. Cleared her throat. Then quickly closed the door behind her and walked off with a suspiciously light spring in her step.

"…What the fuck…" Cinder muttered, eyes narrowing. She huffed air out of her nose, glancing back at Ambrosja, who was lacing up her boots inside their shared room, then to Johann's door, where Donathan was kept overnight.

They gathered for breakfast not long after.

Gunnar was glowing, practically gleaming with the obvious signs of sex. Cinder, meanwhile, looked at him as if he had sprouted horns. Her expression hovered somewhere between disgust and homicidal intent, eyes flicking between his smug face and the visible signs of recent indulgence decorating his neck.

Johann sipped quietly at his water, gaze bouncing between them, clearly waiting for Cinder to stab Gunnar with her fork. Donathan didn't lift his head from his oatmeal, as though staring hard enough at the gruel would make him invisible. But Ambrosja? Ambrosja watched him. Closely. Every twitch of his fingers. Every fidget. She studied him the way one studied a new map—trying to find the hidden trap beneath the ink.

Around them, the inn buzzed with morning life. Travelers clanked their cups and traded sleepy banter. Locals scarfed down eggs before heading out to work. But for this group, the next destination wasn't a road or a city. It was something darker. Something nestled deep in the unknown.

Ambrosja's voice sliced through the breakfast bustle, only loud enough for the table. "Where do you reckon this mining camp might be, Donathan?"

Donathan glanced up nervously, meeting her golden stare. "Uh…" He cleared his throat. "Probably somewhere deep in the Bramble. Still northern, but... tucked in."

"The Bramble?" she asked.

He looked surprised. "Yeah. You know, the forest just past Greenfield?" His brow furrowed. "I thought you were from Wintersong?"

"Never said I was not."

"…Then you should know the Bramble?"

Before Ambrosja could respond, Gunnar spoke, leveling Donathan with a look. "Not everyone's had time to study their geography, lad. She's got other things on her mind."

Donathan shrank a little. "Right. Sure, but—everyone knows about the Bramble and how you shouldn't venture far into it or you risk catching the Veil-like gaze of the Mourntalon." He shuddered just thinking about it. "These are stories everyone is told as a child, the Bramble is thick with dark woods in the deepest parts of it, tales of trees being alive, vines stealing your coin, creatures stalking you." He shrugged. "I just figured everyone knew about the Bramble's history—"

Cinder interrupted, tearing off a piece of bread without looking up. "Alright, well, thanks for the history lesson," she muttered, then bit into it. She then glared across the table at Donathan. "Don't care why you joined the *Black Asses*—survival or not—you still helped torch places."

Donathan didn't argue. He just stirred his oatmeal. And then Cinder leaned forward. "You know what I'm real curious about?" she was glaring into Donathan now.

Donathan looked unsure. Eyes wide. Looking between everyone,

then back at Cinder. "W-what?"

"You said you were waiting for Blondie here to get all weak so you could torch her…" Donathan swallowed. Cinder continued, "But here she is… You telling me there wasn't an opportunity once?"

Ambrosja's gaze fixed harder on Donathan. Waiting for his answer.

The young man looked at Ambrosja nervously. Shifting in his seat. "…She wouldn't stop walking. Not even to sleep. When I got tired, she kept going. And… I got scared. So, I didn't do it."

Ambrosja spoke then, "But you tried in the woods?" She jerked her head towards the door leading outside.

"Yeah — I got even more scared, and I just stopped thinking."

Gunnar rumbled in thought, but he changed the subject. "Let's focus on the matter at hand. If it's a mining camp, I'm certain we can find it fairly easily by listening to the sounds of picks meeting stone or carts rolling around."

Johann, always the tactician, nodded as he sipped. "We could ask a blacksmith around here, too. I'm certain if they're trying to keep up appearances, then they would sell their ore from time to time."

Cinder spoke around a mouthful of bread. "Or… hear me out… maybe they don't give a shit, and they've got a big fucking sign that says *Welcome to Black Hand* with everyone dressed like funeral guests."

Johann dragged a hand over his face. "I don't think it'll be like that."

Gunnar, however, looked thoughtful. "Could be."

Johann looked like he wanted to kick Gunnar in the shin. "Gods, you had one good idea, and now you're following her off a cliff?"

Donathan cleared his throat meekly. "Maybe we could… keep it down?"

Ambrosja stood without a word. "I shall look around."

"Look around?" Gunnar watched Ambrosja move around the table to leave. "Lass, you didn't even know the forest was called the Bramble. Don't go wandering off without a—" But she was already moving, boots carrying her through the inn's door and into the cold, misty breath of morning.

Gunnar sighed, his massive hand scooping up the remaining sausages from his plate. "Impatient little thing," he muttered, already rising and heading toward the door.

"Are you serious?" Cinder scoffed around a mouthful of eggs. She called after him, "I'm still eating, you giant fuck!" A nearby mother gasped, clutching her child's ears. Cinder caught the look and waved her fork dismissively. "Oh, fuck off, you cow! She'll be cursing better than me by the time she's ten." She rose with her plate in hand and stormed after Gunnar, still shoveling food into her mouth with the other.

Johann, looking as if another patch of gray had just bloomed at his temples, stood slowly. "Apologies for my compatriots," he said to no one in particular. "They lack any semblance of decorum." He collected his plate with one hand and dropped a few coins onto the table with the other. "Right. Let's go, boy." Donathan followed without a word, his eyes downcast.

The innkeeper, a round man, balding at the center of his scalp, caught sight of the departing dishes and shouted, "Hey! You can't just leave with the damn plates!" But he didn't chase after them; too tired and weary from travelers of the night before who thought themselves gods after a successful hunt on a rabbit that took seven of them to even capture.

Outside, Ambrosja was already striding toward Greenfield's outskirts. Gunnar's long legs closed the distance as he followed, still chewing on breakfast. Cinder trailed just behind, food in hand, weaving between townsfolk with the grace of a hungry, foul-mouthed cat. Johann and Donathan walked more cautiously, Johann whispering apologies to every person Cinder nudged or brushed past. Ambrosja climbed a flimsy wooden fence with ease. Gunnar didn't bother—he simply lifted a leg over it.

"Alright, easy there," he called, clutching his last sausage like a *Drakesmoke*. "We don't have a proper plan yet. Best idea so far is sneakin' you in as a follower, not stormin' the place like it's a battlefield. We need to be smart. Hunt them before they hunt us."

Cinder leapt the fence with surprising grace, barely spilling a crumb. "Normally, I love the idea of charging in, arrows blazing... but Gunnar's right. Let's say there's fifty of them out there. We'd be fucked. Maybe ease up before you go tits-first into a Black Hand blade."

Johann ducked under the fence. Donathan scrambled over.

"Ambrosja," Johann called gently, "slow down, please."

Donathan added, more urgently, "The Bramble's huge! We can't just wander. If they're really out there, we might stumble into their blades before we even find the path."

Ambrosja paused mid-step. She sighed, golden eyes closing. "You are right." She turned to face them. "But the longer I do nothing, the more risk there is of someone else getting hurt by them. I will slow down, but I cannot stop."

Donathan stepped ahead, his gaze catching on a cart rolling toward the outskirts, following a messy, mud-filled path onto the main road in Greenfield, its bed laden with chunks of glinting ore. "Wait—" he called softly, hurrying after the others. "Look, a mining cart, right? Let's just follow the path, I'm sure that's it."

The others followed his gaze.

Cinder gave a crooked grin. "Well, shit, Flame Boy... guess you're not a wet torch after all." Donathan's chest swelled slightly with pride.

Gunnar gave an approving nod. "Good thinking." His eyes followed the path the ore cart had taken, tracing the grooves left by its wheels. "Still... can't go askin' around too loud. Might give folks the wrong idea—like we're looking to rob the place." He turned and started off again. "Come. Let's say we're... birdwatching." The others trailed behind him without question.

Their boots met soft ground, their pace slowing as they ventured deeper into the Bramble. The forest thickened, closing in around them with mossy trunks and hanging branches. The sound of Greenfield faded into memory—the rustle of carts, chatter of merchants, and clang of saws replaced by creaking limbs and the distant call of birds.

They followed the trail: wheel ruts, hoofprints, and pressed leaves— the subtle signs of heavy movement. For a long while, they said nothing, their silence almost reverent. Until Cinder spoke.

She kept her eyes forward, voice quiet, but not so soft that Ambrosja couldn't hear. "So... is it vengeance or guilt?"

Ambrosja looked up, pulled from her thoughts. "What?"

"This crusade of yours," Cinder clarified with a small shrug. "Are you chasing the Black Hand because it's noble? Or because it hurts too much to stand still?" Ambrosja didn't answer at first. Cinder went on. "I get it. I watched my family burn. I was the only one left. Some nights I…nevermind." She shook her head, looking away from Ambrosja.

The men said nothing. They kept walking, quiet as shadows, giving space.

Ambrosja's pace never slowed, but her voice came eventually—soft and weighted. "They were my responsibility," she said. "I promised I would keep them safe. I failed. And they died... while I lived." A long breath. "So, if I charge ahead, or make poor decisions, or press on without thinking, it is because I do not always know what else to do. And standing still feels worse."

Cinder nodded slowly. "Yeah—I know exactly what you mean... That feeling? I—I get it." There was no teasing, no grin this time, just heavy and honest words. Silence settled soon after between them again, filled only by the sounds of the forest and the steady tread of five travelers, all carrying burdens heavier than any blade.

Clink.

The sound was faint, but sharp. Not loud enough to alarm, yet distinct enough that every head turned toward it. They stepped forward—until Cinder threw out an arm, halting them like an older sister reining in a band of foolish siblings.

"Wait, you idiots," she hissed. "We have no idea what that was or how close it is. What if it's the Black Hand? You want to just stroll into their camp?" She narrowed her eyes on each of them. "Let *me* scout ahead. This is what I trained for."

Gunnar gave a single nod. "Very well, lass. Be safe—and swift."

Johann stepped closer, clutching his holy symbol, his thumb rubbed along the face of the dragon. "Maybe you have the skin of Nymera, the guidance of Marezora, and the strength of Vorthunal, Cinder."

"I'm just scouting, Johann." Cinder scowled at him, but there was no cruelty in it.

Ambrosja stepped beside Cinder, her tone sincere. "It feels wrong to allow you to go alone... but I will place my trust in your abilities, even if I have not yet witnessed them."

Cinder grinned, raising a thumb. "Relax, Blondie. You've never seen me sneak because I'm just *that* good." With a wink, she vanished into the underbrush, low to the ground and silent as a whisper.

Her steps were soft. Every motion controlled. She crouched low, her legs moving in a wide spiderlike gait as she glided from bush to bush. Her sharp eyes swept up into the canopy.

No one ever thinks to look up, she mused. *If this is a front... they'll have archers perched in the branches.*

She did glance downward occasionally. *And traps, always traps...* But there were none—yet.

Clink.

There it was again. Closer this time. She stilled, angling her head to the southeast.

Clink.

Again. Steady. Rhythmic. *Picks on stone,* she thought.

Moving with measured caution, Cinder's eyes darted to every tree trunk, every patch of disturbed soil, every bush too conveniently placed. Then, in the distance, she saw it: a tall wooden fence, just visible between

breaks in the foliage. Behind it came muffled voices, heavy wheels crunching earth, the grunt and rhythm of labor, the clink of picks. The creak of carts.

She crept along the perimeter, not too close, until her gaze landed on what might have been an opening. Two guards stood at its flanks—dressed in black leather, tall, vigilant.

Worst case, I outrun them... she considered. *But that risks the whole mission. I can't be seen.* She pulled back carefully, scanning the area around her. Her gaze drifted upward. A plan formed.

Circling a nearby tree, she drew both daggers—gleaming with faint light. *Too much noise and I'm dead,* she reminded herself.

She plunged one dagger into the bark and pulled herself up, burying the next blade a little higher. Her boots pressed against the trunk. She ascended slowly, the soft *thunk* of steel on wood drowned beneath the distant cacophony of working miners.

At fifteen feet up, she reached a thick branch. She sheathed her blades and crouched low upon it, knees bent like a waiting cat. Still not high enough. She climbed further—twenty feet—fingers curled tightly around the bark. She steadied her breath, inching toward the edge of the leaves, parting them with care.

And there—at last—she saw it: guards stood at every post; all clad in black. Men and women wielded picks and hauled ore-laden carts, entering the mouth of a mine at the far end of the camp.

Donathan was being honest, she realized. *It's them.*

A cart rolled by beneath her, and Cinder's sharp gaze caught the glint of the cargo it carried—a black, jagged ore with blue streaks pulsing faintly through its core.

Her breath caught. *Nythralt... That's Nythralt. Damned ore. That's not good.*

Then she heard a voice—loud, commanding. Her eyes snapped toward the source. A man strode through the camp with strawberry blond hair and freckled skin that had been bronzed from being outdoors. He was barking orders. His shirt was open at the collar—and branded across his chest was a black hand: human in shape, monstrous in design. Just like Donathan's.

That's The Black Hand, alright. Cinder exhaled inwardly. *Time to go back.*

Carefully, she began her descent, lowering herself until she reached the broader limbs of the tree, limbs thick enough to hold her steady. She didn't dare move too fast. One crack of bark, one misplaced shift, and the mission would die with her fall.

Cinder moved with deftness, appraising each branch beneath her boot with the care of a jeweler studying the band of a noble's ring. One foot at a time, every step deliberate. But the descent was trickier than the climb—the branches grew thinner, less reliable. Worse still, she was nearly fifteen feet up before a branch thick enough could catch her weight. She paused, gaze flicking to the next tree. Its limbs were sturdier, spread wider. If she moved fast, she could cross.

She tensed, fingers curling tight around the bark beneath her. Then she pushed off—light, nimble—feet crossing swiftly over the narrow branch, and then she *jumped*.

Her boots landed on the next branch with feline grace. Her hands caught the trunk to steady herself. A soft breath of relief passed her lips. "Thank fuck..."

A voice rasped from just ahead: "What the—?"

She froze. Head turned, eyes rising. Another archer. Perched just around the bend, black-leathered and cloaked in shadow. There was silence between them for just a moment. Then he turned, hand raising near his mouth as if to yell—Cinder didn't waste time. Steel flashed as she drove her dagger into his thigh. The man choked on a cry, then grabbed the blade, wrenched it free, and slashed at her arm. Cinder reeled back. Her foot slipped. She crashed onto the branch below—her landing uneven, jarring pain shooting through her ankle as she hit and slid back against the trunk.
Thuk!

An arrow thudded into the tree, inches from her head. Her gaze snapped up. A second archer, somewhere on a neighboring tree, was already nocking the next arrow. But the first one—the wounded man—was faster. He dropped to the branch with a heavy thump, her dagger in hand.

"You bitch," he growled, blade raised.

Cinder's chest rose and fell rapidly. Her eyes darted once—toward the distant archer. Then she moved. She lunged forward, pain forgotten. Her hands grabbed the man's leathers and pulled him forward—just as the next arrow flew and used him as a shield.

The shaft was buried deep into his ribs. The man gave a wheeze, then crumpled. Cinder didn't stop. She reached for the arrow sticking out of him, yanked it free—he screamed—and jammed it up beneath his jaw with a sickening crack. The body spasmed, then went still. She shoved it off the branch. The second archer, shaking now, loosed another arrow. But she was already drawing. Her fingers flew to her bow, string already pulled, the stolen arrow already nocked.
Thuk!

Right into his eye. Blood coated his cheekbone down to his jawline.

The man tumbled, dead before he hit the ground.

Cinder winced, pressing a hand to her throbbing ankle. "…This is a fucking mess," she muttered.

She began to descend, branch by branch, slower now. At the last length, she dropped, letting the first archer's corpse cushion her fall. She hit with a grunt, then lay there a breath longer than she meant to.

Her hand reached out and gave the dead man a pat. "Nothing personal. You were going to kill me first." She rolled off him, rose with a groan, favoring her ankle. Then she crouched and searched his corpse. Her dagger was the first to go back in its sheath. Next came his quiver, and then his bow. "You will not be needing this."

Ambrosja, Donathan, Gunnar, and Johann waited beneath the trees, postures relaxed, though only in appearance. Their eyes shifted restlessly between the path Cinder had vanished down and the trail where miners trudged to and fro.

Gunnar scratched at his beard, a huff of frustration escaping him. "Damn it, where is that lass?" He pushed off the trunk and took a few paces forward, gaze sweeping the wood line.

Ambrosja moved, brows furrowed. "It was foolish to let her go alone!" she growled—at herself, not them. "I should go find her. This is my fault. My plan."

Johann stood up, hand reaching to halt Ambrosja, "Ambrosja, please…" Johann looked between the tense Ambrosja and the pacing Gunnar, "She is fine. Cinder can handle herself."

Gunnar scoffed, "Of course she can. I trained her, didn't I?"

"Not in archery or subtlety, you didn't." The voice cut clean and sharp. It was Cinder—limping slightly, her bow and quiver where they belonged, an extra quiver at her hip, but she used the stolen bow as a cane.

Gunnar paused, then surged forward, crossing the space in quick strides. He caught her in a hug that lifted her halfway off her feet. "Spitfire of mine!" he boomed. "I thought I was going to have to adopt another damned orphan."

"Ha ha…" Cinder was sarcastic and glaring at him, but there was no real venom; she simply leaned her weight into him.

The others looked visibly relieved at her return. But Ambrosja's sharp eyes found what the others missed first.

"Your ankle—are you harmed?" she asked, already stepping close.

Gunnar steadied Cinder. "What happened?"

"Archers in the trees," Cinder muttered. "Missed a step thanks to them. Took a fall... but I killed 'em. Don't think they were the only ones posted up, though."

Ambrosja offered a nod and gently guided her to a nearby log. "Sit," she said with a soft tone. Without waiting for protest, she knelt, hands already unfastening the buckles of Cinder's boot and loosening the laces. She rolled the leather down to reveal the ankle—already turning a deep bruise-purple. "I can mend this."

Johann approached, crouching beside them. He removed the holy symbol from beneath his collar and let it rest over his palm. "Let me help, I can heal as well. We'll mend her together."

Ambrosja inclined her head. "That should ease the strain."

Both sets of hands hovered over the injured ankle. Light bloomed—Johann's a pale, steady yellow; Ambrosja's, warm gold with glowing flecks like burning embers. Cinder groaned, wincing as her muscles shifted beneath skin, knitting and realigning in ways mortal minds were never meant to fully understand. Then the glow faded.

Cinder shifted her foot—then scowled as she felt the throbbing creep deep within her muscles. "The fuck? I thought you *healed* it."

"We did, girl. But your body still needs time to catch up."

Ambrosja nodded in agreement. "The wound is gone, but Johann is right, your body needs time to realize what has happened. In thirty minutes—perhaps an hour—you will walk unhindered."

"God, must you always sound like a proper princess?" Cinder grunted, then muttered, "...Thanks." Gunnar helped her to her feet with ease.

Johann looked over Ambrosja with curiosity, "You're a healer and a fighter, I presume your father was the one who taught you to fight..." He was watching Ambrosja, studying her.

"Yes," Ambrosja paused. "After my mother passed, he taught me everything he knew."

Gunnar tilted his head. "Hm, you said your father died in battle, right? Which battle?"

Cinder, leaning against a tree, gave a snort. "Alright, ease off. We all know what she is—she's Nordorner. Which makes it painfully obvious which battle it was." She looked directly at Ambrosja. "Nordorner... But here you are, protector of Wintersong. A hamlet *in* Vaestoria. Not Nordorn."

Silence fell, heavy as snowfall.

Ambrosja's gaze moved from one face to the next. Donathan, however, looked between all of them, confused. "Wait, what battle?"

"It was not just a *battle*," Ambrosja clarified, her stance wider now, her tone? Defensive. "It was a war… A country from the continent of Aldorwyn decided that it didn't want Nordorn to be the leading force anymore… And the rulers of that country, *Braxia*, proved exactly why Nordorn's people are not to be threatened." She said too much—*Damn it.* Ambrosja closed her eyes and exhaled slowly. "Is this where we part ways… or draw blades?"

Gunnar shook his head, "A fucking Nordorner hiding in a Vaestorian hamlet…" his arms were crossed, his expression unreadable. But ultimately, he moved, closing the distance. "I knew it…" His hand came to rest on her shoulder. "Neither, lass, you could have kept your healing touch to yourself. But you didn't. You healed Cinder—no hesitation. Still…" his voice dropped, "…this is strange, can't fault us for poking and prodding. What were you *truly* doing in Wintersong?"

Ambrosja met his gaze directly. "They are my people," her tone was firm. "Wintersong was founded by Nordorners—folk who broke away centuries ago. They no longer follow the old ways, and I was sent to bring them back."

Gunnar crossed his arms. "And you believed they would follow you back?"

"I hoped they would…" Ambrosja's eyes met the ground for a moment. "Times have changed. Nordorn is no longer the brute hammer it once was. We do not flatten kingdoms or raise mountains for sport. We seek unity." Ambrosja shook her head, scoffing at herself. "…if I had done a better job of convincing them to follow me… They would still be alive."

Cinder waved a hand dismissively. "Alright—unity, honor, whatever." She pressed on, her tone darkening. "There's definitely a mine. Definitely a cover-up. I saw a man there—same black hand mark as Donathan."

Gunnar scratched his beard. "Well, shit. Looks like we're finally sniffing the right trail."

"Now, we just need to think of a backup plan," Johann's brows furrowed. "We send Ambrosja in there with Donathan… and then what? We need to be close. Not close enough to blow her cover, but not so far we can't help if it turns sideways."

"I agree, old man," Cinder was resting one boot on a rock. "We can't just let them waltz in alone." A pause. Then she sat straighter. "Oh. And by the way? They're mining Nythralt."

Donathan shook his head, "That's impossible. Nythralt is only far north."

"But we are in the northern Bramble…" Gunnar glanced at Ambrosja, "Did you know Nythralt veins ran through here?"

Ambrosja shook her head. Her voice cracked, "No, I hadn't a clue about it…"

Gunnar took a step closer, "You had no clue? A fucking Nordorner had no clue where Nythralt was…"

Ambrosja took a step back, "I assure you, I did not—"

Gunnar closed the distance, the ghosts of what he'd seen—what he'd lost—tightening his fists before his reason could catch up. His hands found Ambrosja's shoulders as he pinned her against a tree. "Don't fucking lie to me, lass… I've seen what that thing can do to the minds of men and women!"

Johann stilled, for only a second, "Gunnar! Stop!"

Gunnar wasn't listening to him; his hands didn't leave her shoulders, "Tell me you're not lying to me, lass… Not after everything, after we let you tag along, after Cinder risked her life!"

Cinder's eyes widened, "Hey—Big guy! Ease it!" she pushed herself upwards, limping and nearly stumbling, "Shit! Gunnar! Stop it!"

Ambrosja's eyes flared with a glow like a threat, her hands shot to Gunnar's, "I'm not lying! I didn't know! It's not why I'm here!"

"Gunnar!" Cinder called out again, but he wasn't listening to her.

"Do you even know what Nythralt can do to people?!" his voice was filled with barely restrained rage. "You think it's just ore? I've seen it boiled down—turned into ash and powder and *hate*. I've seen men crumble from it and for it! I've had to bury my own soldiers who thought they could finally become heroes if they got a *boost* from it!"

"Yes!" Ambrosja choked out. "Yes, I know…" her voice was hoarse now. "It is a rite of passage for warriors in Nordorn."

Johann stepped forward, hands on Gunnar's bicep, trying to pull him back, "Gunnar, stop it! We've discussed this before—mind over matter!"

Gunnar's hands tightened on her shoulders… Then faltered slightly, his eyes were on Ambrosja's face, he saw the slight glow of them, like she was ready to strike if needed, but how it flickered with restraint, Gunnar's chest heaved. He realized then what he looked like—like he was slipping into the man he once was. But it didn't matter.

It was Donathan who stepped forward with urgency next. His hands grabbed Gunnar's arm. "Stop!" He tried to pull.

Gunnar ended up elbowing Donathan, the edge of the armor scrap-

ing across Donathan's forehead, a droplet of blood splattered onto the metal. Gunnar froze at the sight, the blood threw him through memories of his fallen friends, and brought him back. Gunnar's hands fell slack. Cinder rushed with a limp, trying to steady him along with Johann, who joined her side.

"Lad…" Gunnar spoke low, "…Damn, I'm—"

"I don't care!" Donathan wiped away the blood on his forehead. "This isn't what the Black Hand is about! I didn't lose my family over ore!" His hand dropped, fingers curled into a fist as his other hand tugged at his tunic to show the mark branded on his chest. "I didn't fucking sell my godsdamn soul for it either! And I am *not* going to lose whatever I have left because you two want to fight over honesty, Nordorn, ore, or whatever you've got going on!"

His hands flared again—nearly catching fire this time—but he clenched his fists, trembling as tears threatened to spill. He stared down at his shaking hands, then at the earth. His voice cracked. "…I don't know what's going on. But I'm too fucking scared to let this all go to hell. I don't want to be a puppet. I don't want to keep killing. So, please, let's just go and focus on what matters."

Gunnar exhaled sharply. "You're right." His shoulders slumped. Sorrow weighed in his eyes as he glanced between Donathan and Ambrosja. "I'm sorry, lass. I'm real sorry… What I just did—what you just saw? That was a part of me I thought long buried, but I guess not, and I'm sorry."

Ambrosja's hands moved to her shoulders, fingers rubbing the plates of her armor—armor that, only moments ago, had been pinching her skin. "It is alright," she said softly. "I understand… I do not blame you." She looked at Donathan. "…I made a vow," she said, stepping toward him. "And in this vow, I said nothing would stop me. I meant it. I will see this through." She stood beside him now. No hesitation. "When you are ready… take me to the camp."

From the journal of Guinyldr Thorn,
Bjarnvakt, 10, 997
THE BRAMBLE

THE BRAMBLE

Few regions of Stonehaven inspire such wary reverence as The Bramble. Stretching across the northern expanse of the regency and creeping into the borders of Alarion and Greymire, the forest stands as a living boundary between the known and the untamed.

To travelers, it is a place of whispering leaves and uneasy quiet—a realm where the ordinary laws of nature seem to falter. Tales speak of vines that steal coin from the pockets of the careless and shadows that move without wind or reason.

The outer woods are said to be passable, even fair in their own wild beauty, but the deeper one ventures toward the heart of The Bramble, the thicker the gloom becomes, until even sunlight dares not intrude. Whether it is beast, spirit, or the forest itself that guards those depths remains uncertain—but few who have gone far into The Bramble care to return and tell of it.

CHAPTER FIVE
THE THRESHOLD

The mining camp loomed ahead. Ambrosja and Donathan could see it clearly now—the towering wooden fences more akin to walls, and the open gate flanked by two guards clad in black. The distant clatter of pickaxes striking stone echoed faintly in the air.

"Halt!" one of the guards called, raising a hand. "Who goes there?"

Donathan didn't answer immediately. One hand rested firmly on Ambrosja's shoulder, holding her just ahead of him like a prisoner. With the other, he tugged down the collar of his tunic just enough to reveal the blackened brand upon his skin.

"One of yours," he replied.

The guard tilted his head. "That may be—but it doesn't explain the woman beside you."

"Servant," Donathan answered bluntly. "Found her in one of the northern hamlets. Serve, or die. She made the right choice."

The two guards exchanged a look before the silent one stepped forward, scrutinizing Donathan. "Which unit were you with?"

Donathan didn't falter. "Unit? What, is that a trick question? We don't use 'units.' We serve under Hands. I was with Evander's Hand."

"Shit, you really were far north," the guard muttered, nodding. He removed his helmet, giving Donathan a better look, then turned his attention to Ambrosja. "What's your name?"

"Donathan—"

He was cut off. "I was asking the woman."

Ambrosja held his gaze a moment longer before answering, "Amber."

The guard reached toward her. She did not flinch as his fingers threaded through her hair. "Never seen hair like this before…" His eyes wandered over her as if assessing fine craftsmanship. Then he caught her chin between his fingers, lifting her face so gold eyes met his own dark gaze. "Looks like trouble." At last, he stepped back. "Go in, both of you," the guard said, gesturing toward the heart of the camp. "Find something to keep yourselves busy. The Commander will see you, I'm sure."

Donathan's heart gave a jolt. *Commander…?* he thought. *What in the hell is a Commander of the Black Hand doing all the way out here?*

Ambrosja steeled herself, focus sharp. Her fingers twitched, longing for the blade Gunnar had taken from her to preserve their cover.

Up in the trees, Cinder whispered, watching her companions from above, "They got inside."

Johann shook his head slowly. "This is still madness."

Gunnar's shoulders were tense, though he made a deliberate effort to appear calm—there was no use in spreading panic. "They'll manage. It's the best plan we've got. Let 'em snoop around a bit. Anything they find will help."

Ambrosja and Donathan entered the mining camp, their gazes sweeping across everything within reach. Most of the structures were wooden—crude but functional. Toward the back loomed a building more fortified than the rest, rising perhaps three stories. Guards patrolled every corner, watched over each station, and accompanied every mining cart that emerged from the mouth of the cave. The scent of sweat and metals clung to the air. Grunts of the working man and woman, and laughter from guards that seemed drunk on power, only made the camp feel more suffocating. Once they were far enough from the two guards at the entrance, Ambrosja lifted a gloved hand and wiped her chin. Her nose curled in visible distaste.

Donathan noticed. "Sorry about that."

Ambrosja blinked and looked his way, surprised. "Sorry? For what?

You were not the one who laid hands upon me."

"No... you're right. I wasn't. But you are here because of me."

"No, I am here because I chose to be."

Donathan exhaled, giving a nod. "True enough."

Before further words could pass, another guard approached. He wasn't tall, but thick with muscle; his strawberry blond hair bounced with every angry step this man took. His black cloak billowed as he closed the distance.

"The fuck are you two standing around for?" he snapped.

Donathan didn't flinch. "Brought someone in looking to serve. Was told to wait for the Commander."

"*Oh*, told to wait for the Commander, were you?" The guard echoed the words with a sneer. "Well, guess what? You're talking to Lieutenant Berric right now, so go ahead and make yourselves useful in the damn mines."

Donathan didn't hesitate—he placed a firm hand on Ambrosja's shoulder and gave a gentle push forward. "Right. We're going."

"Good. You better pray he likes your face, or you're next."

A window for planning, this is what we need. Ambrosja gave a subtle nudge of her foot to Donathan's, an attempt to ease him.

Ambrosja said nothing as she moved silently toward the mine's opening with Donathan, accepting a pickaxe from a nearby guard without a word. Donathan took one as well and followed closely behind.

"There's a tunnel they just opened up—southeast corner, third fork to the right, don't go too far in though, roof ain't exactly stable," the guard called after them. He was already turning away, mind elsewhere.

They walked along the cavern edge, one hand trailing the wall for guidance as dim oil lanterns offered a flickering path toward the tunnel in question. Workers were already there, chipping and hauling. Ambrosja said nothing—just stepped forward, found an open spot, and began to swing. Donathan winced at the sight.

"Gods, your form is dreadful," he stepped closer, dropping his voice to a whisper. "You've never mined a day in your life, have you?"

"No," Ambrosja said plainly, still swinging. "I have not."

Donathan's smile was tight, and his brow was twitching. After a moment, he leaned closer, murmuring with serious but subtle concern, "Cinder's theory about you being royalty is starting to sound a lot less like a joke."

"Yes, well," Ambrosja replied crisply, "I suggest we focus on matters of substance and not Cinder's *theories* about me."

"You're right..." Donathan muttered, but with a smirk. "Again."

Ambrosja's tone lowered, almost conspiratorial. "Do you know this Commander?"

"I don't know any of them personally," he admitted, voice kept to a hush. "Only heard of the Northern ones. I followed Evander after my hamlet fell."

Ambrosja tilted her head slightly. "And where was your hamlet?"

"Stonecreek Hill. Mining hamlet in the northwest—just beyond the mountains."

A slow glance was cast his way. "So *that* is why you were critiquing my form."

"Possibly," Donathan answered with a grin, though it faded just as quickly. "...But more pressingly, sounds like we've found ourselves a Commander with a temper."

"Which we could use to our advantage, maybe?"

"Hey! Less yapping, more mining!" a guard barked as he passed the tunnel entrance.

The conversation halted. Both turned back to their work, pickaxes striking stone in mechanical rhythm.

Nearby, a stranger—a miner, not a guard—glanced at them, specifically at Donathan. He studied them for a moment, then returned to the wall he was chipping at. Under his breath, just loud enough to be heard, he muttered, "Strange... Dressed like one of 'em, but here you are, chipping stone with the rest of us."

Donathan caught the miner's muttered comment but kept his tone light, nonchalant. "Isn't that what they always do?" he scoffed, swinging his pickaxe. "Make the newcomers do the manual labor? Easier on the conscience than writing death orders."

The miner glanced over again. "Hm." His pick struck the stone a bit more gently this time. "Makes sense... never seen you around before."

"Yeah, I kept north. Was with Evander's Hand." Donathan gave him a sideways look. "You know which Hand runs this camp?"

The older man grunted, pausing as if rifling through vague memories. "Listen, son. We're just here to pull ore from stone. Don't know much about which Hand's in charge of where. But..." he hesitated, "...from what I've heard? Last Hand was removed. Demoted. Commander didn't like something about him."

Donathan's rhythm faltered. He turned to face the man more directly. "Is he always like this? Aggressive? Easily set off?"

The miner gave a low chuckle, pickaxe still in motion. "All I know is

that man could hear you breathe wrong from fifty feet and start planning your burial." He shook his head slowly. "No one here crosses him. He hires us, pays us, and leaves us alone. We return the favor. That's the unspoken rule."

Ambrosja finally spoke, her tone calm and measured. "Has he been stationed here long?"

The miner didn't pause, but his brow furrowed in thought. "Less than a month, I think. He came to close the ledgers, or so they said. Left the last Commander in pieces too torn for the gods to name. We stopped asking questions after that."

Ambrosja tilted her head, expression unreadable. "Has he done such a thing to others? Or was that simply... a singular lapse in restraint?"

The miner shook his head, his grip tightening around the wooden shaft of his pickaxe until his knuckles whitened. "No... I think every step that man takes is calculated." His voice dropped as he shook his head more forcefully this time, as if warding off a thought too grim. "It's only a matter of time before he decides the lot of us aren't worth the effort of the paperwork..."

Ambrosja watched him. His shoulders trembled faintly as he returned to his task, and each swing of the pickaxe landed heavier, less precise.

The sharp peal of a bell echoed through the cavern. The miner froze, then muttered something under his breath. Ambrosja's gaze darted to Donathan. He was already looking around. One by one, the miners dropped their tools and began scrambling for the exit. Without speaking, Donathan nudged Ambrosja's arm and gave a small tilt of his head. They followed.

At the mine's mouth, a formation was taking shape. Miners on one side, guards on the other—two rigid lines facing each other, with a wide, deliberate gap in between. All eyes were on the main structure, the stone edifice at the back of the camp. Ambrosja and Donathan took their place among the miners. They glanced towards the building, and they noticed the stance of Lieutenant Berric had sharpened, but his gaze looked bored.

"Oi," a guard hissed toward Donathan, brow furrowed. "You're on *this* side, boy. You wear the Hand, not the collar."

Donathan hesitated. Just for a breath. His eyes flicked sideways—toward Ambrosja. She stood tall, posture flawless, hands folded neatly behind her back, the picture of discipline. She did not look at him, but she dipped her chin in a subtle nod. Donathan understood. He crossed the divide and took his place among the Black Hand.

High in the trees beyond the camp's edge, Cinder hissed down through the branches. "Something's happening."

Gunnar looked up sharply. "What kind of something?"

Johann shot him a sharp glance. "Hush."

Cinder shook her head. "Not sure. But the miners and guards are lined up. Facing each other."

The heavy doors of the stone building groaned open. The first to emerge was a Black Hand guard, his pace brisk, almost anxious. He took his position at the front of the assembled lines, standing apart from both sides.

Ambrosja and Donathan now stood directly across from one another—six paces of open air between them. But her sharp eyes caught the flicker of change in his expression. She saw the way his gaze darted toward the doors again. The way his eyes widened for only a moment, then snapped back to her. She saw the breath he drew—and held.

Ambrosja followed his line of sight.

Him.

His boots struck the wooden steps with purpose, each step slow and resounding, like an executioner pacing toward the scaffold. He was a towering figure, made for war—broad across the shoulders, his arms thick with muscle, hands large enough to break bone without effort. Shoulder-length black hair framed a face darkened by sun and battle, the bronze of his skin accentuating the pale scar that slashed from the bridge of his nose down to a jawline sharp enough to shame a blade. Thick strands fell like a curtain across eyes the color of forged steel—cold, gray, and unyielding.

He did not spare them a glance. His eyes stared forward—cold, half-lidded, and full of disgust. When he spoke, his voice scraped the air like steel dragged across stone. "I have beaten men for lesser offenses than stealing from me..." he began, walking between the lines of bodies like a ghost gliding over graves. "And I am more than willing to do far worse when I discover who has been siphoning Nythralt from this camp."

Cinder froze where she perched. She craned her head and whispered down, "Some brute just walked out... Built like *you,* Gunnar."

The man halted in the center of the formation. His voice carried easily. "Some of you know me. Some of you don't. I am Killian Thorn. Northern Region Commander of the Black Hand."

A beat of silence.

"And I am the one who shall deliver judgment today." He resumed walking, slow and deliberate. "The last Hand in charge of this site," he continued, "tried to help himself to our Nythralt. I removed him." His tone was flat, almost bored. "But he did not act alone."

He reached the end of the formation and stopped—squarely between Ambrosja and Donathan. His head turned. Not to Donathan. To her.

"You're not a miner," he said simply. He faced her completely, his icy gaze sweeping over her with slow, unhurried appraisal. He exhaled through his nose, as if disappointed. Ambrosja did not blink. Her golden eyes held his stare, unmoving. His jaw ticked once—something grinding behind his teeth.

From her perch, Cinder narrowed her eyes and leaned lower, whispering to the others. "He's just standing in front of Ambrosja..."

Gunnar's hand crept toward his axe, fingers curling tight. "Don't," Johann hissed, grabbing his arm. "She's new. She stands out. He's likely just assessing." Gunnar didn't move. "Mind over matter," Johann murmured again, firmer. "Mind over matter."

Gunnar gave a low, frustrated sigh. "...Fine."

Back in the camp, the commander's gaze remained fixed on Ambrosja. His eyes dropped to her armor, lingered, then returned to her face. "Remove it." Ambrosja didn't move. "Remove your armor, soldier."

Donathan stepped forward, his voice shaking despite himself. "Forgive me, Commander... She came with me. From Wintersong."

The commander didn't turn—only tilted his head, casting a glance over his shoulder. "And that is supposed to mean something to me, boy?"

Donathan inhaled slowly. "She's not a threat."

Killian turned back to Ambrosja. "That remains to be seen." He studied her a moment longer, then gave a slight tilt of his head. "Go on. I'm not asking you to strip to your linens. I'm ordering you to show whether there's a spine beneath all that leather and steel... or if you're just a doll playing soldier."

Ambrosja stood motionless for a breath longer. Then her hands moved. With calm precision, she reached for the buckles at her ribs, unfastening the straps securing her breastplate. She pulled it up and over her head, sliding it free from her left arm with practiced ease. Next, her fingers moved to the plates fastened around her thighs. One by one, the metal fell to the earth with soft, echoing thuds.

When finished, she stood tall once more, adorned in dark gray leathers. Her hands returned to rest behind her back. Still and unshaken.

Killian's eyes moved over her, but gave away nothing—not a nod, not a flicker of approval or interest. Just that same cold, unblinking stare. "So. A soldier, then," he said at last, his voice low and slow—like the sky just before a storm breaks. "Which means you've seen blood. Spilled it."

Ambrosja's gaze didn't waver. "Yes, Commander."

"Good." He turned from her and raised his voice for the camp to hear. "Now I need not concern myself with beating a man half to death in front of a lady."

Then—*Crack. Bone snapped.* Again and again. Killian's hardened fists met flesh. Knuckles striking across the face—once, twice—then low in the stomach. A body fell. But Killian didn't stop. He raised his heavy boot high and slammed it down upon the ribs. Sickening snaps and a guttural crunch could be heard. Ragged gasping from a punctured lung could be felt. Killian's eyes never left the figure on the ground, and his cold stare never faltered, just as his strikes didn't.

Ambrosja flinched despite herself, her eyes wide as blood splattered, spattering across her pale skin and soaking into strands of her ashen hair. The miner that once stood beside Ambrosja had slumped to the ground, unconscious and in a pool of his own blood. Finally, Killian's steel-toed boot shoved the broken miner aside, rolling him like a discarded sack.

Killian's hand, slick with blood, rose to brush his black hair from his face with eerie calm. Then, finally, emotion crept through; his voice thundered across the yard, "This is what happens when you steal from me!" His gaze swept the gathered crowd, fire in his voice now. "Do not test my patience. Do not test my limits. You will find I *have none.*"

Then, just as quickly, he straightened, rolling his shoulders as though nothing had happened. Turning toward Ambrosja. She was still frozen. Her composure, so carefully cultivated, was cracked. Her eyes lingered on the broken body. Still. Too still.

"What," Killian stepped closer, "you wish to lift him up? Pity him?

Reward betrayal with mercy?" Ambrosja's throat tightened. She said nothing. Her eyes remained on the bloodied form below. Killian's hand snapped up to seize her jaw, fingers digging into her cheeks with bruising force. "Look at me when I speak to you, soldier." His grip tightened. "What will it be? Will you undo my sentence with kindness? Or accept his punishment for what it is?"

Ambrosja didn't answer. Her face didn't move, didn't twitch—but Killian saw it. The flicker of something behind her eyes. Rage, maybe. Or fear. Or something worse.

He released her with a shove, sending her head tilting back slightly. "In my office, soldier," he said coldly. "Seems we have paperwork to discuss." He turned toward Donathan. "You too."

Without another word, Killian strode back toward the stone structure, vanishing behind its tall, heavy doors. Ambrosja drew a long breath, quiet but sharp, steadying herself, while Donathan's pulse kicked hard beneath his collar.

The strawberry-blond man, Lieutenant Berric, stepped forward, clapping his hands to shatter the stunned silence. "Alright, show's over! Back to work!" Then he called out, "And none of you touch this man." He pointed towards the slumped body of the miner. "Not unless any of you would like to end up just like him!"

Cinder's hand remained over her mouth, her wide eyes frozen on the courtyard. Gunnar glanced up sharply. "Lass..." his voice dropped to a whisper. "What in the fuck is going on? You've been quiet too long!"

Cinder didn't answer right away. She watched Ambrosja and Donathan disappear into the building. Then, without a word, she dropped—her feet finding branches as she descended like a squirrel fleeing a wildfire. She hit the ground with a soft thump.

"...That big one," she muttered, turning to Gunnar. "He just *pummeled* a miner into the dirt. No hesitation."

Gunnar's jaw tensed, nostrils flared. "That's what the shouting was?"

Cinder nodded. "And—he made her take off her armor. In front of everyone."

Gunnar's face darkened like thunderclouds gathering. "He *what?!*"

Johann's expression shifted into deep concern.

Cinder fixed her bow slung over her shoulder, "They're inside. With him."

Gunnar's breath came through gritted teeth. "We need to get closer. Now."

Johann ran a hand through his hair. "We're already too near, Gunnar. Any closer and we risk patrols—or worse, another archer like the ones Cinder ran into." He took a deep breath to steady himself. "I know you're worried," he added quietly, "but we must trust them. Just a little longer."

Gunnar gave a slow, reluctant nod. "Fine."

He turned to Cinder. "Let's at least get around the back of that building. Stay low, stay distant. You think you can guide us to it?"

Cinder nodded and was already moving. "Opposite side. Might get a glimpse if I find a tall enough tree." She didn't wait for approval. "Let's not waste time."

From the journal of Guinyldr Thain,
Bjarnvakt, 13, 997

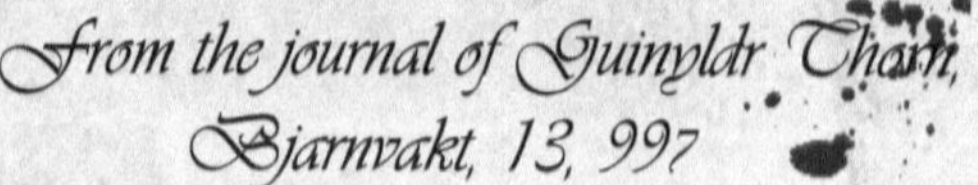

NYTHRALT

Deep beneath the stone veins of Nordorn lies Nythralt—a black ore streaked with veins of luminous blue.

The dark metal, harder than iron and sharp as legend claims, has long been prized by Nordorner smiths for forging weapons of remarkable strength. Yet it is the living veins within Nythralt that give it its fearsome renown.

When distilled into liquid, this essence is consumed in the ancient warrior trials of Nordorn. Those who endure its searing passage are said to emerge hardier, their endurance unmatched.

Those who fail meet a death both excruciating and unforgettable—so much so that even the bravest hesitate before the cup. Thus, Nythralt stands as both gift and curse: the ore that tempers not only steel, but the spirit of those who dare its power.

Mythralt

Black as obsdian, bearing its
elegant sheen, yet harder and
truer than iron.

The Veins of Mythralt

"The Blood of Brynhjora" -
scholars believe this is all that
remains of the empress; when
refined, the substance is used in
perilous rites of endurance.

By the time they reached the staircase, Ambrosja had already buckled her armor back into place, her fingers moving with the kind of speed only born from years of battle. She and Donathan ascended the stairs, taking one step at a time as they followed behind Killian. Donathan's heart thundered in his chest, his fingers trembling despite the effort to still them. Ambrosja reached across the gap between them, her hand closing gently around his in a firm, reassuring squeeze. His eyes shut tight for a beat. Then came a slow, sharp exhale—and a nod. By the time they reached the landing, Killian had already thrown open the double doors to his office.

The sconces lining the walls remained unlit, allowing the full light of the afternoon sun to spill in through the tall, open windows. The office was expansive. A dark, heavy desk of solid wood dominated the center, stacked with haphazard piles of books and parchment scrawled in aggressive strokes of ink. The floor was wide-planked and seamless—not a creak escaped even under Killian's weight. A round rug in shades of crimson, plum, black, and gold adorned the center. Bookcases lined the curved back wall; across another hung pinned maps marked with tacks and red thread. Near the hearth, two deep chairs sat angled around a black-stained table, their cushions upholstered in blood-red velvet. A shelf of liquor—clearly expensive—stood quietly in one corner.

"Come in," Killian called without looking back.

He moved behind the desk, lowering himself into a chair that groaned softly beneath his bulk. He didn't lift his gaze. One massive hand dragged a paper closer, the other dipped a quill in ink and began to write.

"So then, young Black Hand. What is your name?"

"Donathan."

"And the woman?" Killian asked without pause, though this time his eyes did rise, fixing on Donathan with cold precision. "Her name?"

"Amber."

Killian's gaze flicked to Ambrosja. A moment passed. Then it returned to Donathan, "You brought her from Wintersong," he said slowly. "That is no short journey... About four days at least." He returned to his writing. "If that's the case, you served under Evander's Hand. Yes?"

"Yes, Commander." Donathan swallowed, straightening, his hands clasped behind his back to mirror Ambrosja's poised calm. "I was among those left behind to ensure no survivors remained."

Killian gave a thoughtful hum, the soft scratch of the quill continuing. A silence stretched between them. "Then why bring her here?" His tone was unreadable. His eyes rose again, fixed on Donathan with a quiet, searing intensity. "Why not return her to Evander?"

Donathan hesitated. His breath faltered. "Well—" he clasped his hands harder. "I was trying to follow the same protocols that occurred when I was brought in. I was taken, chained, and trained before I could officially join a battle. And — Greenfield was closer by that point."

Killian was quiet. A rough forefinger rubbed against his large chin. He remained silent. His gaze never left Donathan's face.

"Is that so?" he said at last, the faintest tilt of his head toward Ambrosja, his storm-gray eyes landing on her once again. "You look like you can hold your own in a fight, I'll give you that." His hands came together, fingers interlacing atop the desk. "But we're not short on blades. Veterans of half a dozen wars. Former bounty hunters. Cutthroats. Mercenaries." His tone darkened. "We don't need another soldier... *Amber.*" The way he spoke the name—*Amber*—dripped with quiet contempt, as though he tasted something bitter just saying it.

Ambrosja's brow did not flinch. But her eyes did flicker. Just once. Still, she took a step forward. Measured. Intentional. "I am a fast learner," she said, voice as smooth as it was formal. "You'll find that I am quite skilled in fighting and healing."

Killian's face remained unreadable. Not a twitch. No sound. Then his hand lifted lazily, gesturing toward Donathan without even looking at him.

"Leave us." Donathan hesitated. Briefly. This time, Killian's gaze snapped to him, "I said leave us."

Donathan dipped his chin, turned, and stepped out, closing the doors behind him with a soft, hollow click. Killian's gaze remained locked on Ambrosja. The silence between them stretched, long and unmoving. She did not shift, did not fidget. Her posture was statuesque—shoulders square, hands behind her back, chin held with quiet authority.

Finally, he gestured toward the liquor case across the room. "Go on. Choose something that catches your eye. I insist."

She remained still—not from hesitation, but calculation. Her gaze searched him, reading the posture, the pitch, the smallest betrayals of intent. But Killian offered nothing. No tells. No flicker of mischief or threat. After a moment, she turned and moved toward the cabinet. It was beautifully crafted, dark, polished wood catching the light like wine. Inside, an array of glass bottles gleamed—deep ambers, shadowed greens, obsidian blacks, and silken reds. Her fingers traced along the pane, light and deliberate.

"Take your time," Killian called behind her, already returning to the papers on his desk.

Her gaze found a pale blue bottle, its glass frosted and swirling with faint white tendrils. Strange. Delicate. She chose it. Behind her, Killian's eyes flicked up, noting the choice, then returned to his writing without comment.

Ambrosja drew the bottle free and closed the cabinet. She turned back to face him, holding it with an effortless grace. "Is this a test?" she asked, one brow arching. "A judgment of character based on my taste in spirits?"

Killian looked up from his desk. Then he stood. The chair creaked as it released him, his form rising to full height. He moved toward her with heavy, unhurried steps and reached for two glasses from a nearby shelf— wide-bowled, with tapered rims shaped for savoring.

"Snowkiss, an excellent choice," he said. When he reached Ambrosja, he was tilting his head slightly. "And no, I am merely being a gracious host."

He set the glasses down on the table between them and took the bottle from her hands. His grip engulfed the glass, steady and sure. With a slow swirl, he disturbed the white wisps inside—the tendrils rising and dissolving into a soft, celestial shimmer. He uncorked it, then poured. The liquid shimmered, light catching in slow-moving swirls.

Killian lifted his and tapped it once against the rim of hers. A polite clink. He drank. Ambrosja held her glass for a moment longer. Her fingers curled around it. She inhaled—herbs, berries, something sharp and ancient. Then she drank. It hit sharp—bitter, then dark with berries and smoke. A warmth spread down her throat, soft and slow. She swallowed. A quiet hum left her lips, involuntary. Killian was *watching*.

His head tilted slightly as he observed her, one brow arching just so. "Funny," he murmured, "a person's taste in drink tells you more about a person than blood ever could."

He took another small sip. Then, he moved. He stepped closer, slowly, but not aimlessly. His body shifted forward, looming—his free hand pressed against the cabinet behind her, pinning her on one side. Not touching. Not quite. Just close enough.

"…Don't you agree, *Empress?*"

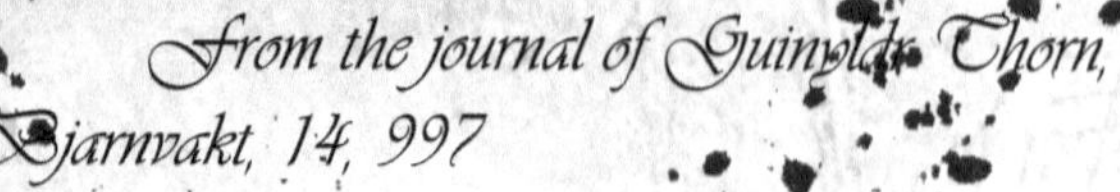

SNOWKISS

A spirit favored in the high halls and wind-bitten outposts of Nordorn. Its making requires patience and cold in equal measure.
Clear as glacier melt, it strikes first with frostleaf's
bite before yielding to the smoke-dark sweetness
of nightberry. When poured, the air about it hazes
with pale mist — a breath of winter itself.
Locals claim the first draught tests a traveler's
worth: if you flinch, the mountain knows
you do not belong. The second warms
the blood, and by the third, the drinker
swears to feel the slow heartbeat of the
earth beneath their boots.

Base: Start with a clear winter spirit (like a distilled grain alcohol or fermented root sap) kept chilled in snow or ice caves.

Bitterness: Steep with frostleaf—herbs that grow only in frozen soil and have a naturally biting, mint-bitter flavor.

Depth: Add a syrup brewed from nattbær, small black berries that grow beneath the snowline and have a smoky, jam-dark taste when roasted.

Finish: Serve it cold enough to mist when poured. Traditionally, the rim of the cup is dusted with powdered frostleaf ash to sting the lips.

Result: The drink bites first, then blooms dark and heavy

Nattbær
The syrup of nattbær darkens the spirit and warms the veins.

Frostleaf
A hardy alpine herb whose serrated leaves hold their own frost even in sunlight. Crushed leaves release a sharp, mint-cold scent used to clear the mind and steady the breath.

Cinder was hoisted up—Gunnar's hands clasped tight at her boot as he boosted her toward the tree's lower branches. With a grunt, she caught the nearest one, swung her leg over, and scrambled higher. Her foot had fully healed by now, as she climbed with urgency this time. But despite the urgency, she remained cautious—pausing now and again to glance behind her, judging her height.

At last, she settled onto a sturdy branch and turned her eyes toward the building. She glanced down, nodding once to Gunnar—she had a clear view now. Her gaze scanned the windows methodically, one by one. Then her eyes narrowed. She spotted him—Killian. His hand braced against the liquor cabinet. If not for the familiar cascade of thick, wavy blonde hair, she might not have spotted Ambrosja at all. The commander's towering form nearly obscured her.

Inside, Killian remained precisely where he stood. Watching her. Ambrosja's breathing had finally slowed.

Her brow arched, her head tilting slightly. "Is that your chosen nickname for me?"

Killian's lips curled—just faintly. A smirk, sardonic and fleeting. "Charming."

He pushed himself away from the cabinet, moving back toward his desk. As he walked, he lifted his glass and drained it, exhaling a quiet sound of satisfaction as he held the empty vessel up to the light.

"*Snowkiss,*" he said, admiring the glass. "Illegal in Vaestoria. Banned purely for being a Nordorn craft. Difficult to acquire… but gods," he set the glass down, "one of the finest things I've ever tasted." His gaze flicked back to her. "You mistake my brutality for ignorance. Assuming I wouldn't know who you are…"

He turned fully now, facing her, though keeping a broad distance of ten paces.

"I find myself wondering," he said, his voice almost inquisitive, "what the Empress of Nordorn is doing in a camp owned by the Black Hand."

Cinder's eyes flicked across the windows. She couldn't hear a word—but the tension was evident. She saw Ambrosja still standing, untouched, and sighed in relief. But her brows knit quickly—Donathan was gone. She glanced down toward the men below. "Donathan isn't in the room anymore," she whispered.

Johann and Gunnar exchanged a look. Johann's hand moved swiftly to catch Gunnar's wrist. "Give it a moment," Johann said calmly. "He might have been dismissed. He is one of theirs, after all."

Killian leaned back against the edge of the desk, powerful legs braced, arms folded. He said nothing, waiting. Ambrosja remained still. Her glass was untouched now, her fingers clenched tightly around its stem.

Killian studied her a moment longer, then let a small, humorless smile tug at the edge of his mouth. "You think I intend to turn you in. Or kill you. Don't you?" He shook his head slowly. "Neither serves me. Your death would mean war. Vaestoria versus Nordorn." He lifted a brow. "And that would… inconvenience my ambitions. All those hamlets I still need to burn. All those mouths I must silence."

That was the spark. The *crack* in her restraint.

Ambrosja stepped forward—deliberate, forceful. One boot struck the floor, then the other. Her drink dropped to the floor with a dull *clunk,* rolling out of her grasp. Her hands collided with Killian's chest, shoving him hard against the desk. "*You!*" Her voice was low, venomous, her face a storm

of grief and rage, "You are the one who commands the slaughter!"

Killian didn't resist. He let her push him, his back hitting the desk with a thud. His hands remained at his sides, calm, unmoving. He only smiled. "That boy—Donathan," Killian said softly, "he mentioned *Wintersong*." The name lingered like ash between them. "Must have meant something to you."

Cinder's hand flew to her mouth. Her breath hitched. From this distance, all she could see was movement. But that was enough. Ambrosja—charging. Practically on top of him. A body pressed to another on a desk. No weapons drawn. No fighting back.

"*Wintersong was mine!*" Ambrosja shouted. "My people. My blood. My responsibility. And you let them burn—like weeds stripped from a garden! I carried a dead little girl to lay beside her grandfather's corpse!" Her fists balled in his collar. She yanked him up once, then forced him back down with all the fury of a woman who had no one left to bury. "She was no older than six! *Six!* Why?! How can you *live* with this?!"

Killian let her scream. He absorbed the violence, the heartbreak, like a confession at a temple altar. When he spoke it was quiet. A controlled rumble that seemed to shake the air between them. "I am removing a plague." His words were not cruel. But they were not kind. "Northern hamlets cannot feed themselves," he said. "They starve through every winter. The kingdoms bleed resources into them—feeding the weak, sheltering the dying. And in doing so... they weaken themselves." He paused for a moment. "Ripe for forces like Nordorn."

"You're a fool if you think Nordorn would go to war just because your people lack the spine to govern." But her voice didn't stop there. It rose, but didn't shout. It sharpened, and cracked like a whip, "You risk a nation's wrath when you dare slaughter my people."

Killian's hands moved at last—snapping up to seize her wrists, cold and unyielding. "Your people?" he growled. "The ones born on Vaestorian soil? Raised under our taxes, buried under our banners?" He laughed. Low. Cold. A sound that didn't need volume to hollow the space between them.

Ambrosja's voice trembled—not with fear, but fury. "Then you are a monster. Not a brute. Not some misguided soul pretending to better his homeland. Just a monster."

Killian didn't flinch. He studied her tear-brimmed eyes with a gaze devoid of triumph, pity, or pain. "Sometimes, to preserve humanity," he said softly, "you must be willing to abandon it." His grip loosened. One hand slid to her waist—not possessive, just firm. He lifted her, setting her aside as he sat up. Then he looked at her. And for the first time—saw her. "As Empress of the most feared and savage nation on this continent," he spoke with a quiet and sure voice, "I expected you to understand that."

Killian set her down. Ambrosja stepped back without a word, fury still coiled hot beneath her ribs. But she said nothing. Instead, she crossed to the nearest window. With a sharp clack, she unlatched it, letting the cold rush in to fill her lungs. Her shoulders trembled. Her knuckles tightened against the frame.

"My great-grandmother bled to change how the world saw Nordorn," she said quietly. "She forged peace. She offered kindness where there had once been only blood." She turned. Her golden gaze burned despite the calm in her voice, "My grandmother upheld that law. My mother upheld that law. And now—I will." She stepped forward—not closing the distance, but letting her words carry across it. "I arrived at Wintersong alone. No guards. No blades. No banners. Only the truth—that Nordorn had changed."

Killian stood still, unreadable. That same cold mask remained. "It changes nothing," he said. "Those people were Vaestorian. Born here. Sworn here. Their deaths do not belong to you." He stepped forward as well, voice low, "Are you truly prepared to start a war over them?"

Ambrosja didn't flinch. "Perhaps I should," she said—calm, but deadly. "Perhaps I raze the land just to ruin your designs. Or perhaps I simply take what belongs to me." Her eyes narrowed. "All of it. Every hamlet. Every inch of soil that holds Nythralt beneath it."

Killian stilled. "Is that so?" his voice was like a blade unsheathing.

Ambrosja met him without blinking. "That is what you want, is it not?"

A long breath. Then a curl of his lips—slow, sardonic. "Well, well," he murmured. "The little Empress *does* have a mind behind all that moonlit hair."

Ambrosja's smile was not soft. "Let's not pretend this isn't what you're after." She tilted her head, her chin angled with dangerous precision. "Nythralt is blessed by a Nordorner god; it is and has always belonged to Nordorn. That ore is rightfully ours. Only the strong may wield its power. And those who are not strong enough…" Her voice faded for a moment Then she finished, "They perish. And not gently."

Killian said nothing. He turned, walked to his desk, and began straightening the scattered papers she'd disrupted. Ambrosja watched him, jaw tight.

"That's it?" she asked. "No denial? No challenge?"

Killian didn't look up. His hands moved with quiet purpose. "If you wish to wage war, then do so," he said. "But it will not be with the Black Hand." His eyes lifted—sharp. Empty. "It will be with all of Vaestoria. And I do not believe you are foolish enough to prove the world right." He leaned forward, elbows propping on his desk, fingers lacing together. "That Nordorn hasn't changed at all."

Ambrosja stood still—one breath, then another—then she struck. Her hands slammed against the desk. The inkwell jumped. Papers flared once more. The sound cracked like a whip across stone.

"What about *you?!*" she shouted. "Would you really drag this continent into ruin for your ambition?!" Her voice shook, "Vaestoria wouldn't survive Nordorn's wrath." She leaned forward, closer, heat pouring from every word, "You think you're protecting your country by slaughtering the desperate. By killing miners and mothers and children in the dark—" Her eyes burned. "But Nordorn will flatten the entire godsdamn world if needed."

Killian didn't move. He let her scream. Let her breath come ragged. Let her grip bend the corners of his maps. "Are you finished?" His voice was soft. Dry. Dismissive enough to flay.

Ambrosja's fury twisted. Her chest rose and fell, the anger scraping at her lungs. "I *hate* you," she said. Low. Bitter. No less true for the way her voice cracked.

"You're dismissed, Empress."

That was all Killian said before looking down at his papers.

the
AMBER of the
NORTH
EMPRESS
AMBROSIA NORDRAVN

From the journal of Guinyldr Thorn,
Bjarnvakt 20, 997

THE EMPRESS OF NORDORN

The Empress of Nordorn stands as both sovereign and symbol — the living bloodline of Brynhjora herself. Each Empress bears the first empress's mark: skin pale as snow, hair paler still, and eyes of burnished gold. By ancient decree, the crown passes from mother to daughter upon the latter's twenty-fifth year, when youth and strength are said to align with divine favor.

Until her marriage, the Empress commands Nordorn's armies by her own hand; thereafter, that duty is entrusted to her consort, though her word remains law above all. None may rule in her stead. unless necessary, for it is held that the Empress alone carries the will of Brynhjora — unbroken, unchallenged, and eternal.

Each Empress is also granted a name by her people — a title earned through deed or temperament. Some are remembered as "The Iron Dove," others as "The Amber of the North." These names endure long after crowns have changed hands, woven into song and scripture alike.

CHAPTER EIGHT
CORNERED

Cinder had seen enough to make her stomach twist. She couldn't hear the words—but Ambrosja's fury and Killian's stillness told her plenty. Cinder witnessed Ambrosja's staredown. The slamming. The silence. Cinder sighed; the air was shaky as it left her lips. She climbed down more slowly this time, boots finding each branch with care. Then dropping herself in front of Gunnar and Johann.

Cinder rubbed the back of her neck, "Well, Ambrosja seems physically fine, but looked like she had a fight with him."

"Do you reckon we should just go in there and get her out?" Johann looked at Gunnar now, waiting for his old friend's thoughts.

Gunnar simply stroked his beard in thought but also in worry, "The plan was for them to snoop around, but they've already been noticed by a damn leader. I doubt they can snoop as easily now."

Crunch. A twig snapped behind them. They all turned, hands moving to their weapons. But stopped. Donathan.

"Lad!" Gunnar called out, already pulling Donathan into a hug.

Donathan's body trembled in Gunnar's hold. His hands suddenly shot up, gripping Gunnar's furred cloak. "Thank you…" his voice trembled, "…Unexpected, but—I really needed that."

Johann, however, didn't waste time waiting on news. "Sorry to break up the family reunion, but, what went on in there? And how are you simply out here?"

"I asked to do a perimeter check," Donathan explained, catching his trembling breath as he stepped out of Gunnar's hug. "Met a Commander," Donathan said. "Black Hand. Killian Thorn." His shoulder twitched. Even saying the name seemed to sting. "He wanted to know why I brought Ambrosja all the way here instead of reporting back to my Hand. I think…" his voice dropped, "he doesn't trust her. Maybe doesn't like her. I don't know." Donathan exhaled. "He dismissed me. Said he wanted to speak with her alone."

Cinder scratched her knuckles, her fingers flexing as she tried to recall every detail. "I could barely tell what was going on, but—it looked bad. Mostly on her side, like a fight. While he was just a damn rock."

Johann's eyes narrowed. "He's trying to rattle her, I bet. Get under her skin. Maybe make her confess to spying. Silence can make people say things they shouldn't."

Gunnar's fingers tightened on his axe. "I need to stop letting women do things on their own. Makes me twitchy."

A cold voice cut in. "Keep twitching, and we'll spill your guts."

Three blades pressed into his back—one center, two at his sides. A Black Hand guard had spoken, flanked by four more. Cinder cursed under her breath. Johann sighed. Donathan didn't move.

"Let's go, birdies," the lead guard sneered. "Commander'll want a word. If you behave, he might decide against beating you to a bloody pulp, before roasting you."

Gunnar and Johann exchanged a look. They complied. Cinder didn't move at first. Not until a shove from behind forced her forward.

One of the guards fixed his glare on Donathan. "You too, boy. Commander'll want to know why you're whispering with spies."

Donathan's eyes darted between his comrades. Fear bloomed in his throat. "I can't—he'll kill me—" And then he ran. His leather boots beat down upon the grass with desperation as he sought his escape.

"Boy!" Gunnar called out, ready to chase, if it were not for the blades at his back.

"Go," the leader barked, causing the guards to move instantly. Two broke off, leaving the rest to secure the trio. "Bring him back!" He bellowed. He stood for a moment, then shared a glance with the others. "The rest—we take."

Ambrosja stepped from the building. The moment she spotted her friends—disarmed, surrounded, and her sword in the hands of a Black Hand—her pace quickened. "Stand down," she called. Her voice rang sharp and commanding. "They are with me."

The guards froze—not in fear, but amusement. One chuckled, stepping forward. "Just 'cause the Commander let you walk out doesn't mean we'll take your orders."

"Lass," Gunnar warned. "We're fine. Don't—"

She didn't move. But her jaw locked, and her fingers twitched as she eyed the hilt she no longer wore, now tainted by a Black Hand. Behind her, the doors creaked open again. Killian descended the steps like judgment itself. Slow. Heavy. Hands flexing.

"What now?" he muttered. "More recruits? Or bodies for the fire?" Killian looked between them, then noticed the extra bow being carried by a Black Hand guard — a bow that was all too familiar. He took note of that.

Gunnar, meanwhile, was frozen in place. His eyes were fixed on Killian now. Staring at him as if he had just seen a distant memory come to life.

The lead guard stood straighter. "Caught them in the woods behind your quarters, Commander Thorn."

Killian's gaze drifted over the group again—cold, clinical. "Then stack them with the rest." He turned.

"Wait." Gunnar's voice cracked through the tension. "Killian Thorn… I didn't place the name at first. You're Aaric's boy, aren't you? Spitting image."

Killian paused. His shoulders rose—then fell. He didn't look back. "Killian Thorn is dead to Aaric Thorn." His words sounded like a knife dragging across stone. Then he walked away.

Gunnar's voice rose like a war drum. "Your father bled beside us. And this is how you carry his name?"

Killian stopped. Slowly. His shoulders straightened. His fists curled—white-knuckled. For a moment, no one breathed. Then he turned. Not like a man—but like a blade. His boots struck the dirt. The guards parted without a word.

Rain battered against the stained-glass windows, casting fractured colors across the curved chamber. Stone arches met the dark honey wood of the walls, where dragons coiled in carved relief, slithering from the double doors to the windows at the far end. At the chamber's heart stood a vast round

table, its edges etched with a dance of twisting patterns—elegant, poised, almost alive. Five tall-backed chairs were filled except one; that one was tucked against the round table, as if no one would claim that seat any time soon. The seventh chair, a towering seat raised higher than the rest, sat empty, its broad silhouette highlighted by the gloomy light from the stained windows.

Chatter rang through the stone chamber—sharp, clipped, urgent.

The double doors burst open. The chatter halted. A young courier staggered inside, soaked, panting. He crossed the chamber in haste as he left puddles beneath his every step. The courier hunched beside the tallest man at the table—broad-shouldered with scars decorating the back and sides of his neck, hinting at more beneath the fabric. He was every inch a soldier. Black hair swept back from a strong brow. His deep blue eyes flicked over the message. Then he dismissed the boy with a nod.

The doors slammed shut behind him. The room fell still.

An older man leaned forward—shoulder-length hair threaded with gray. His fingers were laced, his green eyes sharp. "Well, *Lord Jareth*?" he asked, his voice smooth with the edge of condescension. "Another hamlet gone?"

Jareth rose. "Wintersong," he said. "Destroyed. A week ago, maybe more."

A chair scraped. Lady Rosalind stood, long and dark braided hair falling over her pale shoulder, brown eyes flashing. "This is going to destabilize Stonehaven's economy. If we keep letting these hamlets fall, the cost to rebuild them will bury us."

Jareth nodded once. "I agree," His gaze swept the table. "But we cannot act blindly." He turned to the older man. "Lord Varian. Your men were stationed there. Surely someone survived?"

Varian's jaw tightened. "Given that a courier delivered the news and not one of my soldiers… No." His fingers curled into fists. "None of our soldiers made it out."

Rosalind scoffed as she retook her seat. "Some military." Varian shot her a glare at that.

A throat cleared. Lord Oswin, dark hair brushed back, rounder than the others, but no less sharp. "We should send scouts. Order them to observe—hidden. Not engage."

Jareth's gaze snapped to him. "Just observe? While people die?"

"You said it yourself—we don't know what we're facing."

"I said we shouldn't strike blindly," Jareth growled. "Not that we should *watch* our people die like lambs waiting for the slaughter."

Rosalind shifted her gaze to a man who had been seated and quiet

throughout all of this. "Well?" Rosalind's leg crossed over the other, foot tapping with pointed irritation. "You're awfully quiet, Lord Emeric. No thoughts on this disaster?"

"For what?" Emeric replied, brushing a blond strand from his face. His green-grey eyes didn't lift, raking instead across the parchment in front of him. "Every time the Lord of Arts and Culture speaks, I'm laughed out of the room. Why waste the breath?"

Jareth sighed, "We don't have the luxury of ignoring ideas, Lord Emeric. Not now."

Emeric looked up, finally. He leaned forward, elbows on the table, fingertips pressed together. "Send both," he said simply. "Scouts and soldiers. Not one or the other. It's not a bold strategy—it's common sense."

"That would stretch our forces thin!" Varian snapped. "What if no more attacks come? What then? We'll have men scattered across empty fields instead of guarding our city!"

Jareth slammed his fist onto the table, the force of it shaking inkwells and glasses of water. "We weren't chosen for this council to gamble lives like dice, Varian!"

"*Lord* Varian," Varian hissed. "Do *not* forget my title, *boy*."

"I'll use your godsdamn title when you act like a man worthy of it."

Rosalind stood. She clapped her hands once—sharp as a whipcrack. "Gentlemen. Enough," Her eyes moved between Jareth and Varian, "We're here to stop homes from burning—not each other."

Oswin sighed, rubbing his temple. Emeric leaned back, arms crossed, looking like he'd seen this performance a dozen times.

Jareth rubbed a hand down his face aggressively. His patience was razor-thin. "As Lady Rosalind said, rebuilding will bleed us dry. And the Regency's image? It's already cracking."

Killian's footsteps stopped right before Gunnar. Killian stood like a statue—but a vein ticked at his temple, and his jaw was tight as iron. Cinder's hands slowly moved, readying herself to take back her bow and arrows. Johann looked to Gunnar, ready to follow his friend's lead.

"Wait—" Ambrosja's hands met Killian's chest.

Killian stilled completely as he felt her touch there. His expression had changed. What once appeared as a calm rage now appeared as confusion. Killian looked down. She wasn't pushing him. Just placing space between

them. Quiet and intentional.

Killian took a deep breath, trying to steady himself. "Remove your hands."

Ambrosja's fingers twitched; they slid lower, stopping at his ribs. "What do you want... so they walk away?"

Killian's brow arched, "Interesting—" his eyes looked over Ambrosja, scanning her face, "—Actually offering an exchange instead of pleading for the safety of your allies? That is refreshing." His gaze cut back to Gunnar. Assessing him. Finally, he spoke to the guards, without looking away from Gunnar. "Take them to the mines—their sentence will be served in labor."

The guards moved in, shoving away at their backs to urge them towards the mines. One guard grabbed Ambrosja's wrist, "Alright, come on—" only to feel his own wrist being tightly grasped with a bruising force. "Hey—!" he froze when he saw Killian's hand.

"She's not part of them."

"Apologies, Commander—I simply thought–"

"You thought wrong. Leave."

The guard dipped his chin nervously and pulled his hand away once Killian's grip loosened.

Killian's eyes settled on Ambrosja once more. "Very well," he stepped closer to her, "And what exactly are you going to offer me?"

Ambrosja's gaze shifted subtly as she looked into Killian's, tracking each eye at a time. "I'm—" she took a deep breath, "What do you want?"

"You had nothing prepared. Just a desperate attempt to avoid your allies being beaten like disloyal dogs." Killian leaned forward, strands of black hair falling in his face, "See… The reason I held off is not that you *could* offer me something, but that you did. That your first instinct wasn't to beg. It was to barter."

Then he straightened himself. He raised one hand, lifting two fingers, and gestured to Berric, the man with the strawberry blond hair. The man took note, and his face had soured at the sight of those two fingers. He walked forward, stopping three paces from Killian.

"Commander?"

"Take her to my chambers, Lieutenant Berric."

Berric wrapped his hand around Ambrosja's bicep and nudged her along, "Right away, Commander."

Ambrosja looked down at the guard's hand, then up at Killian, "Your chambers?" she repeated.

Killian didn't answer. Just watched—as his lieutenant pulled her toward the very place they'd stood as enemies moments before.

From the journal of Guinyldr Thorn,
Bjarnvakt, 27, 997

THE ROUND TABLE

In the earliest age of Vaestoria, beneath banners of gold and fire, the First King and Queen called forth their dragon riders to council. They gathered not in thrones nor in galleries of rank, but around a single round table — a symbol of unity, where none might sit above another. There, under the vaulted sky of the First Hall, oaths were sworn in flame and blood to serve the realm as one.

When the royal line was later fractured, and the Regencies rose to rule in its stead, many of the old traditions withered — yet the Round Table endured. Its shape became the emblem of balance and shared dominion, a reminder that even power must turn in circles. Each regency maintains its own table, carved from the heartwood of the elder groves and ringed with seven seats. Six belong to the lords and ladies of governance, and the seventh, set at the table's crown, to the High Regent, whose word seals all matters of state.

At times, the council may debate for hours or days. When voices clash and votes are tied, the Regent's judgment breaks the stalemate — their voice the quiet axis around which the realm turns

The High Regent
The Diplomat
The Reeve
The Justiciar
The Marshal
The Treasurer
The Cultural Steward

CHAPTER NINE

SHADES OF RED

Ambrosja sat still on the red cushions of the velvet bed bench, her lower back pressed against the edge of the canopy bed. Her ashen locks were damp, curls forming at the ends. A massive black towel swallowed her frame. Across the room, the brass knob turned. Ambrosja's golden eyes snapped to the sound and hugged the towel tighter around her. The door creaked open. Killian entered, head bowed as he shut it behind him. He took two steps—then stopped. His eyes lifted. Landed on her. And held.

Killian's eyes swept over Ambrosja's form and the ridiculous way that the towel engulfed her. "You bathed…" Not a question. He rolled his jaw slightly, "And you used *my* towel."

"It was the only one."

"But *why* did you bathe?"

"Your Lieutenant told me to."

Killian stared. Then he chuckled. The sound was unrestrained and genuine.

"I do not understand. What is so funny to you?"

"He thought I was going to *bed* you."

Ambrosja's expression cracked—caught between offense and disbelief. Her voice shook—not with doubt, but insult. "You are aware I did not offer such a thing, correct?"

Killian's amusement hadn't faded, "I am aware, yes." He moved towards the table at the center of the room and pulled out a chair, but didn't sit yet. He unfastened each button of his leather tunic—never looking away from her. "I am aware that the Empress of Nordorn cannot bed until she is twenty-five, for that is the age she weds by." He tilted his head, "And given that you are *here*, you are not wed. Because no husband worth his title would've let you risk yourself like this."

"You know plenty of my home's customs."

"History has always been my favorite subject." He dropped his gaze to the towel, "Are you dressed under there?"

Ambrosja snapped, "Of course! You think I would be nude in your chambers?!"

"Well…" his lip twitched, another grin forming. "I didn't think you'd bathe in my quarters. Or steal my towel. But here we are—apparently, I keep underestimating you."

Ambrosja's eyes dropped—just briefly—to his hands. "What are you doing?"

Killian didn't look away from her as the final button came undone and began to slide the tunic off his broad shoulders, tugging with ease. "I am getting comfortable in my chambers." He tilted his head, "I don't recall any laws that the Empress couldn't see a man shirtless."

"There are no such laws regarding that."

"Then what's got your cheeks burning?" His tunic was off at last, now tossed to lie across the seat he had pulled. His torso was a battlefield. Every line carved by war, not vanity.

Ambrosja's eyes flared with insult now, as did her voice. "I assure you, there is no *burning* on my cheeks. It is simply the red of your drawn curtains."

"Is that right?" Killian bowed his head, his gaze still fixed on her, "Yes, I'm sure it's just the curtains."

He grabbed his tunic and slung it over his shoulder, walking to step behind the folding screen that hid away the bathing area. Ambrosja watched as the sunlight behind the red curtains outlined his silhouette. She caught a glimpse—his hands pulling at leather, then fabric sliding. She looked away—fast. Looking at the opposite end of the room. She could hear the ruffling of fabric now. His boots coming undone, and his steps moving about.

She finally broke the silence, "What did you want me *here* for?"

"I'm still deciding," Killian admitted, "I couldn't leave you wandering around the mining grounds." There was silence once more. Killian stepped from behind the folding screen, approaching his bed. His eyes narrowed. "… Hm."

Ambrosja looked behind her and immediately looked away as she saw

Killian standing in just his fitted, dark nethercloths. She swallowed, "What is it?"

"...I had laid out my evening clothes here."

Ambrosja shrank beneath the towel, "Oh, that was for you?"

Killian's head jerked in her direction, his cold eyes glued to the back of her head, "No..." he whispered as realization dawned on him. "...You're wearing *those* too?"

She fixed her posture. "I think it is safe to say that—given how the events played out, being told to bathe, finding a single towel, then finding fresh clothes on the bed... Makes sense, yes?"

Killian exhaled sharply. He moved, walking beside the bed until he was just next to her form on the bench. He leaned down, dark strands of hair dancing in her vision, "...Comfortable, are they?"

Ambrosja swallowed. She looked briefly at Killian, up into his piercing stare that was hovering over her, then straight ahead at the door across the room, "Quite."

She moved with practiced grace—but her nerves still flared beneath it. She pressed her hand into the cushion, gliding to the far end like it was effortless. And gliding away from Killian's hovering presence. Killian noticed, a genuine smirk pulled at his lips.

"Very well, Empress, keep them."

He set his eyes on his dresser now, already walking away. He pulled on the golden bars of the dark wood drawer and reached in for a fresh set of clothes. Black again. Ambrosja kept her posture straight, though her eyes flicked anywhere but him—walls, the hearth, the window—anything that wasn't the sound of fabric sliding over skin.

She took a deep breath, "Your father is Aaric Thorn?"

Killian stilled. He exhaled sharply, "We're not doing this."

"What?"

"*This.*" He gestured vaguely between them, "Discussing personal affairs and familial connections like we have been lifelong friends. As if you don't hate me and you're not desiring to rip my face to shreds with your dainty little Empress claws."

Ambrosja took a deep breath, "Very well. I suppose only one of us is allowed to provoke the other here with grief." She was silent now, looking out towards the red curtains that bathed the room in a warm hue.

"Your allies haven't been beaten," Killian spoke as he moved towards the table, fixing the arrangements there, "in case that's been plaguing you. They are going to work in the mines, but fear not, they will be treated like the other miners from this point onward." Killian's gaze shifted back to Ambros-ja, "They will have a place to sleep, eat, shit, and bathe. Provided they don't try anything stupid… Such as killing my archers. Again." Ambrosja froze at that, and Killian saw it. So he continued, "They're fortunate that you're here, if not — I would have dragged them to the flames and burnt them myself."

The word *burnt* clawed at her. She was now meeting Killian's eyes with her own. A calm fury stirring beneath them. "Just like you've done to all the hamlets?"

Killian only gave a cold and cruel smirk at that. "Yes."

Ambrosja's nostrils flared. She stood far too quickly, clutching that towel that hugged her even more tightly. "How long will you keep them here?"

"However long I decide to keep you here."

"You cannot keep me here."

"No…" Killian agreed, "I cannot keep you here, not for long. If I kept you here too long, I'd invite Nordorn's wrath, risk your execution, and help drag two countries into ruin. So no, I can't keep you here—*for long*. But I can and will keep you here for *as long* as I deem necessary."

There was a silence that settled between them as their eyes remained locked for moments that stretched for too long.

Finally, Killian took a step back, "We will have dinner togeth-er." He turned away, walking towards the door, "Then we will en-gage in conversation like civilized people–" he opened the door and looked back at her "—who do not throw bodies at the table."

He shut the door behind him.

"Civilized," Ambrosja muttered, a slight scoff as she burned holes into the door with her golden stare.

Ambrosja sat still for a moment. Counting under her breath, waiting for the distance between Killian and the door to increase. Then she stood, dropping the black towel onto the velvet bench and moving. She stepped to-wards his dresser, opening the drawers with one hand while the other began to dig through his clothes in swift shuffles, trying to feel for anything or spot anything that didn't belong.

He has to keep something somewhere hidden…

She pressed her fingers into the panels of the drawers, feeling for a hidden compartment. But nothing moved at her fingertips. Ambros-ja abandoned the drawers, moving towards a low bookshelf in the cor-ner of the room. Her hands moved along the spines, tipping each book back and giving a gentle wiggle to see if anything came loose. Her pa-

tience became thin. One by one, each book was removed instead, opened with a quick flip of pages to check for more secret compartments. Ambrosja's brows knit closely. Her eyes darted from book to book until all was put back. She stood up and gave another glance around the room.

Her fingers were already on a frame. Gently tilting the painting of a cliffside waterfall upwards to get a look behind it. She slid her hand upwards, feeling for anything.

"What are you doing?" Killian's voice called from behind her.

Ambrosja turned, her hands dropped from their task, and let the frame bump against the wall with a *thukk*.

"Admiring the framework," she said, her eyes catching the wide tray in Killian's hand, two cloches over it. "Is that dinner?"

Killian arched a single brow. His eyes traced the oversized shirt tucked into pants that were only being kept up by her belt that cinched the fabric at the narrowest part of her waist. The rolled pant legs to avoid tripping, and her bare feet pressed against the wood.

"It's dinner, yes." The slightest smile tugged at his lips as he stepped inside, closing the door behind him and then locking it. He walked towards the table, setting the tray down, and looked at her from a closer distance now. "Would you like socks?"

Ambrosja looked down at her feet, suddenly feeling exposed. "If you do not mind sharing."

Killian stepped towards his dresser and opened the top drawer. He paused, just long enough to notice things out of place. "You were admiring the framework of the painting, hm? But were you not content with the organization of my drawers and felt the need to meddle with my fabrics?"

Ambrosja didn't look at him, simply kept her posture. "That must have been your doing. I did not *meddle* with your clothes."

His hands closed around a pair of black socks. He stood beside her, towering over her, "I hope you are a better fighter than you are a liar, Empress, because one day, someone not as merciful as I may cross your path." He extended his hand. "Here. Socks."

"If you believe yourself to be merciful — then the world is doomed, Commander." Ambrosja's gaze slid from his down to the socks and her gentle hand grabbed them.

"Thank you." She dipped her chin once. Despite the animosity between them, she kept her grace. Or at least she tried to.

The bed dipped beneath Ambrosja's weight, and the black socks slid on as Killian was back at the table, removing the cloches on the tray. The

scent hit Ambrosja's nose immediately. The smell of garlic and herbs, melted butter, and grilled greens. She had to hold back the unladylike sound that was about to escape her throat. She stood up, slow, maybe too slow, as she tried not to appear desperate for the meal that sat ten feet away from her.

"Roast chicken," Killian said. He stepped aside and set a plate near her at the end of the table. "I made sure you'd have your own bird—all to yourself."

Killian grabbed his own plate and sat at the furthest end across the table from her. Ambrosja crossed the floor and paused at the chair. She took the meal in before her. It had been weeks since she had something this nice, this *much*.

"What is your attempt here?" She looked at him, trying to see any hidden motive.

Killian did not budge. He was seated now, bringing his plate closer to him, forearms braced on the edges of the table, "Perhaps I'm trying to turn you into a house pet. A cat, maybe. Feed you well, keep you docile—even as you fantasize about sinking your claws into my face. You do look like you would be a cat. The fluffy white kind."

Ambrosja wasn't amused. She sat down and shifted her gaze from Killian to her plate. The mashed potatoes glistened with the gold hues of butter, and grilled greens sat on the side, covered in seasoning. The chicken itself was crispy; the skin was a deep shade of gold and orange. Her hands reached for the cutlery placed by the side, and she began to gently cut into the meat. The slightest tremble was evident in her fingers, as if she couldn't cut fast enough.

Her eyes snapped up to Killian as she spotted the man pick up the chicken with his bare hands and dig in. The fork and knife in her hands were momentarily forgotten as she watched him. "You are eating with your hands?"

Killian didn't set the chicken down, didn't apologize. "And for some reason you aren't."

"I was told Vaestorians used utensils."

"Some do, some don't." Killian tilted his head. "Why are *you* using them? Nordorners typically eat with their hands when it comes to meat."

"That is true, but—"

"—but you were trying to appease and blend in with this country."

Ambrosja nodded, "Yes."

"That is nearly impossible given your appearance," Killian spoke, finally setting the chicken down and wiping his hands with a cloth. "But it's

true that how you act and behave can help minimize the number of eyes on you." Killian exhaled, eyes fixed on Ambrosja. "Is that why you speak so proper?" A chuckle escaped him. "Because from my studies, Nordorners are typically… *Vulgar* with their speech."

"I am simply trying to be respectful to this country's customs."

Killian shook his head, "You never need to hide who you truly are, not from *me*…"

A silence settled between them. Ambrosja kept her glare on him, a glare between confusion and hatred; while Killian kept his cool cold gaze of gray on her.

He gestured to the chicken, "Go on, I already know who you are, you can drop the act now."

She was still for a moment. Just a moment. Then fingernails dug into the crispy skin, the meat lifted off the plate, and Ambrosja sank her teeth into the thigh. A sound escaped her—low, involuntary, like a hum reserved for under the covers of a lover. She didn't meet his eyes. Killian watched her. His hold on his cup had paused near his lips once he heard that sound. He exhaled, his bottom lip rolling between his teeth.

"Stop staring at me…" Ambrosja had spoken, her voice muffled by the food, her accent slightly thicker. "I can't enjoy this if you're just going to keep watching me."

Killian nodded. His own eyes set back down to his cup as he drank, only to shortly rip into his own plate. His fingers dug into the meat, parting the roast chicken in half. His massive hand wrapped around the leg, the other gripped the breast as he dug in again.

They sat at opposite ends, in silence as they devoured their meals. The only sounds were the cracks of crisp skin, the dull scrape of metal on plate, and the rustle of cloth across knuckles. But the silence was only momentary.

"Tell me something, Empress," Killian cleared his throat after taking a sip from his drink, "what were you hoping to achieve in Wintersong?"

Ambrosja paused her chewing, grease stained her lips, her eyes met his. She grabbed the cloth beside her plate and wiped her mouth. "Why? Are you looking for new ways to provoke me? I thought you wanted a civilized conversation, not for me to slam you, yet again, into another table."

Killian chuckled, the sound was low and the strength of his body made the table vibrate. "I am curious, as I said earlier, I wonder what the Empress of Nordorn was doing in Vaestoria. Unannounced. Uninvited. Hidden." He cocked a single brow. "Well?"

Ambrosja rolled her jaw, her brows lowering. "If you must know, I wanted to bring them back to Nordorn. The people of Wintersong were once children of my country."

"Yes, I'm aware… But why? Why go there alone? Why make the effort of bringing back, what, one hundred people or less?"

"Because they're mine."

"Sounds like you sought to own them, as if they're property, Empress."

"No–" Ambrosja took a deep breath, she closed her eyes for a moment before continuing, as if she could sense his provocation slither between his words. "No, when I took the throne, I was taught to see my people as if they were my own children. Compassion, love, but willing to hold a firm hand when necessary. Never as toys, pawns, or lives that I can just freely discard. Unlike some."

Killian raised a brow at '*some*'. "And you believed you had to bring the people of Wintersong back? That you were a mother trying to convince that the home was safe yet again for your children to live in?"

"Something like that."

"Ambrosja," Killian's voice was softer now, he leaned forward, his eyes locked on hers, "Wintersong had been part of Vaestoria for about three-hundred years. At that point? They were no longer your children. No longer people who would recognize the country or be recognized. Could they even speak your tongue, Ambrosja? Or did you mistake blood for belonging?"

Ambrosja didn't answer immediately; her fingertips rubbed at her forehead. "No, they didn't speak my language…" A heavy breath left her then, like a sigh filled with sorrow. "Not anymore."

"My advice?" Killian brought the cup to his lips. "Go home, Empress."

The scrape of a chair cut through the quiet. Ambrosja stood, her expression carved from glass. "My appetite's gone," she said, dabbing her lips with a napkin that might as well have been a war flag before she dropped it on the table.

As she passed, Killian's hand caught hers. "I've aggravated you." He rose with her, his shadow nearly swallowing hers. "That wasn't my intention. I was trying to give you the best advice I could offer."

Ambrosja didn't pull away—she turned, golden eyes meeting his storm-gray with unflinching heat. "You call *that* advice? Telling me to crawl home and pretend the blood on my hands is not there?"

"Not *pretending*," he said evenly, "just accepting that the people of Wintersong stopped being yours the moment they left Nordorn."

"I refuse to accept that."

"Why?"

"Because they died while I was still there, *trying* to be their Empress, their protector!" Her voice didn't tremble; it struck like a blade. "And I cannot live with the fact that I was too weak to protect them!"

Killian tilted his head. "So this is all about selfishness?"

"Do not come to me about selfishness! You are a man who has acted on nothing but selfishness!" Ambrosja tore her hand away at last. "I'll admit, it's admirable that you can be the one to make the hardest choices—hells, I could even respect you! But what respect does a monster deserve when he has no heart? When there is no love? Those choices aren't the hardest anymore— they're nothing. They simply *are*."

Killian's reply came softly, but the sound rumbled through the floorboards, low and resonant. "I could love," he said. "If I wanted to."

Ambrosja looked him up and down, her vision stuttering where her words failed. She wasn't sure she believed him—gods, she *didn't want to*—yet her fists clenched all the same, her heart thudding hard against her ribs. *But why did those words affect her?*

Killian noticed her stance, her stare. The rise and fall of her chest. But he didn't engage in her reaction; he turned back to the matters at hand. "You seek to prove yourself to your people; you are upset not that Wintersong perished, but that you *failed* your quest." His arms rose slightly, hands spaced wide apart as he gestured towards her. "Tell me, Empress, how is that not selfishness? How is this whole ordeal not about you?"

"Fine!" Ambrosja snapped. "It is about *me*. It's about the fact that everyone expects miracles because every Empress before me could shit starlight and move mountains, and I—" Her arm swept across the table in a flash of fury, silverware and candles crashing to the floor. "—couldn't even save one godsdamn person in a hamlet—" Ambrosja nearly choked then, but reined her emotions in, "—that I couldn't protect that little girl…"

Killian didn't interrupt Ambrosja. He let her unleash her anger, let her shout or shake like he did when he first brought her to his office, when he first revealed that he had known who she was. He simply knelt down, picking up what had fallen.

"I was once part of the Vaestorian Military. Specifically of Stonehaven's Regency." Killian's voice was lower than usual. "I've been where you are. I've spilled enemies' blood and my own to protect my people." A sigh escaped him, heavy and low. "But there is only so much a soldier can do." He stood, placing the fallen objects back onto the table, "So I tried my hand at politics.

Turns out I wasn't polished enough for courtrooms. Or charming enough to climb ladders that don't reward blood." He looked at Ambrosja now. "There is only so much a soldier can do—only so much an empress can do."

Ambrosja's glare softened, but her fists were clenched tight. "And now, instead of protecting the people, you *kill* them."

"I do," he said without hesitation. "Because too many mouths and too few fields can destroy a kingdom faster than any sword. I do what I do, because I love."

"That's not right." Her voice cracked—strained with fury. "Don't you dare dress slaughter up as strategy. Don't dress up cruelty as justification for love."

Killian's fist twitched, his control fraying at her tears. "As I've said before, Empress," he said, low and rough, "you must abandon your humanity to preserve it." He turned away, forcing a calm that didn't quite fit. "Let's finish dinner."

Ambrosja stared at him for a long moment. Her breathing was fast at first, then she took one deep inhale to calm her nerves, her eyes closing gently then. She gave a nod, a silent agreement of civility, and moved to return to her seat. She looked over her shoulder, "You have got a talent for ruining meals, you know that?"

Killian's mouth twitched—a ghost of a smile. "So do you, Empress." He looked into his cup. "I think some of your tears have fallen in here."

Ambrosja turned sharply. "Tears?! I did not cry!" She took a step forward. "I will show you tears, Commander."

"Easy." Killian chuckled, low and rough. "Or I might think you're flirting with me, Empress."

Ambrosja's eyes widened just slightly. Her brows then furrowed as pink crept across her cheeks. "I am not flirting!" She moved back to her chair and sat down with more force than necessary. "I would not flirt with a mass murderer."

"Shame," Killian said, bringing his cup to his lips. "It's been a while since a pretty woman has flirted with me."

Ambrosja stilled mid-motion. The linen in her hands went perfectly still as if she'd forgotten what napkins were for. She didn't look at him — wouldn't — not when her pulse gave her away faster than her tongue ever would. Instead, she straightened, shoulders squaring, chin lifting just enough to pretend composure.

"You mistake disdain for affection, Commander," she said. Her voice was smooth, but anyone with a keen ear could hear the slightest tremble. "A

common delusion, I hear."

Killian's smirk deepened, the faintest heat flickering behind his steady gaze. "Then I'll take comfort in being common." He finally took a sip of his drink, then set the cup back down. "Has your husband-to-be already been chosen?"

Ambrosja's eyes snapped to Killian, her brows pinched, lips parted in disbelief. "This is how you choose to change the subject?"

"I'm simply trying to understand the woman before me and the boundaries at hand."

Ambrosja sighed, "Yes, he's been chosen."

"Do you love him?"

"He respects me."

"That's good to hear. But—that's not what I asked."

Ambrosja was silent as her eyes narrowed onto her meal before her. "He and I have an understanding. He is free to bed any woman he so desires until we marry, *if* I decide to marry him."

Killian scratched at his chin with rough fingers, the corner of his lips twitched, one eyebrow arched as he looked off to the side. "So," now his lips shifted into a smirk as his gaze set upon her face. "No love there, hm? I suppose that eases your mind when you travel, when your gaze lingers on forbidden fruits. There are no feelings of betrayal, I could only assume." Killian let his words linger before continuing. "Have you been with other men, Ambrosja?"

Ambrosja froze yet again, but not with bashfulness as before. Whatever she was preparing to eat next was forgotten. Her golden gaze burned at the thought of his question. Her cheeks became rosy, the freckles nearly blending into the blush there. "That is entirely inappropriate to ask." Her brows furrowed, hands gripping the edge of the table. "How would you feel if I asked *you* that same question?"

He shrugged. His broad shoulders lifted once with nonchalance. His wide frame leaned to the side in his chair, one forearm resting on the table. "As I've said, I simply seek to learn more about the woman before me. From the moral compass that you intend to wield and the lines that you draw. I want to know your comforts and discomforts."

"Asking me about my life within the sheets is *quite* uncomfortable."

"Allow me to make you extremely uncomfortable, then." Killian leaned forward, forearms bracing against the edge of the table. "I cannot leave you alone. For your safety. I cannot allow you to go far from me. As I said, I will keep you. And at night? You will be with me, in my bed."

"That—is not happening."

"I'm not suggesting we have sex. I am not even suggesting we touch hands." Killian relaxed now, taking a sip of his drink, then setting the cup down slowly as he watched Ambrosja's cheeks flush. "I assure you I have no intention of peeling off the fabrics — my fabrics — that adorn your body." He tilted his head, more inquisitive now, "Tell me, Empress, would you risk your crown—your identity, out in the camp? I've no doubts that you are wit-ty—that you can think quickly on your feet. But me? I am quicker. I have been playing dangerous games since I was a boy. This—" he gestured between them with his free hand, "—this is not about possession. This is about protection."

Ambrosja was silent. But Killian saw the way her fingers flexed, the way her chest rose and fell beneath that ridiculously large black top that belonged to him. He spoke again, his voice softer now, "Allow me to protect you, Empress."

The Empress was silent for a bit. Her brows were lowered, knitting the space between them into fine lines. Then finally, "No," she continued, "I do not trust you to protect me. You stand against me, and I, you. I am to be married, and I refuse to share a bed with another man. There is nothing you can do — that I cannot do to protect myself, Commander."

Killian leaned forward, elbows firm against the table, so firm and heavy that the wood creaked. His fingers interlaced in front of his mouth. His own brows had lowered, but the look he had seemed calm. "So — you would risk your own crown? Your bloodline?" He let the words settle for a moment, then continued before she could retort, "If someone recognizes you beyond these walls, no one will come to your aid, Empress. Not unless I am there. If I let you walk? Whispers will be spoken, soldiers curious on why I let the woman with the friends who killed *two* of my archers simply walk free." He continued, leaning back now, a hand smoothly grabbing his cup, "Besides, I know you already — and I know you will walk — walk from this camp, into another, trying to find the justice you seek. Isn't that right, Empress?"

Ambrosja didn't speak. She refused to give in to his questions. And Killian noticed. He noticed everything. A smirk pulled at the corner of his lips.

He tilted his head slightly. "Hm, how about your allies?" Ambrosja's gaze snapped to his at that. And he continued, "I'm only allowing them to live because you sit here at my table."

Ambrosja's head turned begrudgingly, as if she didn't want to look at him headon, despite her eyes being unable to peel away from his form, from that *infuriatingly* relaxed pose of his. He was right. And she knew it. If she left this outpost, she would just try to find the next one, and if someone else recognized her… *Who knows what will happen to me?* But worst of all, she did not want to abandon those who helped her get this far.

"Fine." When she spoke, her voice was firm, though it shook on some words. "If we *must* lie in the same bed—I demand something between us. A barrier of some sort."

Killian nodded, "If that's what it takes to put you at ease, fine." He raised his cup towards Ambrosja, "That much I can give, Empress."

THE BINDING OF THE EMPRESS

Among the most sacred customs of Nordorn is the Binding of the Empress, the ceremony through which the divine ruler takes her consort. The Empress's suitor is chosen long before her coronation — a man of renown and strength, proven in battle and in bearing. Though he may be known to her in youth, no union is permitted until her twenty-fifth year, when she is deemed fully ascended to Brynhjora's favor. From her twenty-first year onward, courtship may blossom beneath the watchful eyes of the court, yet chastity remains law until the wedding night.

Upon the day of their joining, the Empress and her chosen consort share a single sword between them — hands clasped upon the hilt as they whisper their private vows before speaking them aloud to their people. When the ceremony concludes, the suitor becomes Hrafnwarden — royal consort, sworn protector, and chief advisor. Their rings may rest on any hand, so long as they touch when their fingers entwine; a symbol that duty and devotion must ever meet.

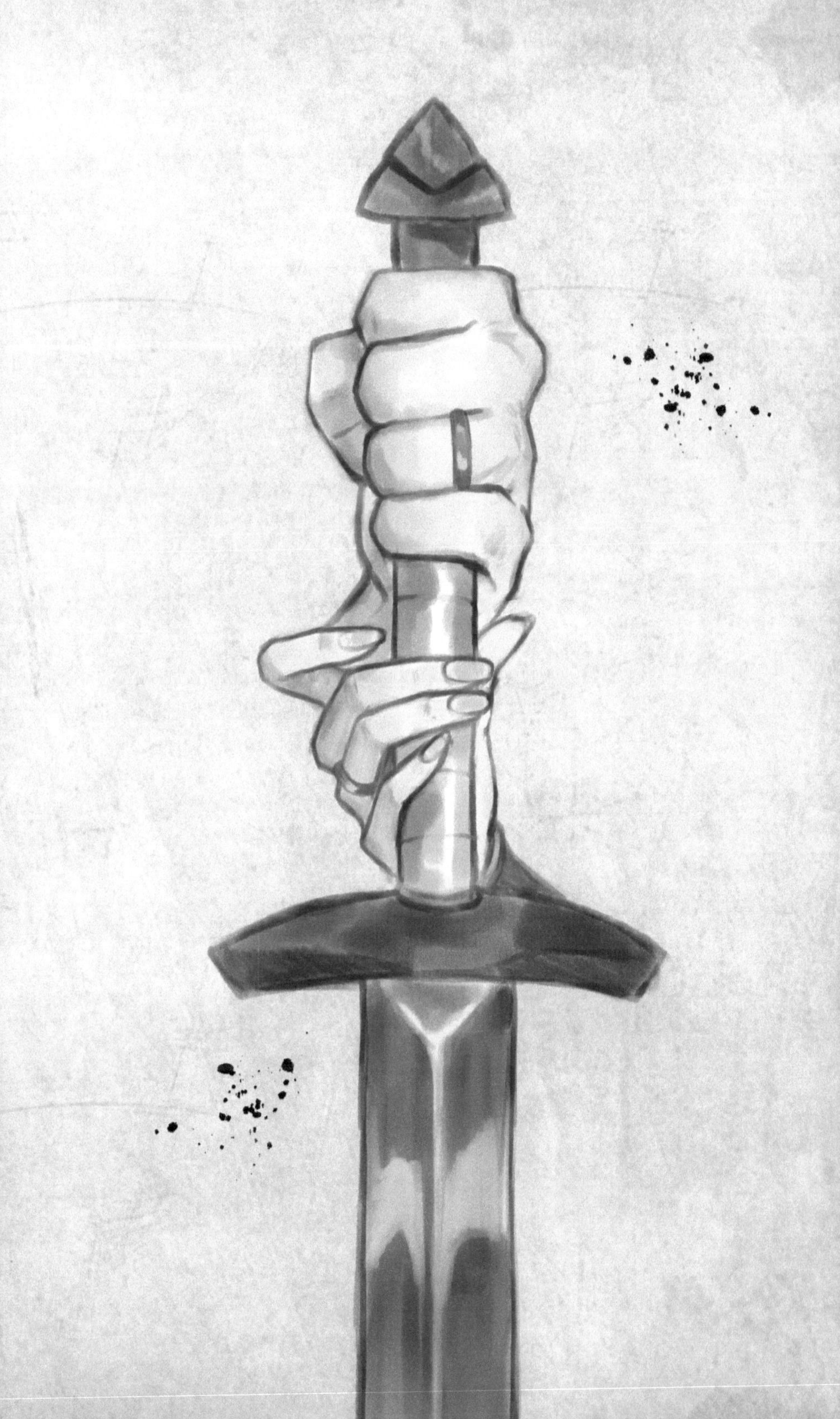

SCARS BEYOND SKIN

ootsteps creaked on the wooden steps as two guards dragged Donathan between them. Donathan's own movements were heavy and defeated, his eyes downcast at the wooden grains of each step.

"I'm telling you—this is a bad idea," muttered the rear guard.

"We need to figure out what to do with this little shit," the other growled, giving Donathan a shove. "Fucking traitor to the Black Hand."

"It's past midnight. The Commander's lights are out," the first warned. "You really want to wake him for *this*? Just toss the brat with the others and cuff his hands. No magic, no trouble."

"And let him roam? What if he bolts again—or worse, stirs up more trouble?"

The first guard grabbed his partner's shoulder, halting him at the final step. "What's better? Watching him till dawn—or getting your face bloodied because you were too damn impatient?"

The second guard exhaled hard, dragging a hand down his face. "Fine." He glanced down at Donathan. "You're lucky, boy."

Beneath the flicker of a low flame, Cinder, Gunnar, and Johann lay under a torn canvas. Their bedrolls were thin, the earth unforgiving. Cinder grunted, shifting again as another damned rock jabbed her spine.

"We're really just going to stay here?" she muttered, dragging a hand across the ground, searching for the next lump waiting to bruise her ribs.

Johann sighed. "Even if we tried to fight our way out, there are too many Black Hand guards swarming the place."

"It'd be suicide," Gunnar rumbled.

"Alright!" a voice barked from outside. "Get in there, boy!"

The trio shot upright at the noise. Donathan stumbled through the flaps and shoved hard. His balance faltered—his hands still bound behind him.

"Lad," Gunnar whispered, a tinge of relief and worry crept beneath his voice. He rose slowly, eyes looking to the guards outside before stepping forward.

Donathan flinched at the sudden voice of Gunnar. He turned, and a shaky breath escaped him as he spotted the towering man. He picked his way forward, his steps careful despite his shakiness. Doing his best not to step on the sleeping miners strewn across the floor.

"I—I'm glad you're all alright," he said, taking a deep breath as he tried to calm his nerves.

Gunnar caught his arm, steadying him, guiding him back toward the bedrolls. His eyes caught the swelling near Donathan's eye, the bruises along his jaw. "They beat you." Gunnar's voice was low, a whisper of a growl beneath it.

Donathan wavered—half a nod, half denial. "Yeah… but it could've been worse." Donathan let Gunnar guide him down to a worn bedroll. His gaze darted around. "Where's Ambrosja?"

Johann scratched at his beard, chewing on the memory. "Last we saw, the Commander pulled her aside."

Cinder scoffed, "Yeah, that *Commander*—real sweetheart—threatened to gut us." She thumbed at Gunnar. "Big guy pissed him off. Ambrosja had to step in before we got turned to mulch."

"Whatever she said, it worked," Johann muttered. "Calmed the bastard down enough to turn us into miners instead of ash."

Donathan's head dipped. "So… where is she now?"

"I imagine she's still with him," Cinder said, blowing air up at her messy bangs. "I overheard him tell a guard to take her to his chambers."

Donathan's throat bobbed. "Do… Do you think he's hurting her?"

Gunnar's lip curled, another growl rising—but he shook it off. "No.

Ambrosja doesn't seem to be the kind to take a beating lying down. If he laid a hand on her, she'd walk out painted in blood—and none of it hers, I bet."

Cinder smirked. "Yeah, the only reason these two relics are still here is 'cause we're waiting on her."

Johann laid a calming hand on Donathan's trembling shoulder. "What matters is you're back. We were worried when you ran."

Donathan's head lowered again, cheeks flushed with shame, eyes locked onto the ground. "I'm sorry. I panicked. After watching that Commander nearly beat a man to death… I just— I didn't want to be next."

Gunnar gave a low grunt. "Fear's no shame, lad. It keeps us alive." He clapped Donathan's back. "Try to rest. They might toss us back in the mines tomorrow."

Cinder groaned, flopping onto her bedroll. "Yay. Rocks."

Morning light spilled across the crimson sheets, catching the shimmer of silk in soft gold. Killian stirred, his broad frame stretched on his side of the bed. A hand ran down his face as he slowly came to. He pushed up onto one elbow, breath steady but low. Through a thin slit in the curtains, Killian watched as golden light filtered in—trees washed in green and rust.

A soft breath whispered beside him. He looked down. Ambrosja lay still, facing away from him—pillow barrier untouched, exactly as she'd demanded. Her ashen hair fanned across red silk. The blanket had slipped to her waist. One shoulder was bare, the black shirt fallen askew—revealing something beneath. Dark markings, like twisted roots, curled over her pale skin.

Killian's gaze narrowed. His hand—large, lethal—moved with disarming care as he drew the fabric lower, only slightly. His fingertips traced the lines, moving from her shoulder to her neck. Without warning, Killian felt a blade at his throat, the cold of it kissing his skin.

Ambrosja's golden eyes were burning into his. "We made a deal," she reminded him, "no touching."

Killian's eyes glanced down at the blade. "We did." His hand retreated slowly. "I see you decided to sneak in the butter knife from our dinner last night."

"For this exact reason."

"Smart." His tone was almost approving. Killian's eyes looked into Ambrosja's once, then dipped back to the markings on her skin. "That is the consequence of chaos magic, isn't it?" His gaze found hers again. "The kind of magic where the faintest of whispers can open the earth."

Ambrosja didn't lower the knife.

"You really plan to use a butter knife?"

"Yes, because if it comes to it… It will be painful."

Killian leaned in closer, forcing his throat against the knife, letting the smooth curvature of it press into his skin. "Go on," he whispered, his breath mingling with hers from how close they were. Ambrosja's eyes didn't widen, but her breath did catch in her throat as she looked into those icy-gray ones that seemed to read her soul.

She didn't move. Killian's hand slid up her wrist slowly, fingers curled firmly. His eyes remained locked on hers as he pressed her hand against the headboard. His other hand reached for her fingers that were tight around the handle of the knife. He pried one by one off. Then tugged the knife away, tossing it over his shoulder, hearing a soft *clang* against the ground.

"Bold," Killian murmured. "But you and I both know you won't kill me. Not yet."

He let go of her and moved away, sliding to the edge of the bed and standing up. Ambrosja lay in the same spot, hand resting against the headboard, her chest rising and falling slightly. Her cheeks were flushed. And she remained like that for mere moments longer. Only her eyes tracked his every movement until he disappeared behind the folding screen. She could hear the rustling of fabric, and clothes were tossed to hang over the screen.

Ambrosja sat up at last. Her hand pulled the flimsy shoulder part of her shirt back over her. Her breathing was slightly heavier than before, possibly nerves—or something deeper. She shoved the rest of the blankets off her and moved off the bed as well, heading towards the curtains to pull them open.

She caught sight of her allies below, moving out of a tent, "They're alive…" A shaky sigh of relief escaped her. Her fingers curled into the frame, nails digging in as her leg bounced.

I feared they'd be gone… I must get them out of here, they can't stay. Not for me…

Sloshing of water was heard. Ambrosja looked over her shoulder to see the faintest silhouette of Killian's form lowering himself into the tub. She looked away, her hand reaching for the shoulder he had touched.

———┼⚜┼———

Jareth's form was bare, hunched as he sat at the edge of the bed. Sunlight peered in through tall windows, dancing across his scarred back. He rubbed his jawline with force, fingers scratching against stubble. A sharp exhale left him as he looked down at papers clutched in his other hand.

"Jareth?" A woman's voice called sleepily. "Come back to bed."

Jareth looked over his shoulder, glancing down at her exposed form that was barely covered by the blanket. He brushed a lock of auburn hair away from her face, his knuckles grazing her cheek. "I am in bed."

"You know what I mean…" she turned over, facing him now, brown eyes narrowing, "Get under the covers and put your damn work away."

"Mira…" Jareth sighed, "Being a diplomat means taking my work everywhere, even in bed."

"Then I'm not doing a good enough job if the first thing you think about in the morning is *work*." She sat up now, her hands moving to support herself on his broad shoulders, her bare chest squishing against his back as she looked down at the papers in his hand, "Is it about the hamlet of Wintersong?"

"It is," he nodded. "Another hamlet gone. That's the fourth in the last year. The first time, we thought it was bandits—random. The second… maybe more organized. We posted bounties, shifted guards. By the third, we knew better. And Wintersong? That confirms it."

"Jareth…" Mira kissed his shoulder, "It's just a hamlet. Stonehaven can't afford to weaken itself."

Jareth moved, letting Mira fall as he stood to his full height. "It's not *just* a hamlet, Mira. It's people." He turned to face her, his eyes cold. He tossed his papers onto the bedside table with force, and Mira flinched slightly. "I don't give a damn about the land—it's the people. Families with nowhere to go but down. Because everyone is too scared to take a risk!" He ran a hand through his black hair. His voice was lower now. "I'm sorry, this is just—getting to me."

Mira had grabbed the blankets to cover herself, eyes on Jareth. She nodded, "I know…" her legs moved to slide off the edge of the bed. "Listen, why don't we see about writing a neighboring Regency? Or maybe write to Marrowind?"

"Marrowind?" Jareth looked at Mira, one eyebrow arched. "Why would we write Marrowind? They're on the complete opposite side of the country from us."

Mira stood, the blanket falling away as she stretched. Sunlight slid over bare skin as she crossed the room. Jareth's gaze followed—from shoulder to heel.

"They *are* the regency known for its vast military." She shrugged. A smug smile crossed her lips as she caught Jareth's stare. She didn't comment. She didn't have to. "They might have some forces to expend."

Jareth scoffed. "If our letters even reach Marrowind in time, they're weeks away, and without proof, they probably wouldn't even lift a pinky."

"Perhaps. Perhaps not." Mira reached the tall white door, pushing it open with her delicate hand as she looked at Jareth over her shoulder, "Now…" She leaned against the doorframe, "Are you going to bathe with those papers of yours? Or are you coming to bathe with me…?" Her smile curved as she stepped backward once into the bathroom, disappearing from Jareth's view.

Jareth's chest rose once as he inhaled deeply and exhaled sharply. "Damn it," he muttered, his tongue dragging over his teeth. He moved, stepping forward and making his way to follow Mira.

Mira descended into the tub, "Oh! It's cold!"

"Cold?" Jareth echoed. "Make room. I'll warm it up for you."

Jareth closed the distance in three strides, settling behind her in the tub. The water shifted, sloshing over the rim. His broad frame made the tub feel claustrophobic—in the best way. His strong arms wrapped around her waist, bringing her spine flush against his chest.

"My hero," Mira teased. She tilted her head to look up at Jareth from over her shoulder, "Perhaps we can catch a carriage together on the way to work?"

"Together? If we're seen in the same carriage, then it'll start gossip that we've rekindled things."

"Would that be so bad?" Mira purred, the tip of her finger reaching over her shoulder to graze down, moving from his lips to his chin. "Or do you fear that no other woman will lift her skirt for you?"

"Funny," Jareth muttered, though his tone said more than words ever could. "I just don't wish to confuse the public. Last thing I need is a sketch of us splashed across the front of *Stone's Gazette*, with half the city speculating on rekindled courtships and wedding bells."

"And you've always cared about your public image, huh?" Mira didn't look back this time. "Everything came before *us*—your work, your name, your image. When the papers speculated about infidelity, you were more worried about clearing your name than ensuring *I* was okay."

Jareth's arms loosened around her, "Mira." His tone had dropped. "That's not fair. You knew I didn't cheat. The public didn't."

Mira ran her fingers through her damp auburn hair, brushing the moment off with it. "Let's just bury this and enjoy ourselves. Enough drama for one morning." She leaned into Jareth, closed her eyes, and let her shoulders fall—like none of it mattered.

Ambrosja glared at Killian from across the table. Her golden eyes burned into him while leaves fell around them, surrounding the canopy of the raised platform. The sounds of working men and women filled the air.

He just sits there. While they sweat and bleed for him.

"You're staring," Killian spoke, not even looking at her, his eyes fixed on a parchment before him. "What is it?"

"They break their backs for you—and you're sitting there slicing eggs like you've earned the right to rest."

"By Dragon's Breath," Killian muttered, biting down on a piece of bacon. "If I had known you'd be such a delight to eat breakfast with, I would have invited you to my table years ago."

"We didn't know each other years ago."

Killian's eyes finally met Ambrosja's, "That was sarcasm."

"Oh…"

Their gaze remained locked — until Ambrosja had to look away.

"You're not used to engaging in simple conversation, are you?" Killian tilted his head, looking at Ambrosja like she was a puzzle with too many of the same piece—every edge the same, none of them fitting.

"Does it matter?"

"Perhaps not." Killian smirked, leaning forward. "You *are* quite refreshing."

"Commander!" A Black Hand guard called, dragging Donathan behind him, "We've been waiting all night for you! This one here—" he shoved Donathan towards the wooden platform in which Killian's table sat upon, "—was caught speaking with them three we found yesterday! Bastard ran away and put up a fight, but we got 'im!"

Ambrosja shot to her feet, the chair scraping back. "Donathan—" Her heart seized. *Gods above…* Bruises bloomed across his jaw, blood darkened the collar of his shirt. *They beat you.* Her hands curled into fists. *This is my fault.*

Donathan could barely raise his eyes to meet Ambrosja. As if he was too ashamed—or didn't want her to pity him.

Killian raised a hand as he stood to his full height, "Put up a fight, did he?"

"Yessir, Commander," the guard nodded, "but we brought him back. So, what do you plan to do with him? Beat him?" Donathan flinched at that. "Throw him into the next burning hamlet?"

The commander's eyes simply moved over Donathan, sizing him up once. "Let him go."

"What—"

"Did I stutter?" Killian's gaze snapped to the guard, "He put up a fight, he's still standing. Let him go. Set him to the mines with the other three and leave him be."

Killian sat down again. Ambrosja glanced between the three figures, itching to leave her seat and tend to Donathan, but she caught the most subtle shake of Killian's head. A warning to stand down.

"But Commander—"

Killian's fist hit the table. Donathan took a step back out of instinct. The sound echoed through the camp, catching the eyes and ears of many there.

"…Yes, Sir." The guard disappeared from the commander's sight, dragging Donathan in tow.

Ambrosja remained standing for a moment longer, until Killian's eyes settled on her.

"Sit down, Ambrosja. Unless you wish to draw even more attention yourself." Killian leaned back in his chair, picking up the parchment and looking at it more closely.

Ambrosja faltered. Only for a moment. Her steps made their way across the wooden platform, but her wrist was seized sharply. Killian was standing now, towering over her and bringing her close enough that their bodies grazed. This brought the attention of a few Black Hands nearby, including Killian's lieutenant.

"I've given you comfort in both a bed and a meal." Killian hunched slightly, his face inching closer to hers. "And now you are disobeying me where my soldiers can see." His voice dropped to a deadly whisper, "You know I won't kill you because of who you are, and soon, others will question why I won't beat you senseless. Are you trying to out yourself? Or are you itching to piss me off, Ambrosja?"

Ambrosja's eyes snapped down to Killian's firm hand around her wrist, then up to his cold gray eyes. "He's just a boy. And they've beaten him."

"He is a young man," Killian tilted his chin once as he corrected her.

"And I've let him go instead of beating him myself." Killian caught the stare from Berric across the field. And finally, he let go of Ambrosja's wrist with a slight shove. He raised his voice loud enough, "Go! Make yourself useful and grab a pickaxe." Then he turned.

Ambrosja stood there for a moment. Killian didn't look back at her as he sat once more, reviewing his parchments. She exhaled sharply, nodding to herself as she understood what Killian had done, at what he had *allowed*. Ambrosja moved towards the mining equipment just a few feet away. Her boots kicked at rocks unintentionally, throwing dirt behind each heel that dug into the ground a bit too forcefully.

"Here," a Black Hand guard spoke with a tone of impatience. He handed her a pickaxe before giving her a push into the mines.

It wasn't long until Ambrosja noticed the hulking figure of Gunnar. He swung his pickaxe with more force than necessary. Cinder had one arm up, shielding her eyes. Johann seemed to deliberately place himself at least ten feet away from Gunnar, as if he knew that at some point, a rock from Gunnar's side could shoot out and cause injury. Donathan was beside him, his gaze was vacant, and his body seemed to be simply moving without much thought.

Ambrosja stepped closer, "Gunnar! Cinder!"

Gunnar stopped swinging abruptly. "Well, damn," Cinder muttered with a smirk. "It's about time you showed up, Blondie!"

Johann looked over his shoulder at Ambrosja, "Are you alright?" He turned completely now, meeting Ambrosja halfway, along with Gunnar.

Gunnar circled Ambrosja, "You don't look like you've gone through a scuffle... Your hair is brushed, no bruises..."

"And she's wearing clothes that are at least ten sizes too big for her," Cinder chimed in, "So..." Cinder got closer to Ambrosja, "I saw you and the Commander having breakfast together. Did you sleep with him or what?"

Ambrosja's brows twitched at the question. She could feel her cheeks flush from the incredulity of such a question. "No! I did not lay with him romantically if that is what you mean!"

Cinder chuckled, then returned to her spot in the mines. She gave a glance over Ambrosja. "Fine, I'll bite — what happened? Where were you?"

Ambrosja sighed. "I *was* in his bed. But — not like that. He… wants to keep me close."

Johann squinted at that. "Why?"

"I — I am not entirely sure."

Cinder groaned, "Ugh, so you get a nice cozy bed? Lucky you. But

— at least I don't have to sleep next to a man. I bet he smells bad up close."

Ambrosja tilted her head in thought. "He sort of smells like an oak tree with dark berries. But — I want to stay with you —"

Cinder immediately interrupted Ambrosja with her hand, slicing through the air. "First off, I don't want to know how you know what he smells like. Second — you should stay in his chambers…" her voice dropped to a whisper, "Take the opportunity to look around." Before Ambrosja could protest, Cinder thumbed towards Donathan. "Can you talk to him? He hasn't been himself since last night."

Ambrosja looked towards Donathan, leaning on one foot as she tried to read him. "He seems… disconnected." She walked forward, her hand found Donathan's shoulder, "I saw the bruises… Are you alright?"

Donathan stilled for a moment. His hands shook around the handle of the pickaxe. Then… it dropped. He turned just a bit to look at Ambrosja.

"S-sorry…" his breath left him shaky, "Ambrosja?" He bent down to pick up his pickaxe, "The others figured you were fine… I'm glad to see you are…" There was a pause as he straightened once more, "Are you… Fine?"

Ambrosja nodded, her eyes swept over Donathan, "Hey, what is wrong?" She raised her right hand, slowly towards his face, her fingertips began to glow, ready to heal.

Donathan's hand snapped to hers, seizing her wrist, not strongly, just quickly. "Don't… Don't heal me. I don't deserve to be healed."

Gunnar exhaled sharply, looking between them with concern. Johann stepped closer, and Cinder had stopped mining completely, just watching now.

Ambrosja shook her head, "But you do not deserve—"

"Yes, I do," Donathan interjected quickly, his hand loosened around her wrist and dropped, "I deserve this. And I want to wear it as a reminder. A reminder of the consequences of my cowardice…" His head dipped and he shook it, "…Just as I wear my mark of the Black Hand. A reminder of a choice I made…"

A sudden voice came from the entrance of the tunnel, "Oi! Mine and talk! This isn't a damned place for a tea party!"

Donathan flinched slightly and quickly turned, already resuming his mining. The others joined. Ambrosja joined last as she watched Donathan for a moment longer.

For moments that were too long, the silence simply stretched. Only filled by the sounds of iron meeting stone and the bits of rock that fell and met the ground.

"None of us care," Cinder said suddenly. "We get it, Donathan, okay? You ran away. You panicked. I get it. You barely know us. If I were in your shoes? Shit – I'd probably run away, too."

Gunnar grunted, a smirk playing on his lips. "Oh, and she has. Sort of." Cinder shot him a look, but Gunnar only grinned wider. "Weeks after Johann and I first met her, we encountered these ruins, deep in the southern woods of Redharrow, not too far from the border of Mercinari. Pretty sure these were the ruins that belonged to an ancient dragon-worshipping temple. They looked like they hadn't been explored in months. We found packs on the outside, but torn with bite marks and books that were barely legible from the rain that must have beat down upon it. The ruins? Nasty things were inside, I could hear it—hells, I could smell it. Probably necromancy gone wrong, y'know how Vaestoria frowns upon that sort of thing. Anyway—" He swung his pick, sweat was dripping down his forehead, but he didn't stop smiling. "A little rock fell... And Cinder bolted. She closed the doors on her way out, sealing us inside. And she ran."

"Shut up, Gunnar," Cinder muttered aggressively with a scowl.

Johann laughed. "But you know what? She came back a day later, unlocked the doors, and apologized profusely. She was so sorry... She actually cried."

Donathan paused, "Cinder... cried?"

"Oh, shut it! All of you! I was trying to reassure Donathan!" Cinder stopped mining, scowling at the two older men now, "But now you've gone ahead and shared something that didn't need to be shared and ruined the moment."

Ambrosja bit her lip to stop herself from joining in on the laughter. "But Cinder is right," she said at last, her eyes moving back onto Donathan, "It makes sense, anyone would have run in your shoes."

Donathan shook his head, "It's — it's not just that..." He sighed, looking down at the ground, "I did this back when my hamlet burnt down as well. I ran. I was scared. I left my family behind like – like a—a coward!" His grip tightened on the handle of his pickaxe. "I don't deserve any of you. Your kindness, your words of encouragement... Or that second chance you all gave me back in the woods."

Everyone was silent now. Their eyes locked on Donathan's trembling frame.

It was Cinder who moved first. Her arms wrapped around him, "We're all a little cowardly, okay?" she whispered, "We've all done things we're not proud of, things that will haunt us until we die... Doesn't mean that we *deserve* to die."

Donathan was frozen in Cinder's arms. Then his eyes closed tightly. His pickaxe dropped, and his arms came around her as well. Ambrosja, Gunnar, and Johann were silent as they watched the scene. They all remained quiet as Donathan and Cinder had their moment.

NECROMANCY

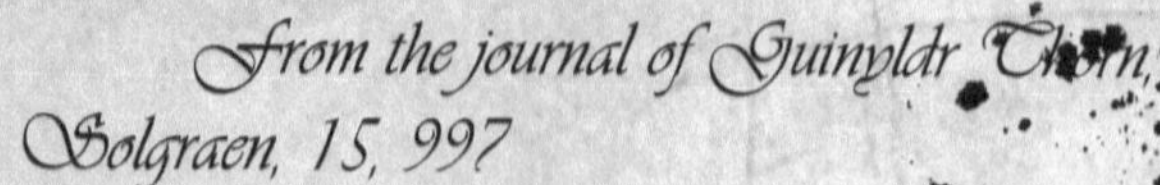

Necromancy, the most perilous branch of Veil Magic, concerns the calling of the dead back across the boundary of life. Practitioners claim it to be an art of restoration — of summoning the departed from beyond the Veil — yet all lawful scholars of Eldorwyn hold it to be an abomination.

It is forbidden throughout the realms, for it is believed that what returns to the flesh is not the soul that once dwelled there, but something else wearing its shape. The act severs the balance between the living and the dead, and those who attempt it are said to invite the gaze of what waits beyond the Veil itself.

THE RUINS OF RED HARROW

Once a grand temple where the Dragon Worshipers of Vaestoria gathered in reverence, the Ruins of Red Harrow now lie broken in the southeastern reaches of Marrowind. Lost in the war between Vaestoria and Mercinari, its halls are long fallen to ash and time — though some say the stones still remember the wings that once passed overhead.

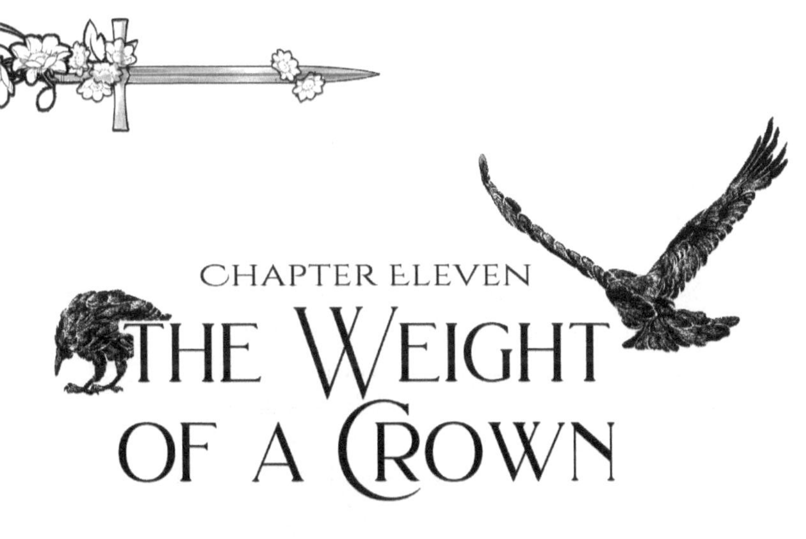

CHAPTER ELEVEN

THE WEIGHT OF A CROWN

Jareth pushed open the heavy council doors. The same chamber he'd sat in only yesterday felt colder now. Dull murmurs buzzed through the chamber—until Jareth's steps faltered. His gaze snapped to the front, the chair that was empty yesterday had been filled with his father's form. He wasn't much shorter than Jareth, though age had silvered strands of his hair and sharpened the blue in his eyes. His presence, however, made the room feel smaller. Jareth straightened and continued, walking right up to his father's seat.

"Father," Jareth said, his tone nearly a whisper. "I thought the High Regent was only needed when matters were grave." A chuckle escaped him, "What happened? Did Lord Varian lose another heirloom and demand a search party?"

Aaric's lips twitched, though he tried to hide the amusement. "Yes, well..." Aaric began to speak, glancing briefly over at Varian, then up at Jareth, "Varian did indeed summon me here, apparently regarding our long-gone hamlet, Wintersong."

Jareth immediately fixed his posture, "Varian summoned you? Without even consulting the Council first?" His brows pinched as he tried to read his father's face. "We just learned of Wintersong's destruction yesterday; we haven't even announced its fall to the public yet."

Aaric tilted his head, adjusting the parchments in his hand, "I know, but he said he has reason to believe I should be here today, so, here I am. Besides," the smallest grin formed on his lips, "it gets boring in my office. Might be fun to see you all bicker."

"Well," Jareth exhaled, something between amusement and exasperation. "I still don't quite care for him going around us to summon you. If you'll excuse me, I'll take my seat." He didn't go far; the Diplomat's seat was always beside the High Regent's, a seat that mostly remained empty, except for today.

Oswin leaned into Aaric, his voice dropped to a whisper, "Varian summoned you here, old friend? Any idea why?"

Aaric did a slight shrug and whispered back, "He only said it involved Wintersong. You know how Varian likes his drama."

"Unfortunately."

Varian stood from his chair and cleared his throat, "Since all members of the Council are present, let us begin, hm?"

The sound of chairs scraping and papers shifting echoed in the chamber as everyone took their seat and adjusted their parchments. Their eyes drifted between Varian and Aaric. But ultimately landing on Varian.

Varian relaxed his posture; he dipped his chin once he had everyone's attention. "After yesterday's news with Wintersong's destruction, I decided to revisit the reports of other hamlets that were attacked." Varian hunched over his side of the table, his hands shuffled parchment. Then he moved again, moving along the table, placing a parchment in front of each council member.

"I've taken the liberty of organizing my notes and conducting theories." He kept moving, passing Aaric and Jareth now, "The very first hamlet that was attacked was Willowfen. Sloppy work." He added, "When I went over the costs of repairs and what was taken and ruined... The guilty stole the hunting dogs, leathers, and meat."

Once Varian finished going around the table, he was back at his seat, letting the silence stretch with only the shifting of parchment being heard as each council member looked over the gentle script before them.

Rosalind spoke first. "Of course, Willowfen's primary source of income and production is from hunting. That *would* be the biggest loss."

Varian nodded, "Yes, and for the destruction of that hamlet, the casualties were almost none. Mostly hunters who were defending their hounds and goods. Very minor burning." Varian gestured to his own parchment, "In fact, it was noted by our guards that the burning came from arrows. No magic, no torches. It was done at a distance, specifically from near the shores."

Emeric sighed, rubbing his chin. "And what about Mareholt? What do you gather from that?"

Varian grinned, "Mareholt? That was the sloppiest, but the numbers were higher. Thanks to Mareholt being so close to Vaelmoor, the military was close by. Granted, they did indeed do more damage. More arrows, more fire. Burnt down a stable. They took some military gear. But... No horses."

His hand rubbed his chin, "And in those reports? They mentioned that hounds were used in this attack."

Oswin's eyes roamed over the parchment, "Yet no hounds were used in Willowfen?"

"Correct, because the hounds taken from Willowfen were used against Mareholt."

Aaric laced his fingers together, his cold eyes were set onto Varian, "I assume you are connecting a pattern here, Lord Varian? This will eventually come to an idea, or preferably an answer as to who is behind this, yes?"

Varian tilted his head, "Of course, let me hurry this along." He bowed his head before gesturing to the parchments once more, "If you look at the mining hamlet of Stonecreek, you will see that the reports were nearly catastrophic. Homes were burnt down, a lot of deaths, and quite a few missing people that we never found. Ores were taken. Weapons. Tools. And now..."

His finger moved down to where Wintersong was listed, "Nothing. Just a report of the hamlet of Wintersong being burnt down to ash. No survivors. And although we've yet to receive a complete report on what was taken, if anyone is missing, the information given to Lord Jareth shows that no homes were left standing and there were bodies scattered about."

Jareth's piercing gaze moved from the parchment to Varian, "And I trust you have sent at least a handful of soldiers, a strategist, and an investigator to take into a proper account of what happened there."

"Of course, Lord Jareth," Varian finally took his seat, "it wounds me that you would even bring that up. I'm a well-prepared man."

Jareth didn't say anything, but his jaw clenched, and there was the faintest scoff from his side of the room.

Aaric's voice sharpened. "You've walked us through every attack. Every missing dog and burnt tool. I'll ask plainly—what are you suggesting, Lord Varian?"

Varian smiled, and it wasn't a kind one. "Nordorn."

That earned a few glances.

Aaric's voice turned cold, "Nordorn?"

Jareth leaned forward, forearms pressing into the edge of the round table, "That is ridiculous. Are you really blaming Nordorn?"

Varian waved dismissively. "*Think*, young Lord Jareth." Varian gestured to the parchment in front of him, "I've listed that the arrows came from the shores. It seems every attacked hamlet was along the edges, near the shoreline. The horses from Mareholt were not taken, but the hounds from Willowfen were."

"That means nothing," Jareth snapped, his voice cold. "You really want to blame an entire country for what could be far more likely as a group of bandits that are simply becoming more organized and more lethal as time goes on?!"

"Lord Jareth," Varian spoke with a cool level, "inside voices, please. There is no need to raise our tone."

Jareth ran a hand down his face, shaking his head in disbelief. "Lord Varian, right now, you are accusing another country of attacking our regency. You do realize what you are currently doing is nearly proposing war? We cannot simply accuse another country without further evidence. There has been *nothing* to indicate Nordorn besides—" Jareth pushed his parchment from him, his hands falling heavily only to armrests as he leaned back aggressively, "—apparently the *arrows came from the shore.*"

"And they didn't steal horses." Varian reminded him.

"By the Stone Dragon!" Jareth barked, raising his hands into the air as he rolled his eyes, "They didn't steal horses! That is your other reasoning?! You're accusing a sovereign nation over arrowheads and the fact that there are no missing horses? You *know* that's how wars begin."

"Lords," Aaric responded cooly with a raised tone, "Settle. Down."

"I'm not saying Nordorn is guilty," Varian said, almost too gently. "But if this were a game of patterns... they fit the shape." Varian braced his hands against the table, looking at each council member. "You need more pieces to this puzzle? Nordorners do not use horses; they use snowbears and wolves. They come from the sea with their fleet of barbarians and archers." He tilted his head. "Let's not forget, raiding? That is what Nordorners have excelled at since the beginning of time."

Emeric spoke, shaking his head as he read over the parchment, "Truthfully — Nordorn? That is... Not very likely..." He studied it closely, then looked towards each council member as he began to explain, "That country has been working to make allies since Empress Inghild reigned over three centuries ago. Besides, they have the strongest army and the strongest fleet. Why would they bother with hamlets? If this is the '*work*'—" Emeric gestured with a dramatic wave of his hand that echoed the disbelief in his tone, "—of Nordorn, it must be rogue raiders. Not from the official word of the Empress."

"And—" the door opened, Mira stepped in. Her auburn bob was neatly brushed, curling inwards at the ends, her slender frame was draped in a fitted gown of honey-brown silk, its cloak-like sleeves edged with golden embroidery along the hems, "—that is why I think we should send word to Greymire. After all, that is the closest regency to Nordorn's borders. If they have been through something similar recently..." Mira gave a shrug, "...Then perhaps it is indeed Nordorn."

Jareth's eyes snapped up as soon as he heard Mira's voice. He stood and gave a bow to her as she approached him. "Miss Harte, to what does the council owe the pleasure?"

"I apologize for barging in." She looked to the council members, bowing her head, then her eyes landed on Aaric, and she deepened her bow. "As Advocate of the court, I believe we should find time this week to discuss the losses suffered at Wintersong and prepare a letter of our deepest and most sincere apologies, but also a promise to take better care of our hamlets. We all remember what happened after Stonecreek," she paused, letting the memories catch up. "With silence, we risk riots."

Jareth fixed his throat, adjusting his cravat. "You are correct, Miss Harte."

"I'm glad we agree, Lord Jareth, as the Diplomat and the *temporary* Justiciar of Stonehaven—" Jareth's gaze flicked to the empty seat beside him before returning to Mira. "—you must be the one to ease the concerns of the people." Mira smiled, stepping closer to Jareth and giving the slightest bow of her head. "But I am always here to help you and the council." She looked at the other members. "I can begin writing a tightly fitted document that will protect the council's honor while also aiding those who are suffering from Wintersong's loss."

Varian glanced between Jareth and Mira with interest. He smirked, exhaling a slight puff of smug air before speaking, "Well, Miss Harte, the council certainly appreciates the eagerness that our advocates approach us with, but... We had not exactly disclosed Wintersong's situation. This was meant to be private..." His eyes moved over onto Jareth's form, "Unless someone shared it beforehand?"

Mira smiled sweetly, "Oh, you got me, Lord Varian." She turned her body to face him completely. "Truth be told, and I do sincerely apologize for this, I was eavesdropping. I heard what sounded like an argument and couldn't help myself. Also... It's very possible the other advocates and I have a secret betting pool on who is going to throw the first punch in this room." That earned a few chuckles in the room. Including from Aaric.

Emeric was one that didn't chuckle. Instead, he studied Mira. His brows lowered, his eyes tracing her face. "You *are* awfully prepared for someone who overheard our conversation."

Mira didn't miss a beat, "That's what being an advocate is all about, Lord Emeric, thinking on your feet."

"Thank you, Miss Harte." Rosalind dipped her chin in appreciation, "Do come see me after this, if you have the time, of course. We will discuss the costs and possible settlements towards the kin of those who lost their lives in Wintersong."

Mira bowed one last time, "Of course." She straightened herself, "Before I make my leave, should I speak with our strategist to work on a letter to send to Greymire? If we get it out before sundown, we might just get an answer within two weeks."

Aaric nodded, "Yes, that would be useful." He turned to look at Jareth, "After this meeting, be sure to check in with Miss Harte and your strategist about the letter."

"Of course," Jareth agreed, then looked at Mira. "Allow me to walk you out."

Jareth walked close to Mira. His hand settled on her lower back as they walked side by side. Varian and Rosalind noticed it, they exchanged a glance and Rosalind arched a knowing brow. Emeric simply shook his head as he took a sip of his water.

"...Are they together again?" Oswin whispered as he leaned into Aaric's side.

Aaric shook his head. "As my wife says with all of her Vaestorian elegance, *Jareth is fucking around.*" Oswin chuckled. Aaric did not.

Jareth opened the council doors, leaving them ajar behind him as he stepped out with Mira.

"Don't tell me you're entertaining Varian's fantasy," he muttered, keeping his voice low.

Mira's gaze drifted up the hallway, thoughtful. "Entertaining? No. But dismissing Nordorn entirely? That would be naive."

Jareth's brow twitched. "Mira—"

"Jareth," she interrupted, a hand brushing lightly against his jaw, "If we fail to even *consider* them... how do you expect to prepare for what they're capable of?" Her fingers lingered, cool and poised. "It's not about accusation. It's about readiness."

He caught her hand—gently, but firmly—and lowered it, as if he were creating distance between them. "That's not a strategy. That's suspicion

dressed as foresight." He stepped back, adjusting the front of his tailcoat, jaw tight. "I'll see you after lunch."

Her lips curled, the faintest curve of mischief. "Try not to miss me." She walked off, hips swaying a touch too deliberately. Before rounding the corner, she turned—blew him a kiss.

Jareth didn't smile. But his eyes tracked her longer than he should have. He turned back toward the council chamber. Inhaling once, smoothing his brow, he pushed the door open.

"I apologize for the interruption," he said with cold ease, returning to his seat as if nothing had ever touched him.

Cinder's brows arched, her brown eyes tracking the hulking figure of Killian. She scoffed, and the slightest pull of amusement crossed her lips.

"What?" Gunnar looked up from his bowl of stew. "What's with the smirk?"

"Killian has looked over at Ambrosja over twelve times now. I counted." Ambrosja's eyes quickly met Cinder's, and Cinder's lips pursed thoughtfully. Then she grinned, looking at Ambrosja, "You should seduce him."

Ambrosja nearly choked on her stew. Her hand quickly came up to wipe the remnants from her chin. "What?!" she gasped low, her head nearly bumping into Cinder's from when she turned.

"Hey, we all want to continue our *little* adventure towards Stonehaven," Cinder gestured dramatically with a hand into the distance. She set her bowl down beside her. "I'm just saying, he's into you, and if it isn't romantically... then it is definitely with hunger."

Ambrosja shook her head, "I do not think that is what's going on, Cinder..." She dared a glance—and instantly regretted it. Killian's steel-gray stare had already found hers. Like he'd been waiting. Her heart may have stumbled, but she couldn't tell if it was from Cinder's influence or just the smallest thrill she felt.

Johann sighed, idly twirling his spoon in his bowl, "Cinder, please don't encourage nonsense that could sentence us all to death."

Gunnar grunted in agreement, "Yeah, please don't try to throw our friend into the lap of our enemy."

Donathan actually chuckled for once, though the bruises made every movement ache. "I mean—"

Gunnar's head snapped towards him, "Not you, too, lad."

Donathan shook his head, smiling gently. "I'm not saying Cinder is right, but she doesn't have the *worst* idea. Besides, it's true. The Commander has been glancing here nearly every other minute, and when he doesn't see Ambrosja immediately... He *searches*. Not only that..." Donathan smiled, leaning into the group like a child spilling a secret. "Whenever it looks like Ambrosja is about to look at him? He looks away. Tell me that's not the reaction of a man who is crushing on a woman."

Cinder slapped her leg, barking while chewing, "See?! I'm not the only one noticing!" Cinder swallowed her food and leaned forward. "Listen," her voice dropped to a whisper, only adding to the conspiratory tone between all of them, "I'm not saying she should sleep with him... I'm just suggesting she use her feminine wiles to get information out of him. That's what we need, right? Something concrete, something substantial to present to Stonehaven. It's the only way they'll do anything that requires more than sending one extra guard to each hamlet."

Gunnar shook his head, "Well, that's not up to me, Cinder." He pointed at Ambrosja with his spoon, "That's up to *her*."

Everyone looked at Ambrosja. Ambrosja looked between all of them.

"I do not think that would be wise..." She cleared her throat, now looking down at her stew. "Besides, flirting out of nowhere would be... odd. Do you not all agree?"

Johann nodded immediately, "It would be odd."

Gunnar shook his head, "Not really."

Both men stared at each other for a second.

"Really?" Johann sighed, narrowing his eyes at Gunnar, "You don't think it would be strange for Ambrosja to walk up to the man out of nowhere and start batting her eyelashes?"

"Depends on how it's done," Gunnar shrugged, "If she is obvious, sure. If she's subtle, no."

Johann just stared at Gunnar for a moment, frowning deeply. "You're not the man to ask this. You will sleep with anything that is warm, wet, and curvy."

Gunnar looked momentarily offended, then tilted his head as his eyes opened wider, as if a revelation had dawned on him. Then nodded quietly and went back to eating.

Donathan spoke gently, looking at Ambrosja, "Listen, you don't have to do this, but it might work. We might get to leave sooner. It's up to you."

"I will think about it," Ambrosja muttered, her eyes downcast at her stew once more.

Cinder's smile thinned, "Except—" Cinder looked at Ambrosja, there was no smirk, no jest in her eyes. "—We don't have all the time in the world. Every day we sit here waiting, someone else dies screaming. That's the part you're not thinking about."

Ambrosja's brows furrowed, her eyes met Cinder's, "I *am* thinking about that."

"Are you? Because you are the only one in the perfect position to *maybe* seduce the man that we need information from."

"It's not easy," Ambrosja said firmly. "I—I—" Ambrosja clutched her bowl. Then her eyes found the raven in the distance. Its gaze set on hers. She looked down. "...I am promised to someone else."

Cinder dropped her spoon. Donathan almost dropped his bowl. Gunnar stopped eating, and Johann calmly set his own meal down.

"Promised?" Cinder narrowed her eyes. "To who? Since when? Where the fuck is he? Please tell me he's on his way to find you."

Ambrosja shook her head. "N-no, he is not. He is away. It is… an arranged marriage."

"Arranged?" Cinder scoffed. "Then you're not promised. Hells, he's probably off slipping his sword into different sheaths right now."

Ambrosja froze completely. Her body had gone still except for the slightest movement her breathing made, but even then, that looked nonexistent. Johann and Gunnar immediately noticed the stillness.

Johann glared at Cinder. "It's not your business, girl. Don't go around saying things you know nothing about."

Cinder looked at Johann, slightly offended. "Oh, please — I'm just saying… An arranged marriage barely counts. She's not married yet. She might as well get all the meat she can before she's forced to settle down."

"Cinder!" Johann gasped.

Gunnar still had his eyes on Ambrosja. He noticed how her fingers curled tightly around her spoon. "Lass," he said calmly, his own gaze set back down to his bowl. "If he is doing such things, he's not worth the trouble. Or the wall you are trying to build around yourself at this moment."

Ambrosja's eyes met Gunnar's face. Simply listening. But she couldn't speak. She felt that if she did, her heart might tear its way out through her throat.

Gunnar noticed. He didn't comment. He simply continued, "A man worthy of you — arrangement or not, wouldn't be leaving you to dust while he busies himself with women he shouldn't be busying with."

The Empress looked down then. Staring into her own reflection in

her stew that was becoming colder by the minute. A twirl of her spoon disrupted her reflection—as if she couldn't bear to look at herself.

There was silence now. It was uncomfortable. Johann looked over Ambrosja, trying to read her, to see what she needed. Cinder looked ahead, watching the leaves fall around the canopy of their lunch area, looking like she hated what she said, but she was too proud to apologize. Gunnar was tracking every miner there, who they spoke to, and where they sat to eat. And Donathan watched Cinder.

Ambrosja risked a glance again. Her eyes traced Killian's figure, how he moved, how he walked. The way his jaw shifted every time he spoke, how leaves seemed to never land on him but around him, like a force that none could dare touch. And she saw the way his eyes did indeed find hers again. And how their stares lingered towards each other. A kind of stare that she can't recall ever receiving from her betrothed. Her heart did another flip— her lips parted as if her breath had escaped her without permission.

Killian forced his stare away, now turning completely in the opposite direction.

Until he glanced up at the sun, those gray eyes of his turning silver. He raised a hand, his palm open wide, until the Black Hands surrounding him had silenced themselves and stepped aside. Killian's hands moved, undoing the tunic that hugged his broad frame until his scars and muscles of his bronze skin were all that was bare. His boots and pants remained, however. Everyone watched him, and he was unbothered. He simply marched towards where the tools were held and took hold of a pickaxe. Examined it briefly before moving into the mines.

Ambrosja's head was tilted with pure curiosity. She scooted closer to Gunnar now. "What is he doing?" she asked quietly.

Gunnar didn't answer at first. He glanced around, looked at the sun, then at everyone else. He noticed the heat. The sweat. "Dragon worshipper," he simply said. "He's testing his body's limits."

Ambrosja's eyebrows pinched. "How do you figure that?" She only seemed more confused and more curious.

Johann chimed in, "We are approaching the hottest hour of the day, and it is Vorthenday." He nodded, as if almost approving. "He is not just a worshipper of any dragon, but a Vorthunal worshipper. Those who worship Vorthunal test their body's limits and try to push past it. They are about endurance, of the mind and body."

Ambrosja stared now, into the entrance of the mine where the faint echoing of steel meeting stone could be heard. Cinder caught this.

"Mmm, I suppose Blondie has a thing for men who are hard working, hm?" Cinder rested her chin in the palm of her hand, all mischief in her expression.

Ambrosja's eyes darted to Cinder's. "I am just… shocked, I suppose… I may have judged him harshly earlier, claiming that he had no interest in helping the miners."

Donathan shrugged. "Why would he? He is a Commander, not a Foreman. He has hired these miners; they're not slaves, Ambrosja."

She looked at Donathan and gave a small dip of her chin. "I suppose you are right, that one miner we spoke to did say they were hired… Only those who have betrayed Killian have been forced to work to pay off their sentence…" Ambrosja shook her head suddenly. "Still, I would work beside my people, pay or no pay. And not beat them half to death."

"That is the only reason why I am not praising the man," Johann sighed, "but I can respect his dedication to his prayers."

Cinder scoffed, scraping her bowl harder with her spoon. "Why? Because he's a damn dragon worshipper like you?"

Johann's brows lowered heavily, staring at Cinder with a disapproving look. "Cinder, these dragons are the bones of our people. Our ancestors."

"Sure," Cinder agreed, "but that doesn't mean you should respect a damn man who—" she dropped her voice suddenly, a harsh whisper towards Johann, "—is associated with those burning down hamlets!"

Ambrosja had stopped listening to the bickering at this point. Her eyes were on the entrance to the mine entirely. She pushed her bowl away from her and stood, heading towards the mines as well. The group looked at her. Gunnar went to move after her, but Cinder immediately latched onto his wrist, giving a slow shake of her head.

Deep within the mines, the grunts of Killian echoed. It didn't take long for Ambrosja to spot the hulking figure moving with strength that was near graceful, given how his muscles flexed. Or maybe it was the low-light of the oil lamps. Or maybe it was because it had been a while since Ambrosja had seen such a man at work, so her eyes couldn't help but linger.

The Empress cursed herself for every second she stared, but she didn't pull her eyes away. She stopped five paces away from him. Just staring. He looked at her once, but he didn't stop to greet her or question her and he returned to work.

"Why do you keep looking at me?" Ambrosja had crossed her arms. "You kept staring at me during lunch."

Killian rumbled. Then slowed his movements, standing straight and wiping sweat from his forehead. His eyes slid over to where Ambrosja's form stood. "I could say the same, Ambrosja. Every time I looked at you, you were looking at me." He then placed his forearm onto the stone wall, his gray eyes locked on her golden ones. "Do you see something you like—" his voice dropped to a whisper that was meant just for her, "—Empress?"

Ambrosja's lips parted, jaw going slightly slack from the audacity. Her brows pinched close together. "Hard to see a creature with cruelty embedded into its bones as attractive, Commander." Then she took a step forward. "And don't call me that."

The corner of Killian's lips curved. "What are you doing here? Did you march your pretty little blonde head all the way down here to scold me for peeking at you?" He mock-bowed then, "Forgive me, my lady — I didn't realize that keeping an eye on you was the most unlawful thing I could have done."

She squinted at him. "I don't quite care for that tone of voice; it sounds like the one you used with your sarcastic remark."

"It is the same one."

"Well, I don't like it."

"Hm," Killian hummed, "and you know what I don't like?" he took a step forward, leaning down, "Being disturbed while I am trying to work. If you're going to stay here, grab a pickaxe and... Get. To. Work."

Ambrosja stared at him, her eyes glaring into his. Then she turned, grabbed a leftover pickaxe from the ground, and took a spot on the wall opposite him. Killian watched for a moment, then returned to mining... Only to flinch at the *godsawful* scraping sound. He slowly turned; those cold-steel gray eyes of his had locked onto Ambrosja's form. Messy. Inexperienced. Her posture was poor, and the grip on the pick was wrong.

Killian abandoned his own pickaxe now. Setting it aside against the wall he was working on and moved behind Ambrosja. When she lifted her pick overhead—Killian's hand shot at it—he stopped her from swinging, staring down at her from above. Her own head slowly tilted up, tilting back until their eyes met, until she could feel the back of her head grazing his bare chest.

"*That* is not how you mine," Killian said, his hand now moving down to rest over hers.

Ambrosja's pose was forcefully shifted. He gently shoved at her boots with his own, forcing her stance to widen.

"Excuse you," she hissed, but Killian didn't stop.

He adjusted her grip, holding her hands tight to keep them steady. Then his hands moved down to her hips, tilting her body just right. Then his hands found her waist—she swallowed, her heart pounding within her ribs—his one hand squeezing there while the other traveled to press against her lower back, forcing her to straighten.

"You want a straight back—don't hunch. The last thing you want is your spine ruined." Killian was instructing her, his hands grabbing at each relevant part of her. "Keep your knees bent but not locked. Stance wide for support, hands spaced apart on the handle." He took a step back then. "When you raise the pick over your head, let the weight of it deal the blow to the stone. Guide it. Don't force it, you'll just exhaust yourself faster." He gestured towards the stone before her. "Go on, try."

Ambrosja was still for a second. Trying to fight the creeping heat in her body and the fluttering within her stomach. She felt insulted, and she felt the most damned itch within her. Like she had taken a bite out of something forbidden and found it delicious. *How dare he touch me like that — and damned me for even letting him.*

She brought the pickaxe overhead, then swung, not forcefully, just guiding the pick down and then letting the weight follow. Her posture was better, she didn't grunt as loudly, or stagger.

"Much better," Killian said, now returning to his wall and resuming his task. "Don't forget to shift your stance occasionally. It'll ease the strain on your body."

"I should put some strain on your body," Ambrosja had muttered.

He paused everything once those words left her lips. He angled his head, eyes on the stone before him as he processed her comment. His jaw shifted. Then he turned just enough so his eyes could lock onto her.

"You would put strain on my body, Ambrosja?" He angled just enough—enough that when Ambrosja had turned, the light from the lamps was making the sweat glisten just far too perfectly on his battle-sculpted body. "Careful, a man might take that the wrong way."

The Empress's brows had lowered dangerously. She dropped her pickaxe and turned to face him completely, keeping her eyes on his gray ones. Not daring to look down at his *infuriating* form.

"I will make you take something the wrong way," she snapped back in a hiss.

Killian only blinked once. He was facing her completely now. Then he laughed, the sound was short but deep, curling around the air and vibrating within the rocks of the mine. "Is that right?" he leaned down, bending slightly at his waist to hunch over her frame. "Sounds like another invitation."

Ambrosja scoffed, "There is no invitation. I would rather be mauled by a *snowbear* than entangle myself with a mindless and violent beast like you."

His tongue ran along the inside of his cheek, gliding across his teeth. "Mindless? You wound me." He leaned down just a little closer. "I think what you mean is unconscionable, Empress."

"It matters not!" She sliced her hand through the air. "I would never touch a man like you!" she took a step closer, "Arrogant!" another step, "Violent!" and another step, until she had to crane her neck to look up at him, "Cruel! And remorseless!" she leaned up, getting onto the tips of her toes. "Do not. Flirt. With me. And do not touch me ever again as you did this morning!"

Ambrosja didn't see it coming. How could she? She would have never thought that in this moment, Killian would have done what he did; he raised his hand, and without warning, his long, thick finger came down, gentle, far too gentle for a man like him, and *booped* her right on the nose.

The Empress's lips made the shape of a silent gasp. Her eyes focused on that *stupid finger* inches from her. Then her gaze — blazing gold — snapped to his. She slapped his hand away, not gently, but not hard enough to leave a mark.

"How dare you! I said *do not* touch me!" Ambrosja proclaimed.

Killian smirked, then leaned back, no longer hunching over her. "Are you done, Ambrosja? I have a task to tend to." Then he turned away, already adjusting his grip on the pickaxe.

"You—" her fists clenched tightly.

Ambrosja reached over, grabbing his shoulder to get him to face her. Killian didn't resist because the man was amused. He turned, a smirk already forming, only to drop when her fist flew through the air, slamming into Killian's nose and snapping his head back. He barely staggered, but he still moved. Just a half step back.

He remained silent. Head still tilted back, then slowly rolled his shoulders as he lowered his head to glare down at Ambrosja.

Blood was dripping from his nose, a nose that was now angled slightly to the side. Ambrosja looked surprised for a second. She didn't mean to punch him that hard, or at least that's what she told herself. She definitely did not mean to break his nose. But Killian said nothing. His hands simply rose to his face, his cold gray eyes set on the Empress's as he fixed his nose back

into place with a soft crunch.

Killian stared at her. Silent. Unmoving.

Gunnar was looking at the entrance to the mines. He was squinting at it, as if its very existence was offending his own. Cinder noticed this.

"What are you staring at, Gunnar?" she mumbled as she scooped up the last bit of her stew.

"Once more," Gunnar waved his hand in the direction of the mine, "I let a girl go off and do something and it's making me twitchy. She's been in there for a bit."

"Maybe she accepted the quest of seducing him," Cinder grinned.

"Please," Johann was already looking at the sky, "do not say that."

Cinder was definitely going to make another remark — then they all heard the sounds of a rambling, angry woman and fists pounding against flesh. Everyone turned their heads toward the mines, and there Ambrosja was: her body slung over Killian's shoulder while her fists pounded into his back, demanding he put her down.

Killian didn't flinch or seem bothered by every fist that met his spine. He stopped directly by the side of Gunnar's table, and without ceremony, he dropped Ambrosja, letting her fall back onto her rear. The Empress released an oof sound as she felt her body meet the dirt. Her chest was heaving, eyes boring into Killian's. No one dared comment on Killian's bloody nose.

"Are you done?" Killian asked, no smirk, no jest. "Because if you're going to act like a brat, you are free to return to the room and pout there for the remainder of the day."

Ambrosja gripped the dirt beneath her sides. And without a word, she tossed a bit at Killian's body. He only stared down at the specks of dirt hitting his pants and torso. Then his gaze met hers once more as she sat up.

"I will go back!" she said, "And when I am there, I shall keep the door locked so you cannot enter!" Ambrosja turned sharply, moving back to the Command Hall.

Miners and Black Hand guards parted for Ambrosja. But one guard looked at Killian, as if waiting for instructions. Killian gave a shake of his head, a silent sign to leave her alone. Cinder saw this. She squinted at Ambrosja's form that just disappeared, then at Killian. Killian didn't notice, or he pretended not to. He simply turned, heading back into the mines.

When Killian was out of sight, Cinder leaned into the group.

"...Huh, did she break his nose?" Then Cinder shrugged, giving a half smile. "Yep. They're obsessed with each other," she muttered, which caused Gunnar and Johann to both groan, but Donathan nodded, immediately agreeing.

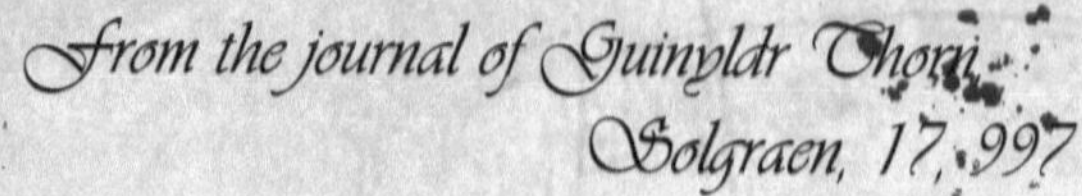

VORTHUNAL,
THE SPINE OF STONE

Vorthunal, the Spine of Stone, is revered across Stonehaven as the enduring guardian of the realm. His hide, harder than any metal, bears a ridge of jagged spines that gleam like carved granite — said to be unbreakable even by the breath of other dragons.

In ages past, Vorthunal is said to have shed his scales willingly, gifting them to the Vaestorian legions to forge armor and strengthen the walls of Stonehaven itself. Thus, the city's indestructible ramparts are not merely stone, but legacy.

Among the dragons, Vorthunal embodies endurance, resilience, and justice. He is a creature of immense patience and wisdom — one who listens before he speaks, yet whose words carry the weight of mountains. To the people of Stonehaven, he is both protector and paragon: the silent heart of the realm.

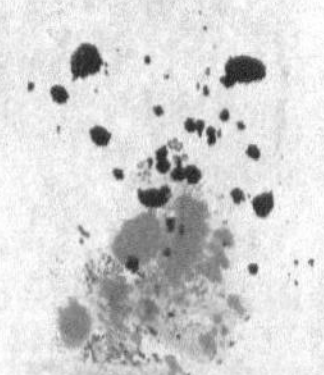

CHAPTER TWELVE
THROUGH VEILED EYES

Ambrosja was seated at the table within Killian's chambers, a parchment crumpled in one hand. She had one window open to let the calm summer breeze drift through. The red curtains swayed faintly with every push of the wind. The Empress could hear the miners outside, barking with laughter over dinner. She stood up and approached the window, looking out over the entire camp. She noticed everything in the camping grounds had been shifted slightly, seemingly to create more space; tables were pushed to the side, tents shifted to the very edge of the tall wooden wall.

The Empress's attention was caught by Cinder's laughter. She had started some sort of game. That's when Ambrosja could take in the shapes of everything she was looking at: the tables were pushed to the side to create a long, narrow yet spacious… *court?* And in the center, there were three piles of rocks, each at different heights — resembling what she could only understand to be some sort of posts with what seemed like twigs that were tied together to imitate circles at the very top of each.

Ambrosja crossed her arms, watching intently as she saw how Cinder was speeding ahead, kicking… *a ball?* Ambrosja laughed at the scene. Miners — younger ones — were trying to steal it from her. Cinder managed to kick the ball between one's legs, passing it to Donathan on the other side. Then Donathan kicked it into the air, launching it through the poorly made twig circle that stood on the highest post. Cinder cheered, running into Donathan and launching onto his back like he was some sort of pony.

The Empress tilted her head back, laughing silently at the scene. Then she relaxed... She continued looking. She saw how the Black Hand and the miners were always spaced apart; they never ate or sat together, probably to keep what the Black Hand was truly doing in hushed whispers. Whenever a Black Hand approached, a miner backed away, like an unspoken understanding. The miners didn't want to meddle, and the Black Hand didn't need more trouble than they already had. And the miners took even bigger steps away whenever Killian was around.

And that's when she really looked around... She hadn't seen Killian this entire time.

Knock. Knock. Knock.

Ambrosja jumped. Almost forgetting the crumpled parchment in her hand. She shoved into her pocket, her hands coming down to smooth out her dark blouse and fix her hair.

"Ambrosja," Killian's deep voice came from the other side of the door. "Unlock this."

The Empress didn't move. She stared at the door with brows that were knotted into a scowl.

"Ambrosja," Killian spoke again, his voice dropped, more firm, more tired. More annoyed. "You broke my nose. You locked this door. You locked *me* out of *my* room. And right now, you are testing my patience. Open. This. Door."

After another moment, Ambrosja finally moved. She marched to the double doors of his room, unlocking it and swinging it open. Their eyes locked. She and Killian stared at each other for a long, silent moment. Killian's jaw was rolling, his nose had a paste over it, something honey-colored mixed with pieces of healing flora, no doubt. Then his hands moved to press into the doors, pushing them open as he stepped in, forcing Ambrosja to back up.

"You've left these doors locked for—nine—hours, Empress..." Killian closed them shut behind him. His massive hands pushed them, not slamming, but close to it as the *thud* echoed and vibrated against the walls. "...I wanted to clean myself, to tend to my written work, to take care of my nose, and you stopped me from that because you wanted to be a brat."

Ambrosja's lips twisted downwards. "Oh — I apologize, you are just so *clever* and *strong*, I simply thought — surely you'd find a way to open these doors with your intellect — or just smash them open with your strength."

Killian stared at her for a moment longer, then stepped past her, shaking his head as if he decided he would not engage in this battle of tongues. He headed to the screen that separated the bathing area from the bedroom.

"I will not break down my own doors because you've decided to act like a petulant empress." His hands moved, undoing the laces of his pants and letting them fall down his thighs as he kicked his leather boots off. "You've missed dinner," he reminded her calmly. "Are you hungry?"

Ambrosja turned to look at him, then immediately away as she caught a glimpse of him partially nude. She didn't let the heat rise to her cheeks. "No, I am not hungry."

"You should eat."

"I do not want to."

"Why?" Killian looked at her from over his shoulder, his body standing on the threshold of the bathing corner and the room.

She risked looking over her shoulder. Their eyes locked. She couldn't speak for a moment. Then she looked away. "After being manhandled, my appetite has disappeared."

Killian rumbled, then disappeared behind the screen. "Very well, Empress… But if you do get hungry, let me know, and I will bring dinner to you."

Ambrosja didn't reply. She only heard the sloshing of water, a sign that Killian was nude and bathing. Another sharp inhale as she cleared her mind. Her hand drifted down to the pocket of her pants, grabbing the parchment to bring it out — looking over the simple greeting once more.

Ambrosja,

Never *beloved,* never *dear,* never something that should have spoken of a bond. She shook her head, shoving the parchment back into her pocket again, and she moved to the bed, pulling the red blanket open and dropping herself onto the soft mattress and plush pillows.

Her eyes fluttered open as she felt a shift beside her. It was still dark out. She turned over and saw Killian's broad back from what she could see over the little barrier. He was still shirtless; she could see every scar, presumably from his time in the Vaestorian military. His war-carved physique was impossible not to stare at, even if she hated it.

Ambrosja glared at—or—ogled his back for a few, long, *long* moments. Her eyes tracked the muscles, the scars, the sheer width of it. The heat his body was providing, even in the distance that they had, separated by

barriers, reached her skin like a summer caress. It was a welcoming and new sensation for her after spending years living in a cold mountain. Now that she thought on it, the feeling of Greenfield's summer was odd compared to Wintersong's summer. The two places were just days apart, but their weather was nothing alike; *possibly the cold winds of Nordorn influenced Wintersong's temperature*, she thought.

The Empress risked getting just a bit closer. *Just for the warmth*, is what she told herself. But at this distance, with this closeness, Cinder's words echoed in her mind… *If it isn't romantically… then it's with hunger.* The idea thrilled Ambrosja, the idea that someone could be hungry for her. But she squeezed her eyes shut as tight as she could.

Do not think of such things, she thought to herself. *You are betrothed… And this… man beside you is a monster. Do not feel flattered by the idea. He is just another creature with primal urges.*

But even as she thought this, even as she reminded herself — her eyes opened again, slowly, drifting back towards Killian's back, now up to his shoulders. That's when she remembered Cinder's idea, to seduce him, to grab whatever information she could. She immediately shoved that thought back down. Her hand gripped the pocket that held the parchment.

Ambrosja took a steady breath, her hand drifted into the small space, pulling out that letter again. She looked at it once more.

Ambrosja,

That's all *he* had ever called her. That or *woman*, never anything kind or sweet. She crumpled the paper again. Her hand found the edge of the blanket, pulling it off of her gently, careful not to rouse Killian, and she stood up. Her bare feet met the wooden floors as she made her way to the hearth. It hadn't been lit in over a day, but she was sure it would be soon.

She pulled out the letter again. This time, reading beyond the greeting.

Ambrosja,

Woman, you said you were only going to Wintersong. Now it has perished, and you seek to venture further into that pit to chase after so-called 'justice' for a hamlet that wasn't even part of our people? You were not built for this. You are delicate. You are exactly as the people call you: an amber. Now, come back.

Hådvard

She tore the letter up, nails digging into the parchment with a quiet hurt.

Killian shifted then. "Ambrosja?"

Ambrosja paused. She looked at Killian. "I thought you were sleep-

ing."

"I was not." He fixed himself, still lying on his side but angled slightly differently to look at her better. "I was reading. I heard you awake, I figured you were going to get your dinner." He gestured with his elbow toward the table.

The Empress looked at the table behind her. And sure enough, there was dinner. A plate with a cloche over it. He had brought it to her regardless of her statements of not being hungry. He must have done it in the short time she slept.

Ambrosja looked longer at it. Then at Killian. Then back at the letter, continuing to tear it up. "While the gesture is thoughtful — I meant it when I said that I am *not* hungry, Commander."

"Very well," he returned to his previous position, "when you are — it will be there." His eyes glanced at her again from his book. He noted the parchment she was ripping. But he didn't ask. His eyes moved back down to read the words on the pages before him.

When Ambrosja was done, she moved back to the bed, sliding back beneath the blankets and inching slightly closer. Then Cinder's *damned* words reached her again. *Seduce him.* She thought of that letter, the damned greeting. She scowled at nothing.

Why should I feel bad about flirting? Why should I care? It is for information, for survival. Nothing more…

She bit her bottom lip. Her heart pounded. Then she thought about Wintersong. And her eyes closed even harder, the hardest it ever had. But she took a deep breath. *This is for them.* Her thoughts were a mess. Constant reassurances. Reminding herself that it doesn't have to go far, just far enough for there to be some sort of trust.

Finally, she moved, just slightly. Just a bit closer.

"Killian?" Her voice was a gentle whisper.

Killian's back was still to her, his eyes still downcast on a thick book that was nearly dwarfed by the size of his hand. Dragons were engraved into the borders of the cover. "Hm?" His eyes didn't peel away from the words before him. "Yes, Empress?"

"What are you reading?" She propped herself up to peek over his shoulder.

Killian took a deep breath and released a slow exhale. "I am reading one of many stories about the dragons of my homeland."

Ambrosja perked up at that. "Dragons?" She leaned closer now, climbing over the barrier that was there to separate them. A line she had drawn, and she was now crossing. Ambrosja hovered over him. "Do you know much about dragons? Is that why you said *Dragon's Breath* this morning?"

Killian's body went still when he felt her chest pressing into his shoulder. His book was forgotten when he felt her hands clamp onto the thick muscle of his bicep. He could feel her trying to peek and read. Killian turned, forcing her to retreat behind her barrier as his gaze was now on hers.

"Is there something you need, Empress?" His voice wasn't cold, but it was cautious.

Her cheeks had bloomed to a gentle pink, though she wasn't quite sure why. "I do not often get to read about dragons, I suppose I am curious. Gunnar and Johann spoke a bit about it during lunch but—I was distracted," Ambrosja shyly admitted as she pressed herself impossibly close to the barrier, "Dragons—they are the big, flying, horny creatures, yes?"

Killian's eyes almost betrayed him by widening. His throat worked. There was a moment of silence. Killian stared ahead, not turning to look at her yet. His brows were furrowed, eyes narrowed. He exhaled sharply—then turned at last, closing his book and setting it onto the bedside table. And he saw her. Close. Hugging the barrier. His breath caught in his throat. He had to lean away, just a bit.

"Horned…" He corrected her. "You mean horned. Not horny."

Ambrosja shook her head, echoing his words with the faintest bit of confusion, "Horned? Not horny?"

"No, Ambrosja… Horned. Horned is the right way to describe them… Horny is — arousal."

"Oh…"

Killian cleared his throat then. "You want to know about the dragons?" He cocked a single brow, "You do realize the hour, yes?" Ambrosja nodded. Killian sighed, "Very well." He sat upwards and dragged himself so his back would lean into the headboard of the bed. He looked down at Ambrosja, "Do you have any knowledge about the dragons at all?"

"Only that they disappeared shortly before the Fracture."

"I suppose I could give you a summary," Killian muttered, his hand moving to rub the side of his neck as he thought. "Dragons were the noble beasts of Vaestoria. Not many of them, but not few either. Those chosen by the dragons were said to have the heart of a king or queen, to be as noble as the dragon itself."

He looked at Ambrosja. "Some legends, those written by those who are not Vaestorian, claim that our dragons had immense strength and power. And while some did, it wasn't as nearly as described. What our dragons had

was knowledge and wisdom. Inner strength."

Killian leaned down again, supporting himself on one elbow, his body angled towards Ambrosja. "Those chosen by the dragons could ride them. They were our companions in battle and law, often helping us shape the world around us. Vaestoria was once ruled by a King and Queen, this started when everyone said that only a dragonrider should be able to take up the crown due to its *character* and so began the reign of King Pierce Lockhart and Queen Sybilla Lockhart. They rode the dragons named Olyr and Marezora."

Killian looked down, noticing that Ambrosja was still listening, staring straight at him. He cleared his throat, he could feel heat creeping across his neck, he tried to shake it off by rolling his shoulders. "Vaestoria was ruled by a King and Queen for quite some time. When King Pierce and Queen Sybilla passed away, their dragons chose new riders. None of which were the children of the Lockhart line, which put *quite* the strain on the country, as the people believed only dragonriders should be crowned. To ease the people, the kin of King Pierce and Queen Sybilla took up council from dragonriders." Killian smirked, leaning in slightly. "Which, believe it or not, are actually still present throughout Vaestoria to this day."

Ambrosja's golden eyes widened. She propped herself up onto her elbow. "Truly? The descendants of dragonriders still rule the rooms of politics today?"

"They do," Killian nodded, "although not every single person on a seat of power is a descendant of a dragonrider, every descendant of a dragonrider has taken a seat somewhere along the lines of power and politics. Such as in Stonehaven, the Thorn family has a seat of power, and their ancestor was once a dragonrider of the dragon named Vorthunal, *the Spine of Stone*."

Ambrosja tilted her head, "Thorn?" Her eyes raked over his face, "Your last name is Thorn..."

"It is." His voice filled with pride, his lips curving at the corner into a genuine smile.

Ambrosja let out the smallest gasp. She leaned forward, almost leaning over the barrier of pillows. "You're a descendant of a dragonrider?" She sounded excited, in awe. Whatever plan of seduction she was forming had clearly slipped from her mind.

Killian's cheeks may have dusted with pink from her reaction. But he would never admit it. "Yes—" he cleared his throat, "—supposedly I am. Though... It is a name I'm not sure I've lived up to." He found himself rubbing the side of his neck again and he stopped. His eyes had to look away from Ambrosja. "As I was saying... Dragons... Each dragon had its own unique abilities, areas of resolve. So, after they had gone missing, to honor them, the Vaestorian people made them into gods. And each day of the week, we worship a different dragon."

Ambrosja bit her bottom lip, listening intently. "And what day of the week is your dragon associated with?"

"The first day of the week, what you know as Kaldheimar—" Killian spoke, his voice dropping to something of warmth and calm, "—I know as Vorthenday."

She shifted forward, laying gently atop the pillow-barrier, eyes lifted to him as though lured by a storybook voice. "Oh—I remember something about this, Johann said how you are a worshipper of Vorthunal, so on Vorthenday you push your body."

"That is true." Killian nodded. "On Vorthenday, early in the morning I pray, and I swear to the dragon Vorthunal that I will endure all that comes my way, I wear a stone pendant that resembles the face of Vorthunal." He added, "I also tend to push myself to work harder on both my body and mind."

"What does Vorthunal represent?"

"Resilience," Killian hummed. "Endurance... Justice."

Ambrosja tilted her head, getting more comfortable on the pillows, "And do you feel like you represent justice on Vorthenday?"

Killian let out a chuckle, "Do you ask this because you think I am not just?" Killian lowered himself closer to Ambrosja, his voice dropping to something of a teasing rumble, "I suppose I have not given the best impression of myself. But I assure you, Empress, justice is not always pretty. And I've never been known to deliver pretty things."

Ambrosja's breath hitched from the proximity, the plan that she had forgotten was back. *Damn it. He's so close...* But she couldn't pull herself away. Her eyes nearly dropped to his lips, but she caught herself. She shifted—closer—just slightly. *Why am I moving closer? Why am I entertaining this plan?* Her mind was a storm. *This is Cinder's fault, she has gotten into my head. Think of Wintersong. This is for them.*

"What are your other dragons?" She finally asked, her eyes fighting to stay locked onto his.

"Well," Killian rubbed his chin, "There is Vorthunal the Spine of Stone," He began to count them on his fingers, voice low and rhythmic—as though reciting old scripture. "There is Sylaera the Blooming Ash, Caeldryss the Goldtongue, Nymera the Emberforged, Olyr the Hollow-Eyed, Tharnyx of the Falling Star, and Marezora the Wind-Mother." Killian added, "At least those are the dragons written as being the changing and aiding force of Vaestoria. But we have had others."

Ambrosja smiled, "I was going to say, strange that your history only has seven dragons when it sounded like Vaestoria had far more."

Killian chuckled, "As far as my studies have shown me, Vaestoria had around fifty dragons. Possibly less. It is truly uncertain."

Ambrosja beamed a serene smile, her face resting half into her hands and half into the pillows. "Could you tell me more?"

"Hmm... No." Killian then turned, laying on his side, facing away. "Go to bed, Empress."

Ambrosja's lips were parted. Her brows furrowed in the absolute audacity of this man. She leaned over the barrier, her hand found his bicep, "You cannot expect me to sleep now! You've teased me with a half-tale and locked the rest within your mind."

Killian grunted, "Well, you could always turn over, count the stars and try to bore yourself to sleep."

"You would really do this to me?"

"Do *this* to you?" Killian echoed, chuckling, "You mean try to make sure you get decent sleep? I suppose I would. I'd do worse to protect those I'm responsible for. Sleep, Empress."

Ambrosja stared at the back of Killian's skull, burning holes into it with her golden eyes that were currently ablaze with petty fury. "Fine," she grumbled, turning away, staring out at the window. Then she purposely tugged on the blanket, bringing more of it to her side. "Goodnight, Killian. I hope your nose does not mysteriously break again throughout the night."

The Empress's breath misted in cold air. Sweat dripped down her forehead, mingling with the dark kohl that lined her eyes. She looked all around her as flames ate away at homes. She felt as if her body was dragged from one spot to another. Placing Mora behind a tree. Pulling a boy out of the way. Her sword clashing with another. Her pommel hit a man's temple. Then — the air left her lungs as a kick to her chest knocked the wind out of her. Then darkness.

Footsteps creaked across the wooden floorboards. The mattress dipped beside Ambrosja. The warmth of movement drew her from sleep. Her hand moved to gently rub her face as she turned. She sat upright, her ash-blonde locks fell over her face and shoulders. Her mind was pounding for a few moments, her fingers rubbed her temples.

The Empress saw Killian at an angle, just enough to see his nose. "Your nose looks far better."

Killian was lacing up his black boots, he glanced at Ambrosja from over his shoulder. A grin curved across his lips, "Nothing a little healing magic can't do." He turned away again, lacing his other boot up. "Would you like to work in the mines again? Remain close to your friends?" He stood up, adjusting his belt, pulling bits of his black tunic over it. "Don't worry, I won't be in there today, so there will be no need for you to march in there and confront me."

"Is this a rare moment of free will?" Ambrosja rested her chin into her palm, her eyes not quite open yet, her form moving to and fro with sleep.

"Yes." He rolled up his sleeves, exposing his thick, veined forearms. He moved to grab something from the other side of his folding screen, then came around, tossing it onto the bed. "Put that on. The sun is beating down today. Even some of my guards have removed bits of their armor for relief."

Ambrosja blinked a few times to adjust her vision. She reached for it. Her hand held a decagonal glass jar, its contents were a creamy, pearlescent color. The label around the bottle said *Sunshade Salve*.

"You fear I will get burned?" She looked up at Killian.

"You're so pale I'm surprised you don't glow in the dark." He had just finished unbuttoning his tunic down past his tanned chest. Killian turned to face her. "You will apply that to your skin. Or else you will remain inside."

Ambrosja narrowed her eyes. "Are you actually restricting me?" She sat up straighter. "Am I a child now? If I do not put this on, I cannot go outside and play with my friends? So much for free will."

Killian chuckled, the sound was short. He looked at her, his brows lowered, "I am not letting you burn yourself. Put that on."

Ambrosja dragged herself to the edge of the bed, glass jar in hand as she swung her legs over the mattress and stood up. She momentarily dropped the jar onto the blankets as her hands moved. She pulled off her blouse, baring her shoulders. Beneath it, a fitted leather bustier hugged her torso— strapless and tight. Killian looked. Briefly admired. But his gaze didn't linger on her form or shape, no. They lingered on those dark root-like scars that he had seen yesterday in the morning. He watched her as her hands reached for

the jar again, opened it, and scooped out a handful, spreading it over her arms and shoulders in slow, rhythmic movements that might have tempted weaker men. But Killian wasn't thinking about temptation.

Her scars... He thought to himself, *A gorgeous consequence of power.*

Ambrosja looked over her shoulder. She caught Killian staring. Her cheeks became a reddened shade, whether it was from embarrassment or shame, it was uncertain. Her hands moved to grab her sleeves, tugging it back up.

"You're staring," she muttered, grabbing her ashen locks to lay over her scarred skin, despite the black top already covering it.

"I know, I'm sorry." He dipped his chin once, stepping forward. "You never did answer me about your scars. They are the consequence of uncontrolled chaos magic, aren't they?"

Ambrosja swallowed. Her eyes cast down once, then met him again. "What *do* you know of chaos magic?"

"Only that it runs through the Nordravn bloodline, the royal bloodline of Nordorn." He continued, "Forcefully passed down from Brynhjora, the Raven of the North, the woman who caused the Fracture." He leaned in, just a little closer. "And it is so strong that if used without control, it will scar you." He gestured to her scarred side, "Is that what happened? Did you lose control?"

Ambrosja looked away, "...I had no intention of using it. It was an accident. And I swore never again."

"That's not wise, Empress." Killian studied her expression. "You have a gift, a gift that is a curse, but it is yours. And you should learn to embrace it. Not fear it. Sometimes fear is what makes us lose control."

Ambrosja tilted her head to the side, her eyes still locked on his, the gentlest shake in her head. "Of course, the man who thrives on power would suggest I wield mine as well."

Killian smirked, only slightly. His broad frame leaned against the wall beside the window; his arms crossed over his chest. "There is nothing wrong with power, Empress, as long as you know how to wield it."

Ambrosja's eyes raked over Killian's form. They were close, but not too close. The proximity caused Cinder's voice to echo through Ambrosja's mind once more. *Seduce him,* those words repeated back. Ambrosja abandoned the vial onto the bed; her hands laced behind her back. *I can do this,* Ambrosja thought to herself. *Just something to entice him, nothing too strong.* She approached, hips slowly swaying with every step.

"Do you love power, Killian?" Her voice dropped, turning into a tone more velvet.

He noticed it all. Her hands behind her back, the sway of her hips, and the dip in her voice. He chuckled. Then laughed. Not cruelly. But genuinely amused.

"You're trying to seduce me," he spoke through his chuckles, a broad smile crossing his lips. "Oh, that's new. Can't say I'm used to it."

Ambrosja froze. Her cheeks were red again. But now with fury *and* embarrassment. She turned sharply, her hair snapping behind her like silk in a breeze

Killian was still amused, "What? Did I say something wrong?"

"You could have just turned me down instead of laughing in my face!" She grabbed at the vial again, opening it once more with more force than necessary and scooping in again, dragging it across her skin with a grumbled roughness.

Killian tilted his head, the smirk still pulling at the corner of his lips. "I'm not laughing at you, not really." He leaned further into the wall, watching her. "Look at me, Ambrosja." Ambrosja turned around, staring at him with an expression that bore no emotion besides annoyance.

He lifted his hand, gesturing for her to come to him. "Don't stop now, Empress. I'm curious to see how far you're willing to go." Ambrosja scoffed, she began to turn away again—until Killian's strong hand found her arm. Dragging her back towards him. His other hand moved to her lower back; he pressed her close to him. Her breasts flush against his ribcage, her hands pressing against his chest, the jar had been forgotten and slipped from her grasp. Her eyes were wide, looking up at him.

He dipped his head, inching close to her, his lips near her temple, but not touching. "Careful, Empress..." He murmured. "You look at me like that—and I'll forget about the barrier in the bed." Ambrosja's breath hitched, her lips were parted, her cheeks a vibrant pink. "That's how you seduce," Killian whispered against her hair. Then he leaned back, his hands still on her, but his lips nowhere near her. Bearing the most smug expression on his face.

Ambrosja pulled away. "If this is what you find amusing then go poke fun at someone else!"

Killian didn't let go. In fact, his hands now found her waist, dragging her back to him. "Wait," he murmured, turning her to face him, "You're doing this on purpose." His cold gaze studied her, "You're not freely flirting. You wouldn't. Not the woman who demanded a barrier of pillows to protect her tradition, her purity. Not the woman who is promised to someone else."

Ambrosja groaned at that, a quick roll of her eyes. Her hands pushed

against his chest. "Oh! What does that bastard care about this union any-way?!" She growled those words, fingers clenching into the fabric of Killian's shirt.

Killian was still, just for a moment, breathing low, eyes reading the Empress's face. "So, what is it you are up to then? Betrothal aside, Ambrosja, you wouldn't do this, not you, and definitely not with the man where you only see Wintersong's death."

She didn't say anything. She didn't want to. Her eyes looked away from his, brows only furrowed more.

"Ah," the Commander nodded, as if realization had dawned on him. "You want information. Fine. What do you want to know, Ambrosja?" He kept her near him; he didn't ease his grip once. "Do you want to know about the attacks? Who does it? Who leads the charges?" Killian continued, "I've already told you why I do what I do; I must place myself into a role that everyone detests, and the answer is that no one can do what I do. What I must do. Because no one else will."

He let the silence stretch between them. As if their eyes were saying things their lips couldn't. He caught the shake of her irises, the nervous stare, the flushed cheeks. *Damn it,* he thought to himself. *Damn woman… I'm letting her get under my skin… And—I like it.*

When he spoke, his voice was still cool, never a hint of heat within his words. "Would it put you at ease to know I'm not the one who ordered the attack on Wintersong? That I'm merely the one assembling the Hands — the one constructing the plans for battle — but not the one who decides what burns… I just — help with strategy. When it comes to who burns… my hands are tied."

Ambrosja hesitated to speak at first. *So, he has no say in this war?* Her brows lowered, eyes fixed on his face as if she were studying every line, searching for any hint of intent he might be hiding. "Why are you telling me this? You've made it very clear you were *purging a plague.*"

"I did say that," Killian agreed, his voice had dropped lower, turning into a calming rumble. "Because there is truth in it, but not one you are ready to hear just yet." Killian still didn't let go of her. "Maybe one day—and when that day comes—maybe you'll be able to look at me without seeing the death of Wintersong."

"…You're spilling an awful lot to me, Killian," Ambrosja murmured.

"Perhaps, I hope that one day you will trust me enough not to hide a butter knife beneath your pillows. Or between the mattress and the frame like I had found *this* morning," Killian teased, but Ambrosja blushed at that.

"Trust me, Empress, even if you cannot trust me with anything else, trust that I keep you near because it is safer, and I need to protect you."

Ambrosja parted her lips; nothing came out at first. Her eyes simply stared into his. Her fingers curled softly, as if she was trying to find some sort of inner strength. When her voice came, it was soft, tentative, "...Are you sure it is because you need to? And not that you want to?"

Killian stilled. His breathing had paused for a second—two seconds—before he inhaled deeply and exhaled just as sharply. Then at last he spoke, "Trust me, I am a man — there is want. But I am not the mindless creature you think I am. And I will not act on my desires." He forced himself to let go of Ambrosja. He bent at his hips and picked up the dropped jar, gently handing it back to her. "I will see you downstairs for breakfast, if you so choose to eat with me."

Then Killian walked away, heading towards the broad door, gripping the golden handle to twist it open and walk into the day.

The Crown of
Marezora

The Crown
of Olyr

King
Pierce Lockhar

Queen
Sybilla Lockhart

From the journal of Guinyldr Thorn,
Solgraen, 19, 997

THE REIGN OF LOCKHART

King Pierce and Queen Sybilla Lockhart stand as the first crowned rulers of Vaestoria — the mortal hands that steadied a realm once guided only by dragons. In the elder days, the people of Vaestoria looked to the dragons for wisdom and command, until the great beasts themselves confessed: they do not lead, they only follow. From that revelation rose the need for sovereigns of flesh and blood.

Pierce and Sybilla were the fiercest of Dragon Riders — he, bonded to Olyr, the wisest of dragons; she, to Marezora, whose gentleness could turn to ruin when roused. When the people sought rulers, none questioned their worth, for dragons choose their riders by virtue of heart — nobility, honesty, wisdom, and bravery.

Thus began the Lockhart Dynasty, crowned not by divine right, but by the will of dragon and man alike. Their reign ushered an age of order and unity — though, in quiet sorrow, none of their children ever bore a dragon's bond again

CHAPTER THIRTEEN

A Court Buried in Ash

Faded and torn curtains swayed from the cold air that swept into the dark, stone chamber. Snowflakes drifted in, falling onto the long, cracked table and onto the black cloaks of the men and women surrounding it. None sitting. All standing. All waiting. All adorned dark-steel armor atop even darker leather. The shoulder plates were broad, making their figures appear even more imposing as their capes draped over their forms. One woman, looking out a broken window, called out, "Evander has arrived!" A man shifted, muttering, "Finally, I was growing impatient."

Evander descended from his thrask, the enormous creature shifted, its muscles flexing to shake off the snow building on its scales. Evander adjusted his plated bracers and made his way inside the snow-covered ruined tower. Behind him, men and women remained nearby, their eyes always watching across the snowy lands.

Evander's boots hit the stone steps with thundering force. The man's face was unreadable as he moved upwards. Everyone else in the room had their eyes set upon the archway where the steps lay just past. And soon enough, they all saw him appear. His hands came up, grabbing at his helm and slipping it off with ease to reveal a tousle of brown hair. Cold, brown eyes looked around the room. His skin, although light, was rosy from the cold; the flush on his chin highlighted the scars that decorated his skin.

"Not quite the welcoming party I was hoping for," Evander

smirked, looking over everyone. "I'm glad to know you all took my message very seriously."

"Yes, well..." One woman with tanned skin crossed her arms, "It's not every day we have the honor of discomfort from a sorceress invading our minds, requesting our presence in the most frigid region of this miserable country."

Evander tilted his head. "At least it was just a message that my sorceress, Ziraxia, sent and *not* a scream. That would have been... Far more uncomfortable, I imagine." The woman's lips pursed, but she said nothing.

The man at the head of the table, tanned skin with short hair that had gone white from age, and brown eyes that remained sharp, spoke, "General Evander, *you* summoned us here, requesting our presence as soon as possible."

Evander bowed his head once, "I did," he flexed his gloved fingers, adjusting it as he looked ahead, "And I thank you for coming here, Grand Marshal Gaspard." He examined the room once before speaking. "My last attack was on the hamlet of Wintersong. It was successful, and as far as I could tell, no survivors. All their goods taken. Homes burnt. I left behind a promising young man to ensure the bodies would turn cold." He paused, keeping everyone slightly more rigid. "However, when he hadn't caught up, I sent a rider to go back to Wintersong and investigate the area further."

Evander smirked, a cruel look across his scarred lips. "And guess what I found?" He braced his hands on the stone-cold table. "My rider reported that he didn't find the boy, but something far more interesting, and *far* more dangerous."

Gaspard's eyes narrowed onto Evander; he tilted his chin slightly, caution crossing the lines of his face. "And what was that?"

Evander approached the open windows and gestured outside, "See for yourself." Then he looked outwards and down onto those who had arrived with him. He released a sharp whistle. "Unwrap it!"

The men and women who waited outside looked up once and moved to the back of a wagon, pulling away at a flimsy sheet that revealed a portion of a rowboat.

Gaspard shook his head. "The bow of a rowboat?"

"Not just any bow of any rowboat," Evander said, pointing at it. "Does that carving mean anything to you, Grand Marshal?"

Gaspard squinted in the distance. He traced the design with his eyes, "A raven? A raven with a crown?" Then he froze. "The Nordravn insignia." Everyone else froze in the chamber now. His jaw clenched, his head snapped

towards Evander, taking a step forward. "General Evander..." His voice had turned ice-cold. "Did you end up murdering the Empress of Nordorn in Wintersong?"

Evander shook his head, "If I am to speak plainly... I'm not quite sure." He scratched at his chin. "It was all a blur of blood and fire." He continued, "I didn't think I had to be on the lookout for blonde-haired women of royalty."

Gaspard pinched the bridge of his nose. "Fantastic," he muttered. Then his hand snapped, slapping a goblet off the table, denting it as it hit the wall and fell to the ground. "The last thing we want is Nordorn on our fucking doorstep! We've always attacked from the shore, you didn't think to look for any possible vessels bearing the mark of the Empress of Nordorn?!"

Evander's jaw clenched. "That rowboat wasn't even at the shore. My man found it hidden in the woods nearby. As if someone was intentionally trying to hide it."

Gaspard turned away, running a hand down his face. "I take it that your rider found no evidence of a Nordorner within Wintersong?"

"Correct."

"And did you bother tracking the boy down, yet?"

"No," Evander admitted. "I figured you all wanted to be here for it, see if maybe the Empress tagged along, just in case." Then he smirked wide and knowing, leaning in just slightly, "Or of course to simply witness Ziraxia's power." A few of the Black Hand shuddered at the thought. But not Evander or Gaspard.

The tanned woman from before spoke, "And what makes you think he didn't simply run away? Why would the *Empress* of Nordorn be tagging along with him?"

Evander inhaled deeply, then exhaled slowly, a smirk playing at his lips once more. "Well, Sister-Hand Serana, who knows? Perhaps she charmed him. Perhaps she killed him. Perhaps he felt bad or perhaps—I am simply seeing to seal every breach in the wall."

Gaspard was still looking down and away, trying to calm the raging storm erupting deep within his bones. *"Then get to it."*

Evander nodded. He looked out the window again. His eyes found the figure of a slim woman, skin pale like death, hair as black as the darkest void. "Ziraxia." He gestured with a tilt of his head.

Ziraxia nodded once, turning in her long, dark gown with red embroidery that decorated the hems in the shape of floral patterns. Her long coat trailed behind her, wiping away her prints in the snow. Her walk was a dance between serene and haunting, her body barely shifted as she stepped, as if she was gliding instead of walking. Everyone at the base of the tower parted for her, their movements fast, none of it was about respect—but instead fear.

As everyone in the chamber heard her steps approaching, they tensed, just slightly. Evander smiled cruelly at everyone's reaction.

Ziraxia stepped in, her eyes were just as black as her hair, moving slow as she looked over ever single person within the room before settling onto Evander. "General Evander?" Her voice was breathy, yet haunting. "Would you like me to track Donathan Wren now?"

Evander stepped aside with that smug smirk, giving an encouraging gesture to the table. Ziraxia stepped forward, standing where Evander once stood. She reached into her long, loose sleeve, and pulled out a dark orb. She set it on the table in front of her, and everyone in the room, except Evander and Gaspard, felt uncomfortable. Hands itching to rub at their own Marks beneath their clothes. Ziraxia's hands moved, fingers twitching and bending in a manner that no fingers should. Within the orb, smokes of dark purples swirled, and Ziraxia's palms became dark, as if smeared in blackened ash.

"He is not far... Five, maybe six days away..." Ziraxia whispered. "He is within range of Greenfield." Her hands stopped moving, and the smoke dissipated from the orb.

Serana, the tanned woman, looked at Ziraxia, "You couldn't give us an exact location? See through his eyes? Try to spot if that Nordorn whelp is within his reach?"

"I could, Sister-Hand Serana..." Ziraxia's voice never stopped being unnervingly calm. "But if I pushed it... Saw through his eyes, he would know. And I was informed to not alert the boy."

A man with shoulder-length brown hair that waved at the ends, a face where half had been scarred by blade and fire, with calm viridian eyes, had been watching from the corner of the room, near the chair where Gaspard once sat. He leaned off the wall and took a few steps forward. He looked at the orb—then at Gaspard. "Greenfield... Isn't that where Commander Killian Thorn is overseeing?"

Gaspard grunted, nodding. "Yes, Marcus. Thorn has been recently overseeing the mining operation of Nythralt at our camp in the Bramble."

Evander chuckled darkly. "Is that wise? Having a Thorn within the regency of Stonehaven? A regency where his family has influence?"

Gaspard tilted his head, looking unkindly at Evander. "I think it shows us if Killian Thorn is willing to watch his own people die. Lets us know if his heart is in it." Gaspard exhaled, calm yet laced with impatience. "Now, if we're

done just sitting around... We clearly have other priorities." Gaspard exhaled sharply, he looked at Serana, "I want you to dispatch your riders to Greenfield." He looked at the others, "We will postpone our attack on Greymire's hamlets.

He continued, "If we keep aimlessly killing while the Empress of Nordorn prances through the lands of Vaestoria—she might end up being another body in a grave. And then... Then Nordorn will come. And we do not want to get caught in a war between Vaestoria and Nordorn."

Gaspard looked over his shoulder at everyone, "You are all dismissed. Return to your camps unless I've given you orders that state otherwise."

Various boots of leather and metal descended the ruined spiral staircase. Each Black Hand made their separate ways once leaving the tower. Ziraxia remained close to Evander.

"Never change, Ziraxia," Evander spoke while smugly smiling, fixing his helmet back on once he felt the snow hit his skin again. "You are perhaps the only thing in this world that could make delicate look so unnerving."

"You think I am delicate?"

Evander stopped. He turned around, looked Ziraxia up and down—then barked a laugh. "My dear, you aren't delicate. Oh no." He chuckled. "You *look* delicate. You look like you could be snapped in half by the gentlest hug." He stepped closer and leaned down. "But don't worry. I think your gentle look is what makes you so disarming, because everyone knows that behind that dainty face lies power that is beyond comprehension."

Serana made her way to her horse that stood with a group of others. She saddled up and grabbed the reins. "We're heading towards Greenfield." She looked to the riders that were right beside their horses. "You are all tasked with trying to find a woman, a Nordorner. Pale skin and pale hair." Serana continued, "We will also visit the mining camp that is being seen by Commander Thorn. None of you are to give away the reason for our visit without my say so. Is that understood?"

Serana's riders grunted and nodded in unison, already grabbing the reins of their own steeds and saddling up to prepare for the ride ahead. With a single command she headed southwest, and her riders followed her. Evander stood back and watched for a moment before ascending onto his thrask once more. The giant beast let out a grumbled roar within its throat before shaking off the snow gathering on its skin. Gaspard watched from the window of the ruined tower. His brows lowered, the lines on his face spoke clear of his disdain and the thinning patience.

Marcus still lingered near Gaspard. "And what are you to do if Sister-Hand Serana finds the Empress?"

Gaspard turned. "I have two options, Marcus." He took a step forward. "I can either kindly inform her she should go back to her castle and tend to her own court and politics... Or I can be the most gracious host." He turned away, eyes now looking over the cold mountains in the distance. The mountains that acted as the border between Vaestoria and Nordorn. "Killing her isn't an option...." He turned from the mountains, back into the cold dark. "...Yet." The wind crept through the broken glass like a whisper of war.

From the journal of Guinyldr Thorn,
Solgraen, 21, 997

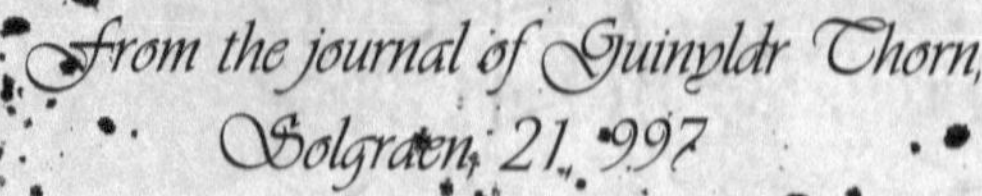

THE THRASK

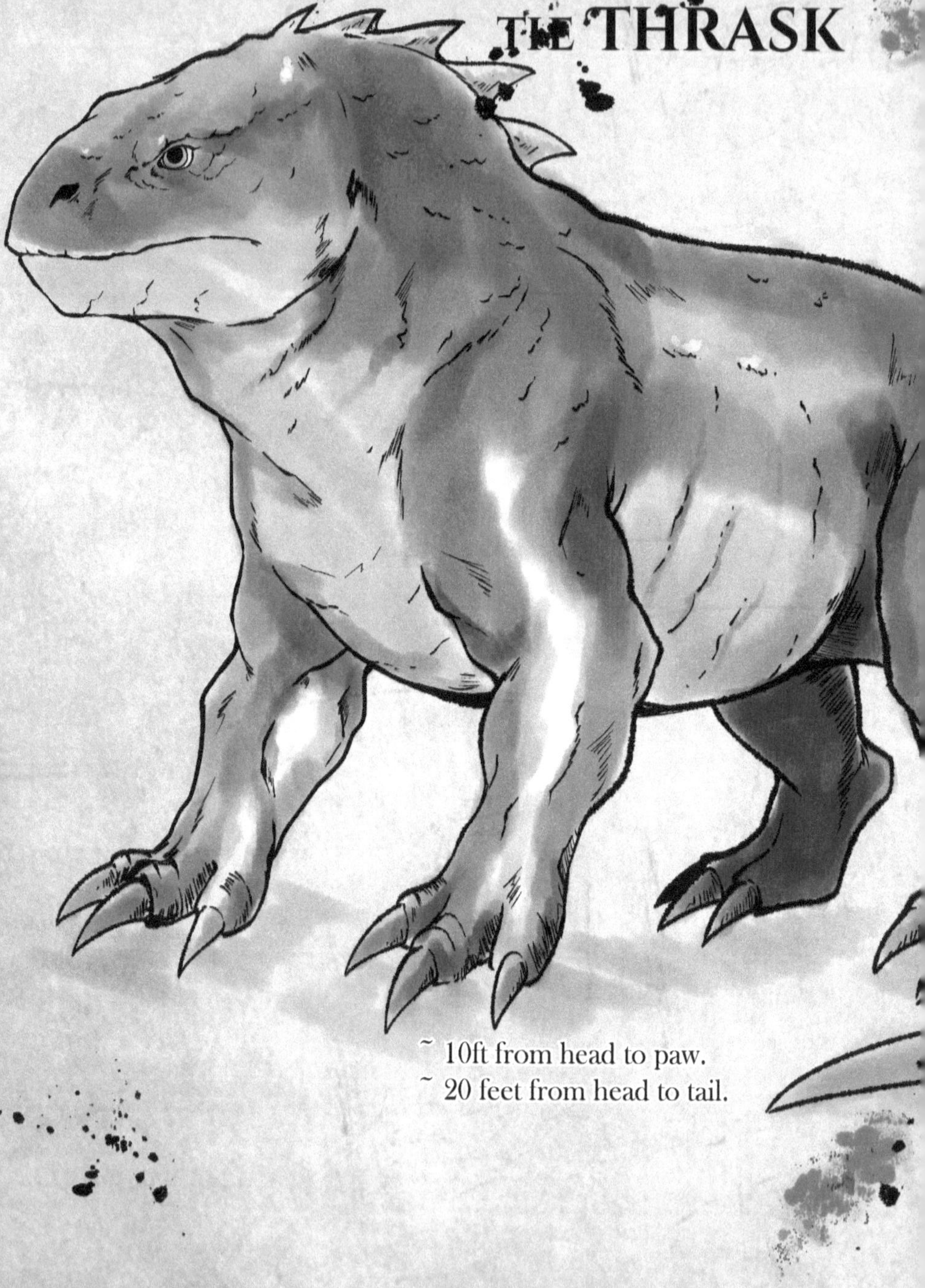

~ 10ft from head to paw.
~ 20 feet from head to tail.

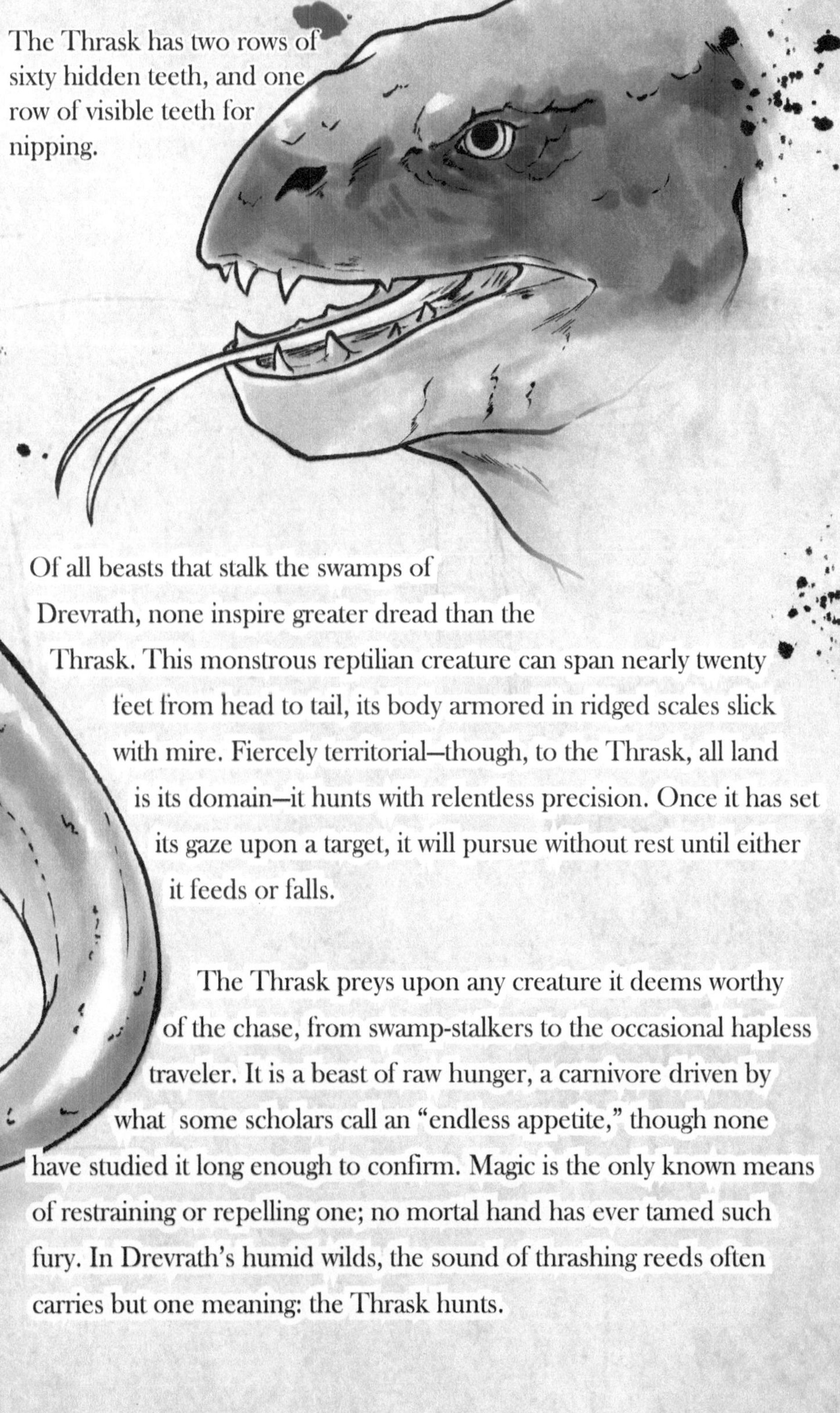

The Thrask has two rows of
sixty hidden teeth, and one
row of visible teeth for
nipping.

Of all beasts that stalk the swamps of
Drevrath, none inspire greater dread than the
Thrask. This monstrous reptilian creature can span nearly twenty
feet from head to tail, its body armored in ridged scales slick
with mire. Fiercely territorial—though, to the Thrask, all land
is its domain—it hunts with relentless precision. Once it has set
its gaze upon a target, it will pursue without rest until either
it feeds or falls.

The Thrask preys upon any creature it deems worthy
of the chase, from swamp-stalkers to the occasional hapless
traveler. It is a beast of raw hunger, a carnivore driven by
what some scholars call an "endless appetite," though none
have studied it long enough to confirm. Magic is the only known means
of restraining or repelling one; no mortal hand has ever tamed such
fury. In Drevrath's humid wilds, the sound of thrashing reeds often
carries but one meaning: the Thrask hunts.

CHAPTER FOURTEEN

BURNING THREADS

It had been a day since Ambrosja had asked Killian about his *want*, and since then, she only found herself *wanting*. But she would do her best to shove those thoughts down. Especially this morning, after waking up from what she assumed would be another nightmare — or just another fragmented memory of Wintersong. She struggled, struggled to remember everything and struggled to accept that she could not see the pieces of her own life clearly; this struggle only made her more frustrated, more impatient. From her time of being in this camp, she had to rein in every violent thought of wanting to slam a Black Hand into the ground.

She reminded herself: *Do not bring attention to yourself. Get answers first. Always look for the threads. That's what Grandmother would say.*

The Empress stabbed at her porridge with a spoon. She was not accustomed to fine meals; it wasn't a luxury for warriors, and although she had only been part of one war, she had grown up preparing for it. Still, she *hated* porridge. Ambrosja took a deep breath, trying to think of Wintersong, reminding herself to stay steady, to think of her grandmother's teachings.

But still… She found herself distracted by the girlishness of things.

She wasn't eating with the Commander this morning. She didn't see him. He had woken up earlier than her, only leaving that Sunshade Salve and a note warning her to put it on. *Or else.* Although her allies were talking, discussing strategy and ideas on what to do while they're here — Ambrosja kept finding herself thinking of him. That was the distraction plaguing her right now. Not a harsh thought like Wintersong, or a comforting thought like her grandmother… This was something silly that made her stomach twist and flutter. She scolded herself any time she realized she was thinking about him. She *had* to force those thoughts down again.

Ambrosja's gaze was locked onto the breakfast before her, doing her best not to look for Killian. *Wintersong*, she reminded herself. *Think of Wintersong. Of… of little Mora.* That hurt. Her eyes fluttered shut, as if she could feel the weight of Mora in her arms once more as she tripped through the snow.

"Alright," Cinder muttered, angling herself to face Ambrosja, "I'll bite. What's up your ass?"

Ambrosja's eyes snapped open, staring at Cinder. "W-what is up my…?" Her brows pinched. "Nothing goes up there!"

Gunnar slammed a fist onto his chest, turning away to cough through a wheezing fit of laughter. Johann buried his face into his hands, not amused but also not not-amused. Donathan's cheeks had gone a soft red; he bit his lip so hard it trembled.

Cinder just stared. "Glad to hear," she deadpanned. "You know that's a figure of speech, right? I am not asking if something literally goes up there or if something is *currently* up there… I am asking you: what's gotten you in a sour mood?"

The Empress looked mortified from the misunderstanding. Her lips moved to speak, yet no sound came out. Her cheeks had turned pink—and for once, Killian Thorn had nothing to do with it. "I…" She looked as if she wanted to throw herself into the mines and never come out. She covered her face, "By the Gods, I am so sorry — please just toss me into the depths of a cold mountain and let a *Frost Troll* smother me and eat my remains…" She dragged her hands down her face, still embarrassed, "…I am not in a sour mood."

Gunnar barked, "Ha! Could have fooled me! You've been so quiet — I thought you might have gotten a cold."

Ambrosja shook her head. "No, I have no cold. I am simply tired."

"Tired? Tired of what?" Cinder looked slightly insulted, though not viciously so, as she leaned into Ambrosja's side. "You're not obligated to work the mines; you get a nice cozy bed, under a proper roof. What are you so tired about?"

Ambrosja angled her head just enough to glare at Cinder. She dropped her voice into a whisper as she pointed aggressively at Cinder. "First off, you

are the one who said I should remain with Killian to snoop around. I did not want to stay in that room, especially in his bed. I would have been more than fine with sleeping on the dirt or on a rock."

Cinder tilted her head. "Hm, speaking of the Commander…" she cocked a brow, "did you… think about the whole —" she shimmied her shoulders, "— seduction thing?" Ambrosja's cheeks went red, and her brows pinched. Cinder noticed. "Oh! You did! Did you do anything?! Did anything happen?!"

"I have no desire to speak on this matter," Ambrosja muttered as she grabbed her mug of water and took a very annoyed sip.

"Oh…" Cinder leaned back slightly.

Gunnar also echoed that *oh,* as he stared at Ambrosja.

Johann *tried* to interject, "Cinder, do not provoke—"

Cinder did indeed provoke. "You did try something, and now you're here pouting." She leaned forward. "Did he reject you?"

Ambrosja flinched. She whipped her head toward Cinder, "You are so rude. Who simply asks that?! I would never ask you if a man rejected you."

"Pft," Cinder shrugged. "I don't care enough about men to get rejected." Then she placed her forearm onto Ambrosja's shoulder, tugging her pale-haired ally closer to her. "Come onnnnnn…. What happened?"

Ambrosja was silent for a bit. Well, for long enough that Cinder began sing-songing *come on* again and again. The Empress's shoulders were hunched and drawn in tight. Then finally, she set her bowl down with far too much force.

"Fine!" Ambrosja finally spoke. "I tried, and he saw through it."

That's when everyone froze.

Donathan was the first to speak, "You tried seducing him… And he saw through it? And you're alive?"

Gunnar's eyes narrowed, then he scoffed. "Of course she's alive, the man wouldn't kill a woman for trying to seduce him. He's violent, sure, but I doubt seduction is on his list of reasons for murder."

Johann shook his head. "So, he saw through it, is that why you two have been at arm's length?" He leaned forward, elbows bracing against the table. "I've noticed the past day you two hardly spoke, not that you spoke much to begin with… But…"

Cinder added in for Johann, "…You two weren't stealing glances as often."

"He embarrassed me." Ambrosja sighed. She took another sip of her water before speaking. "He laughed at my attempt. He thought it was amusing. So, I have kept my distance."

Donathan whispered to Gunnar, "...That sounds far more terrifying than if he were pissed about it."

Cinder's lips curled into a thoughtful frown. "Well, I guess that means the seduction plan is off the table..."

"He did reveal something to me," Ambrosja admitted, and everyone turned their attention to her, "he did not organize the attacks on any of the hamlets, including Wintersong. He simply oversees recruits and apparently helps strategize battle plans."

Cinder whistled low. "Well, damn, Blondie. If he told you that — he is *iiiintooo* you."

Gunnar shook his head. "Possibly, but it doesn't say much; all it does is poorly wash his hands of blood. But he *has* indirectly caused bloodshed to the hamlets." The old warrior rubbed his beard in thought. "You should take this time away from him to look through his things."

"I already tried," Ambrosja leaned forward, defeated. Her chin rested in her hand. "The first night, I tried looking through his things. I found nothing. If he has anything... It might be in his office. And I doubt I could just wander in there."

"The office is...?" Gunnar questioned.

"Second floor," Cinder said as she took a bite of her porridge. "I remember from when we were first trying to spy into this place. An office like that is probably guarded."

Ambrosja nodded. "The only way I could think of getting in is with Killian's permission."

Donathan shrugged then, "So, get his permission."

The Empress groaned lowly. "How? How would I get his permission? By getting close to him? No, I have no desire to. I cannot — I cannot be near him and not think of Wintersong — I already have a hard time walking by these monsters without wishing I could grab my sword and cut them down."

Donathan's brows lowered, his eyes narrowed. "And you think I don't? Why do you think I'm enduring, Ambrosja? Because this hurts. It *hurts*. I see this damn marking on my chest, and I see the death of my family and my cowardice." The young man released a heavy breath and eased back then. "Sorry, I'm not trying to fight... We are putting a lot of pressure on you, and that is... unfair."

Ambrosja looked momentarily taken aback, but also ashamed. It was true, after all, that Donathan had lost his entire family in the attack and was taken into servitude, enduring all that he had just to survive.

"I know," Ambrosja whispered. "I am sorry as well, I just —" her throat worked as she tried to shove the words out, "when I was at Wintersong, I was not there for long, but long enough where... I felt closeness and belonging... Then... Mora..."

"Mora?" Gunnar asked, leaning closer to give Ambrosja his full attention from across the table.

"She was a little girl, she was so sweet, and I tried to hide her, I left her behind a tree — I left her," Ambrosja confessed through shaky breaths. "And still, she died... She wandered back, probably for her grandfather... And I found her body. And I can't stop thinking about her." Ambrosja closed her eyes then. A tear slipped down her cheek, hitting the wooden table.

Gunnar lowered his head. "We're sorry, girl, this isn't fair of us to ask of you. And as Donathan said, we are putting pressure on you, and it's not right."

Johann whispered, "I am sure Mora is chasing dragons beyond the Veil, along with her grandfather." He put a steady hand on Ambrosja's, attempting to comfort her. Then his hand retreated as he looked at Gunnar, "I don't think she should be risking getting close to him. Not in this state. I think we should stick around, try listening to the Black Hand, try to find ties and connections."

"That's not enough," Gunnar reminded his friend, "we'll get rumors, not... evidence. We need something that we can hold as proof before councils. Besides," he waved dismissively towards the miners and the guards in the camp, "the Black Hand stands far from the miners; this is all deliberate. A means to not reveal more than they should. And the miners are too scared to get close enough. They're just here for their coin."

Cinder didn't say anything for a bit. She was simply thinking. Then she leaned closer to Ambrosja. "He spilled something to you once, which means he feels comfortable confiding in you... Or he feels guilty by looking at you." Cinder continued, "And if he feels guilty... It has to mean he likes you, whether that's through attraction or something else... He feels something."

Gunnar scowled at Cinder. "Girl, where are you learning these things?"

"Life," Cinder muttered, scooping up another bit of her porridge. "But—he could just not be as tough as he lets on, which might be why he's so violent." She gave a shrug. "Who knows?"

Donathan looked thoughtful; his eyes roamed over the camp. The long tables were spread out, and miners were deep into their morning routine before work. Some of the Black Hand were guarding the outposts, circling the camp, while others were having their breakfast at their own tables, far from the miners.

"Maybe I can get close to the Black Hand again," Donathan finally said, "it won't be easy after being branded a traitor. But maybe if we're going to stay here… I can try to mingle. Might just mean we can't be as we are anymore. I'll have to distance myself."

Cinder immediately slapped her hand onto Donathan's from across the table. "No," she said with a calm finality. "Too risky, too obvious. You're ours."

Donathan stared at Cinder's hand over his. His cheeks went red. His eyes darted away. Cinder didn't seem to care. Johann wasn't paying attention. But Gunnar was; he scowled ever so slightly at the contact but didn't push.

And after that…

Silence fell over the group. Each of them thought of answers, eager to leave the camp behind. Ambrosja had lost herself inside her mind. She wasn't thinking about Killian; she was thinking about Mora again. About the Elder. The people. The little boy who was crying in the center of the hamlet while a rider approached with a swinging blade. She thought about how she awoke to find herself surrounded by blood and bodies.

Ambrosja's thoughts were soon interrupted by Gunnar.

"So, lass," Gunnar's gaze was settled on Ambrosja, "we barely know anything about you besides that you're a Nordorner, you've been trained for battle by your father, and you are… apparently betrothed." He made sure to keep his voice low as he spoke. "How did you come to be in an arranged marriage? I wasn't aware that was a Nordorn custom."

Ambrosja shifted uncomfortably. Her spoon scraped into the bowl. She chewed on the corner of her bottom lip. "It is a custom to some families," she explained, staring back into her porridge, "sometimes a family might try to form some sort of bond or an agreement with another, typically this is between lands. The best way to form this *agreement* is by… arranging a marriage between two people. And this is normally done when betrothed are young — so they cannot reject the marriage, and by the time they are old enough to do it… they feel the pressure and simply accept what has happened."

Gunnar's arms crossed, forearms bracing on the table as he hunched forward, staring at Ambrosja. "Sounds awful," he said, "is that what happened to you? Set up when you were young? And now that you're grown, you don't want to disappoint the family or something?"

The Empress was quiet. She took a deep breath. She didn't want to

lie, but she couldn't reveal the truth. "Not exactly. Not much of a family left. You all know my parents passed. I have my grandmother now. I am simply upholding my end because it feels like a dishonor if I do not."

Donathan fixed his throat then. "So… I know you said you felt weird about trying to…" his voice dropped to a whisper, "…flirt with Killian while promised to someone else. Does that idea plague you more than just being near Killian because of Wintersong?"

Ambrosja thought for a bit. "No… The thought of trying to get close to him hurts far more because of Wintersong, but — I would be lying if I said I did not feel guilty over it because of my betrothal." She sighed, chin resting in her hand. "Though I have no idea why, maybe I feel an obligation; when my father fell in battle, my betrothed carried him until he found me… So I could say goodbye to my father…"

Gunnar was silent, staring. The old warrior's brows creased as they pinched together in deep thought. Then he softened. "You know, lass, when I was younger, and I mean almost fifty years younger… I knew a gorgeous girl named Penelope."

Johann immediately turned to look at Gunnar at that. "P-Penelope? The name you muttered in your sleep as you tried to hold me against you? That's a real woman?"

Gunnar laughed, clapping a strong hand onto Johann's shoulder. "Sure was! Never spoke of her because it felt like a love long buried. Something I couldn't get back. But that love taught me more than I realized." He looked at Ambrosja again. "Penelope was a sweet soul. We grew up together, but didn't talk much until we hit our adolescence. She was on the thicker side, and some boys mocked her for it. Me? I didn't give a damn about that—or about the fools doing the mocking."

Gunnar scratched his beard, recalling old memories from long ago. "One winter day, some brat lobbed a snowball at her. And lass, I tell you— something in me snapped. I charged like an enraged Vaestorian dray. I was bigger than most boys my age, mind you, so when that snowball hit her, I barreled straight for him. Knocked him into the snow, scooped up armfuls of the stuff, and dumped it on his wriggling backside." He grinned, his beard shifting with the stretch of his lips. "I looked back at her, expecting tears… but she was smiling. Laughing, even. Then she covered her mouth like she knew she shouldn't be enjoying it."

Gunnar's cheeks turned pink, he rubbed the side of his neck. "That laugh made me fall in love. And her little lip-covering, too. So I introduced myself proper, and within two weeks, I was courting her. We stayed together for three years." His smile faded then. "Then one night, she came to me crying. Told me her father disapproved. Said he wouldn't have his daughter marrying a man bound for the Vaestorian military—scraping by on a soldier's wage, raising children alone while I slept in trenches. Or worse, for her to be widowed by twenty-five."

He leaned forward then, angling himself to better reach Ambrosja, "And you know what I did girl?" Ambrosja kept her eyes on Gunnar, so he continued, "I let her go." He closed his eyes, as if the memory still burned. "I let her go, because I didn't want her to feel as if she were disobeying her father, or turning back on her family…" he shook his head, fist rising to press into his chin, clenched with anguish, then—his fist relaxed. "And you know what I learned? Family, friends—none of them are worth your happiness more than *you* are. I should've fought for her. Should've told her it would work out. But I didn't. And now she's gone. Married some noble in Alarion."

Gunnar straightened, rolling the tension from his shoulders. "The point I'm makin', lass… don't stop yourself from wantin' what you want. Don't let duty, tradition, or anyone else's expectations chain you down. If you don't want the man you're betrothed to, then don't stay with him out of obligation — even if he did something good for you once."

He brushed at the front of his tunic, trying to shake off old ghosts. "Now, don't get me wrong. What he did — carryin' your father until he found you? That's honorable. That's grand. But if he's hurting you?" Gunnar's voice dropped, low and steady. "One act of greatness doesn't wash away a lifetime of hurt. Don't cage yourself for his sake."

Ambrosja kept her eyes on Gunnar, then looked away. Her brows lowered, as if his words had struck somewhere deep that she didn't want to admit, because *if only things could be that simple.*

Cinder was staring at Gunnar, not in the playful or sour way she usually stared—but in a manner that showed just how caught off guard she was by the revelation.

"I… I can't believe you never shared that bit of you, Gunnar," Cinder whispered, almost as if she were hurt. "We've spent years traveling side by side, not once did you mention being in love."

"Ah, girl," Gunnar waved his hand, as if dismissing the thought, "what would be the point? To make your eyes wet? To drown the atmosphere in sorrow? Nah," he waved his hand again. "I only share what I feel needs to be shared."

Johann scoffed at that. He turned to look at his old friend. "You only share what you feel needs to be shared?" Johann echoed. "Right, that's why after spending a night with a woman you immediately tell me how she moved and what she bit."

"Ew," Cinder and Donathan said in unison, though Cinder was disgusted and Donathan was amused.

The atmosphere shifted immediately when a manacle of some sort was slapped onto Ambrosja's wrist. Ambrosja's eyes snapped to it, arm recoiling as if preparing to strike, but then she looked up to recognize the threat, and she saw the furrowed brows of the strawberry-blond man, Lieutenant Berric.

"What is the meaning of this?" Ambrosja stood now, arm raised between her and Berric.

Gunnar stood as well, and so did Cinder.

Berric didn't care. He crossed his arms. "You're going out beyond the gate to hunt." He leaned forward, his eyes boring into Ambrosja's. "Go to the armorer and grab a weapon of your choice. And be sure to be back by sundown." Then he straightened, and with a jerk of his chin, he gestured to a tanned blonde woman not too far. "She'll be keeping track of where you go, so don't go thinking of doing anything cute."

Gunnar slammed a hand down on the table. "She's not going out there, she doesn't know the godsdamned Bramble."

Berric's gaze slid to Gunnar's; he looked impatient and bored. An expression that seemed to be marked permanently on him. "I don't care. She's been chosen out of the prisoners, so she's going. We've got archers in the trees. Though… we used to have two more… Funny how two of 'em turned up dead the day you lot arrived." Then he shrugged, unkind and uncaring, "She won't get lost."

Berric began to walk away then. Ambrosja exhaled sharply and moved from the bench. Gunnar reached over and grabbed Ambrosja before she could head away, his hand wrapped around her forearm.

"Lass, what are you doing?"

"It is fine," Ambrosja insisted, giving Gunnar's hand a gentle pat. "I think this will be good, I need to clear my head—just for a bit."

Gunnar snarled, but he let go of Ambrosja. "Fine."

The group watched Ambrosja walk away, heading to the Black Hand that was guarding the weapons rack. Gunnar sighed, annoyed and frustrated with himself.

Cinder slouched over her food. "We have archers in the trees," she mocked Berric. "Then send *them* to go hunting."

The Empress made her way through the gates. Her hand clasped tightly around a sword that she was very much displeased with. She sighed, giving a single glance over her shoulder at the Black Guards watching her leave. Then straight ahead again.

Ambrosja didn't go very far. She kept to the woods closest to the mining camp. She twirled the hilt of her sword in her hand while she walked and kept her eyes on it. Brows pinched close together, a small frown on her lips. She thought about her past, her training, everything that her grandmother and her father had prepared her for as she sat upon the Nordravn throne. But nothing had prepared her for mining… Or espionage. Ambrosja had always been taught to be a force of nature. To keep slamming even when her enemies fell, whether that was by blade or words. But now… she was reduced to *this*: a young woman struggling to keep lines drawn, struggling to keep her mind clear. Ambrosja was nearly ready to pummel Berric's face when he slapped that manacle on her — but the idea that she could leave the camp freely—even if for only a few hours—was a refreshing change, and the only thought that kept her steady while her mind wasn't.

What am I even to bring? She thought to herself as she made her way further into the forest.

Despite her eyes glancing around for anything that would be suitable for a camp mostly filled by grown and tired men, the Empress found herself breathing far more easily than before. As if the heavy air that had filled her lungs wasn't just from the mines, but from being caged by the very people who helped to take Wintersong from this realm. Finally, now out in the open, the weight that was buried beneath her ribs had lifted just slightly.

Mora, Ambrosja remembered the little girl again. Her mind bounced in different directions. She was questioning herself now. *What am I even doing anymore? What is the goal here? If the Commander has nothing to share… Why am I even bothering to remain?* She glanced back in the direction of the camp. *Could we really not overcome the Black Hand of that camp?*

She stopped paying attention to where she was walking. At this point, she wandered aimlessly. Until she heard the slightest scrape of something against wood that pulled her from her thoughts. And that's when she noticed the forest had been quiet. Not that silence had surrounded her, but as if the forest shifted because a predator was within. But despite that feeling of danger lurking around… it also felt serene.

Ambrosja walked softly until she reached a tree, following the sound of scraping. She looked around the trunk, pressing some of the brush of bushes down so she could see clearly. She had expected maybe a buck, or something with tusks to create the scraping sound of wood. But instead... she saw the hunched form of Killian sitting on a log. His shoulders were shifting, and with every shift she noticed that same scraping sound again.

She hesitated before moving closer. She wanted to see what he was doing. What had Killian so unguarded within the forest. Or so relaxed where it no longer seemed as if his body was coiled tight like it normally was within the Black Hand camp.

The Empress stepped around. Following a curve around the trees until she angled herself enough where she could see exactly what Killian was doing; she wasn't too close, but she wasn't so far that she had to squint to see.

She saw it clearly now: the small blade in his hand, carving away at a crudely round piece of wood in his grip. His gray eyes, normally cold and sharp, seemed less cold and more focused. Ambrosja looked over the Commander; she noticed his armor had been undone and set aside on the empty spot of the log for the moment. His sleeves were rolled up, resting just beneath his elbows. Along the ground there was an uneven line of these rounded, carved figures.

Dragons? Ambrosja asked herself as she stared at the small figures. *Are these pieces to a stonegame?*

Her eyes drifted back up to Killian. It was odd. She had grown accustomed to the image of a man with cold eyes and hands that were drifting across parchments with quill and ink that might be signing the deaths of soldiers and civillians... But now... his hands moved with care as he carved life into something. He looked... human, and not the monster she was trying to build in her head.

"Killian?" Ambrosja found herself calling for him without thinking about it. She was already halfway through the brush. At some point she had moved on her own.

The Commander's gaze lifted up immediately upon hearing her voice. His movements had halted. He became still. Not still in a manner that made him seem as if he had been threatened, but still in surprise as he met Ambrosja's gaze.

"Ambrosja," he called back, his tone softer than usual, but still unmistakably deep. "Why are you outside of the camp?"

The Empress took another step forward, this time lifting the hand that held the sword. "Hunting, that is what your Lieutenant told me to do."

Killian's brows lowered at that. He sighed heavily, then moved back down to the wooden piece he was carving. "He shouldn't have done that," he rumbled, his voice deepening now. "I told him you were supposed to be left alone." Killian ran his tongue on the inside of his cheek as he shaved off another layer of wood, creating the curve of a tail. "I will talk to him upon my return." His eyes slid back to Ambrosja, observing her. "Either you just got started, or you have been unsuccessful."

"I just got started," Ambrosja said, taking careful steps closer to Killian while her eyes kept looking at the little figurine taking shape in his hand. "What are you doing? Are you crafting pieces to a *stonegame?*"

Killian gave a curt nod, gesturing to the pieces on the ground. "Yes. But we call them board games—played on timber boards, carved pieces. Old Vaestorian tradition." His eyes met hers again. "You seem interested."

"I have never seen you like this."

"Like what?"

"Focused," she explained. "You look… different without being surrounded by your camp. More at peace, I suppose."

Killian gave a small grin as his blade glided over another piece of the wood. Horns coming into shape. "Doesn't everyone feel more at ease when they are away from duty, Ambrosja?

"I do not." The Empress placed a hand on her hip, the other still holding the sword, her head tilted to the side while her eyes shifted between watching his face and his hands.

"Probably because your entire being is attached to duty." Killian didn't look at her, he simply turned the dragon piece in his hand, inspecting where to carve next. "You will never relax." His gaze met hers then, his voice dropped lower, more to a whisper just for them, "You are an Empress, forever bound by your role. Even as you leave, even as you cross borders to new lands, you will forever be plagued by duty." He looked down at his wooden dragon then.

Ambrosja's nose scrunched slightly. "You do not need to remind me."

"Hm," Killian rumbled. He scooted slightly to the side. "Come, sit with me, Ambrosja."

"I'd rather not."

He chuckled. "Ah, that's right. You'd rather be mauled by a snowbear than be touched by me, hm? I bet you'd rather have your bones gnawed on than sit near me. Yet," he cocked a brow as he met her eyes once more, "you sleep very comfortably at night when you're beside me. You tend to fall asleep before I do, and I hear that gentle little snoring from you."

"I do not snore!" Ambrosja proclaimed, taking a step forward, one fist clenched while her other hand waved her sword at him. "I should slice

another scar onto you just for that comment!"

"Oh no—" Killian stood to his full height, "another scar on my very scarred body, *how horrible*. Why don't you try breaking my nose again? The number of times my nose has been broken is far less than the number of scars I have on my body."

The Commander grinned, walking closer to Ambrosja until he was a two steps from her. He looked down at her sword, then over her.

"Sit," he said it again, gesturing with a tilt of his head back at the log. "You can hunt later. Besides," he was turning now, "you'll need my help with hunting."

"I have been trained in hunting. I know how to hunt."

"I'm sure you do, but hunting in a forest is different from hunting on snow-covered lands." Killian sat back down. "You will require different skills. Skills that I have. Besides," he went back to carving, "I've said this before, but I will not let you get far from me. So, just sit down."

Ambrosja sheathed her sword and crossed her arms. "Fine." She moved closer. But she did not sit next to Killian. She placed herself upon a boulder that was across from him. "So, you are making pieces for a… board game. What for? Do you plan to play something? Did you break your own pieces in a fit of violence?"

"Hm, you shoot questions one after another." Killian didn't look up; he kept carving. "It's like you don't know how to be patient. Or quiet. If you're not talking to me and making some backhanded comment along with it, you are glaring into my skull. It's almost as if you forgot we spent a night talking about dragons."

"Ha!" Ambrosja angrily crossed her legs. "Spent a night? More like minutes of you telling me wonderful stories then deciding enough was enough and turning over!"

"It was late at night."

"So? If you cannot finish a story then do not start it!" She tilted her chin up defiantly, angled just slightly away with delicate precision.

Killian observed her posture, her chin tilt. And he couldn't stop the smile that formed on his lips. "By the Dragons, you are…" he took a deep breath, "…adorable."

The Empress wasn't expecting that. Not *that*. Not a compliment out of nowhere. Not that smile on his face. She swallowed just a bit. Her cheeks went pink. She wondered, *When was the last time a man called me adorable?* The answer was clear: she had never been called such a thing, or managed to pull a smile from a man quite like that.

She didn't give in. Didn't soften. "I wish I could say the same for you, but I have met Frost Trolls who were far more handsome."

Killian barked a laugh at that. Actually hunching over. His shoulders shook, and the log beneath him almost rolled as he leaned forward. "Cute, very cute," he murmured, his body relaxing as he returned to carving.

"So," she returned to glaring at him, "why are you carving pieces for a *board* game? Are you making your own? Lost your pieces?"

"No." The Commander's voice was calm. "I am creating these pieces for someone special to me."

Ambrosja felt as if a pin had been slipped past her ribs and pierced into her heart, not a stab but an aching pinch. For a moment, she didn't recognize why she felt this. But she knew this feeling. It was far too familiar, it was the kind of pain that always hit every time Hådvard had done something upsetting in front of her. *Jealousy.* The Empress scolded herself internally once she recognized it.

"Someone special?" She echoed. "A lover?"

Killian's eyes moved from the figurine to look at Ambrosja. He didn't say anything at first. Just watched her for a moment. He bore no smirk, nothing that gave a hint as to what was crossing his mind.

"Perhaps," he said at last. "Why?" He leaned forward, forearms bracing on his knees. "Jealous?"

"You wish," Ambrosja replied immediately, far too quickly. "It is called curiosity, Commander."

"Hm," Killian smirked, leaning back. "Curiosity," he echoed, carving again. "It is for my sister."

A flicker of surprise passed through Ambrosja's eyes, and the slightest breath of relief left her lips. She couldn't stop that reaction from slipping through. Killian immediately noticed it.

"What was that, Empress?" The Commander's eyes immediately locked onto her lips, then her eyes. "Was that alleviation? And here I thought you preferred a Frost Troll."

"You mistake my reaction." Ambrosja stood up then, wiping the dirt from her pants. "I was just merely surprised that a man like you would have a sister. Much less care for her enough to be carving dragons into wooden pieces so small I am shocked you haven't crushed it with your abnormally massive hands."

Killian's smile was broad. "You act like you hate my hands, but whenever I touch you—you tremble."

"That trembling is disgust!" Ambrosja turned away now. "I will go hunting, I fear if I stay here any longer I will end up taking you as the meal for the camp. Though I can't imagine your meat would be satisfying to eat."

Killian's lips twitched at her comment. His voice was calm, betraying just how bold he felt. "I've been accused of being… satisfying."

The Empress stopped walking away. She stood still for a moment before she faced him again. She couldn't stop the warmth from spreading over her cheeks. "You are… repulsive." She turned away sharply then. Marching far from Killian. *Why do I keep letting him provoke me? Stupid man. Monster. Murderer.*

Killian watched Ambrosja stomp away from him. The smallest curve of a smile graced his lips. "Difficult woman…" he whispered to himself, bending down to gather the figurines he had carved, settling them into his belt loops before following after the pale-haired woman.

The Commander didn't let the Empress far from his sights. Even as she marched ahead.

"You're just going to scare away every single beast within a hundred feet if you keep stomping through the forest like that, Ambrosja," Killian called out after her, not bothering to catch up or rush his pace. His long strides did that well enough for him.

"And I shall simply find them!" Ambrosja shouted back. "I do not need you, Commander! Go off and play with your wood!"

Killian sucked in a breath of air. *That was intentional*, he thought to himself. "You are not proficient in hunting in a forested area. Be as stubborn as you want, but at least be good about what you wish to be stubborn about."

Ambrosja stopped in her tracks and turned around. "What could be so godsdamn different about hunting in a forested area compared to frost-filled lands and mountains?!"

Killian stopped right in front of her. Arms crossed now. He tilted his head to the side as he looked down at her. "Tell me, Ambrosja," he uncurled a hand from his bicep, gesturing to the woods, "how would you track a beast here?"

"I would look for prints."

"And have you been looking for prints?"

"…Not yet, I was trying to get away from you first."

Killian's lips stretched into a thin line. "Right…" he shook his head, "Alright, now tell me: how exactly were you planning on finding these tracks?"

Ambrosja scowled at Killian. "First off, I am not a child. Do not treat me like one. Second, on the ground, of course." She crossed her arms then, mirroring his pose.

"And how would you identify these tracks?"

"By looking into the dirt!" Ambrosja looked impatient now. "What sort of question is that?"

Killian lowered his arms. "It's not just the dirt, Ambrosja." He stepped closer to her now, so close he was behind her. His hands lifted, hovering just near her face. "May I?"

Ambrosja looked at where Killian's hands were; she could see them out of her peripheral, just hovering near her face. "Why must you touch my face?"

"I am simply going to guide you where to look," he reassured her, "gently."

She was silent for only a moment, then gave a dip of her chin. "Fine, *just* guiding."

"Of course, I would prefer to keep my nose intact this time," Killian teased.

His hands moved, slow and sure to cup Ambrosja's jaw; he didn't force, he simply turned her slightly, directing her vision not to the dirt, but to the brush and trees. The Empress's heart did that thud again, not painful like before, but still traitorous. She resented this. This feeling. This… *want.*

"When in a forest, you must look for the smallest details," he explained, "like a broken branch or a trampled flower. Those can indicate when something has moved nearby." He continued, "A human tends to be more conscious of where they step if they are not in a hurry. Often, they'll find themselves making sure to not crush a flower… But an animal," he then moved her head to look at a trampled flower nearby, "would not care for such a thing."

Ambrosja took a deep breath. "Fine." She deliberately placed her hands on his—she had to—and pulled his hands away from her face. "You just have different tracks, I can still hunt."

Killian's lips twisted to the side. His sharp gray eyes were staring down at the crown of Ambrosja's head. He took a step back, hands raising then falling to his sides. "I'm not doubting your skill Ambrosja — I am trying to show you that hunting in the woods is far different than hunting in the snow."

"I know!" Ambrosja turned to face him. Then she took a deep breath; and a step back. "I know. I—" she knew. She knew that Killian wasn't doubting her skill. She knew he wasn't talking down to her.

Her eyes met the ground beneath them, then his eyes again. She could tell he was trying to read her. In the short time she had been near him, she had also managed to understand some of his own tells, such as his eyes doing a subtle narrowing when he tried to read her. She hated it whenever he tried to read her.

"I am struggling right now to be near you," the Empress confessed.

"That's not surprising," Killian admitted, already agreeing, "I'm not a man you should want to be near, given everything that's happened. It makes sense that my presence is uncomfortable for you."

The Empress didn't answer. She looked away again. Chewing the inside of her cheek. Killian looked over her posture, her expression.

"You're attracted to me," he said simply.

Ambrosja's eyes snapped to him. Her cheeks went red—not with girlish softness—but with vexation. "Must I repeat the Frost Troll line again?! Is your skull so thick you cannot seem to understand the meaning of my words?"

"Oh," Killian chuckled, not warmly. "I understand meanings just fine, Empress, but you forget, I have been reading people since I was a boy, and you—you are not very subtle."

The Empress scoffed, waving her hand dismissively. "Just — let us hunt and be done with this." She quickly added, "But… not too fast, please, I—I enjoy not being inside the camp." Ambrosja met his eyes again, now waving her finger at him. "But stop that — that thing that you do!"

"I do a lot of things, Empress," Killian leaned forward, his hands resting on his hips, he gave a smug shrug, "you'll have to be more specific."

"That too!" She pointed at him now. "You're not as cute as you think you are!"

Killian gave a half smile, half smug, half genuine. "So, you think I am cute, just not cute enough, huh?"

"Shut up," she turned sharply, walking until she met the trampled flower and crouched beside it.

Killian didn't follow; he remained still, but he couldn't help but bite his lip as he watched her reactions.

Ambrosja observed the entire area that was crushed. She could barely make out the shape. But she focused, trying to outline the best she could. Her fingertips grazed the soft edges of what was beyond the threshold of the flattened surface. She looked ahead along the ground a bit, searching for a hint of something, an understanding of the direction the creature took.

The Commander said nothing, simply crossed his arms and watched Ambrosja, letting her hunt, letting her learn how it must be done in a forest. Though his gaze couldn't help but soften the longer he stared at her.

The Empress, still crouching, took an awkward step to the side, where she noticed deep grooves like claws in the dirt.

"I think it's a wolf print," Ambrosja said, looking at Killian from over her shoulder. Then she looked ahead, following the path, and noticed a thick branch had been crushed; there was weight to the paw. "Huh, perhaps a big wolf, that branch is crushed, then the claws, the size." She stood then, wiping her hands to dust away the dirt.

"A wolf," Killian echoed the idea as he took a step closer, now crouching to examine the print. "A Gray Tyrant…"

"Gray Tyrant?"

"A Great Wolf. Your people would call it a Vargr. Which means hunting is out of the question. If a Great Wolf has been nearby—then all prey animals have likely fled elsewhere and won't return until they feel that the threat is gone."

Ambrosja grumbled, her nose scrunched slightly, glaring at the flattened flower once more. "Then what do you propose? Your lieutenant seemed adamant about my return before sundown with something for the camp."

"You mean the lieutenant who had directly disobeyed me by sending *you* to hunt?" Killian looked annoyed at the mention of Berric. He stood to his full height. "I am Commander, whatever *my* lieutenant had ordered you to do is meaningless now." Then he turned, heading up a faint trail through the trees. "Let's go to Greenfield. We'll buy whatever meat we can from the hunters there."

The Empress stood, she followed a few paces after Killian before lifting her arm, "And what about this?" she pulled her sleeve upward and gestured to the manacle, "Your Lieutenant slapped this on my wrist."

That's when Killian paused. "He did what?" His eyes were sharper now, falling on the manacle that Ambrosja revealed as he turned.

His boots hit the ground with heavy and quick steps like a thunderstorm approaching. For a moment, Ambrosja's eyes went wide, her muscles had coiled, but she stopped when Killian stopped right before her; his eyes glaring at the manacle.

The Commander didn't ask for permission, but his touch was soft. He lifted her arm back up, his hand steady despite the way his nostrils flared just once as he stared at the metal band around Ambrosja's wrist. Then his other hand rose, grasped at one side, the hand holding her, grasped the other. His fingers curled into the space between the metal and her wrist… And with a controlled but powerful pull—the manacle snapped open.

The manacle was off of Ambrosja's wrist, but now gripped tightly in Killian's hands. The air around the manacle cackled with a faint magical

essence — then it dissipated. The Commander kept the manacle in his grasp before hooking it around his belt.

"Next time he does such a thing..." Killian spoke, his voice steady despite the intensity in his eyes, "...you have *my* permission to break *his* nose." He turned, but looked at Ambrosja from over his shoulder and added, "I'm mildly offended that you didn't." He gave a half smirk, then turned completely and began to walk back up the trail to Greenfield.

Ambrosja stood there for just a bit longer. Eyes fixed on Killian's fading form while her hand glided across her wrist, fingers moving in soft motions that betrayed her. She shook her head sharply, curls snapping in the air.

The walk had been quiet through the forest. Ambrosja kept a few paces behind, but not too far. This proximity was... *maddening*. Her eyes kept glancing towards Killian every few steps. They had been silent as they walked. This was something she had noticed about Killian—he was always silent. He always let people speak before he spoke. And if he did speak first... it was because he sought some sort of reaction. At least that was her personal experience.

Ambrosja couldn't help but squint at the back of Killian's head as if she were trying to pry open a book and read the words of a language unknown to her. She had witnessed his violence, his nonchalance towards human life, his cocky attitude. But sometimes... he felt too normal. Sometimes he seemed caring.

The Empress looked away, recalling her memories. Then... softly, her eyes met his form again. And suddenly—everything felt like it was making sense to her. He was... *familiar*. Like home. Killian reminded her of the warriors she grew up training under and fighting beside; they were fierce, cruel if needed but they could also be warm.

She remembered his touch. Then immediately, Ambrosja recoiled as if her whole body had been scorched.

Still!

Ambrosja shook her head again, this time shutting her eyes, hand clenching tight around the grip of the borrowed sword. *Familiarity does not excuse his crimes*, she thought to herself.

The silence continued to wreck the Empress. It had become so loud that whenever her eyes drifted back to Killian, she had to force herself to look elsewhere, even glaring at a bird. She couldn't take it. She never handled silence well to begin with.

"So, you have a sister," Ambrosja said as she continued to walk behind the Commander.

"I do," is all that Killian replied.

"What is her name?"

"Why?"

"What do you mean why?" Ambrosja's voice rose slightly. "You mentioned you have a sister — so now I am curious."

But there was only silence.

Ambrosja growled. "Fine! Do not share her name, could you at least tell me what she is like? Is she anything like you?"

Killian laughed at that. "Oh no," he said as he continued his walk up the path, "my sister is quite short. And small. Well—" he looked over at Ambrosja and gave her a once over, "—she is a bit taller than you. But she has the typical Vaestorian build that most women of this country have," Killian gestured vaguely in the air, continuing his walk, "tall and thin."

Ambrosja squinted at him. "Are you trying to say I am short?"

Killian tilted his head, smirking, though Ambrosja couldn't see, but quite possibly felt it through his voice. "For a Nordorner — you are... quite short."

The Empress glared at the back of Killian's head but said nothing. At first. "And you are ridiculously tall for a Vaestorian man."

Killian grumbled an agreement. "That is true. There are rumors that I have Nordorner ancestors," he then looked at Ambrosja from over his shoulder with an arrogant smile. "I guess we are not *that* different after all, Empress."

"Oh you fu—" Ambrosja was abruptly cut off.

"Hello," a small voice rang out just to the side of them.

Both Ambrosja and Killian turned, their eyes landing on a young boy, no older than seven. He had a small, brown fur coat that was wrapped tightly around him with a belt far too long, a long brown tunic that had weeds stuck to it, and brown pants neatly tucked into leather and fur-lined boots.

Killian took a step forward—Ambrosja immediately reacted, eyes wide, her hand ready to stop Killian from getting close to the child, but... she stopped... Killian got on one knee so he was more level with the young boy.

"Hey there," Killian's voice didn't soften, but he tried to relax his shoulders, "what are you doing all the way out here? Don't you know you're in the Bramble?"

"Yeah," the boy wiped his nose with his sleeve, "I was playing *Hush and Seek* with my friends but... I got lost."

"Is that right?" Killian hummed. "What's your name?"

"Heston."

"Heston?" The Commander echoed the name then gave an approving nod. "That's a fine name for a boy brave enough to venture into the Bramble without crying…" Killian leaned forward a bit. "Tell you what, I'll help you get back home, but promise me you won't go this far again until you are old enough to be a hunter."

Heston looked hesitant to make such a promise. His fingers curled in his tunic and his brows lowered. Killian noticed it all and simply cocked a brow at the young boy. Then the boy sighed.

"Fine," Heston grumbled. "I promise."

Killian gave a small smile and stood to his full height. "Let's go then, Greenfield isn't too far."

The Commander took a step — then froze once he felt the small hand of the child wrapping around his finger. He looked down, and there the boy was, close and ready to return home, and *far too trusting*, Killian thought. Ambrosja watched this, and she felt a twisting flutter in her stomach, like a knot that didn't feel wrong… as much as she wanted it to.

"Hi," Heston interrupted Ambrosja's thoughts as he looked back at her, extending his hand for her to hold as well.

Ambrosja's eyes widened just a bit. Then softened. As if she saw Mora all over again. She gave Heston a smile, "Hi," she said back, her voice softer and far kinder than Killian had ever heard. She walked closer, wrapping her hand around the young boy's. "Let's get you home, hm?"

Berric stood close to his captain. Arms crossed tight against his chest. He stared down at the hands of the tanned, blonde-haired woman as she waved her fingers over a small multi-layered compass. His eyes tracked the woman's fingertips as she slid her nail around the circular object. She adjusted the layers — making sure north stayed true, then brushing her finger over the middle layer until it glowed, and finally flicking the top dial, which flared to life before fading again.

"Well, Lilian?" Berric grunted, growing impatient. "What happened?"

Lilian shook her head. "The *Lockward* went dead—either the clasp was forced open, or the ward was severed."

The Lieutenant huffed. He turned around, "Alright, soldiers, gather the archers, see if they've seen anything—"

"Seen what, Berric?" Killian called out with bags of wrapped meats hoisted over his shoulders.

Berric turned immediately and stood straighter. "Commander Thorn, we sent a prisoner out to hunt, but it seems—" his words cut off as the manacle was shoved into his chest by Killian's hand.

"You sent out the wrong prisoner," Killian growled, his voice barely controlled. "I gave orders to let the pale-haired woman be, so explain to me *why* you sent her out to hunt."

Berric looked down at the broken manacle, his hands catching the device as Killian pulled away. "Commander," Berric said lowly, "I was doing as we have always done: randomly select who goes out to hunt. We do that with our own guards and with our prisoners. She *is* a prisoner."

"She is *my* prisoner," Killian corrected, his voice barely above a whisper. "And you will *not* tell her what to do, ever again."

Then, Killian walked away, heading towards the butcher's table to drop off the wrapped meat. Ambrosja was near the gate, carrying what seemed to be sacks of greens and harvest goods. She observed the encounter at a distance. She couldn't hear the details, but she followed Killian to the butcher's.

The Lieutenant still stared at Killian. Then called out, "This was our *only* manacle, Commander!"

"So it was," Killian said calmly, already heading to the Command Hall, "I suggest next time — you do not disobey me."

From the journal of Guinyldr Thorn,
Solgraen, 23, 997

THE FROST TROLL

The Frost Trolls of Nordorn are no mere legend. They dwell deep beneath the glaciers and mountains, lurking in tunnels carved by their own frozen hands. Born of the Frost Giant Jötunhr, they were shaped from ice and loneliness — his cruel answer to the silence that haunted him. It is said he breathed malice into their chests, commanding them to slay any Nordorner who dared trespass beneath the ice.

A Frost Troll's body is formed entirely of solid frost, its sinew and bone translucent as glacier glass. Because of this, they cannot endure the sun; even a touch of warmth sets their skin to weeping water. They prowl only by moonlight or in the endless dark of caverns, where their growls echo like cracking stone.

To ward them off, one must carry flame. Fire and light are the only powers that turn them away, for they remember the sun as a thing that burns and unmakes. Many Nordorners still whisper an old saying before venturing into the frozen tunnels: "Carry fire, and the frost will fear you.".

CHAPTER FIFTEEN

EYES OF COLD

Killian's boots were kicked up onto his broad desk. His posture was relaxed. Fingers carefully holding another wooden dragon figurine as his other hand applied just enough pressure to shave off a layer of wood. At one side of the desk, a neat stack of parchment, from orders that needed to be signed off to instructions and strategies that needed to be written, waited for him. His quill had yet to be dipped in the inkwell that day.

The doors to his office shook as heavy knocks echoed through. Killian didn't care to fix himself.

"Come in," he called out, his eyes never lifted once from his carving.

Berric stepped in, his boots hitting the wooden floor harder than necessary. Possibly from frustration. Possibly for show. His hands laced behind his back, he stared at the stacks of paper that had been untouched, then to the dragon figurine taking form in Killian's hands.

"Have you drafted the requisition for a new manacle yet?" Berric asked, his voice laced with impatience. "Or do your new duties involve crafting dolls, now?"

"You might want to go to a healer, Berric," the Commander spoke calmly, "I fear your eyes may be failing you, Lieutenant," then finally he looked at Berric, his own gaze growing sharper, "and I don't need a blind lieutenant working under my command."

Berric said nothing for a bit. He flexed his fingers behind his back. "A few of the boys and I are curious, Commander, if you'll enlighten me…" his tone wasn't kind, but he waited before speaking.

Killian's brows lowered, eyes narrowing. "And what could you all be curious enough about that you've come to bother me?"

The Lieutenant took a step forward. "The pale-haired girl…" he tilted his head, "Is she really that good in the sheets that you would break our only manacle?"

The sharp, gray eyes of the Commander had gone cold. He eased his boots off the desk and *slowly* rose from his chair, standing to his full height. He set the dragon figurine down, his knife as well, and braced his massive hands against the desk.

Killian then spoke, far too calm for the rising fury behind his eyes, "Speak of her like she's only flesh for use, and I will remove your jaw from your face."

Berric didn't flinch. He simply inhaled sharply. "Well, guess the Commander has either become smitten… or you're not the cruel man you play the part of."

Killian raised a hand, closed fist with his forefinger extended. "You mistake my position, my role, and my cruelty for the kind of man who would speak down about a woman. You will find that I will do no such thing." He lowered his hand then, moving to step around his desk and walk until he was a pace away from Berric. "I will never lessen someone to their sex; do not insult me by expecting such a thing." Then he leaned closer, his gaze inches from Berric's. "And *never* speak of her that way."

The Commander straightened, his hands lacing behind his back, and he turned, walking towards an open window. He raised one hand and waved dismissively—a clear signal for Berric to leave the room. And Berric did so.

When the doors shut and the Lieutenant was gone, Killian allowed his gaze to drift out the window, falling onto Ambrosja's form. He raised a brow as he caught the Empress in a rather compromising situation. He watched as Cinder was holding Ambrosja tight in a hug, yelling something about *not knocking it until trying it* while trying to get a tomato into Ambrosja's mouth.

Killian sighed, not disappointment, but a small air of amusement. "That's right," he whispered to himself, "tomatoes don't grow in Nordorn. She probably has no idea what it is." He gave a half smile as he observed the scenery once more before turning back to his desk.

The seat groaned as Killian took his place in it again. He leaned forward, elbows bracing against the desk and fingers lacing together. His eyes relaxed on the dragon figurine that was so close to being done. Another

breath of air escaped him. This time deeper. The exhale made his shoulders relax and move down, softening his broad and brutal posture.

"How will I ever get this to you, Lyra?" He grabbed the dragon figurine, turning it over in his hand.

The small smile he gave the little dragon was genuine, warm, and full of nostalgia. He turned it again, his mind drifting off…

"Killy!" A little girl cried, running through the garden where purple and blue flowers bloomed. "They pushed me again! They said I can't play because I-I'm a girl!!"

The young form of Killian turned from where he was training with a sword as he saw his little sister approaching, eyes puffy and cheeks stained with tears. Her long black hair, normally straight and perfect, was knotted as if someone had pulled on it. Her blue dress, her favorite one, was dirtied. But Killian noticed it. He always noticed everything very well since he was a young boy.

She wasn't *just* pushed, he noted. She had been dragged, too.

Killian didn't hesitate. He met his sister halfway with furious steps. Fists clenched tight, the sword dropped onto the freshly cut grass. Dark strands fell in front of the young gray eyes that had stopped being innocent years prior.

"Lyra—" Killian placed his hands on his sister's shoulders, "what *exactly* happened?" He hunched lower to be more at her level, "And don't lie to me, don't lie to me to spare them."

Lyra choked on a small cry. "They pushed me—" she whispered, trembling, wiping her eyes. "Said girls are too stupid to play Drakeward! Then — then they dragged me out of the park by my hair!"

Killian's gaze went cold. He set his sister aside and marched off towards the park.

The dragon figurine hit the desk harder than he meant to. His finger immediately dragged over it, as if giving an apology.

Killian's eyes moved to his knuckles, knuckles that were often bloody as a kid and well into his late adolescence.

"Killian!" Aaric's voice crashed like lightning. "What were you thinking?! What were *you* thinking?! Were you even thinking?!"

Aaric paced across the room. Killian sat still on the long, dark blue velvet couch, decorated with gray embroidery that shimmered. His cold eyes were set on the hearth that was burning before him. Then drifted off to the side, spotting a worried Lyra peeking from around the corner. He gave a single shake of his head, a quiet request for her to go back to her room. But Lyra simply shook her head back. He sighed. He didn't want to bring attention to his sister.

"They were smaller than you, Killian! Younger, too!" Aaric kept arguing. "You broke one kid's arm! You broke another's nose! You dislocated one's shoulder! Do you know how this looks?! You are a Thorn, by Dragon's Breath! Act like one!"

That's when Killian stood up to his father, only inches shorter than him. "Younger?! Smaller?!" His eyes were glassy, his brows twitching, his hands clenched tight with bruised knuckles. "They didn't think the same of Lyra when they pushed her and dragged her by *her hair* out of the park! All because, what, she's a girl?!" He continued yelling. "What kind of man would I be if I let my sister, or any girl or woman suffer that same fate?!"

Aaric was still. Frozen in place with a quiet fury. "Do not raise your voice to me, boy," he said calmly. "I am well aware of what Lyra went through, she told me, but that does not excuse your behavior."

The older man had to pace away, hands behind his back. He sighed heavily.

"Father?" Jareth called out, stepping through the door. "You called for me?"

Aaric nodded. "Yes, Jareth," he looked up at his older son, then at Killian. "I think it is time your brother joined the military with you. It is time he learned restraint and control. Before he tarnishes the family name…"

Killian was silent. His eyes had gone wide. But before he could say anything, a cry cut across the room, and his side was hit hard by Lyra's small form.

"No!" The little girl cried. "Don't send Killy away! Please! He's my best friend! Jay-Jay stinks! Mommy is too busy, and you're always away, Daddy!" She hugged Killian tighter. "Please don't send Killian away! He didn't mean it!"

Killian immediately lowered himself. He hugged Lyra, "Hey—" he whispered, his voice terrifyingly gentle. "Don't cry. I'm sure it'll be a few weeks before I leave. But until then," he wiped a tear from Lyra's tiny cheek, "I'll play Drakeward with you, alright?"

Lyra shook her head quickly and insistently. "No! I don't want you to go!"

Killian tore his gaze from his knuckles to the stack of papers that sat on the opposite end of the dragon figurine. He forced his hands to pull the pieces of parchment closer. His eyes roamed over them, reading words that requested logistics, new information. Others had proposed new trade routes. A different stack requested new strategies and teachings for Black Hand recruits.

The Commander grabbed the quill, but his hand was unsteady. He trembled just slightly, knuckles tightening, fingers flexing, his eyes roamed to a word on the parchment: *control*—and the quill snapped in his hand. His eyes locked onto it. Then he crushed his hand around it. Without thinking, Killian stood up and pushed his desk over. Sending the stacks of parchment flying into the air. He raised a heavy boot and slammed it down onto the desk. Again and again as he yelled at it. His gray eyes were cold and devoid of warmth. Filled only with rage.

He then came down onto tossed pieces of parchment, twisting his foot above it. Tearing it into pieces. Killian only stopped when his eyes shifted to the fallen dragon that was rolling across the floor. Only stopping once it touched the foot of his liquor cabinet. He moved fast, meeting the figurine in a few strides, hand swiping it up then bringing it to his face in a tightly closed fist.

Killian's eyes closed, exhaling sharply as he held the figurine in his hand. When his eyes opened, they fell onto the liquor in his cabinet. He opened the door to it, his hand immediately grabbed a bottle of something dark and amber.

The Commander's massive frame eased into a velvet seat. Legs sprawled out, the dragon figurine in one hand, the bottle in another. He brought the bottle to his mouth, teeth closing around the cork, snapping it off, then spitting it out.

The swig that Killian took wasn't a swig. It was a pour of something burning down his throat. Like a request for numbness that would only be temporary. He didn't wince, didn't recoil from the taste or the feeling, he embraced it, as if his fire had to meet fire to keep control.

His brow twitched when he heard yelling outside. It wasn't aggressive, but more like a barked command and then some mocking. Then he recognized the tone of voice. It was Ambrosja—she was mouthing off to someone. Killian immediately stood from his chair and made his way to the window. Never abandoning the dragon or the bottle in his hand.

Upon approaching the window, he saw it. Ambrosja was getting into it with a Black Hand guard who was approaching far too closely, staring her down. Ambrosja was gripping the pickaxe tightly. Gunnar stood up, standing right behind her with arms crossed. Another Black Hand joined.

"HEY." Killian yelled, and it was somehow calm. Everyone looked up at him. "I am running a mine here! Not a godsdamn brawling pit! So, back off!"

The Black Hand immediately backed off, but Ambrosja stood there, turning the pickaxe in her hand, watching the Black Hand walk away. Gunnar didn't leave her side—just in case.

When Ambrosja met Killian's gaze again, Killian motioned her to come to him with a tilt of his head. "In my office," he called out, "now."

Killian watched as Gunnar hovered protectively, and Ambrosja looked back at her allies. But when she began moving towards the Command Hall, that's when he backed away from the window.

His form was back on the velvet seat, taking another swig of his drink. When the door opened, he didn't bother looking over at Ambrosja. Meanwhile, Ambrosja had frozen upon seeing the broken desk, the scattered papers and the cabinet that was left open. She took a cautious step inside.

"If this is about what happened outside—" she had started to speak, only to be cut off.

"It's not," he said calmly, "you can relax." Killian glanced over at Ambrosja, "Come in, close the door behind you. Lock it so we're not interrupted."

Ambrosja hesitated once he told her to lock it. But she closed her fists tightly, and nodded, turning around to close the door—then locking it. She met the room again, her eyes tracking the broken wood, the torn papers, and the fallen inkwell that had spilled onto what was once a pristine, gorgeous carpet.

"Tell me a tale," Killian said, still not meeting Ambrosja's eyes, "something of your home."

"A tale?" she echoed, taking a few steps closer, her eyes trying to read the torn bits of parchment. "What kind of tale would you like?"

"Anything." Killian took another swig of his drink.

Ambrosja looked at the mess again. "What happened?"

"Nothing you need to concern yourself with, Ambrosja, just tell me a tale."

The Empress noticed his grip tightened around the neck of the bottle. She gave a polite nod, even though he wasn't looking at her.

"Perhaps I should tell you the story about Skeldr, our Shield-Father." Ambrosja started pacing calmly, hands resting in front of her, fingers lacing together. "Skeldr was a man turned god." She approached the fallen desk, eyes focusing on the papers. "He lived his life as a warrior; competent, skilled — he was said to be a man of great honor and valor. Always protecting those who were weaker."

She crouched now, fingers drifting over the parchment, trying to understand the words, despite the bootprint that obscured most of it and the torn and twisted pieces that made it hard to read.

"But he did not get to be a god because he was a good warrior," Ambrosja explained, "he became a god for his deed, for his *sacrifice*." Ambrosja's eyes squinted, murmuring to herself the words that she could make out; her hands moved to fix the papers now, gathering the destruction before her. "He—"

Killian turned and saw her fixing the papers. "Stop it," Ambrosja's eyes snapped to his form once he said that.

He set his bottle down, never releasing the dragon. The Commander moved to step beside her quickly; it looked as if he might touch her, but he stopped himself, fingers curling into a fist, restraining his hand at his side. Ambrosja's eyes were tracking him, trying to read him.

"It is my mess," he said firmly. "Don't try to fix my mistakes. It is not your burden."

It took a moment before Ambrosja nodded; she could tell something was bothering the Commander. "Very well," she said, standing up. "Then I will just tell you the story of Nordorn's Shield-Father."

The Commander gave a polite dip of his chin, "Thank you." He moved back to his seat, grabbing the bottle, but not sipping yet.

The seat that was beside Killian's, but separated by a low table, was taken by Ambrosja now. "Skeldr was a warrior like any other man. But his endurance—his resilience, was unparalleled." She kept her eyes on Killian, even though he wasn't meeting her gaze, just staring down at the bottle in his hand. Ambrosja went on regardless, "After the Fracture, Nordorn was already at war with Braxia, our once sister-country. Braxia would invade Nordorn again and again, attempting to knock it from its title of being the most brutal and fearsome land. The Braxis were filled with rage from what Brynhjora had done, so they deemed us forever as an enemy, hoping to one day enslave Nordorners."

The Empress crossed her legs, relaxing into the seat. "Braxia invaded, and this time, no one saw it coming… Because they took a route none had expected. They went around the northern seas and docked at Mornskald. Attacking us from a place that most would be foolish to attack."

"Because of the snowbears?" Killian asked.

Ambrosja let a proud smile slip. "Yes, because of the snowbears." But her smile soon faded, not because she let it slip, but because the tale didn't call for a smile. "We were foolish not to think ahead. The Braxis came with oil and fire prepared. They aimed for the huts where we kept our snowbears." She sighed. "We lost a lot of our cubs and snowbears that day… And we… were at a great disadvantage then. It was the middle of the night, huts burning down, homes as well, losing warriors and children in the same breath."

The Empress stood, as if she were unable to keep still as she told the story. "Many had to flee. But Skeldr? He was among the warriors who stood behind and held the line. He guarded the gate that led from the region of Mornskald into the region of Nordravn; he stood behind to make sure everyone could make it to the mountains. Wave after wave of enemies rushed him," Ambrosja took a step closer to Killian, her finger flexing as she told the story, "but he stood tall, he kept moving through the fire, the ash and blood, even as he took arrows, even as he felt fire touch his skin… then… then he spotted three young children."

Killian met Ambrosja's gaze then. He didn't interrupt her.

"And that's when Skeldr was no longer a berserker, but a shield." Ambrosja paused, her voice softening, her eyes downcast. "His body became a shield. Skeldr moved from one home to another, guarding the children with his entire body, even as the Braxis came pouring in — he never once let a single blade touch the children. He had guarded Mornskald for twelve days, he found the children on the ninth, and it took him three days to reach the gate… It is said he had taken twenty-eight arrows, ten to his chest, eighteen to his back. A spear in his ribs, an axe in his shoulder… and a sword in his heart."

The Empress lifted her gaze once more, meeting Killian's. "Only when he got to the gate, only when he saw the children make it far up the mountain, and only when he managed to seal the gate… ensuring no Braxis could breach further, did he fall." Ambrosja paused, eyes looking down once more, but not at the floor, at the dragon in Killian's hand—

then she met his gaze again. "We named him Nordorn's Shield-Father, for protecting those that could not protect themselves, for bleeding for three days straight for children that were not his own, for using his body as a shield, for guarding our home for twelve days…"

Killian was silent. His eyes locked onto Ambrosja's. After a moment, he looked down. Rolling the small dragon figurine in his hand. "Skeldr… chose well. His ending was worthy."

"Indeed," Ambrosja dipped her chin. "It was."

From the journal of Guinyldr Thorn
Solgraen, 24, 997

SKELDR, THE SHIELD-FATHER

It is carved into the stone of Nordorn's mountains that Skeldr, the Shield-Father, was the last of the berserkers to stand against the Braxis — the eternal rivals of the North. When the northern lines fell and retreat was called, Skeldr did not follow. He turned and held the pass so that others might live, his roar shaking the peaks as waves of enemies broke upon him. For nine days and nights, he fought alone, sustained by the blood of his kin and the fury of his gods.

Yet on the ninth day, the fire of wrath gave way to something greater. Amid the ruin and smoke, Skeldr found three children hiding among the fallen. He laid down his madness and took up his purpose — becoming not the sword, but the shield. With the children held close, he carved a path through blood and stone until he reached the gate of Mornskald, the last threshold into Nordravn. There, he set them free and watched as they fled into the safety of the mountains.

Only when they were gone did he turn once more to face the enemy. He closed the gate, sealing the path behind him, and met the Braxis blade-first — not in rage, but in resolve. It was there that Skeldr fell, willingly and unbowed.

From that day forth, Nordorners have called him Shield-Father, guardian of the helpless and protector of the innocent. His followers take up his creed: to stand when others flee, to defend where others destroy, and to place the lives of the weak above their own. In the temples of Mornskald, his name is still spoken not with fear, but with gratitude — for it was Skeldr's sacrifice that taught the North that true strength lies not in fury, but in protection.

The young sorceress's delicate fingers picked up the Dragon-King, capturing it into her pale hand and looking it over before shifting her gaze up to her opponent.

"Your Drake… has no ground left," Lyra said in a calm and sweet voice, her blue eyes glinting with victory as she stared at her older brother.

Jareth's fingers were curled tight around his chin. He exhaled sharply as he watched his King be taken by his sister. "So, it is." He leaned back in the high-back chair, taking a sip of tea sharpened with something stronger. "You only won because Killian taught you all the dirty moves."

"No," Lyra cleaned up the pieces as she clarified, "I won because Killian understands strategy better than most men. Even you— which is quite impressive, given that it's been said that you surpass father's intellect with battle."

Jareth grunted but didn't deny it. "It's true, Killian always did have a brilliant mind when it came to war. It's a shame he let his violence speak louder."

Lyra's eyes snapped to Jareth's, blue against blue. "Don't speak about our brother that way," she said firmly, "everything he has done has been for our country—our family."

The older sibling sighed, but said nothing; he knew it was useless to push against Lyra when it came to Killian. She was the only one allowed to insult him in the household. Instead, Jareth simply took another sip of his tea.

"Have you heard from Killy?" Lyra asked, trying to read her brother.

"No," Jareth responded calmly, keeping his tone neutral, "I have not heard from Killy, not since his exile, Ly."

Lyra hummed, crossing her legs, hands fixing her dark blue dress that had silver beading laced through it, appearing as if it were stars on a dark blue sky. She laced her fingers together. "Very well, Jay-Jay."

Jareth recoiled instantly. "Do not—do not call me that."

"Why not?" Lyra smiled widely, lips stretching with sibling mischief. "You are Jay-Jay. You will always be Jay-Jay."

"Yes, and I remember Jay-Jay being stinky."

"He still is. Quite stinky." Lyra nodded while still beaming. Then her expression shifted, one to cautious thoughtfulness. "When will you and Daddy tell the people about Wintersong?"

The air shifted instantly. Jareth ran a hand through his dark hair, lines creasing around his blue eyes as his gaze drifted over the game of Drakeward. His eyes tracked each piece before falling onto the Dragon-Queen. Then he leaned back.

"In about a month, we want… more concrete answers before telling the people, to avoid riots, to provide better comfort this time around," Jareth said finally, "assuming that no one finds out beforehand. Though they shouldn't…" he released a deep air of exasperation, "Though…" he repeated, "it was already found out by a courier doing his rounds…Who knows if he told anyone else?"

"Hm," Lyra hummed thoughtfully. "Hopefully not. Did the courier go straight to you?"

Jareth shook his head. "The courier that delivered me the letter wasn't the one at Wintersong, he was simply the boy working at Stonehaven's Watchstead at the time. The one who received the letter from the courier." Jareth stood then, politely pushing his chair back so his broad frame could rise. "I should head to the council, go over letters, documents, and plans to rebuild Wintersong… If it is even worth it…"

Lyra nodded, chin resting in her hand. "It'll be just like Marrowind's village of Deepwood, huh? Another piece of our country abandoned… and forgotten."

Jareth stopped moving. His head lowered, fists clenched at his sides. "I will do my best to make sure that Stonehaven doesn't forget its own. We have fallen quite a ways down in recent years, yes, but — I will do my best to

raise this regency back up to what it used to be."

"Well," the young sorceress nodded, waving a finger, using magic to move the dragon pieces atop the board, "do not let me stop you, brother."

Jareth's shoes hit the opulent stairs of the council's domain. Each step he took made his hands flex, as if he was releasing a burden from his shoulders, only to shoulder a new one. His eyes didn't track the details of the room or the faces passing him by. The only time he moved was when he gave women a flashy smile as they walked past him and curtsied in greeting; the echoes of *Good afternoon, Lord Jareth*, were not nearly as loud as his thoughts.

"Well, well," Varian called out from over the railing, his pale green eyes catching every shift of Jareth's posture, "I didn't expect to see our young Diplomat in the office today."

Jareth's face immediately turned from neutral to sour. He could— most of the time—control how his face reacted, but when it came to Varian, it was as if not even the Gods could stop the annoyance that the Diplomat felt when within fifty paces of the Marshal.

"Varian," Jareth grinned, not politely, "I could say the same to you."

Only once the men were on the same floor and only five paces shy of each other, did Jareth's voice dip lower, "Did you come here to check on matters of importance? Or to see your wife, Lady Rosalind? Or are you just finding a new spot to dip your quill into an inkwell that doesn't belong to your wife?"

A corner of Varian's lips stretched into a hostile half-smile. "Can't say I know what you mean, Jareth, if I need an inkwell… I will always seek my wife for one."

Jareth scoffed, then walked past Varian, shoulder bumping him on the way to his office. "Have a good day, Lord Varian—should you need me… for matters of the utmost importance… I will be in my office."

The Diplomat turned to face a wide set of double doors, hands grasping at the handles and turning them to enter. His office was wide, square, and everything in its proper place. His desk faced the doors, positioned all the way near the back wall where a tall window shone down upon it. Books and rolled up maps decorated the shelves in perfect symmetry. Five leather seats sat in a semi-circle near his desk, for guests or other lords and ladies, no doubt.

Jareth exhaled slowly, his hand coming to unbutton his pristine dark blue jacket. Shrugging it off his broad shoulders to release some of the tension on him. He made his way to his seat, settling his jacket onto the back of his chair and reached down to open the cupboard built within his desk; he retrieved a bottle of something dark and settled it onto the surface of his desk, a short, round glass joined it shortly.

The lid came undone as it was twisted off. The Diplomat poured a little more than what was necessary but he did not correct it. He took the glass, bringing it to his lips and took a long sip, as if the burn down his throat was a breath he had been wanting to release. He remained standing, as if sitting was a weakness he could not afford to invite.

His fingers, calloused from war, stained with ink, moved the neat stack of papers on his desk. Propositions and proposals that Mira had drafted; plans to where the coin should go as suggested by Lady Rosalind, words to write in letters for the kin of those who perished in Wintersong by Lord Emeric, promises of protection by Lord Varian, promises to do better by Lord Oswin.

A soft knock at the door stopped Jareth from reading further. When he looked up, he saw a familiar auburn bob peeking in.

"Jareth?" Mira called out, always using her *sultrier* voice with him. "I didn't expect you to come in today. I only realized you were here because I heard Varian muttering obscenities under his breath."

Jareth grinned from that. "Yes, I decided to not be as polite today, too tired for pleasantries that aren't deserved"

Mira stepped in fully, closing the door behind her. She walked towards Jareth, always deliberately swaying her hips whenever she was in his field of vision. When she met his side, her brown eyes drifted over his desk.

"Finally reviewing the proposals?" She questioned, her eyes meeting his profile.

"Yes," Jareth gave a curt nod, "the sooner I get through these… the more time I will have to think on how to respond and take action."

Then his gaze drifted to a different stack. A stack of papers that should be done by the Justiciar. Mira noticed this, and immediately her fingers came up, delicately grabbing Jareth's chin, making him look back at her.

"Do not," she said, calm yet firm, "you should *not* be taking on those papers."

"If I don't, then who will?"

"I don't care, Jareth, you are the Diplomat of Stonehaven, not the Justiciar, and if you would accept that your brother's position needs to be replaced then you'd have less weight on your shoulders."

Jareth's eyes narrowed. "No one is taking my brother's place as Jus-

ticiar."

Mira's brows furrowed, almost pinching together. "Jareth, don't be ridiculous. Your brother has been exiled from Stonehaven for years! He has lost his position! He is not coming back to reclaim it!"

"None shall take his seat. Not while I have a vote in this city." Jareth took a step back from Mira. "I will take on my brother's role."

"Jareth," Mira took a step closer, hands closing into tight fists at her side. "You are going to burn yourself out." She looked at the drink in his hand then. "Your drinking has gotten worse. You think I did not spot the four empty bottles this past *Olyr's Watch*?"

"My drinking is fine."

Mira was quiet. Eyes sharp. "If you say so, Lord Jareth, just don't embarrass yourself. *Or me.*"

The Advocate turned sharply then. Hips no longer swaying, heels striking the floor as she made her way to the door, opened it, and closed it firmly behind her.

Jareth didn't flinch. He didn't chase. He set his drink down, and finally took a seat. His hands roamed over the papers, adjusting them into an entirely new stack as he whispered the purpose and function of each parchment before him.

From the journal of Guinyldr Thorn,
Solgraen, 25, 997

DRAKEWARD

Drakeward is a game of wit and patience, beloved by Vaestorian nobles and scholars alike. Its board, set in a checkered pattern of alternating hues, hosts carved dragons as its pieces—each side representing rival flights vying for dominion. The goal is not mere destruction, but the strategic removal of the Queen Dragon and the dethroning of the King Dragon, for to fell the rulers is to claim the sky.

Every set of Drakeward is a work of art in itself. The dragons are carved from the finest woods, each base encircled by a delicate ring of polished stone, colored to signify allegiance rather than square. The process of crafting a complete set can take months, and those made from rare materials are said to be worth more than a noble's dowry.

To play Drakeward is considered a mark of refinement and intellect. Entire courts have been known to pause over a single match, where alliances are tested and tempers quietly sharpened.

The King-Dragon

Carved to be broad
and powerful.

The Queen-Dragon

Carved to be elegant
and serene.

CHAPTER SEVENTEEN

THE HAND THAT APPROACHES

Snow churned beneath thundering hooves. The forest howled.

Serana didn't slow for it either. She leaned forward, cutting through the wind like a spear, her hands tight on the reins as she led her riders. Snow hit against the dark leathers and metals of their armor. Torn cloaks snapping in the cold winds. Heavy hooves tore through frostbitten soil, mist trailing in their wake as the trees whipped past. The heavy breath of each beast cast a fog at the front that was quickly sliced through. Night was here, and it was only a matter of time before Greenfield would be in their view.

Serana raised a hand, signaling to halt as she pulled the reins of her horse and eased into a stop. "Let's make camp tonight!" She swung a heavy boot over the horse and moved off her saddle.

Other Black Hands joined her, swinging off their saddle. Boots hitting the ground. They guided their horses to trees nearby, tying their reins close. They fiddled through their packs, preparing to make camp. They had fire, blankets, and soup simmering over heat sparked from their palms.

"What are we to do if we find the Empress?" One Black Hand asked, settling down onto the blanket beside their horse. "The Grand Marshal wants us to find her and then what, just prays she tags along for the ride?"

"I suppose we have a few options..." Serana hummed in thought. "Depends on how we find her. If she's alive, we'll cross that bridge when we get to it, but—if she's dead? You better pray to whatever God you believe in and beg for mercy, because Nordorn will deliver none."

A few of the Black Hands shifted at that. Knuckles paling beneath dark gloves as they gripped their own arms to keep them steady. A young Black Hand, far more green than he ought to be, stepped forward next. His voice was cocky and curious, a dangerous combination. "And how will we know if we've found her?" He snickered, "We don't know what she looks like for sure besides blonde."

Serana shook her head. "Pale hair," she corrected, "she will have pale hair and sound like a Nordorner."

"But what if she doesn't sound like a Nordorner?"

"And what if she doesn't sound like a Nordorner...?" Serana echoed, eyes now set on the young Black Hand before her. "And what exactly would she sound like?

"...Mercinaris?"

Serana froze. Eyes ablaze. "A Mercinaris?" Her jaw slack with disbelief. Then she stood up fast—kicked snow in the direction of the Black Hand. "I'm a Mercinaris! You oaf!" She gestured to herself, "Dark hair! Dark skin kissed by the sun! If the Empress of Nordorn came from Mercinari she wouldn't be the fucking Empress of Nordorn! Now would she?!"

"Alright, alright," he muttered, wiping snow off his shoulders. "No reason to get bent."

A few other Black Hands chuckled, some whispered, a warning really, telling the man to go to bed. Serana already turned, heading to her blanket.

"If anyone else has a stupid comment or question, I will tie you and drag you all the way to Greenfield," Serana warned them. "Do not test my patience, I'm pissed as it is."

A few muttered "Yes, Ma'am," and "goodnight" before each headed to their own blanket, ready to sleep before another day of riding took them again.

"We ride in the morning." She set down onto her blanket, looking at the Black Hands once more, "Four days until Greenfield. Four days until we know for sure if the Empress of Nordorn is here. Sleep."

The next day provided a new sense of tension.

Serana was seated atop her horse, cloak snug tight, half covering her face from the speckles that drifted from the shared mountains of Nordorn

and Vaestoria. The riders of the Sister-Hand remained close, the snow-laden trees kept them covered.

"What is going on?" Serana growled, narrowing her eyes at a troop of soldiers in the distance.

The soldiers were clad in leathers and furs, their tabards decorated with a dragon insignia that shimmered a silver color.

"Soldiers from Stonehaven," a woman beside Serana whispered. She shifted her shoulder, her dark-feathered hawk adjusted with her. "Judging by their path... they are heading for Wintersong."

"You always did have a sharp eye, Cressida," Serana whispered, her voice tilted with something close to praise.

Another rider, on Serana's opposite side leaned forward. "What would you have us do, Sister-Hand? Stay put and let them pass... or intervene?"

"Stay put," Serana said immediately, "we are searching for the Empress of Nordorn. Our goal is not to meddle with Vaestorian soldiers."

"How have they gotten here so fast?" another rider asked, rolling his shoulders with unease.

"They probably didn't come directly from Stonehaven," Cressida clarified, "might just be troops from the nearest villages making their way..." she scoffed. "Stonehaven wouldn't risk sending their own soldiers."

"The fuck..." a young Black Hand rider muttered, gripping the reins of his horse harshly, his horse neighed and stepped back.

Serana snapped her eyes to him, causing Cressida to reach out and restrain the man's reins. The horse neighed harder, as if sensing the young rider's unease.

"Shut your horse up before it gives us away," Serana hissed, eyes darting between the young rider and the Vaestorian soldiers ahead. But she froze when she saw one soldier in the distance glancing back.

The soldier placed a hand over his eyes, trying to stop the snowflakes from drifting in his vision. Serana could see he was trying to squint through. She remained silent, and Cressida worked to get the horse to quiet down and for the young rider to stay still. The Sister-Hand tensed when another soldier stopped, looking in the same direction.

Tension was short-lived. Another soldier ushered them, waving for them to turn and continue. Serana relaxed.

"What has gotten into you?!" she hissed, staring at the young rider.

The young rider raised a finger, pointing to their right, just a little beyond the trees.

Cressida looked first. She tensed momentarily—then relaxed and sighed. "It's just a Snowbear," she gestured in the direction, but everyone immediately looked. "It won't come closer, its rider—" she gestured again, raising her chin slightly, "—is simply keeping watch. The soldiers probably caught the attention of the Nordorners patrolling the border, and now… now they see us."

Serana eased her horse back. "Fantastic, now we've got Nordorners watching us."

"But only from their borders," Cressida reminded Serana, her piercing blue eyes following the rider's gaze. She outlined the man's shape: large, far larger than any of them, his broad shoulders covered in a gray fur cloak that made him blend more seamlessly with his bear along the treeline. "They won't risk getting closer; their priority is to protect their home, not instigate us."

"That's right, you would know more about them than us," Serana finally looked away from the Nordorner, setting her gaze on Cressida, "you're a Nordorner, aren't you?"

"Half," Cressida reminded the Sister-Hand, "only half." But Cressida nodded, "But yes, I know quite a bit… We can keep going, just as long as we don't cross into Nordorn, they won't bother us."

One of the riders twisted his lips to the side, thoughtful and cautious. "Not sure it's wise to move just yet…" He tilted his head towards the soldiers disappearing into the tree line. "If they're heading to Wintersong, then they'll be passing through Greenfield no doubt… There could be soldiers ahead, so we can't rush past them…"

Serana growled, hands tightening around the reins. "Then we'll keep pace, and we'll walk along the border; we don't have to worry about Nordorners as long as we don't cross the line, and I highly doubt a Vaestorian soldier has the gall to flirt with it."

The Black Hand riders lingered close to the mountains of Nordorn, but never too close. They pulled on their reins, guiding their horses to step on what would look to be the softest patches of snow. The riders kept their eyes ahead, except for Cressida, who would occasionally glance to the side, keeping an eye on the Nordorner rider that trailed near them.

The eyes of Cressida and the Nordorner locked. There was a clear understanding of what was going on. The Nordorner would follow, ensuring

they did not cross, while the rider would keep going ahead, unbothered by the foreign force, as long as they continued following the line they were meant to.

One Black Hand, the younger rider, was gripping the reins far too tightly, still shivering. His eyes kept darting to the side, eager to look behind him and spot the Nordorner that was following them. But a forest loomed ahead, thick and covered in greens and whites, where their vision would be obscured.

"At ease," one rider hissed to the nervous one, "if you keep shivering, your horse is going to kick you off. They can sense your fear, idiot."

"We have a fucking snowbear tailing us," the nervous Black Hand whispered, "if its rider decides, it can just steer into our direction and fucking eat us!"

"Shut up!" Serana looked behind her. "Or I will personally feed you to the damned thing!" The Sister-Hand twisted better on her seat. "We must remain quiet, just don't cross the damned border!"

"I can't even see the fucking border!" The rider cried. Then he froze as he saw the forest coming into view. "I can't —" he began to bring his horse backwards, causing it step awkwardly, nudging into another rider's horse. "I can't go in there! We'll be easy to pick off!"

Serana saw his horse backing up. "What are you doing?! Stop moving, idiot!"

"I want to go! I don't want to be tortured by Nordorners or be a meal for the Snowbear!" The rider's hands trembled; he kicked his horse, trying to get it to move.

The nervous rider's horse backed up into the other's, its rear hitting the legs of the other. Both began neighing; the second horse had to back up, hitting Cressida's. The snorts and cries of the horses created unrest. The Snowbear let out a bellowing growl — the nervous rider's horse kicked up, turning fast, wandering straight towards the border.

"Wrong way, idiot!" Serana shouted.

The nervous rider held onto the reins, unable to keep his horse from drifting off as it began running to the right—right where the Nordorner sat above his Snowbear, and the Nordorner kept his eyes on the nervous man… and when he noticed his horse cross the tree that had hanging runes… The Nordorner reacted; his massive hand reached for his axe, and once the horse stepped across that border, he pulled it out.

The horse came face to face with the bear, and the horse kicked the rider off as it rose to its hind legs with a cry. It stomped down and quickly turned. The nervous Black Hand gathered himself—only to see the Snowbear looming over him with the Nordorner atop and his greataxe out.

A thundering step from the Snowbear caused the land to tremble. The nervous man began crawling backwards. The Nordorner raised its greataxe, ready to strike —

"Hæt! Hann er kjötskalle!" Cressida shouted.

The Nordorner halted. And in that moment the nervous rider was dragged back by Serana's hand as she rode with her horse, dragging the man back behind the border.

"Við erum ekki á þínir landi!" Cressida continued, pointing at the man that Serana dragged back, "Hann er kjötskalle."

The Nordorner did not answer; he simply placed his greataxe back into his sheath and leaned forward on his saddle. His cold eyes never left the Black Hand.

Cressida felt the tension ease. She turned to Serana. "He's not saying anything — but I don't think he will attack." She looked at the Nordorner again, and she saw how he kept watching them. "He's waiting for us to slip up… He wants a *good* reason to cut us down…"

Serana did not look pleased. She glared down at the nervous man. "You lost your fucking horse. Tell me why I shouldn't throw you over the border?!" She got off her horse then and lifted the man up to his feet and punched him in his gut. "Worthless! Stupido! I should send you back to the Grand Marshal to turn your body into mulch for our hounds!"

"My horse kicked me off!"

"He wouldn't have if you had followed my orders!" Serana slapped the man upside the head. "Now look at me! I will be one rider down! You know why?" She leaned forward, eyes boring into the man's. "Because you will *walk* back to Greymire."

"Walk back?!"

"Think of it as a lesson." Serana kicked him then, shoving him back onto the path they came from. "I've no need for cowards in my ranks."

THE SNOWBEAR
&ITS RIDER

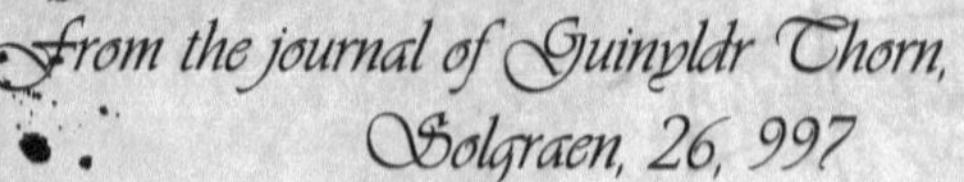

Among the many reasons the
Nordorn military is so
deeply feared, none
inspire greater dread
than the Snowbears
and their riders.
These colossal
beasts, cloaked in white
fur and muscle, stand fifteen feet
at the shoulder and can rear to
heights exceeding twenty-five.
Their jaws are said to rival a dragon's in power, capable of crushing stone
and splintering bone with a single bite. In battle, they move like living
avalanches—unstoppable once in motion, their sheer weight and ferocity
enough to scatter entire ranks.

The riders who command them are no less fearsome. Chosen through brutal trials of endurance and will, they form a bond with their Snowbears that transcends simple mastery.

To outsiders, they appear as madmen; to Nordorners, they are legends. Both beast and rider share a singular bloodlust—the thrill of the hunt, the purity of combat, and the unbreakable pride of the North. Together, they are the embodiment of Nordorn's creed: strength without mercy, and loyalty without fear.

CHAPTER EIGHTEEN
THORNS OF A FLOWER

Since the evening in Killian's office, the Empress had kept herself as far as she could once more, only sharing the bed and meals, but barely. Ambrosja couldn't understand what had happened when she saw his office the way it was, and she understood far less the feeling of something twisting in her stomach, a feeling that was entirely different from what she usually felt. *Not rage*, not something soft and girlish, just something unfamiliar, yet utterly familiar… Something like guilt. *Was it guilt?*

Ambrosja was leaning against the wooden wall of the mining camp. She was looking at her allies. She watched how Donathan had been training with the other Black Hands, forced back in by Lieutenant Berric, insisting they needed all Hands available in case a fight were to come. She watched as Cinder was trying to cheat a miner at a card game. Johann and Gunnar were bickering over something about which Vaestorian regency would win in some grand tournament, a discussion which Ambrosja could barely understand.

Her breath escaped her, heavy and slightly louder than necessary, but not so loud that it stole attention. She kept her arms crossed. Her eyes looked down at the pounded earth beneath her boots, at the pants that were too long, too big for her. *Killian's*. Ambrosja looked at the Command Hall. It was another morning where she hadn't seen him, but she heard him in his office, a mallet swinging, possibly fixing his desk.

She hadn't told her allies what happened. Didn't reveal the broken desk or the torn parchment. Not yet. For some reason, this felt like something that shouldn't be shared…

"Ambrosja," that familiar voice called for her. Warm, deep, vibrating the air like a quake within a lake.

Ambrosja turned and saw Killian. Taking in every detail of his appearance. Killian was dressed for battle: thick, brown leather wrapped his torso, cinched tight beneath a blackened steel chestplate that fit broad across his frame. Spaulders of the same steel guarded his shoulders, each buckle catching the light as he moved. Sturdy leather pants matched the tunic, built to withstand blade and iron alike.

"I've noticed you've been avoiding me." Killian got closer, his shadow fell over her. "I'm afraid that's impossible, I know where you sleep." The Commander saw her face contort, ready to make some remark, and a part of him exhaled, shoulders relaxing when he saw that face, as if it made his chest warm and tighten. Before she could comment, he gave a small grin, already enjoying her reaction. "I am taking on patrol duty today," Killian said, handing Ambrosja's sheathed sword. Her *actual* sword. "And you're coming with me."

Ambrosja's eyes were locked onto Killian's. Then fell onto her sword. Her entire posture shifted. When her hand wrapped around the black sheath of it, she sighed, something similar to contentment and wistfulness, like a piece of her had been returned. Then—she shook her head, blinking as she realized what Killian had said. "Patrol? I am going on patrol with you?"

"Yes." Killian adjusted the fastening of his chestplate. "After what Berric had done, I decided that if I must leave the camp—you will join me." He gestured with a tilt of his head towards the Command Hall. "Go get dressed. I will wait for you at the gate."

Ambrosja's cheeks warmed softly at the idea of her being alone with Killian again, but she quickly tried to bury that. "No—no, no." She shook her head. "I am certain I will be fine while away from you. After all—" she gestured towards her allies, "—I will remain with them."

"She would love to go!" Cinder shouted, suddenly standing not too far. "She's been complaining about how she needs to properly work her limbs, long walks and all! Apparently, that *hunting* outing did wonders for her!"

Ambrosja whipped her head so fast to glare at Cinder, it was a miracle her neck hadn't snapped. Cinder said nothing at the glare, just grinned and gave a thumbs up, giving a lazy call, "I got you!" Ambrosja's nostrils flared, but she didn't fight back, just continued her glare as if that would somehow make Cinder take back her words — it didn't.

Killian's smile was smug enough to blind a god, teeth flashing as his hand settled at the small of her back. Ambrosja stiffened. With the faintest nudge, he steered her toward the Command Hall, silent but undeniable. Ambrosja gripped her sword hard enough that her knuckles had gone bone white. She walked—no—she marched towards the Command Hall, petty fury in every step. Cinder relaxed her hands behind her head, grinning as she watched every step Ambrosja took.

"Cinder," Gunnar whispered, finally taking a seat at the table beside Cinder. "You are going to get that girl so red and so angry one day that not even I will be able to save you."

"I'm sure it'll be worth it," Cinder spoke, not bothering to lower her voice. "Besides, she's been avoiding Killian, typical smitten behavior."

"And he's doing that smile," Johann whispered, joining in on the conversation. "The smile Gunnar makes when he's found a hen he wants to ruffle the feathers of."

"Hey!" Gunnar barked. "I've never—"

"You did it this morning," Johann cut in at once. "To a miner. Said her muscles gleamed just right in the low lights of the oil lamps in the mines. Then you started leaning against the wall, purposely getting her cheeks all red."

"Then you disappeared for ten minutes. With her," Cinder finished, smug.

Gunnar stared at them for a moment before sharply looking away. "A man has needs," that was all he muttered, promptly grabbing his bowl and now departing from his friends.

Within Killian's chambers of the Command Hall, Ambrosja adorned the dark gray leather armor and black pieces of plate she once wore not too long ago. Each buckle fastened like muscle memory, each adjustment made precisely for ease of movement, but each touch of hers lingered too long, as if she sought to distract herself from the touch Killian left on her back, or the way she felt upon seeing him again. She closed her eyes, easing herself back into the role of Empress and into the role of soldier. Now, she was lacing and buckling her boots before giving the tip a gentle kick against the wooden floor to feel it fit her once more—just right—as if she had never removed it.

Ambrosja made her way to the double doors, opening one and clos-

ing it firmly behind her. Her free hand was firmly wrapped around the grip of her sword that was now attached to her left hip, fingers locked around it as if she feared it would part her once more. Her plated boots struck with a clatter; every step down felt like she was charging into a trap with nothing but bare and flushed skin.

Guards flanked the broad double doors that led out of the Command Hall and into the camp. Both guards had their eyes set on Ambrosja. Assessing, not admiring. The breathing of one was steady, but he had his arms crossed tight against his chest, his fingers tapping impatiently against his bicep. The other had her hands on her hips, head angled low, as if she was bored and glaring at Ambrosja's approaching frame was entertaining—or perhaps a challenge. Ambrosja barely glanced at them, chin high, gaze cold, as though they weren't worth her notice.

The Empress spotted Killian leaning against the gates of the camp. His hulking figure dwarfed the Black Hand guards posted around it. She took a deep breath and fought back the heat on her cheeks. She hated this. Hated how, for some reason, just seeing him made her cheeks warm. But she fought it back before she met him.

"Killian," Ambrosja said, her voice carrying a firm and clear tone. She kept her back straight, yet fought to look relaxed. "I am ready for this… patrol of yours."

Killian turned slightly to look down over his shoulder at Ambrosja. That smile of his was creeping back, but smaller, never too wide for the guards, but small enough that it was intimate and hers alone. His calloused hands came to rest on his belt, adjusting the broad leather on his form.

"Very well," he gave a short nod, raising his hand to beckon her to follow. "Let us be off then."

She took a deep breath once and kept walking side by side with Killian. Her golden eyes caught his profile, lingering there, drifting along the lines of his sharp and rough jaw, counting the dark stubbles decorating his skin.

"You're staring, Empress." Killian's lips twitched into something warm and far kinder than ever seen before. His sharp gray eyes moved slowly to the side and down, catching Ambrosja's eyes. "Is this your new tactic now? You've dropped flirting and resorted to staring into my skull? Trying to see the secrets I hide within my mind?"

Ambrosja's cheeks puffed up with air. "I have no interest in learning anything from you. You have made it clear that you do not know much besides *planning* attacks, and whatever else…" She then added, "But if you do know more, I'm sure you will slip up in due time."

Killian laughed—unrestrained. His large shoulders shook, the metal of his spaulders clinked with every shift. His rough hand found the bark of a tree. When his laughing ceased, his hand shifted. For the first time in a while… He let his hand move—invading Ambrosja's space as his rough fingers caressed her puffed out cheek, thumb brushing against her pale skin. "You look like a nibbenscamper with your cheeks like that." His hand cupped her better, bringing her face closer to his. "Hoarding food or fury? Which is it?"

Ambrosja's eyes had gone wide when Killian grabbed her like that. She yanked back, smacking his hand away. "I am hoarding nothing within my cheeks! And I don't even know what a nibscrapper is!"

Killian lowered his hands, his walking resumed once more, and he kept smiling. "A nibbenscamper is a small creature that hoards food within its cheeks. Apparently, the saliva of the creature can keep things preserved, as long as it remains within the pouches. No one quite understands it." He turned to look at her then. "And they look absolutely ridiculous with puffed cheeks. Just like you."

Her eyes didn't meet his. Instead, she kept walking. "I have never had a man speak to me this way," she grumbled. Her boots lifted to avoid crushing plants and flowers. She followed the faint trail that Killian had drifted onto. "Never."

Killian smiled at that. But he didn't comment again. Instead, he focused on their surroundings. The trees grew denser as they ventured deeper into the Bramble, brush, and shrubs forming thick walls of green and amber. Only the music of nature accompanied them; the clamor of the mining camp had vanished entirely—no more chatter, no guards barking orders. Only the buzz of insects, the birds' calls, and the crunch of leaves and twigs beneath heavy boots. The air was cleaner here—pine and earth, divine yet thick in the lungs with a freshness the musty mines could never offer. The sounds were serene, too; a gentle breeze stirred the canopy above while the forest murmured around them. But no matter, Killian's eyes wandered, often, to Ambrosja.

"Tell me something, Empress," Killian spoke, hunching over slightly so his voice could carry closer to her as he walked. "Your betrothed — what is he like? If you are not to bed any man before the age of twenty-five, then what do you two do?"

Ambrosja didn't react immediately, but she did give Killian a sideways glance. "Why do you care?"

"Simple curiosity." Killian's voice was smooth, but the way he kept stealing glances betrayed just how simple it wasn't.

Ambrosja was quiet for a moment. Her eyes looked up into the trees, her mind churned on what to answer. "We engage in conversation."

"Truly?" Killian lifted a brow at that. His hands came down to part the brush away for Ambrosja to pass through. She paused, looked up at him, and gave him a low thank you before walking through. He followed her shortly after, continuing his thought, "I find it hard to believe he does not try to share more than words, like lingering touches."

"He knows better than that."

"Does he?" Killian echoed something close to suspicion. "And what about you?" He moved closer to her now, his presence a heavy weight behind her. "Do you wish he would touch you?"

Ambrosja turned her head to look up at Killian from over her shoulder. "Why are you asking such things? You are being inappropriate again. Like you were at our first dinner."

Killian rubbed a rough finger against his cheek, a sly smile crossing his face. "Well, as I've said before… I've noticed you tremble when I touch you. I wonder if it's because you are not used to such things."

"You're right," the Empress said immediately, "I am not used to *this*," she gestured to all of him. "I am used to men respecting my boundaries, and not crossing lines they should not."

Killian's forearm rested on the trunk of a tree just behind Ambrosja. His other hand found his hip. "But is that what you want, Empress? Men to respect your boundaries? To leave you alone to deal with your problems? To *respect* your space?"

Ambrosja backed up against the tree when Killian leaned in just slightly. Her palms pressed against the rough bark. "That's the proper thing to do."

"Just because it's the proper thing… Doesn't mean it's the thing that *you* want."

She didn't respond right away. Her eyes were on his, thinking about his words. The way they remained within her mind, the way he *said* it. She tilted her face slightly away from him, but her eyes never left his. "It has never *really* mattered what I want, Killian. When you are in my shoes, your wants are not as important as the needs of others."

"But we're not talking about that, Empress." He bent at his hips just a bit more, just so that he was closer to her. "We're talking about desires, love… Courtships, if you will. What you do behind closed doors has no

reflection on your people." He let silence settle between them for a moment as he studied her face, every flicker of her eyes, every little adjustment she made against the bark of the tree. Then he continued, his voice went lower, huskier, his words rolled off a little more slowly, "So, what do *you* want? Not as an Empress, but as a woman—as you, Ambrosja."

Ambrosja's throat could barely work as the proximity between them seemed to slowly disappear, inch by agonizing inch. "You… forget your place, Commander." She then pressed a finger into his chestplate. "And I suggest you take a few steps back before that nose of yours suffers another tragedy."

Killian's hand wrapped around hers, holding her finger against his chest. The size of his hand dwarfed hers. He grinned widely. "I will." He forced her hand open now, pressing her palm flat against his chestplate. "When you answer me."

Her eyes flickered down to her treacherous hand and back up to that infuriating smile he had on. "I suppose I never thought about that." She admitted, not pulling her hand away yet. "I guess I would want someone to push and poke me while I am furious, so I can see that they—they care. That they just won't leave me alone in a room for hours…" She paused there, thinking more. "I want someone fun, someone I can—play with."

"Play with?"

"Play with."

"Play with," Killian repeated. "And what kind of games would you like to play?"

Ambrosja's guard was down now, looking away with a coy smile. "Oh, I don't know—I suppose I would like to get chased."

Killian stared for a moment—then he chuckled. He braced himself against the tree, caging Ambrosja within, but his body was still far enough away to give her space. The Commander tilted his head down; the sound vibrated deep within his chest. "You would like to get chased?" He raised his head to look at her again. "And what do you mean by that?"

"Oh—you know…" She smiled widely, clearly envisioning her every word as her body relaxed against the tree. "Like what you would see those children do, when one chases after the other—but being grabbed tight from behind, tossed over a strong shoulder. I've seen lovers do it through the fields of Nordorn." Her finger had found a curl of her hair, playing with it. "Gentle teasing, playful whispers, lingering glances that say *I can't wait to be alone with you*." She sighed. "I have always wanted that."

Killian saw her—the way her cheeks had dusted to a rosy color, the way she played with her curls, the way she stripped her desires bare before him. His grin had shifted into a half-smile. Something genuine and rare. "Very well." He kept his hands braced against the tree.

"Very well?"

"Mhm," he hummed, straightening himself to his full height. His hands left the tree. "I'll give you ten seconds to get as far away as possible from me…" Ambrosja stared at him, eyes wide with confusion. He continued, "Then—Then I will come chase you down."

But Ambrosja remained there, as if her brain was playing catch-up with what Killian was implying. Her back was flat against the bark, her locks getting stuck on random bits that bent outwards. She only shifted when Killian began counting—his voice low. Teasing. Dangerous.

"One…" He began. "Two… Three…" That was when Ambrosja let out something between a giggle and a yelp and darted from the tree.

Despite the weight of Ambrosja's boots, she lifted her legs high, forcing herself away from Killian as far as possible. She couldn't stop the sounds of joy that left her body, echoing in the thicket of the Bramble. She veered off the path, running down a small mound and heading in the direction of a clearing. The trees spread out further, sunlight beamed down through the open foliage, dancing across her pale locks like fairy dust threaded through each strand. The ground beneath her boots was soft, with patches of grass scattered throughout, and rocks that took on many different shapes and sizes.

The singing of birds had been drowned by Ambrosja's laughter. Laughter that was very much like a young girl learning how to be happy. When Killian reached *ten,* he rolled his shoulders—then sprang into action. His hulking frame barreled down that same mound, and the sounds of metal clinking echoed and mingled with Ambrosja's laughter. His powerful legs carried him to that same clearing in fewer strides. Ambrosja gasped when she heard Killian's heavy footfalls drawing near. She weaved between trees, trying to get herself into tighter spaces that she knew Killian couldn't fit through.

The Commander's laughter boomed through the woods. He didn't bother trying to weave through those same trees; he went around, coming out on the other side to be face-to-face with Ambrosja. Another giggle-yelp left her. She scrambled to the side, weaving around a tree, making her way back to the clearing. Killian didn't falter—he pushed forward.

"You'll find out soon enough that you can't outrun me, Empress!" Killian called out.

Ambrosja could barely get her words through her laughter, "We will—we will see about that!"

She skidded to make a turn. Ducking low as Killian came from behind, his arms moving to wrap around her, but missing as she fell to her knees and began scrambling away. He just stared for a moment, shocked by her determination to evade his grasp. But it was only for a moment—her move only made him want to grab her more.

The drag of the Empress's knees against the grass-covered dirt slowed her. Killian didn't need to run—he marched. His hands came down as he bent at his hips. Ambrosja yelped once she felt Killian's massive hands grasp at her waist, hauling her upwards onto him and tossing her over his shoulder.

"I refuse!" Ambrosja laughed, slapping at his armor. "I refuse to be captured!"

"Nonsense!" Killian bellowed with his laughter, "This is exactly what you wanted!"

Killian carried Ambrosja over his shoulder as he made his way to a thicker patch of grass within the clearing. He adjusted her in his hold, sliding her down to where her chestplate met his, then he eased himself down, bending at his knees until suddenly—he dropped backwards, his back hitting the grass and bringing Ambrosja down with him.

Soft laughter echoed in the clearing, one deep and one soft. The humming sounds of the forest were more present. The clearing felt more serene now that the laughing slowly mingled with bugs and birds. Ambrosja's cheek was pressed to Killian's chestplate. She was breathless with a beaming smile on her face. Her thighs—unconsciously—straddled his broad form. His hands moved low, one resting on her lower back, the other on her thigh. They relaxed into each other, as if they had done this before. As if they had always done this.

Killian turned his head to the side as he spotted a rounded form of fur. He squeezed Ambrosja's thigh to get her attention. His voice dropped to a whisper, "Empress, behold—" he gestured with a slight jerk of his chin in the direction of the creature, "—a nibbenscamper."

Ambrosja turned her gaze to look in the direction that Killian gestured in. At first, she had to look around—squinting between brush, bark, and rock—before spotting the furred creature. Its body was round, the fur was a blend of honey-brown with patches of dark brown near its paws and sides that blended into white fur that disappeared beneath its belly. The ears were short and looked like rounded arrowheads, the eyes were round, big, dark brown, and engrossed in its activity: peeling away leaves that surrounded a red berry. Its fluffy tail seemed to waggle with every leaf that was removed, as if it were pleased with every gentle tug it made.

"That's a nibbenscamper?" Ambrosja whispered, making sure to keep her voice low.

Killian nodded, "Keep watching it, shortly he will place that berry within its pouch."

Sure enough, the nibbenscamper did so. Once the green leaves were stripped from the twig that held the berry, one tiny paw grasped firmly around the stem, the other guided the berry into its mouth, pushing it around until it was firm within one cheek, then at last—both hands gave a firm tug—ripping the stem free from the berry that now sat gently within the nibbenscamper's pouch. Ambrosja's hands rose, covering awe-parted lips once she saw how the cheek of the creature had bulged out.

Her body wiggled with glee upon witnessing the act of the nibbenscamper. The sudden movement caught the eye of the small creature, causing it to retreat on all fours and hop away into the thick brush ahead. She gripped Killian's spaulders tightly.

"Its cheeks!" She released the faintest giggle. "It got so huge!"

"Yeah," Killian chuckled. "They can fit about half of their body weight in their cheeks."

Ambrosja smiled at Killian, looking down at him with the warmest smile she had worn in weeks. Maybe months, even. Then she noticed the proximity—how close they were, how she could smell him—dark berries, something deep with a smoky oak—she had to get up. She removed herself from him, sliding off and pushing herself to her full height.

"That was– very fun," she murmured, brushing the dirt off of her leathers. "Thank you."

Killian's eyes followed her every movement. Steel-gray eyes tracking every wipe and every awkward twitch of her lips. He smiled, small but sincere. "Think nothing of it. I had fun as well."

Ambrosja took a step back, giving Killian space to get up. When he stood, she approached, wiping the dirt off of his back as well as the loose blades of grass that stuck to him and in between his armor. When his back was clean, Ambrosja moved to stand before him, her golden eyes raking over him, searching for every little detail of dirt along his leather and armor. Killian, himself, moved his own hand, massive next to Ambrosja's face, and pulled away a bit of leaves that became tangled in her locks. Their gestures were absentminded, nearly natural—until their eyes locked and they continued. No smile, no words. Just hands roaming to wipe away things that didn't belong. But not each other.

Killian's hand found the side of her neck, his wide palm spanning from her jawline to where his fingers curled behind her neck. He was cupping her face and head. His thumb brushed along her jawline. His touch lingered there. No words were shared, still. Not until—

"Killian?" Ambrosja whispered softly, her eyes searching his.

Killian cleared his throat. "Dirt, on your jaw." He pulled his hand away. "You're clean now." He turned away, making his way towards the mound they had run down. "We should get back onto the trail, Empress."

She remained there for a second longer, her own fingers brushing where his had been—before following after him. "What is this route?"

"A secret one," Killian admitted. "It's mainly used for smaller runs of goods. Take things to and from the nearest outpost."

"And you patrol this weekly?"

"Not always me, but yes, we often take turns patrolling this route." He reached the mound, stepping upwards now, but pausing midway to turn to the side, his hand extending to help Ambrosja up. She took it and he pulled her closer to him. "There are often bandits along this path, or hunters. Can't risk losing shipment or being outed, so it's always best we clear this before the next one goes out."

After reaching the top, Killian began to guide them back the proper way back to the hidden path they had abandoned moments ago. His broad frame pushed aside every branch and brush for Ambrosja. Killian's eyes assessed every inch of the thicket before him. But Ambrosja's eyes? They were on Killian. Her own mind was still caught up with what had happened. Her fingers touched her jaw again.

What is going through his head? Ambrosja thought to herself. *What happened in his office?*

"Are you close with your family?" Killian had interrupted her thoughts.

Ambrosja's eyes flickered up to the sliver of what she could see of his profile. "My family?" She didn't stop walking, but her eyes did drift down towards the ground, brows pinched into something closely resembling distraughtness. "I am close to my grandmother." She looked up again. "She is my only family left."

Killian didn't respond immediately, just glanced over once and nodded. "You took the crown before twenty-five—your mother must've passed early. My condolences." The silence settled for a moment before Killian spoke again, "And what of your father?"

"My father—that is complicated…" Ambrosja took a deep breath, her eyes closing once before she continued. "My father left shortly after my mother passed. He returned years later."

Killian stopped walking entirely. He angled his body to turn halfway, his gaze meeting hers. "I am sorry to hear that. Truly. And what of your be-trothed?"

Ambrosja squinted at Killian now. "You keep bringing up my be-trothed."

His expression had shifted. One brow arched while one corner of his lips tugged into that infuriating half-grin. "Well, you say your grandmother is your only family. But what is he? He is your betrothed, is he *not* family to you?"

"He is a trusted advisor, a great ally, and a fierce warrior."

"Did you choose him?"

Ambrosja narrowed her eyes on Killian. "No, an Empress never chooses her husband—the perfect man is chosen for her by the Elders."

That's when Killian slowed even more, walking beside Ambrosja so he could glance down at her face and keep his eyes there. "And what do *you* think makes a perfect husband?"

She stared at him, lips pressed tight and slightly downturned, eyes still narrowed, but now down to slits as if she was trying to study the fine lines across his form. "I don't know—a kind yet strong man? A man who will stand up for me? Challenge me, but respect me?" Ambrosja shrugged, uncertain and slightly aggressive. "Why are you so interested in Hådvard?"

"Oh—so his name is Hådvard." Killian grinned still. "What does Hådvard look like? How close are you two?"

Ambrosja rolled her eyes. "He is tall, strong, blond hair, blue eyes, the typical Nordorner warrior that every woman desires." Then she waved her hand at the thought, as if wiping it away. "I have told you plenty about him. Now—what about you? How about *your* lovers, hm? And *do not* bring up your meat again."

Killian chuckled. "*My* lovers? Hm, what about them, Ambrosja?"

"Oh—I do not know! Share something as I did!"

Killian genuinely thought about this; that was clear from his silence and how his grin had faded as he pondered Ambrosja's question. "I have been with plenty of women," he admitted, "and as deep as the romance could get — it all eventually became fleeting."

"Have you ever been in love?"

He stopped completely. He looked briefly down at the ground—then at her. "Can't say that I have, Empress." Then he continued down the path.

Ambrosja followed after Killian. "Who was your last lover?"

Killian chuckled, "Oh, Dragon's Breath — a contagiously happy woman named Capricia."

The Empress's stomach twisted differently this time. But the same as it did days ago. *Jealousy.* She took a deep breath, chest rising and lungs filling beyond what was needed.

"You sound fond of her, Commander," Ambrosja said, trying to sound cold, watching Killian attentively now. And she *hated* it. Hated how much she watched him. Hated how much she felt this ugly feeling.

Killian nodded. He scratched his chin, still walking. "I suppose to a point I still am. She's a good woman. I hope the world has treated her kindly."

Ambrosja swallowed. Telling herself to keep her mouth shut — but her throat hurt, as if the words *had* to leave. "And what was she like besides *contagiously happy?*" The last bit was *almost* mocking, almost bitter.

The Commander heard that tone, but he said nothing about it, just smiled to himself. "Physically? Blonde, brown eyes. Last I recall, she was built healthy, I hope she is still in good health." Killian continued to think, "Personality? She's kind, a good woman. Always excitable, and she always wanted to go on an adventure."

The Empress's lips formed a thin line. "She sounds perfect."

The twisting sting inside her stomach was too much to bear. Her chest rose faster, fell harder. She swallowed again. Biting her tongue for the moment. She had to shift the conversation before she let her jealousy rise.

"And your family?"

Killian slowed when Ambrosja asked that question. "You know I have a sister, do you need to know more?"

"…I *want* to know more," the Empress admitted.

The Commander's pace slowed even more, eyes glancing back at Ambrosja. Then ahead. "I have an older brother, and both of my parents are alive."

"Is that all you are going to tell me, Commander?"

"There is nothing else to give."

Ambrosja stopped walking. Killian felt this and stopped as well, facing her.

"Nothing else?" she echoed, "I feel as though I have opened myself up and you still give me nothing—" she stopped herself, growing frustrated. "Fine, give me this…" She took a step closer, almost challenging him. "Do you feel remorse?"

The Commander's eyes narrowed. "Why does that matter?"

"I *must* know," she got close enough where her chin tilted up so her eyes could meet his. "I must know if what stands before me is a monster, or a man, because what I saw in your office was a man who wasn't sure if he enjoyed being a monster or not."

Killian watched her; he always did. His brows had lowered into a scowl. "I do not feel remorse."

"I do not believe you," the Empress said firmly, fists clenched at her sides, only for a moment before her voice rose and her hands gestured in the air, "I refuse to believe you did not feel an ounce of remorse as you beat that poor miner!"

"I didn't," Killian growled, lowering himself. "I delivered a punishment. He had stolen from me."

"He nearly died," Ambrosja hissed.

"But he didn't," Killian lowered himself further, inches from her face, "healers tended to him shortly after. Then he was sent back to Greenfield on a wagon."

Ambrosja remained firm; she didn't back down, didn't stop challenging, and didn't stop scowling. "How you or whomever you ordered to tend to him after does not excuse your violence."

Killian didn't back down either. "And his circumstance does not excuse his theft."

The Empress stared at the Commander, fists clenched at her side. Then she walked past him, following the trail, but Killian wasn't done.

"Don't act like you're better, Empress," he followed after her, "Nordorn would do worse to a thief."

Ambrosja turned sharply, hair snapping and hitting Killian's chestplate. "Worse?! Tell me how much worse we are, Commander!"

"You would have enslaved him until his debt was paid in full," Killian growled, "do not think of me as a man who knows less of your country because I wasn't born beneath the same gods."

"That is different—"

The Commander immediately cut her off, "You're right," he agreed, "it's different. I delivered my sentence in one minute. You would have delivered a punishment that could have stretched over the course of days. Tell me, Empress, what is better: a punishment that is handled and done within a day, or one that is stretched for days, or maybe even years?"

Ambrosja's hand came clean through the air, as if slicing his words. She shook her head. "It is not that simple!"

"You're right again," he didn't raise his voice, just spoke calmly, even with his growling, "and that's the thing, Empress; nothing is simple. I dealt a punishment fitting of the crime under my system; you deal yours under *your* system. Yet you do not see me condemning you."

"I am condemning the actions you took!" Ambrosja took an angry step closer, her jaw tightened, while her finger hit the Commander's chestplate. "I am judging you for the way you acted! For the violence you dealt without showing a single bit of humanity!"

Killian's jaw clenched. He didn't look down at her finger hitting his armor, just her. "I already explained myself, I've no remorse for thieves or criminals."

"What about Wintersong?!"

That made the Commander freeze. His scowl almost dropped. His jaw twitched.

Ambrosja went on, "How about for the innocent lives? The children, Killian! Those who could not wield a weapon! They were all slaughtered in cold blood or burnt alive! Do you feel any remorse for them?!"

Killian kept that stone-cold face on for a moment longer. Then raised his hand to grab onto the bark of a tree. His voice, when it came, was hoarse. "Yes… I do…"

Ambrosja wasn't expecting that. The change in his voice, the way he reached for the tree, or how his eyes closed.

"I feel remorse for every hamlet lost," Killian continued, his voice growing weaker yet angrier, as if the words were in the pit of his throat and he had to force them out, "I feel guilt. I feel… responsible, even though I was not the one who had cast the fires or swung the blades… I still feel it—the weight, the guilt, the pain… I feel all of it, Ambrosja. Is that what you wanted to hear? That I hurt just as you do? Because I do. Very much."

Ambrosja's glare was gone completely. Her lips were parted, taking in calm yet deep inhales of air as she watched Killian. She didn't get closer, didn't get further either. She simply watched how his eyes closed, how his fingers flexed against the tree, how his other hand was grasping at the leather on his thigh.

Then… finally… her hand moved to rest beside his against the trunk he was touching. Their skin nearly brushed, but Ambrosja did not get closer. But she also didn't speak, though her throat burned. The bark was cold, just as was the distance between their hands.

The Nibbenscamper is a small, round forest-dweller, easily recognized by the white streaks along its back and the short, arrow-shaped ears atop its head. Its cheek pouches can hold nearly half its body weight and possess a curious enchantment that preserves whatever is stored within.

Once, they were hunted relentlessly for this gift. Trappers sought to harvest the pouches, believing the magic could be extracted and repurposed. Such efforts failed. Upon death, the enchantment dissipates entirely, leaving nothing but flesh and fur. When this truth became widely known, the slaughter ceased—not out of mercy, but futility.

In the years since, Nibbenscampers have come to dwell near towers, academies, and forest libraries, often welcomed by mages and scholars who recognize both their utility and their gentle disposition. They are docile creatures, fond of warmth and routine, and form quiet bonds with those who treat them kindly. Many will choose a single caretaker, following them faithfully and allowing only trusted hands access to their pouches.

Though harmless, they are not tools. To mistreat a Nibbenscamper is to lose its trust forever, and a distressed creature will empty its pouches and flee, scattering its contents to the roots and moss. When respected, however, they serve as living vaults—keepers of letters, seeds, charms, and truths best kept safe, carried not by lock and key, but by trust.

THE NIBBENSCAMPER

CHAPTER NINETEEN
PETALS OF INK

Commander Killian Thorn had remained silent. After their hands nearly brushed, Ambrosja and Killian stared at each other without speaking words. His own breathing had been deep and sharp, like a man coming undone, and Ambrosja's was calm, like a soldier waiting to be leaned on. But that moment never came.

Killian had brushed past her, calm but heavy steps. His gaze wouldn't meet hers anymore, and he had returned back to the woods, leading the Empress back to the mining camp.

And now... Ambrosja followed, a few steps behind him.

Ambrosja *ached* to reach out; her hand kept rising further than it would naturally sway, fingers curling like she hesitated to touch the Commander. She couldn't help but wonder if she should have spoken—if she should have offered comfort.

"Killian—" The Empress started to speak—only to release a sharp and haunting gasp as she felt something drag her back into the woods.

Killian turned on his heel immediately, "Ambrosja!" He didn't hesitate. He ran to where he saw her disappear into, following the sounds of her panic.

Ambrosja's hand tried to reach for the hilt of her sword, holding on tight so as not to lose it as her body hit every bump, branch, and rock. Feather and fur were all her eyes could see through the darkened foliage as kicked dirt had blurred her vision. She heard the heavy falls of what sounded like sharp claws ripping through grass and dirt. Roots pulled on Ambrosja's locks, the pale strands now darkening with reds and browns, clumps of the ground entangled into her hair.

Killian wasn't gaining any ground, and whatever had taken Ambrosja was moving faster. The Bramble was turning darker. The greens and ambers of the leaves overhead faded into shades far darker, all a blur to Ambrosja's vision. The sun barely broke through the leaves now.

Killian ran, hopping over logs and rocks. He parted branches with his broad frame, splitting shrubs with his hands like a giant shoving boulders. His eyes had narrowed into slits of fury, and his pace echoed his resolve. "Ambrosja!" He had called to her again. "I'm on my way!" Killian stormed through the darkened woods. His ears followed the strangled gasps and the breaking of branches while his eyes followed the trail of a body being dragged.

"Killian!" Ambrosja had called back, breaking her silence with a panicked cry for help. Her hand wrapped around a root protruding from the ground — briefly — it snapped in an instant as the beast kept barreling forth. She screamed again as the bark broke beneath her fingertips, splinters wedging into her skin. "Killian!"

"Ambrosja!" Killian picked up his pace now, barreling through the woods without a second thought in his head besides *Save her!* The sweat on his brow had gone unnoticed, the ache in his knees was nonexistent—same for the pain that struck his arm from a thick branch, like it hadn't even touched him. His sole focus was on the woman being dragged into the unknown by a creature he hadn't even seen.

The creature had slowed, entering a decrepit clearing where the trees curved outwards and upwards like a twisted spire, encircling the space like guardians from long ago. It swung its tail wide, throwing Ambrosja into the thick trunk of a nearby tree. Her back hit the bark, and just as it did, a sharp breath of air left her lungs. She fell on her side and rolled a few feet from the tree. Her dirtied locks covered her face as she tried to pick herself up; her knees and elbows struggled to pull herself upwards onto all fours. The air felt suffocating, she closed her eyes tightly, trying to steady her spinning mind.

Killian's form broke through the brush and skidded to a halt once he stood before the creature. His eyes widened, his body coiled tight, his back hunched low, and his knees bent as he stared at it. His eyes drifted from the long, dark furred tail to the powerful hind legs covered in black fur. The fur crept up the front of his body, tall and powerful enough to overpower a bear. The fur shifted into feathers around the shoulders and up the head, a raven-like head with a long, sharp beak. White, round eyes decorated each side of its head. Its paws ended in sharp, black talons that clicked against the ground.

The cold eyes of Killian flickered to Ambrosja's weakened form. "Ambrosja," he whispered low—then ran, wrapping around the creature to reach on the other side.

The tail came crashing down, stopping Killian in his tracks. Killian staggered back, just shy of being slammed down into the ground by the powerful tail. He looked at the creature once, their eyes meeting each other, then back at Ambrosja.

"Ambrosja!" He called to her, his voice laced with fury and worry.

The creature's head turned to the side, one eye locked on Killian, the other on Ambrosja's struggling form. Ambrosja had finally managed to pull herself onto her fours—her fingers dug into the ground, her head tilted upwards, her eyes focused on the creature. She pulled herself upright immediately. Her eyes had gone wide now as she took in the monstrous size of the danger before her.

"What in the frozen hells is that, Killian?!"

"A Mourntalon, a monster of the Bramble!" Killian explained with urgency, but his eyes could barely stay on the massive creature, he kept looking at Ambrosja. "Are you okay?!"

Ambrosja nodded, she tracked every movement of the beast. Her feet backed against the thick tree behind her, moving to the side now, inching closer and closer to move around it—until the head of the Mourntalon snapped in her direction, the tail began to coil low against the ground, like a scorpion tail readying to strike.

"No!" Killian shouted, whipping out his sword with the deftness of a man who had done this a hundred times before.

He lunged forward, his sword rose high over his shoulder—only to come swinging down heavily into a point, the tip of the blade plunging into the midpart of the tail. The Mourntalon shrieked and Killian used all of his strength to drive the sword deep into the ground.

The beast yanked its tail with a guttural cry. Killian vaulted over it, palm slapping down for purchase as he flipped to the other side. His feet landed firmly, and he didn't waste a second. He rushed over to Ambrosja, his hands found her shoulders, turning her to him.

"Are you hurt?" Killian's voice was raw—urgent. His fingers brushed away the tangled mess of pale bangs that covered her golden eyes. She shook her head, and Killian released a breath he didn't realize he was holding in.

Then they heard the gritty sound of dirt and stone against steel,

scraping and grinding. The Mourntalon was lifting its tail, dragging the sword out from deep within the ground. Black ooze slopped from the wound. Ambrosja and Killian both stared as the appendage lifted with menacing ease. Then their eyes shifted to meet the beast's face and chest, watching how the feathers rose and fluffed, how its chest puffed like a dragon inhaling smoke.

The shriek was loud, piercing like a glass splintering in the throat, laced with a primal resonance that vibrated from deep within its being—as if the very air trembled to its rhythm. The pitch-black ooze spat from its beak with its scream, like splatters of ink hitting upon parchment. Ambrosja shrank into Killian's arms. He drew her against him, twisting just enough to cover her—yet never once turning his back on the beast.

Their hair was tousled, a mess of knots and clumps of black hung in strands. When the shriek was over, the Mourntalon pulled back, then lunged—Killian pushed Ambrosja away as he took a wide step back. The long beak struck into the tree with a deadly force.

The beak was stuck—for now—into the bark of the trunk. The sound of wood splintering and groaning echoed around it. The Commander immediately turned on his heel, heading for the tail where his sword was stuck. Killian stepped onto the tail, gripped the hilt, and ripped his sword free with a sickening tear of flesh.

Ambrosja was already running to meet Killian from the other side, her own sword removed from its sheath now. She held it with two hands, her eyes locked on the beast as it pulled its beak free with newfound strength and screeched from its flesh being torn by a blade.

"Killian!" Ambrosja called, rushing to his side. "You know what this thing is! How do we kill it? What are its weak spots?!"

Killian shook his head. "This thing can't die, not really," he muttered. "We'll have to just cut it down the best we can."

She whipped her head to stare at Killian. "What do you mean it can't die?!"

"It's a creature from the Veil! Even if we manage to 'kill' it—it'll just come back!"

The Mourntalon turned—slow and deadly—its eyes already locked onto the both of them. Its hips started to sway with a slight bounce to it, the midpoint of the tail followed the rhythm of its legs while the tip was slowly coiling tight. Ambrosja and Killian both took notice.

"Why is it moving like that?!"

Killian briefly looked at the hips and tail, then back to the creature's face. "It's getting ready to swipe with its tail—it's just trying to decide which

of us to target."

"And do you know which?!"

"No! Hard to tell when it's got an eye on each side of its skull!"

That's when the tail rose high and fast—swinging down even faster in between Killian and Ambrosja—forcing the two to part once more. Ambrosja ended up closer to the side of its rear, while Killian was closer to the beak. The Mourntalon tilted its head just enough so each eye was tracking each threat.

"It doesn't want us close!" Ambrosja called out from behind.

"It's not intimidated by being flanked," Killian shouted back, his feet now crossing one over the other as he tried to circle it. "You'll have to move with me—if we're still, we'll be easy to keep track of, but if we're moving—"

"It'll have to focus on us harder!" Ambrosja finished and followed Killian's footsteps, both circling the hulking beast now.

The Mourntalon noticed. It shrieked again, its throat throbbing as it tilted its head back. It spun. The tail came around, slashing wide from behind Ambrosja and spinning until it met Killian. Ambrosja ducked, then swung her sword after it, barely grazing the skin. Killian had to drop low to the ground, rolling onto his side and lying flat on his back as the tail came over him. With his frame on the ground, the Mourntalon lunged—its talons came down onto Killian's broad frame. Its back talon caged him on the right side, while its furthest talon caged him on the left, and two in the center began to push into his chestplate. Killian groaned under the crushing pressure. His sword fell; his hands shot up, straining against the force pressing into his chestplate.

Killian's guttural growl rose into a fierce warcry—echoed back by the Mourntalon, two monsters locked in a standoff. His ears rang from the beast's shriek, but he didn't falter. He only pushed back harder, his hands strained around the talons as he lifted the sharp points from his chestplate, bending them backwards. Ambrosja's cry for him was drowned beneath the roars of both beasts, but Ambrosja ran, dragging her sword behind her with both hands and raising it high as she inched closer to the Mourntalon's foot, then swiped wide across the ankle.

The massive body of the monster arched, nearly putting all of its weight into Killian as the slash of Ambrosja's sword hit deep—not deep enough to cut off, but deep enough where its black blood gushed in thick streams. Killian's eyes narrowed onto the deep gash—he pulled. The beast's cry echoed like nails scraping across glass and stone. Killian twisted his body, a guttural shout left him as he pulled harder—the flesh ripped, a sickening sound followed by the crunch of bone—then the foot was severed.

Sputters of black sprayed in the clearing, like a perfect arch made from death's inkwell. The Mourntalon fell onto its side, and Killian rolled the opposite way, abandoning the monstrous foot. He stood up beside Ambrosja now, kicking his weapon off the ground and holding the hilt with one hand, rolling his wrist to adjust his hold.

"One leg down," Killian growled.

Ambrosja's voice trembled, "I've fought men, Killian—not monsters…"

Killian risked taking his eyes off the beast. "Ambrosja, look at me." Ambrosja obeyed, and Killian saw it all, from her wide eyes to her trembling hands. "There is no difference between monster and man, the only difference here? That creature is huge, far bigger than anything you've fought—but that doesn't make it more dangerous. Trust me." Ambrosja gave a frantic nod. "Good," Killian whispered. "Now, battle like you always have, just be smarter, be aware."

The Mourntalon's shoulders shimmied, its feathers standing along with its fur as it stared at them. Silent. Watching. Weighing. Its pale eyes studied them both. Ambrosja and Killian were wound tight, their chests heaving. The Mourntalon didn't wait another second—it lunged forward. Ambrosja and Killian parted once more as the beak aimed for the space between them. Then it spun again. It extended its tail, this time aiming high, then switching low at the last second. The Empress jumped too late—she tripped—the tail then whipped back and coiled around her waist, holding her tightly while its wing opened, not giving the Commander space to dodge—forcing him to be pushed back. He lost his footing and rolled backwards, losing his grip on his sword.

A talon slammed down, pushing Killian's fallen sword further from reach. He found his footing right as the Mourntalon barreled forward again, using its head to send Killian into the hardened trunk of a tree, then promptly tossing Ambrosja onto him. The two collided with heavy grunts, their chestplates smashing into each other followed by their bodies hitting the ground.

Ambrosja coughed, the air had escaped her lungs from the impact. She moved to get onto her fours. "We have to get rid of that tail!"

Killian grunted, rolling onto his side. "Fine—you get the tail, I'll keep its beak occupied."

The Empress didn't wait another second, her sword was still in her hand and she charged forward, but she didn't go around—no—*The beast would expect that.* She went under it—running fast then dropping to her knees and tilting herself backward, slipping beneath the beast.

Killian moved right after—he rolled flat onto his back and sprang onto his feet in one fluid motion. He flexed his arms, fists circling one another before he hammered a barrage of blows into the Mourntalon's face. Each punch delivered a sharp crack that mingled with the rapid bursts of screeching from the beast. Ambrosja slipped out from beneath it, then used the momentum of her glide to lift her leg, planting her heel into the dirt and turning. Her hand moved fast. Sword swiping forward and down onto the tail. Slicing two feet away from the tailbone.

Blood sprayed again, the Mourntalon released another haunting cry that was soon interrupted by Killian's fist meeting its throat.

Ambrosja moved again. One leg rose, her boot finding purchase on the backside of the Mourntalon's body. When the creature felt boots upon its body, it began to thrash. Killian wrapped his arms tight around the beak, forcing the beast's head to bow against his chest. The Commander growled while using all of his strength to hold the Mourntalon's upper body in place.

The Empress walked along the spine, almost losing her footing a few times. She drove her sword down, stabbing into the thick fur and piercing its flesh. The Mourntalon thrashed harder, its beak straining for another cry. Finally—it shifted its weight onto one side of its body, forcing the duo to roll with it.

A sharp gasp mixed with a grunt escaped Ambrosja when she felt the passing weight of the heavy creature roll over her. Killian grunted. Still attached. Still holding on. He shifted himself, wrapping a leg around the neck to come out above it, but the Mourntalon simply turned over again, lying on its back, crushing Killian beneath its head and neck. Killian roared in pain but refused to release his grip. The beast felt this and began raising its neck to lift its head off the ground—then slamming it back down. Again and again.

"K-Killian!" Ambrosja rose to her feet, one hand clutching her ribs while the other still held onto her sword. Her feet moved before she realized it. She charged for the belly of the beast, releasing a war cry from her lips before stepping onto its body and puncturing the very core of it.

The Mourntalon let out a prolonged cry, its body vibrated with each tremble of its throat. Then a talon lashed upward, flinging Ambrosja from its belly. Claws raked her face as she slammed into a tree. The beast moved again, even while the dark blood flowed out of its body, it rose and thrashed its head from side to side. Its movements were erratic. Unpredictable. Killian began to lose his grip on the neck of the creature, but he released another warcry, forcing his arms to wrap tighter His eyes narrowed down to slits as he bared his teeth and began to choke the Mourntalon with his arms.

The eyes of the beast twitched. It rolled onto its back yet again, attempting to crush Killian into the earth, but the Commander only held on tighter. He shouted like he was vanquishing all of the wrath within his bones.

Gurgles were heard. The crushing of bones. Snapping and popping. The Mourntalon's three legs thrashed in the air as its body writhed from side to side—until stillness took over—but Killian didn't let go. He tightened his hold, then planted the heel of his boots into the ground. He lifted himself up, carrying the beast with him as he groaned, then—*snap*. With a sharp wrench, he squeezed the creature's neck so tightly that the bones within it cracked and crushed. The beast slumped, slipping from Killian's grip to fall.

Killian stared at the beast for a second, then his gaze shot to Ambrosja leaning against the tree. "Ambrosja!" He called for her. He rushed forward, skidding to a halt and falling to his knees. His arms wrapped around her, urgently brushing her hair from her face.

"That burns…" Her voice was a hoarse whisper. Her fingers touched the gashes across her face—three of them—from the edge of her jawline to her forehead.

He fixed his grip on her. He scooped her up into his arms, one hand bracing behind her back, the other beneath her legs. "I got you, I'll get you to a healer." He stood up without a second thought, already moving, adrenaline still pumping.

Ambrosja placed a hand onto Killian's chest. "No, it is fine—"

Killian refused. "Absolutely not, this is my fault, I will—"

"Killian," Ambrosja said firmly with a wince escaping. "I can heal."

"Right. That's right," Killian finally allowed himself to fall to his knees, never once dropping the Empress.

Ambrosja winced when she touched her face. Her skin shifted, like threads joining together, blending seamlessly. And finally, both of them relaxed. Killian fell onto his back. His hand moved to the back of Ambrosja's neck, fingers threading into her pale locks, just keeping her close.

The sounds of something crumbling caught their attention, like large pieces breaking into smaller ones. They looked ahead to where the Mourntalon was. Its body was crumbling, bit by bit, until it turned into a pile of dust. The dust shifted; something was moving within it. Ambrosja was alert, but looked to Killian for guidance. When she saw he was still calm, she looked back at the pile of dust. And out came a Mourntalon chick. Dark feathers fluffed as was its fur, its eyes too big for its head. It looked around, spotting Ambrosja and Killian, prompting a resonant hiss—before disappearing into the woods with quickened hops.

"Nothing to fear," Killian whispered with a smile. "...For a few weeks."

Ambrosja let out a laugh, then outstretched her entire body on Killian's lap. "I feel so disgusting." She wiped the black ooze from her armor.

"Me too," Killian stood then, still carrying Ambrosja but gently setting her back down to her feet.

The two gathered their fallen swords, sheathing it now that the battle was over. They were dragged far from the path, Killian recognized this, and gave a once over to figure out his footing. But he was soon distracted by the Empress's voice.

"Hey!" Ambrosja was looking through the trees, her head turned, tilted slightly downwards. "I think there is a river nearby! I hear the sound of rushing water!"

Killian exhaled deeply. Relief coming over him. "A river sounds like a gift right now," he adjusted his armor and walked to stand beside Ambrosja, this time his hand wrapped around her hand. "Just in case," he muttered. "Wouldn't want you being dragged away again."

Ambrosja's eyes were set on their joined hands, cheeks burning hot like they did hours ago, she didn't bother trying to fight back the heat. "Of course, understandable." But still, she kept her voice cool. "Let's head off, then?"

They stepped forward, moving down a grass-covered mound, one eager yet exhausted step at a time. The Bramble seemed to shift. The canopy above opened up more, the late afternoon sun beamed through the parted tapestry. The leaves and grass were vibrant once more, the trees glowed above them. The song of birds returned and the humming of bugs was soft. The sounds of nature were a welcoming tune.

The gentle rushing of water was no longer a whisper, but a present sound of reprieve. Killian and Ambrosja emerged from the brush to see how the golden sun shone down on the glistening and clear surface. The river was wide and deep enough to swim in. A cascade resided not too far, rocks formed like steps where the water could flow down; descending into the very pool that the duo stared at.

Killian wasted no time—he walked forward, already undoing the buckles of his armor and dropping his chest plate, his spaulders, all of it. He only stopped walking when he reached the very edge.

"I'm going swimming," Killian said, pulling the laces of his leather tunic open and tugging the fabric off of his tanned, broad and scarred shoulders. "You should as well."

Ambrosja watched, her eyes went wide as she watched Killian's hands tug on the laces of his pants now—followed by him pulling it down without a second thought. Her voice faltered, "I–I am not quite sure I should go swimming."

"I thought you said you felt disgusting."

"Oh—I do! But—I am not sure it would be proper."

Killian scoffed, but not coldly. "Ambrosja, there is nothing improper about a woman itching for a bath after a giant bird had bled all over her." He looked at her now. "I promise not to look." He shot her a wink and turned away to shed the rest of his clothing—even his dark nethercloths—Killian heard the muffled whimper that escaped Ambrosja and his grin went wide.

His bronzen-toned body met the surface of the water, the splash of water echoed in the woods around them. Droplets graced Ambrosja's face burnt hot as she noticed just how clear the water was. She wasn't a stranger to the bodies of men; Ambrosja had hosted many parties that ended with bodies on top of each other by the end of the night while she watched from her throne, but with Killian—this was different.

The Commander emerged. His dark hair whipped back, his rough hands rubbed along his face as his muscles flexed all over his body, the sun beat down onto the droplets of water that graced his glistening skin. He then submerged again, swimming in the crystal-clear water.

Ambrosja's one boot moved over the other. She watched for a little bit longer, and the water looked too good. She gave in. Her hands found the buckles of her own armor, and she undid them just as Killian did. Stripping down to her linens. But only there. She kicked her boots to the side, and her feet got closer and closer to the edge of the water. Killian breached the surface once more, but slowly this time, stopping suddenly when he saw Ambrosja. His gaze tracked her every move, unintentional and yet unashamed. Ambrosja looked up and caught this—she covered herself with her hands immediately.

"You said you would not look!"

"An accident," Killian admitted, but he didn't stop looking. "Though I don't regret it." Killian turned away then, out of respect.

Ambrosja sighed with a smile and walked into the water; a gentle hum of contentment escaped her. She moved softly, slowly. Inching closer to Killian's frame. She lowered herself into the water, her lips parted to fill her cheeks. Then she emerged, the movement sudden as she spat water like a fountain onto Killian's back. The Commander froze up, eyes wide in shock, but in an instant his face shifted into something close to dangerous amusement. He turned around fast, scooping Ambrosja over his shoulder

and dragging her into the water with him. She yelped, clawing at his broad back while laughing.

The two of them lingered long in the river. Laughter echoed, and sloshing and splashing were heard. Birds that stopped to drink quickly moved further away to avoid being hit by the splash zone. Ambrosja and Killian barely noticed the sun was beginning to go down.

When they emerged, Killian had his arms wrapped tight around Ambrosja's frame as they walked out of the river together, his hands moving along her arms to keep her warm from the sudden cold that brushed their skin. When they reached their clothes, Killian grabbed his linen long shirt and wrapped it around Ambrosja.

"You can't remain in your wet linens, Empress," He said warmly, "remove them, so they can dry, and you can be warm." Killian then turned away, sliding his nethercloths on.

Ambrosja nodded. She understood the logic, but it felt… forbidden. But she didn't stop herself. Not this time.

She peeled off layer by layer until she was bare. The linen tunic, another article far too big for her, slid over onto her frame, swallowing her figure entirely. She laughed as she looked down, noticing how the ends of it came to her knees.

"What do you find so amusing, Empress?" Killian asked, eager to turn his head, but fighting not to.

Ambrosja walked, still laughing, softer now, and stood in front of him. She grabbed at the midsection of the tunic and pulled it away from her frame. "I keep forgetting how you're so big! It's so ridiculous!"

Killian's lips twitched, a smile forming on his lips. "Yeah—I suppose it is." The Commander forced himself to turn away, to drop the smile, but not the warmth. He looked around, finding something to do. "The sun is setting, by the time we're ready to leave, it'll be dark. We should camp." He rubbed his chin. "The Mourntalon wasn't too far, which means other predators haven't occupied this space. We'll be safe here tonight."

Ambrosja agreed immediately, but for other reasons. "That sounds wise. We wouldn't be able to see properly in the Bramble without some sort of light to guide us."

Killian slid his pants up now. "I'll go get the firewood; you stay here, get comfortable." He gestured to the edges of the woods, "I'll be along the edges, so you'll always see me, alright?"

Ambrosja nodded and moved to organize their clothes, folding the fabrics and laying them over rocks. Killian watched, his gaze softened—then he turned to work as well.

"Alright," Berric called out to the whole camp. "The Commander has been gone for hours. So, we're organizing a little search party to go find him, while I'm off, Wex will be in charge."

"What about our friend?!" Cinder rose to her feet. "She went with him!"

"Yeah, yeah. We'll find her as well." Berric took a few steps forward, looking at Cinder. "In fact, you can come along. You and…" He pointed at Johann next. "You, clergyman. You're coming. We might need all the healers we can take."

Gunnar stood, nearly toppling the table from how abrupt he was. "You aren't gonna take them without taking me."

Berric was already halfway turned when Gunnar called out. Berric rolled his shoulders and looked at Gunnar. "Fat chance I'll let you tag along, next thing I know—you're all trying to escape with your pale friend. Not happening. You'll stay here along with the Black Hand traitor," he gestured to Donathan at that. "Right now, we need a hunter and a healer, not a barbarian and a fire mage. We got plenty of those." Berric called out to the camp next, "Fifteen minutes! Then we move out!"

Ambrosja and Killian were next to each other. His arms were wrapped tight around her, keeping her close—their excuse was warmth, but that was a lie, and they both knew it.

They stared up at the stars together, watching the two moons in the sky. The smaller one had a shade of soft blue and was ever-so-slowly moving in front of the other one, the one that was bigger and brighter with a creamy color.

"Elyra is going to hide Arkenna soon," Killian murmured.

"Elyra is your smaller one, and Arkenna is your bigger one?" Ambrosja asked, looking up at Killian.

"Yes, and yours are Vardmara and Skjoldna."

"Your pronunciation of Nordorner names is quite good." Ambrosja smiled now. "Do you speak any of it?"

Killian shifted them both. Propping himself onto his elbow so he could look down at Ambrosja. He brushed a few damp strands away. "Ja, Sóleygr."

Ambrosja's breath caught. Her eyes dared dip down to his lips, then up to those cold gray eyes that didn't seem so cold anymore. "Sun-eyed is normally a term of endearment meant for a loved one."

"So-er." Killian gave a smug shrug.

"Now you are showing off," her brows furrowed, but she couldn't help but smile.

She turned away, and Killian immediately pulled her close to him, his chest against her back. The slightest exhale escaped her, something close to surprise and need. She felt that creeping feeling of guilt again. She pulled away as Wintersong and Hådvard hit her heart.

"Ambrosja?" Killian looked down at her again.

There was silence from her. She wouldn't meet his gaze. "I am sorry…" she shifted further from him. "I just — I cannot…"

"Don't," he said immediately, "don't apologize." But Killian noticed how Ambrosja curled further into herself. "You're cold…" he thought for a moment. "How about this?"

The Commander turned completely, his back touching hers. Ambrosja felt it, and she softened. The gesture was kind, thoughtful, close without feeling like she was betraying anyone… But she still thought about Wintersong. Her body was still stiff.

"What's plaguing you?" Killian's voice was lower, calmer… kinder.

"I—" Ambrosja sighed. What could she say that she hasn't already said before? She closed her eyes tightly. "I just feel like I am betraying my vow by being this close."

"Your vow?"

"My vow to avenge Wintersong," the Empress explained. "You say you did not bring the hamlet to ruin… and I believe you, but — but I am still conflicted. Very conflicted, because you are still tied to those who did."

Killian listened, and he took his time to respond. "I understand — better than you think, Empress." He looked over his shoulder, "Though I must ask, *why* are you so conflicted? We know where you stand. This—*this*—is convenient. Warmth. Quiet. But when you leave this camp…? I know that our blades will cross."

"Will they?" She looked over her shoulder as well. "Because a part of me wonders if they should—If they must—and truthfully... I wish for them not to cross."

The Commander's eyes were locked on the Empress's, and for a moment, neither spoke. Then, gently, he reached over, his hand finding hers, bringing it to his lips. "They needn't cross, if you ask that they don't, Empress."

The sun beamed down. Branches broke. Killian snapped wide awake, his hand already gripping the hilt of his sword, when he faced the direction of the noise. Bringing Ambrosja close to him. She woke up next, startled. When she recognized the commotion, her hands moved to cover herself better with the fabric of Killian's shirt. The Commander noticed this and immediately shielded her lower half with his body.

"The fuck is this?" Berric questioned, his tone dripping with subtle annoyance. "We travel all night to find you lot, and here you are, cuddling like everything in the realm is perfect."

Killian's arm eased from Ambrosja's frame, only for his hand to grab at another scrap of clothing to cover her. He stood to his full height right after, bare-chested and unbothered. "Watch your tone, Berric, you respond to me."

"Right..." Berric gave a tilt of his head. "Well, now that we found you, can we get on with it?"

Cinder and Johann rushed to Ambrosja's side. Cinder wiped Ambrosja's hair away from her face, Johann turned Ambrosja's arms around, as if they were checking for signs of danger or distress.

"I am fine. Stop—stop doing that, Cinder!" Ambrosja shoved Cinder's hands away, but not aggressively.

Johann sighed, a sound of relief escaping his lips. "She's fine."

"Good," Cinder muttered. "Gods, I thought he took you out here to execute you, or that maybe you executed him and then ran away."

"No—no, we just got lost—fought something, then found a river."

Killian watched the way Ambrosja's allies fussed with her. His gaze was focused on only her. Berric noticed this.

The Lieutenant's voice dropped to a whisper. "Easy, Commander, keep staring at that girl and everyone here will think you've gone soft. Hells, some of us already do."

Killian's jaw clenched, but he didn't respond. He didn't bother because he refused to peel his gaze away from Ambrosja.

THE MOURNTALON

The Mourntalon is among the most dreaded of creatures— an immortal predator, twisted from what was once radiant.

Long ago, these beings were known as Emberion, creatures of celestial beauty that soared like burning stars above the lands, their wings leaving trails of golden light. But when the Fracture tore the world asunder and Chaos Magic bled into creation, their brilliance was undone, now tainted and connected to the Veil.

What once burned with the sun now dwells in shadow — black as the void, cold as the grave.

The Mourntalon is drawn to places where magic gathers thick as mist, feeding not on flesh but on dominance and instinct. It hunts for territory, not hunger, and its piercing cry can shatter silence like a thunderclap, leaving the ears ringing and the mind unsteady. Its talons are said to rend steel and sunder wards, and even in death, the creature endures. When slain, the Mourntalon's form collapses into ash — from which a chick rises, reborn, reaching full strength within weeks. Thus, death is no true end to the Mourntalon, only a breath between hunts.

CHAPTER TWENTY

ACHE, FORBIDDEN

Ambrosja stared at Killian's side of the bed from where she sat at the dining table. The silence around her was deafening. She didn't hear the miners or the Black Hand beyond her own threshold despite the windows being open. She paid no mind to the birds singing. The sounds of work and training didn't reach her.

The only thing that reached her was the memory of Killian's lips against her hand. The memory made her fingers curl softly against the table. The hair along her skin raised.

A raven landed before her and she flinched. Her mind finally snapped itself away from those memories that only made the guilt she carried to bury deeper into her skin. Ambrosja took a deep breath, then looked at her raven properly.

The feathered creature was carrying a letter in its mouth.

"Hådvard," the Empress whispered to herself. She retrieved the letter, unrolling it with an expression that gave nothing away. She didn't frown, she didn't beam. She simply opened it. "What do you want now?"

> *Ambrosja,*
>
> *Come back. Your grandmother worries, the people question, and I grow tired. A Vaestorian hamlet is not worth your time or your heart. I stay put because you trust me to lead Nordorn, and that is not a task I take lightly, but you are the Empress of Nordorn, not of some Vaestorian pit, and I suggest you act like it.*
>
> *Hådvard*

Ambrosja stared at that letter, her brows lowered to a scowl. She looked to Killian's side of the bed again, noting the inkwell and scraps of paper there that he had left behind. She noticed he hadn't been as organized lately. *No matter,* the Empress thought to herself, she got up from her seat and walked to the inkwell — but stopped once she was right there. Her gaze drifted down to Killian's side of the bed. And... her hand tentatively reached out, then pulled away sharply, as if she had been burned.

Fingertips met her forehead as she turned away. *Gods, what is wrong with me?* she asked herself as she released a shaky breath, dragging her hand down her face and stopping at her burning cheeks.

Ambrosja placed her hands on her hips, tilting her head down to glare at the floor beneath her feet. Her fingers pressed into the fabric of her belt. Then—finally—she grabbed the inkwell and moved back to the desk, where she dropped herself to sit at her chair once more, now redirecting her glare to the letter before her. The raven shook its feathers, dropped one right beside the parchment, then took a hop to the side. The Empress didn't waste time. Once the quill was in her grasp she had dipped it into the inkwell.

> *Hådvard,*
>
> *You will remain where you are. You will do as you are meant to. You took my father's position when he passed... Now act like the man you are meant to be and accept my word, the word of the Empress, or step down.*
>
> *Ambrosja*

Ambrosja stared at that letter longer than she meant to. The quill had curved from how hard she pressed down, and her chest was still heaving even after she finished writing. Her curls fell in front of her face as she stared down...

The letter was rolled up soon after, and she handed it to her raven, which promptly hopped off the table and flew towards the window, disappearing into smoke and feathers.

She stared again, but this time out the window, towards the mountains of Nordorn, so tall and grand, rumored to be seen all the way in Mercinari. She sighed, hands finding her neck, resting there as her eyes drifted down towards the wood of the table and her eyes stuttered over every grain.

"Release him!"

Ambrosja stood up abruptly. She recognized that voice. It was Killian's. She rushed to the window, her upper body stumbled out of it as her hands grasped at the frame to steady her body. Her hair fell forward as she looked to see where Killian was.

"I said, let go of him!" Killian repeated, grabbing at the Black Hands

who were restraining Gunnar.

"But, Commander!" One Black Hand was trying to speak before being tossed across the camp.

The Empress wasn't sure what she was expecting to see, but she was not expecting to see Gunnar, enraged, in the middle of the mining camp, being surrounded by Black Hands. He tried to swing towards Killian, but Killian took a step back; he never raised his fists. And Ambrosja recognized that look in Gunnar's eyes… she had seen it once before when he pinned her to a tree. She gasped and quickly retreated from the window — darting fast to the double doors.

"Gunnar!" Johann shouted, "Please! Mind over matter!"

Gunnar wasn't listening; he kept lunging at Killian, fists closed tightly, growling and stomping ahead with every step that Killian took backwards. The Commander didn't seem once prepared to fight back — only dodge. Cinder watched this with a hand gripping Johann's shoulder. She tried to step in, but Johann pulled her back.

"Don't, girl," Johann whispered urgently, "the last thing you need is to get accidentally pummeled by one of those giants!"

Donathan came running out of the mine, skidding to stop beside Johann and Cinder. "What's going on?!"

"Gunnar found a piece of Nythralt," Johann replied, keeping his eyes on Gunnar and Killian, "he's having an episode… I don't think he's aware of where he is."

Ambrosja came running out of the Command Hall at that moment, urgent and with wide eyes as she observed the scene. Her eyes kept darting between Gunnar and Killian. The old warrior reached for a pickaxe now, wielding it like it was his greataxe. The Commander took another step back, fists clenched, his eyes grew sharper.

The Empress stood there helpless. Then she took a step forward. "Gunnar! Stop it!"

"He's not listening!" Johann shouted from across the yard.

Ambrosja saw the trio and immediately ran to them. A few Black Hands approached, ready to try and intervene in the fight between the two men, trying to circle them, but Killian kept firmly raising a hand to halt them while dodging each of Gunnar's swings.

"Do not approach him!" Killian said firmly, "I don't want any of you approaching him!"

Berric stepped forward, hands on a thick and long piece of rope. "He's causing havoc, Commander! We're already behind on schedule as it is!"

"Don't you dare!" Cinder shouted, approaching Berric and trying to snag the rope from him.

"Sod off, girl!" Berric pulled back, shoving his elbow into Cinder, causing her to stagger back.

Cinder gasped, hand clutching her chest where she was shoved. "You fuck—!" she went to charge.

Johann and Ambrosja went after her, but as soon as Cinder got within distance of the Lieutenant, Berric raised his hand and backhanded her. The force was so hard that the crack was audible. Cinder cried and fell to the ground, landing on her knees.

"You're a fucking prisoner!" Berric reminded Cinder with a hiss in his voice. "Try again, and I'll do worse!"

After that smack was dealt… Silence was felt. Gunnar had frozen momentarily, as if the sudden cry from Cinder snapped him from wherever pit he was in, but only momentarily. He turned from Killian, immediately heading for Berric, but the Commander took action without a second thought, wrapping his arms around Gunnar in a tight hold.

"You—" Ambrosja growled, fists clenched, staring at Berric.

But before Ambrosja could get a punch in to avenge Cinder, Donathan had yelled; he threw his leaner form against Berric and landed punches into his gut.

"Fuck you!" Donathan was yelling repeatedly, throwing punch after punch towards the Lieutenant, his hands grew hotter, flames sparking off like droplets of rain.

"Donathan—" Johann began to speak, already rushing to grab hold of the young fire mage. His hands wrapped around Donathan's arm, but Donathan kept wailing.

"Get off of me! You pest!" Berric growled, then threw his own fist into Donathan's rib, which caused the young mage to wince, but Donathan didn't let up.

"All of you! Stand down!" Killian shouted, but no one was listening. He was already grunting with the effort to hold Gunnar still. "I said—STAND DOWN." Still nothing.

The Commander did what he didn't want to. His arms tightened around Gunnar, and with a growl, he lifted the older man in the air, then threw him into the crates, causing Gunnar to roll, wood breaking against his body as his weight dragged him across the ground.

Ambrosja saw this, stunned by Killian's actions, or maybe just stunned by the entire chaos. She took a step back when Killian moved past her, his

massive hands reaching for both Berric and Donathan; one grabbed the back of Donathan's cloak while the other grabbed the collar of Berric's tunic. Killian roared, pulling them apart and shoving them a few feet from each other.

"I said stand down!" Killian yelled. Then he pointed at Gunnar. "Now look! Both of you forced my hand because no one here fucking listens!" He waved his hand over all of them. "Miners! Get the fuck back to work! Healers tend to the prisoner!" Then he looked between Cinder, Donathan, and Berric. "I don't want the three of you looking at each other. Berric, you're off mine duty for the day, look over supplies, but first, in my office." He set his gaze onto Cinder and Donathan, then Johann, "You three… Go sit with your friend."

Killian then turned, walking past Ambrosja as if he had never even seen her. His rough hand came up, wiping sweat off his forehead, marching towards the Command Hall.

The Empress was frozen there. Her heart tugged in different directions. Golden eyes followed Killian's form until he disappeared beyond the doors. Then she looked at her friends. Then again, where Killian went. She growled at herself for even wondering which way she should go… She turned, heading to Cinder.

Cinder was already sitting on her bedroll beneath the canvas of the mining camp. A Black Hand healer was looking over her, but Cinder was shoving the healer's hands away.

"I can take care of myself! I don't need your godsdamn healing!" Cinder swatted again, and the healer recoiled, muttering under their breath and moving away.

"Cinder," Ambrosja whispered, watching as Johann now moved to take care of Cinder's cheek. "Are you okay?"

Cinder bit back a wince when Johann touched her cheek. "My pride hurts more," she bitterly admitted, "that's the first time I've ever been slapped."

"Alright, girl," Johann said gently, his glowing fingers hovering over Cinder's freshly bruised face, a bruise that was fading back to her natural tone, "you'll be fine…. No scar will touch you, no bruise either, but you'll be sore for a few moments longer."

Cinder nodded, then looked at Donathan, who was scowling at nothing. He had also swatted away the Black Hand healer.

"Hey," Cinder called to Donathan, keeping her voice gentle, "thanks for that. That was… brave of you."

Donathan was quiet mostly, but he raised a brow, looked at Cinder, then scoffed. "Well, he deserved to get the shit beat out of him for hurting you." Then he looked away. "I just wish I dealt more damage to him."

"I think you damaged his confidence," Johann spoke with a smirk, "you threw him hard to the ground with your body."

Cinder agreed with a chuckle, "That's for sure, I heard him — wish I saw his face, bet he was surprised."

Ambrosja smiled, but didn't add much. She looked at Gunnar's figure; he had been laid down onto his own bedroll by a few miners and Black Hands that could carry him. She noticed his breathing was steady. A sigh of relief escaped her.

The Empress sat down on the bedroll beside Johann. "What happened?" she asked cautiously, looking between all of them.

Johann ran a hand down his face. "Finally broke through a wall and found more Nythralt... Gunnar was the first one to find it... And he snapped."

Cinder looked down, a face that was normally hardened or smug, was distraught. "Never seen him like that. He started attacking the wall of the mine, almost knocking down a support beam," Cinder explained, looking at Ambrosja, "some of the miners tried to restrain him, he nearly pummeled them... Then Black Hand tried to get in... Gunnar almost beat them... Then finally! Killian shows up and manages to provoke the big bastard to follow him out of the mine."

Donathan sighed. "Sorry, I wasn't there. He looked between Cinder and Johann. "They had me working in a separate tunnel..."

Immediately, Johann waved his hand. "Don't worry about it, Donathan, it's not your fault. Even if you had been there, Gunnar would have had the same breakdown."

Cinder touched her jaw, fingers gliding to her cheek. "You were right, not sore anymore." Then she looked at Ambrosja. "How have you been?"

Ambrosja's eyes widened. "Hm? How have I been?"

Cinder squinted at Ambrosja. "Yeah... You've been distant recently. Ever since the Mourntalon, actually, before that," she gestured vaguely, throwing her hand back as if rewinding time, "ever since the Commander called you to his office... You've been off."

"Ah," Ambrosja said simply, rubbing her arms awkwardly, "I am fine."

Cinder's squint deepened momentarily; she didn't seem to buy it. "Right, fine, sure. Well, what happened in his office? Why did he call for you?"

The Empress thought back. The destroyed desk. The papers that had been stomped on. The bottle in Killian's hand and how he looked as though he were unraveling, but he couldn't bring himself to tell her. Her brows pinched together; she was almost insulted by the fact that Killian hadn't opened up to her. Then she sighed, they weren't close then... *Why would he say anything?*

"Did you at least get to snoop around?" Cinder finally asked, probably feeling a little impatient.

Ambrosja's eyebrows shot up as she realized she had been recalling the office and getting frustrated over *something* that didn't exist at the time. She looked at Cinder, and the truth was that... Ambrosja did try to snoop around at first; she tried to look at the papers. She caught a glimpse, but not enough.

"Not really, no," Ambrosja admitted, "I saw something about an outpost and Greymire on a paper, but that was it. That was all I could make out before Killian distracted me." She shook her head. "If it is alright, I do not want to talk about this further."

It felt wrong... Wrong to expose Killian's secrets when the man seemed to be at his lowest. She gripped her biceps hard, nails digging into the fabric as she thought on this. Why should she care? Why was she so bothered by how Killian looked and the state of his office that she didn't want to discuss plans that could provide them with answers? That could be enough of a means to get them out of camp and take a new step. It was clear the answer could be this *outpost* or *Greymire*, but... Ambrosja just did not want to talk about this.

"Greymire..." Johann whispered, his brows lowered far on his face as he thought on the name, his hand running along his beard. "Greymire's Regency is to the east of here... Cold place, too. What could be in Greymire?"

Cinder looked back at Gunnar. "Gunnar is from Greymire... When he wakes up, we should ask him if he has an idea or something."

Ambrosja took a deep breath and a step back. "I am going back to the Command Hall. Please let me know when Gunnar wakes up, but... take your time... I know you two have known him longer... I just want to make sure he will be well."

"Nonsense," Johann gave a half-hearted smile, "we've traveled together, mined together, and had to deal with Cinder's mouth together," that prompted a *hey!* from Cinder, "We're family, Ambrosja."

The Empress swallowed. She released a shaky breath. She quickly wiped her eyes. "Do not... do not make me cry." She smiled at them. "All of you..." she looked between Cinder, Donathan, Johann, and even Gunnar's unconscious form, "You have been my best friends... I cannot recall someone being near me for longer than they were obligated to… But all of you have…" She took a step back. "I should go." She cleared her throat, and because she didn't know how to exit, she bowed to them before turning on her heel and rushing to the Command Hall.

Ambrosja pushed the door open, passing by the Black Hand guards that were always posted at the bottom of the staircase. She ascended to the second floor and saw that the door to Killian's office was locked, but she could hear them, faint, but there. The Empress stepped closer, one step at a time, until she was up against the frame.

Killian's voice was filled with rage. "We do not hit women in this camp! Do you hear me?"

Berric's voice was muffled, like a disgruntled groan. Then a slam against the very door that Ambrosja was leaning against. She stepped back quickly.

"Do you understand me, Lieutenant?!"

Wood groaned beneath the force. Ambrosja looked down, trying to see the shadows, and all she could make out as one set of boots.

"Y-yes, Commander…" Berric sounded like he was choking.

The Empress looked up. She could tell now that Killian was holding Berric up against the door. Then suddenly, he was dropped.

"Out of my fucking office," the Commander growled.

The handle turned fast, and the door was ripped open. Berric was shoved out, the door slammed behind him. The Lieutenant's gaze fell on Ambrosja; his brows lowered, and he gave her a once-over.

"The fuck are you staring at?" Berric grunted, keeping his voice low as he walked past her, "Fucking harlot."

Ambrosja didn't gasp, but she bared her teeth, looking like she was ready to strike. But… the closed door caught her eye. And suddenly, Berric was no longer important. She waited for the lieutenant to descend the stairs; when his boots had faded, that's when she approached the door and knocked.

It felt like an eternity before Killian's deep voice finally came through, granting permission when she heard those words, *Come in.*

The Empress steadied herself, though she felt silly. She twisted the handle, pushed the door open, and stepped inside. The desk was put back together, a few pieces missing, but minor. A velvet chair had two stacks of parchment; one filled with pages that seemed haphazardly put together, and the other was a neat stack.

Killian looked up from where he sat at his desk, and for a brief moment, his cold gaze shifted into something softer. "Ambrosja," he spoke her

name with a cool neutrality. Ambrosja felt it, and she hated it. "What are you doing here?"

"I am checking in on you," Ambrosja explained. "You did not wake me... You haven't since the patrol. And you have also been having breakfast elsewhere, it seems... I do not see you beneath the canopy outside."

"I've been having breakfast in my office, Ambrosja." Killian looked back down at his papers, writing once more. "Is there another reason for you to be here?"

The Empress's throat burned. She ached to ask him if he's been avoiding her, if he regrets their time on patrol. She's always been stubborn; she's always been willing to slam her shield again and again into her enemies. So, why is it that asking this question seems to make her want to choke? Why is she stuck standing still, making her interlaced fingers grasp and fight each other as her heart fights her mind? Then she forced the question down, replacing it with: *Why should I care?*

"I heard what you said to your Lieutenant," Ambrosja said instead, "I find it quite admirable that you wish not to harm a woman. And... surprising."

Killian's gaze lifted to hers. "Surprising how?" His grip on his quill tightened. "Do you think that poorly of me?"

"What?" Ambrosja took a step forward, her hands waved gently in front of her, quickly denying his question. "No, not at all. I am just — surprised due to..." She paused. "I–I am not quite sure why. I suppose it is because... You... remind me of home."

"Home?"

"You know of Nordorn enough to know how we treat each other," Ambrosja explained, trying to ease herself into the same neutrality that Killian was showing her. "Women and men face the same punishments, the same consequences; gender matters not."

Killian didn't look impressed or satisfied. And this *bothered* Ambrosja. Her fingers curled inward, and she fought the twitch that her brows wanted to do.

"But," the Empress continued, "Cinder had done nothing but try to protect her own friend... And Berric was aggressive without reason, believing he could land a hand on her because she was a prisoner." She took a step closer. "And because, despite her being a prisoner, you still insist that she should not be harmed because she is a woman. That is what I am admiring."

Ambrosja took another step. Then another. Until she sat in the empty chair across his desk.

"But now I wonder, Commander…" Ambrosja crossed her legs, easing into the seat. "When they first appeared in the camp, you were willing to kill her, all of them… What has changed?"

Killian exhaled sharply through his nose, turning his gaze back to his papers. "Nothing," he clarified. "She has earned her time in this camp, and her acting out was her first offense. Berric's reaction was unnecessary. So far, I've yet to spot your friends spying or doing things that they shouldn't, and that is why I haven't thrown anyone to the pyre." Killian paused as he signed a parchment, placing it to the side and starting on the next one. "That is why I disapprove of what Berric has done, beyond her just being a woman. When I deliver punishment," his eyes met Ambrosja's, "I deliver it with reason." Then he looked down again.

The Empress's brows furrowed as Killian looked down back at his papers. The silence between them ate at her. She felt the urge to rip his quill right out of his hand and draw all over him, demanding to know what had changed since the patrol, though the end of the quill would hurt, *but still…* Ambrosja's sigh was silent; she refused to give an inkling of reaction to Killian

"But…" Killian spoke again after a moment, and Ambrosja immediately looked at him, "I still refuse to land a hand on a woman. The only time that may come is if my life or the life of someone I care about is being threatened. Then… then gender matters not."

Silence settled between them. Ambrosja had only given a small nod, approving of his answer, but the Commander still didn't look at her. She crossed her legs tighter, fingers pressing into the fabric of her pants—his pants—and was scowling at him.

"What is going on with you?" she had asked without even thinking.

The Commander finally met her gaze. "What do you mean?"

"You…" she began to speak, "you have been quite distant since the patrol. You are not as…" she tried to think of the words, and she found herself blushing as she tried, "Not as infuriatingly playful as you were before. Now… Now I do not even know what you are. We no longer have breakfast together, or lunch, or dinner, you have locked yourself away in your office, and if you are not in your office, you are off shirtless working on your body or overseeing the camp."

Killian stared at Ambrosja for quite a bit; his chin rested firmly in his hand, his forefinger was pressed into his cheek, while his long finger was over his lips. He pressed harder, as if fighting something. "You often watch me working on my body while I am shirtless, do you?"

Ambrosja leaned back, grabbing the armrests of the velvet chair, her legs uncrossed, boots planted firmly into the wooden floor. "Is *that* what you gather from this?! That I watch you shirtless?! Of all the things I pointed out?!"

The Commander shrugged. Whatever he was fighting with his lips, he had let go as his hand came back to rest against the desk. His lips twitched into something smug and feral; he was rolling his shoulders. "I am just… relishing in being right." He cocked a brow at her. "You are attracted to me."

Ambrosja growled. She stood up, grabbed his papers, and flung them onto his lap, all while she growled, like a cat sweeping a precious token off the edge. Killian watched this and didn't stop her, nor did he stop smiling. He leaned back into his chair and chuckled.

"Why are you laughing?! Stop laughing at me! You always laugh at me!"

Killian shook his head, shoulders still shaking. "I am not laughing at you, Empress, I am laughing at your reaction."

"My reaction is me! You are laughing at me!"

The Commander tilted his head with a half smile, possibly agreeing, possibly not. Just being vague enough to infuriate her further. Then finally, his hands gathered the parchment she had tossed onto his lap, and he organized them—partially—as he simply settled them back onto his desk.

"You did not answer me," Ambrosja said coolly, arms crossed beneath her chest as she stared down at Killian, "what happened?"

His expression shifted, the half-smile was gone, the lazy, cocky attitude disappeared, and his shoulders had straightened once more. "Why does it matter?" He didn't look at Ambrosja, just down at the papers he was fixing.

"Why does it matter?" she echoed, "It matters because I hate that — that I was feeling some sort of warmth from you, and now? Now it is as if we are meeting for the first time, but you could not give a single damn about me as you stare at me with those cold eyes."

Killian didn't say anything, and he still didn't look up.

"I do not like it," Ambrosja continued, "what happened, Killian?" But Killian still didn't look up; his jaw was clenched, brows furrowed, Ambrosja saw this. "Look at me… please."

That *please* broke Killian. Finally, he looked up at Ambrosja. "I am respecting the boundaries of your crown, Empress," he explained, "you made it quite clear about your guilt out in the woods, and I refuse to cause further distress, so… I am distancing myself, as I should have done since the day we met."

"Do not," Ambrosja took a step forward, her fingers finding the edge of the desk, "do not distance yourself from me. I can handle my own guilt, my own feelings… Do not pull away."

"Empress," Killian began to speak, only to get cut off by Ambrosja.

"I do not like this feeling, Killian," she leaned forward, "I do not like feeling warm then cold. It is awful. My heart hurts. Do not do it." Ambrosja felt her knees shake; she felt her wrists shake, too. She couldn't quite understand *why* she was feeling this; normally, if she shook, it was because of rage… not whatever *this* was.

The Commander released a sigh, a heavy one. The kind that vibrated the very wood he was bracing himself against. He looked down again, his eyes searching aimlessly as his gaze crossed over his papers. Then his hand moved so his head could rest against it; his thumb against his temple, while his fingers rubbed his forehead.

"What would you have me do, Empress?" Killian's voice was low, calm, but strained. He took a deep breath first. "You say that you feel guilt from being close, so I do us both the favor and create distance—but now this distance hurts you?"

"I do not understand it," Ambrosja explained, pressing her hands hard into his desk, "but it hurts! And I would rather you be near, and I feel guilt, than you be far and I feel lonely!"

"I–" he stopped himself from speaking further. His hand snapped down, and his head turned to the side, refusing to look at Ambrosja, as if the sight of her alone was unraveling him. He stood up, as if sitting still was worse. He walked around his desk, steps slow and heavy as he approached Ambrosja. He tried to gather his words in the mere seconds it took to reach her.

But as the Commander reached her side… he completely stopped. Ambrosja was looking up at him, her expression was soft, unguarded. And he couldn't help but stare openly. Killian's cold eyes softened as he took Ambrosja in, as if he were counting every freckle that crossed her face. His fingers that were curled at his side—finally relaxed. He couldn't find the strength to peel his gaze away.

Ambrosja couldn't handle the scrutiny, but she didn't want anything less. "Why—why are you staring?"

"Because I never thought I'd live the day to witness perfection…" The words slipped before Killian could stop himself.

He cursed under his breath, his fingers curled again. "Forgive me— that was inappropriate."

The Empress had frozen in place, taking one deep breath as her hand pressed flat into the desk, trying to still her breathing — to not give too much away. But she couldn't help how her eyes remained on his, how the outer edges of her brows tilted down, and the inners curved to meet each other. How could she stop the way her expression shifted or the thud of her heart when the man before her had said something to her that no one else ever had? It felt like a cruel joke, yet the sweetest confession.

"...Do you mean that?" Ambrosja's voice trembled.

Killian's gaze slipped back to hers, as if he was being pulled and he couldn't stop it. But even as he was, he built his wall once more, straightening himself and placing his hands behind his back. "As I've said, that was inappropriate. It would be best if you forget that, Ambrosja."

"You—you cannot expect me to forget that when—not when you said it so—"

"It was a mistake," his voice cut through the air. He turned away sharply, already making his way back to his chair to sit.

And once he did, his gaze slid to her, cold and far away.

"You are dismissed, Empress," he said, unable to stop the way his voice went hoarse as those words left his tongue with a bitter taste.

*From the journal of Guinyldr Thorn,
Dreknfell, 06, 997*

THE RAVENS OF THE NORTH

The Ravens of the North are found only within the frozen skies of Nordorn. Nowhere else in Eldorwyn—or beyond it—do ravens exist. In lands where one might expect them, there are only crows: smaller, clever, wholly natural creatures bound to soil, season, and decay. The distinction is not merely one of size or temperament, but of origin itself.

Ravens belong to no natural lineage. They are most often seen circling the peaks of Mount Nordravn, where stone meets sky and Chaos Magic lingers thinly in the air. They move with a deliberateness that suggests intent rather than instinct. Their eyes reflect no color, only depth, as though they are less creatures of sight than of observation.

It is said they were not born of flesh, but of Chaos Magic itself—threads of creation given form when the world was still unfinished.

Their only known magic is the ability to slip briefly between realms, vanishing into the Veil for the span of a breath before returning elsewhere, untouched by distance or terrain. This alone sets them beyond all natural order.

Their presence has long been regarded as an omen of divine intent.

The Ravens serve no master but the Empress, and no realm but Nordorn. From the time of Brynhjora, they have acted as messengers, carrying word and will across impossible distances, often arriving before riders could have reasonably set out. Their messages are never intercepted. No blade has struck them. No spell has bound them.

Their loyalty cannot be bought nor broken, for their bond is not forged through training or command, but through blood and ancient magic older than the crown itself. The Empress does not own the Ravens; she is recognized by them. When a raven answers her call, it is not obedience—it is acknowledgment.

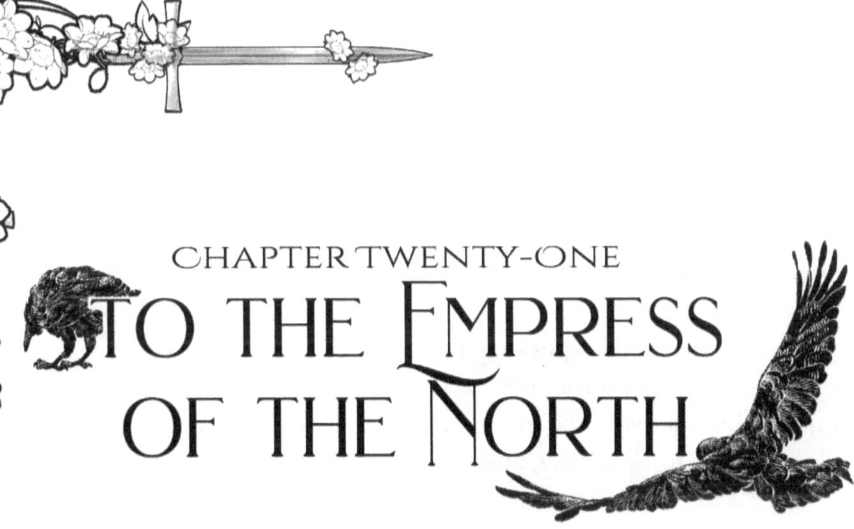

"'Empress Nordravn,'" Jareth spoke, keeping his voice loud and clear as he walked around the round table of the council room, "'By the authority of the Stonehaven's Council of the Round Table, we extend to you formal greetings in the hope that this letter finds you in health, clarity, and continued sovereignty.'"

The Diplomat continued his pace around the table, everyone seated listened as he brought up how reluctant yet necessary it was to write over fear and concerns regarding their hamlets. Aaric's hands were firmly resting against the armrests of his chair, his gaze was calm as he followed Jareth's figure. Emeric had his hands laced tightly in front of him, resting against his lips while his elbows braced against the table. Rosalind was downcast, turning a coin over in her fingers as if it were a nervous tic. Oswin looked optimistic yet still uncertain as he also followed Jareth's figure. Varian remained cool, leaning into his chair on one side, elbow resting against the armrest while his other hand was calm and still on the table.

Jareth continued speaking, reading off the drafted letter, "'We wish to state plainly that this council does not presume guilt, nor do we hasten to unfounded conclusions.'" He gave Varian a quick slide glance, then continued, "'However, the nature of these attacks has compelled us to seek clarity from the only realm whose forces possess both the skill and proximity to enact such strikes with such precision.'"

The Diplomat's fingers tensed slightly around the parchment. Even as he read every word, he couldn't help but think to himself, *Everything could be riding on this single letter.*

"As such, we respectfully inquire: Have any Nordorner troops, warbands, or unsanctioned raiders been dispatched—knowingly or otherwise—beyond your shores, operating independently of your command?" Jareth looked to the council, then spoke again, "'Or, failing that, are you aware of any rogue elements bearing Nordorn arms, or colors who may be acting without your leave?'"

He continued, speaking about desired peace and stability between the realms, expressing that they would be failing their people if they had not inquired about a matter so grave. And therefore, they ask because they must, and they hope to be wrong, and to receive an answer of sorts.

"'We trust in your candor, Empress, and await your response before further action is considered. May this matter be resolved through truth rather than bloodshed,'" Jareth finished, "'With due respect and vigilance, The Council's Round Table of Stonehaven, By collective seal and sworn oath, Vaestoria.'"

Aaric nodded his head. "That sounds perfect. I don't think we can get any more polite or precise than that."

Emeric visibly relaxed. "That letter was well written, it was very respectful to the Empress. If this one is anything like those before her, I am sure she will write back and be as respectful and as honest as possible."

A loud scoff left Varian's throat. "I wouldn't count on that," he explained, "wasn't this Empress the one that waged war on Braxia four years ago?"

Emeric scowled immediately. "She didn't wage war on Braxia; Braxia has been going after Nordorn since the Fracture. This Empress simply decided to take out their entire naval fleet and render them useless for now."

Varian leaned forward, finger tips meeting each other as he set his gaze on Emeric. "And you think this is a woman that's peaceful? One that removes a country's means of oceanic defense?"

"I think—" Emeric was cut off.

"Lords," Aaric said firmly, "if we are to repair our country and remove the rot within it, we must work together. Our Diplomat has drafted a well written letter to the Empress of Nordorn, and this argument of what-if's is not what we need right now."

Oswin immediately agreed, "We need to place our focus on the enemy, but right now… we need to find out who our enemy is."

"Gods forbid it's our own people and we've been blind," Rosalind muttered, smoothing out her dress, "but Emeric is right." She looked at Emeric, then at Varian. "The Empress cut off a thorn in her side, and she made the right call, was it devastating? Yes, but when hasn't a country resorted to drastic measures to bring about peace?" The lady leaned back in her chair. "So, yes, I believe if this is an Empress with sense, she will respond, and she will not react with hostility."

Emeric dipped his head in appreciation towards Rosalind, then looked at Jareth. "Jareth. How do you feel? You are the one that created this letter— is there anything you'd like to add? Or if you need further input," Emeric gave a bow in his chair, "I would be glad to assist."

The Diplomat was distracted, but Emeric's call pulled him from his thoughts. "Forgive me," Jareth said, his hand smoothed over his cravat. "Yes. Assistance, another once-over the letter by a second set of eyes would be appreciated." Jareth walked towards the table, taking his seat once more.

"You look bothered, Diplomat," Aaric said as he gave his son a glance, noting the lines creasing around Jareth's eyes and how his fingers kept flexing against everything he touched, "do you have any thoughts you'd like to share?"

Jareth was silent at first, his eyes narrowed as he weighed his thoughts. When he was ready to speak, he looked up at the High Regent. "I suppose I share similar concerns to Lady Rosalind," he explained, gesturing to the Treasurer, "what if the hamlets burning are our own people? What if this is some new threat that spawned within our very own lands?" He rubbed his chin. "If it is, then it is a call, a call to do better for our country in every way possible... For we create hate and violence out of neglect and unkindness."

Jareth held the door of the carriage open for his father to step in first. The older man released a low grunt when he stepped onto the footplate of the carriage and pushed himself inside and settled against the dark blue velvet seats. The Diplomat followed in after, settling with far better ease than the High Regent.

"This is a mess," Aaric muttered, dragging his hand down his face. "How long do you reckon it'll take that letter to reach the Empress?"

"Gods," Jareth whispered, exasperation entwining with his breath as his hand moved into the interior pocket of his coat and he pulled out a flask. "Luckily Stonehaven is neighbors with a portion of its borders... But I guess it depends on if we can actually reach the Empress." The Diplomat took a swig from his flask as he thought about travel logistics. "One of our carrier pigeons can deliver the letter to Greybarrow within a day… and from Greybarrow they can approach the border — which might take a week, depending on weather conditions. But… we've never sent a letter to Nordorn…"

Jareth's voice trailed off, he sighed and tilted his head back.

Aaric's gaze slid to the flask in Jareth's hand. "Drinking again?"

"I've *been* drinking since I was seventeen, father."

"Hrm," Aaric grunted with a huff, "and I still don't approve." Then he reached over, grabbed Jareth's flask and took a swig for himself.

"Hey!" Jareth's eyes narrowed. "That's a vintage." But he didn't fight it, just laid back and leaned into the side of the carriage's car.

He lifted his foot to rest his ankle onto his knee, his arms crossed. Jareth continued staring outside, watching the sky shift from afternoon into the early evening glow.

"I swear, Varian wants a war, father." Jareth's jaw was tight. "He has been doing all that he can to point his finger at Nordorn, but as Emeric said, there is no guarantee that the Empress is behind this, or even that Nordorners are."

Aaric looked thoughtful. Then took another swig. "Yeah, Varian has been trouble. I can't imagine how this would benefit him at all, so I fail to understand the game he's playing. The last thing we need is war with Nordorn. We've barely recovered from the war against Solymethis. And we have our own bandits and lowlives to deal with."

The High Regent handed back his son's flask to him. His own hand retreated to the inside of his cloak, pulling out a gorgeous cedar wood pipe in the shape of a dragon. Aaric pulled out a long stick next, thin yet sturdy and flicked it across the sole of his boot. The lit stick met the pipe and Aaric took in a deep inhale, then puffed out his smoke.

Jareth watched his father, chuckling to himself. "You still have that smoke pipe? You haven't switched to drakesmokes yet?"

Aaric grunted, taking another puff. "A pipe is timeless, my boy. You and your brother can stick to your drakesmokes." The High Regent's expression softened. He pulled the pipe away, his gaze set on the ground of the carriage. "Have you heard from Killian?"

"Yes." Jareth dipped his chin into his hand, his free one put away the flask back into his pocket, only shifting around to pull out a letter with creased edges. "I got this last week." He handed it to his father, which Aaric quickly took it with an uneasy grasp.

The High Regent's eyes focused on the letter, reading the words over and over again before finally muttering them, "'The scorching flames rise from west to the east, where snow drifts down from the Northern mountains. Places small and unseen, soon to be burnt, caressed with eternal dreams, formed by a black mark.'" Aaric released a sharp exhale. "He didn't sign it," Aaric said as he gave it a once over again, then stopped once he saw the ink stamp of Vorthunal in the corner, small and subtle, "ah. Of course."

"This is the first letter in a year," Jareth's voice went low, his throat going tight, fist clenching around the edge of his seat, "reads like a warning."

"Did you tell Lyra?"

"No," the Diplomat sighed, "I've kept everything about Killian a secret. And I hate it, father."

"I know," Aaric said solemnly, "but we must do all that we can to protect both your sister and mother."

PIGEON CARRIERS

With the passing of dragons and the quiet years that followed The Fracture, Vaestoria turned to humbler wings for the work once borne by legend. Thus began the age of the Carrier Pigeons — birds trained and enchanted to bear messages swiftly across the realm.

Though ordinary pigeons have long been known as "homing birds," Vaestorian mages refined the art. By casting subtle enchantments upon unhatched eggs, they bound each bird to the memory of its birthplace, ensuring it could always find its way home. The magic is gentle, woven into instinct rather than will, and has made the keeping of carrier birds both reliable and secure.

Most settlements now maintain a tower beside the local watchstead, where pigeons and other trained fliers are housed under the care of handlers. Each bird wears a light ribbon about its leg — the color marking its home settlement. When a message must travel swiftly, be it a merchant's ledger, a private letter, or a call for aid, the bird is loosed to the skies, carrying words across the winds that once belonged to dragons.

CHAPTER TWENTY-TWO
UNDER SUN EYES

Killian leaned against the support beam that held the wide canvas to the miners' tent. He watched as Gunnar was hunched over on his bedroll. The older man's shoulders were lowered, palms open and facing him, his old eyes tracked the lines across his skin.

"I think you should go," Killian finally said, approaching Gunnar. Gunnar looked over his shoulder and saw the Commander, and he continued speaking, "I should have known, I knew you were in the military, that was given by how you knew my father; however, I didn't know you had a past with Nythralt."

The older man made a sound mixed with a laugh, a grunt, and a scoff. "Anyone in Greymire's military ranks had some sort of crossing with Nythralt—one way or another." He looked at Killian again. "If I had said something… You would have either sent me to my death or sent me away… and there was no way I would be leaving without the four friends I came in with."

"Four?" Killian echoed, now sitting on the bedroll across from Gunnar. "Do you count Ambrosja and Donathan as part of your crew?"

"Aye," Gunnar confirmed without even thinking about it, "I met both of them at their lowest, I'll be damned if I leave them there, or I at least don't get to see them at their highest."

"They are not your responsibility."

"Neither are they yours."

The Commander was quiet at that. His eyes narrowed. "That may be. Donathan doesn't belong under my command, and Ambrosja — Ambrosja shouldn't even be here to begin with. But she is. And she is under my care."

Gunnar's fingers rubbed his beard alongside his jaw. He tried to relax a little, lowering himself to look less like a threat. "You like that girl?"

It didn't escape Killian what Gunnar was trying to do; despite that, he responded honestly, without giving anything, yet everything away, "She is maddening."

"And she broke your nose."

The Commander smirked, small and rare. "I didn't think she'd manage to reach… Guess she's proven me wrong." Killian shifted, his smirk disappearing, his eyes cold again, setting on Gunnar. "As I said, I think you should go. You may take your friends with you, even Donathan, though, as I'm sure you know… He can be tracked. But Ambrosja? She stays with me."

"Absolutely not," Gunnar said firmly, immediately straightening and curling his fingers, "I will not abandon her. With all due respect, Commander, the only thing I know about you is that you're my old friend's son. But that's where that ends. I've seen your violence, I've heard your rage. I'm not leaving her here with you."

Killian ground his teeth, but he didn't retort, and he refused to clench his fists. Instead, he leaned back. "Fine, stay, but you will no longer be working in the mines. I will make other use of you." The Commander stood up, making his way out of the tent, but he stopped. He turned to look at the older man once more. "One of my captains is proficient in Psychic Magic," he said, "she offered to *numb* your past with Nythralt. I said no, that is something I'll leave to you to decide. Think on it, if you want." He continued his way, leaving Gunnar behind in the tent.

The older man stared at the edge of the tent as Killian disappeared. His fists curled into his bedroll, only to lift his hands so he could drop his head into them, fingers gliding over the smooth surface of his scalp. His chest tightened, yet his eyes closed steadily.

Night had arrived, slow and cruel. The room swelled with thick air that clung to Killian's skin. One hand gripped his chin hard, his other held tightly to a book he was reading. His gaze skimmed the pages, though it flicked often to the wide doors. Waiting. Expecting to see Ambrosja walk through as she should have hours ago. Ever since he dismissed her, they had been distant.

She wouldn't look at him anymore, not even a second glance, and although he told himself he preferred it that way — he hated it with a passion that burned so deep into his bones it was a shock he hadn't torn the Command Hall down just to relieve his stress.

He exhaled sharply. Too sharply. *Where is she?* The thought scratched hot against his skull. He recalled seeing her earlier in the day in the bedroom, standing by her side of the bed. He hadn't questioned a thing, and she hadn't looked at him, but he watched her fold some regular white tunics, then promptly stuffing them into a small pouch. He cursed himself. He was foolish not to ask.

Killian's jaw clenched, then shifted like a man readying for a fight. And without another thought he threw the blankets off his body. His book was forgotten and tossed to the side. He didn't bother putting on boots or throwing on a shirt as he stormed out.

Each step down the stairs hit like a bellowing roar of silent fury. Felt but not heard. The guards posted at the bottom of the staircase flinched as they saw Killian barreling down. They immediately stepped aside, creating a wide path for him out of instinct and self-preservation.

The doors slammed open to reveal the camp under the night, and all looked. Miners, guards, any who could witness this from their seats or their bedrolls. Conversations died suddenly. Throats bobbed, bodies flinched. Ambrosja was just setting down her own bedroll to join her friends. They were mid-conversation when suddenly they stopped. Cinder's eyes went wide, her hand gripping the thin sheets as she saw Killian storming through. Gunnar instinctively sat up, his body coiling for a fight despite the calm conversation that was had earlier. Ambrosja's back was facing Killian, but she felt the silence, then felt the presence and heard the slight footsteps that fell heavy onto the dirt behind her.

Ambrosja turned, and suddenly she and Killian were close. Close enough that his presence was all she could see. His fingers flexing, his fists clenching. His nostrils flared. His body was frozen—for just a moment—with hesitation. Then he moved. Hands sudden and sure, gripping her thighs and hauling her over his shoulder.

"Killian!" Ambrosja gasped, hands falling to grab his broad, bare back.

Gunnar immediately stood up, Donathan's new found courage caused him to rise half-way, his veins were already glowing with magic. Cinder moved to crouch now, her hand found a rock that was wedged into the dirt beside her. Johann sat up from his bedroll, his eyes fixed on Gunnar's posture—

ready to follow his best friend's lead. Ambrosja's voice trailed off, her hands still gripping Killian's back as he walked back towards the Command Hall.

"Hey!" Gunnar shouted as he trailed behind, his steps furious. "You think it's proper to just grab a woman like that?!"

Killian stopped abruptly and turned, "Don't," he said coldly. "I meant it when I said she is under *my* care."

The two, hulking men stared at each other. Black Hand guards already reached for their weapons, waiting.

"It is fine, Gunnar," Ambrosja spoke with a voice that trembled from the angle of her body, not from fear. "Please, go back to bed. Get some rest."

Gunnar's eyes flicked briefly to Ambrosja's hanging form, at least what he could see of her head, before finally taking a step back as he saw all the guards suddenly surrounding him. He sighed, he didn't want to cause another scene or a fight, not after the Nythralt incident. He stepped back, and Killian turned sharply. Heading back inside. The doors closed behind him. Gunnar took a deep breath, attempting to calm himself before he turned on his heel and rejoined his friends back under the canopy of bedrolls.

Cinder narrowed her eyes. "The fuck was that about?"

Donathan, normally quiet and letting people explain first, spoke, "You spoke with the Commander earlier?"

"Yeah," Gunnar scratched at his beard, "he said I should leave because of what happened, that I could take the three of you with me… but he insisted on keeping Ambrosja and I said I wouldn't allow that. So, that's that."

"He was going to let us walk?" Cinder looked aghast, a part of her relieved, crouching and looking at the gates beyond. But she looked at Gunnar. "Did he say why he was keeping Ambrosja?"

"No," Gunnar answered simply, "it's clear to anyone with a set of eyes that something is going on between those two… and honestly? It worries me."

"Agreed," Johann nodded, "we—well, Cinder—told Ambrosja to flirt information out of the Commander and now…" he gestured vaguely at the Command Hall, "Girl looks like she took it too seriously."

Cinder cursed under her breath. "What the fuck are we going to do?"

Killian slammed the bedroom door shut behind him with his foot. His hands were still firm on the back of Ambrosja's thighs. As he reached the bed—her side of the bed, he dropped her. Not carelessly, but not gently. Ambrosja hit

the mattress, her body bouncing once—twice, before stilling. Her pale locks fanned across the silk cases of the pillows.

He paced away once, then sharply turned back. "Were you planning on making me wait all night?!" He growled.

Ambrosja's chest rose and fell, then she sat up, leaning forward as her fingers grasped at the blanket beneath her figure. "Wait all night?!" She echoed his words with anger. "For what? You said that it's best to bury whatever we have. What was I to think?!"

"What were you to think?! Maybe you should have thought about staying near me like we agreed!" He pointed at the barrier of pillows on the bed. "That is there for you, because I respect your lines, I have forced myself to respect your crown, the least you could do is extend that same courtesy and respect my conditions, Empress!"

Ambrosja snapped. "So your presence can further break my heart?!" Killian was silent. Ambrosja was not. "Every time I feel you get closer — you pull away! Do you not think I would ache lying next to you while you insist that whatever lingers between us is best to be buried?"

He still didn't respond. He just turned away from her now, his cold eyes boring into the wooden floors beneath his bare feet, a rough finger dragging across his lips as he forced himself to remain silent. But he could only stay silent for so long.

"I will not indulge in our hunger," Killian said firmly, fists clenched, turning so he could stare down at Ambrosja, "I can be violent, I can be brash, but I am disciplined when it matters, and I will not give in to my own desires and risk ruining you."

The Empress stood up fast, closing the distance between them with heartaching rage. "You would have me starve beneath your *discipline* so you can feel at a comfortable enough distance not to give in." She leaned in. "But I have no desire to starve, and my heart should not need to break because you fear *us*."

Killian remained still when she said *us*. His heart only pounded faster. He could hear and feel the blood move throughout his body.

"Fine." The Commander hunched over her. "I want to touch you," Killian finally admitted in a whisper, "every time I see you, I want nothing but to stare into those sun-eyes of yours and submit beneath your gaze."

Ambrosja's breath caught in her throat. Her eyes widened, flicking to each of Killian's stone-cold yet heated stare.

"Is that what you wanted to hear, Empress?" Killian lifted his hands slightly, as if baring himself to her. "That I think of you more than I should?

That I can't forget how fierce you looked when we first met as you slammed my desk and defended the ashes of a home that wasn't even yours? That I can't get out of my head how you look when you're about to break? When you're vulnerable? Selfish? Or how you wield a blade like it is a piece of your soul?"

Killian closed the distance with his hands; the space between them diminished to nothing but heat. His hands found her waist and dragged her close to him, pressing her flush to his body.

"I understand your traditions, and that is why I haven't pushed, why I haven't sought your lips against mine, because I can't—because we can't, Ambrosja." Killian swallowed, his cold-gray eyes looking into hers. "You already hate me enough for Wintersong, I know it, I see it. The conflict, the guilt. Trust me, it is like staring into a mirror. Everything you are feeling? I am feeling. My skin scorches with desire and want for you—but, I don't want you hating me further… all because I gave in to your desires — as well as mine."

Ambrosja was silent for a moment too long. Killian's fingers flexed, dug slightly, not to hurt, but to ground himself as they stared at each other. He was ready to let go—to step back—then Ambrosja finally spoke, her voice trembled, but it was not with fear. "…I want you."

"You *don't* want me, Ambrosja, you want a man who will give you everything, and hells, I could. I would," Killian whispered against her hair, his nose brushing at the pale strands. "But you do not want a man that is buried beneath the sins of a monster. No woman should want a man like that." He pulled back, just enough so he could stare into her golden eyes. "And if you do, then it is because your knees shake for affection."

Her breath quickened, shallow and wild, as if her heart had taken over her lungs. Her hands met his chest, nails pressing into his skin, "Don't—" she whispered, her voice shaking slightly. "Do not treat me as if I am desperate." She shook her head, eyes glassy but not from sadness. "I am not desperate."

Killian hunched over her, bringing himself closer while pulling her impossibly close. "You are the one seeking fire from the enemy, Ambrosja, how is this not desperation?"

Ambrosja grabbed his biceps, holding on for support. "You want me as well."

The silence was heated now. Neither dared to look away even as Ambrosja's pale skin flushed and Killian's breathing quickened.

"I do," he admitted, quieter now. Defeated.

The space between them evaporated. His nose nuzzled her hair, his breath drifting across her freckled cheekbones. He pulled her closer, lips

dragging across her skin…

"I can't," Killian whispered. "I won't be the regret that haunts you." He tore himself away from her like a man ripping off his own skin. His touch lingered down to her hips—then vanished.

"Killian—" Ambrosja's hand shot out, grabbing Killian's wrist, pulling him back towards her. "You are not even giving me a chance to choose."

"Do you think I want to stop?" he asked, voice hoarse. "Every part of me is screaming to stay. But I know what regret tastes like, Ambrosja. And I refuse to be that flavor on your lips." He looked down. "You are already promised to someone."

"Someone I didn't even get to pick, Killian." Ambrosja shook her head, moving closer to Killian. "Someone who is not you."

"Ambrosja… I am a monster…" Killian's voice had become barely a whisper as he reminded her of the harsh truth.

The Empress didn't step back. She didn't pull away. Her golden eyes remained on his, brows tilting into a softened state. "So am I," she whispered, "I just carry my sins differently."

Killian growled. Something low and deep that vibrated within his chest like a mountain splitting in two. His hands found the small of her waist again, pulling her flush once more, like being away was an ending worse than death. His large fingers curled into the sides of her blouse, holding Ambrosja steady against him.

"You are maddening," he said, lowering himself, hunching so far his nose was brushing hers, "yet you make me ache in ways no other woman has."

"And you enrage me," Ambrosja retorted, leaning in as well, "I can barely stare at you without wanting to beg before you while I claw at you."

"Fuck," Killian growled again.

Like a man possessed, the Commander wrapped his hands around the Empress's waist completely, pulling her impossibly close as his lips met hers with a hunger that neither of them could hide anymore. Ambrosja gasped against Killian's lips at the contact, and he drank that gasp like it was the answer to everything he ever craved. Her fingers threaded into his hair, her lips met his messy and inexperienced, but so needy. Killian could *feel* the inexperience and the need, and it lit him up from within. He groaned against her lips, pushing her until her spine met the wall.

The Commander's hand found the Empress's thigh, lifting it high to wrap around him. His lips dragged from hers to her jawline, then to her throat. Ambrosja's sounds became sweet like a lover's in sheets — and that's what pulled Killian back to reality.

Killian stopped completely. He retreated from Ambrosja's form, staring down at her with hungry gray eyes, but he forced his hands to brace against the wall.

"I want you," he reminded her, "but your crown — I will still respect it."

"Killian," Ambrosja's hands found his chest, fingers threading through his chest hair as her nails scraped at his skin, "I do not want you to respect my crown!"

"I know," his voice was hoarse with want, "I know… But you — you are young. And you are in a situation that no Empress should find herself in. I want you, badly so… But I cannot take you to my bed, Ambrosja. I will kiss you, I will hold you, but that is where I must stop us, because if I go further? And the next thing I see in your eyes is regret? I will truly break."

Ambrosja frowned, fingers trembling against Killian's bare chest. "So, now I must starve because you fear I will regret us?"

"You are not the only one starving, Empress." His hand left the wall and found hers, bringing her knuckles to his lips. "I will starve with you." He kissed her knuckles with reverence while keeping his eyes on hers, never turning away from her sun-blessed gaze. "Starve with me, Ambrosja," Killian begged.

The Empress's heart beat against her ribs like a tree seeking to take root and sprout from within her. Her breath quickened, her lids lowered into something soft and vulnerable. Her free hand found Killian's jawline, tracing the scar right near the edge.

"I will starve with you," Ambrosja answered him, kissing his battle-scarred knuckles in return.

PSYCHIC MAGIC

Psychic Magic is the art of the unseen mind — the power to control, seduce, and distort. Of all the known disciplines, it is among the most treacherous to master, for it touches not the body but the will. Through it, one may alter perception, conjure visions, or weave entire realities within another's thoughts. The physical world remains unscarred, yet the soul may never recover.

Wounds inflicted by Psychic Magic seldom heal cleanly. Victims may question their own recollections, distrust their senses, or feel hollowed by thoughts they cannot name. Unlike broken bone or burned skin, there is no clear moment when damage becomes visible, and no certainty that recovery is ever complete. A mind once reshaped may function, but it is never quite the same instrument again.

Practitioners of Psychic Magic are few, and their craft is tightly regulated throughout the realms. While the arts of telepathy and telekinesis are widely accepted, any use of coercive influence — mind control, enforced suggestion, or the fabrication of memory — is forbidden. Still, temptation lingers. Those who wield this power tread a narrow path, for the mind is the most fragile battleground, and victory there often costs far more than defeat.

CHAPTER TWENTY-THREE
EDGES BRUISED

Snow drifted down from the mountains above, hitting the floor of the large stone-carved balcony. Hådvard's cold blue eyes looked to the snowy land beyond the Nordravn castle. He watched the sun breach the clouds and bounce off of the mountainous walls below, walls that led into the Nordravn region of Nordorn, a region filled with homes of warriors, seers, and families alike.

Hådvard's attention was caught by the black smoke and feathers that manifested out of the cold air, and shifted into a raven carrying a letter.

The raven landed softly onto the stone balustrade, taking a hop closer to Hådvard's form. The warrior reached out with a massive hand and retrieved the letter from its beak. A sharp exhale left Hådvard's nostrils as he prepared to read Ambrosja's letter.

He unfolded it with battle-worn hands, far too big for the letter. And when it was open, he read each word slowly. Brows furrowing deeper with every second that passed. When he reached the words *act like the man you are meant to be* he nearly tore the parchment in half.

An echo boomed across the balcony and into the mountains as his fist came down onto the stone surface before him. Shaking the snow that had gathered there. He grunted, shoving aside a pile, forcing it to fall. The raven flew away, settling on the handle of the open door of the bedroom behind Hådvard.

"That tiny, little — Empress," Hådvard growled, "this is how she treats *me?* The man she is meant to marry? The man taking care of her empire as she skips off for adventure?!"

The warrior lifted his hand, calling the raven back, and so it returned, already plucking a quill with its beak and dropping it into the massive hand as the raven flew over and perched onto the space of the rail in front of Hådvard.

"I don't have time to hunt down ink," Hådvard muttered as he sliced the quill down his palm without wincing once. The blood dripped down to the tip and Hådvard wrote hastily, muttering his words through gritted teeth, "Empress, I do not have the time or patience for your childish nonsense and desire for adventures. It is time you return, or I *will* come to Vaestoria and bring you back myself, Hådvard."

Golden speckles filled the room from the sunlight pouring through the opened red curtains. Ambrosja's fingers twitched gently within Killian's hold. The morning light glowed across her pale skin, her moonlit waves fanned around the red silk of the pillow, and her lashes—as pale as her hair—fluttered open. Her gaze shifted from blurry shapes to clear clarity as her eyes looked down at her hand, resting so softly within Killian's on the pillows that separated them.

Killian's hands were rough, large, dwarfing the Empress's, but held her hand with a gentleness that none would ever believe he possessed.

She could hear the Commander's breathing—relaxed and low—with a slight growl to it that she found herself smiling at, wondering if maybe that's what dragons sounded like when they slept.

Ambrosja's eyes didn't leave their interlaced fingers. Her cheeks warmed just by the memory of last night. Of their kiss, of their promise to starve for each other—even if it hurt. The idea that it would hurt… meant nothing compared to how Killian looked at her, how he held her, how he took her to bed—not as a lover—but as a precious and delicate gem… even if she feared and hated being something breakable… she was willing to be that in his hands.

The Empress inched closer to the barrier, pressing herself to it as if she could reach the Commander through it. It was infuriating to have the barrier there, but it felt all the more special. That's when Killian shifted, trading hands so he could keep holding her, as he turned, his own form facing the barrier now.

"Empress?" Killian's voice was rough with sleep. "I can tell you're awake."

Ambrosja smiled. But she remained silent, testing him.

He continued, "You're not snoring, Empress."

Her lips parted, making a silent gasping expression, and she frowned. She whipped her head towards the barrier, and with her free hand, she grabbed her own pillow and smacked it onto Killian's face.

"How dare you accuse me of such a thing again! I do not snore!"

The Commander didn't chuckle. He didn't growl. Instead, he hummed, a sound of pure contentment. "There's the Empress I know—always beating me."

"I do not!"

"My nose says otherwise."

"Your nose lies!"

"Oh, it really doesn't," Killian chuckled. He propped himself onto his elbow so he could look over the pillows and gaze down at Ambrosja. "Good morning, Ambrosja."

Ambrosja looked up at Killian, her golden eyes met his silver ones, and she was stunned—it was like seeing him in an entirely different light.

"Good morning, Killian," Ambrosja whispered softly, "I hope the way we slept was not uncomfortable for you…"

The Commander was still holding her hand. He brought her hand to his lips, kissing the skin tenderly. "Never."

"I don't know why I haven't moved south yet," a pigeon-handler muttered as he wrapped himself up in thick layers of fur and wool, "I blame you little shits." He narrowed his eyes at the pigeons, filling up the feed for them.

"Shut up, old man," a young man laughed, carrying a pouch of letters. "You love those tiny beasts, and you know it."

The old pigeon-handler grunted, "They behave better than my actual children, that's for sure."

A chuckle escaped the young man, then stopped, narrowing his eyes out the window. "We have a pigeon incoming! From Stonehaven's Round Table!"

Both men made their way to the window, their eyes focused on the pigeon that barreled through the cold winds with a rounded tube attached to its foot, red ribbon dangling about, holding it together. When the pigeon was within reaching distance, the men pulled the window open quickly, letting the pigeon fly through.

The pigeon landed atop the cage of the others, its head bobbing as it moved slowly around the space, shaking off the snowflakes that had drifted into its feathers. It kicked its small foot, presenting the red ribbon.

The pigeon-handler carefully undid the ribbon, freeing the bird and the tube. He undid it gently, as if any mishandling could cause the contents to crumple in his grasp.

As the tube was opened, he slid out a piece of paper out and read it, "'Do not open the inner tube'," he said, giving a glance and noticing a thinner tube within the one he had just opened, then looked at the letter again, "Hand this off to the current Military Captain of Greybarrow and ensure the inner tube is delivered immediately to the Stone of Still Oaths..." his voice faltered then. He swallowed, "... and make sure it lands in the hands of a Nordorner Oathbearer."

The young man's eyes were wide; he stuttered once, "To the S-Stone of Still Oaths? That's the border—the separation between Nordorn and Vaestoria... Stonehaven—the *Round Table* of Stonehaven is sending a letter to *Nordorn*...?"

The old man rolled the parchment back. "Let's find the Captain of the Guard; he'll know what to do."

"Do you think you're going to do it?" Johann asked Gunnar, keeping his eyes on his old friend with a quiet concern.

Gunnar rubbed the back of his neck, staring down at the wooden grains in the table. His lunch was pushed aside. "Not sure," he admitted, "it would be nice to not be haunted by such things anymore... The idea of not having to worry about whether or not I am going to lose myself as I did in the mine... Sounds grand."

Cinder was silent for once; her fingers were just curled around her bowl of elk stew. Brows pinched together. She'd normally have a comment, but as of recently... most things seemed to slip her.

But it was Killian's voice that spoke next as he approached the table. "I don't think you should do it," he said, setting down a list of tasks beside Gunnar's arm, "our wounds of war are ours to carry, and to overcome as we must, not to numb." Then he gestured to the list. "New tasks for you, from helping build crates to fixing weapons, take your pick."

Gunnar grunted. His eyes met Killian's, then the list. "Can't I just rotate the tasks?"

"Sure." The Commander crossed his arms. "Rotate your tasks, stick to one, as long as you don't go into the mine again."

Cinder glared at Killian. "What would you know about wounds of war? You are one of the men causing them." She scoffed, waving Killian off dismissively. "Don't speak of them if you have one; it's not your place."

Killian arched his brow. "We all have a wound," he gestured to the burn scar on her neck, "and you have one as well, I'm sure."

Donathan, mostly quiet, spoke up, "Don't talk about her scar, it's not your business."

The Commander tilted his head, looking at Donathan with something close to being amused but also impressed. He placed his hands behind his back, calmly interlacing them. "I will say, you've grown quite a bit since we first met, Donathan…" He paused and then gave a nod. "I'm almost proud. But watch out, it's not often I accept that kind of tone around here." Killian turned away then. "Carry on."

As Killian walked away, he passed Ambrosja. The two of them locked eyes. Killian gave her that quiet half smile, and Ambrosja gave him her reddened cheeks that only he could do, and just as they passed… his hand left from resting behind his back to drag his forefinger down her arm and briefly hold her fingers before parting as he continued making his way to the Command Hall.

Ambrosja's heart was pounding. Eyes half-lidded with pure contentment. Something she hadn't felt since that playful chase in the Bramble. Or that moment when Mora sat on her lap.

Mora… Ambrosja thought to herself, already cursing her memories and her mind. *Godsdamn it! Why now? I am — I am sorry! I am just trying… trying to be happy! That does not mean I do not care or I stopped fighting for you!*

The Empress stopped walking completely, her hand found the arm that Killian had rubbed, and she dragged her hand down and then up, rubbing it; her fingers pressing hard into her own body. Those lids that were partially closed from contentment had now been trembling as her brows pinched and twitched. She bit her bottom lip hard, not even paying attention that she was still standing in the middle of the mining camp.

He was not the one who lit the fire. He was not the one who brought down the blades! Why must I feel so guilty about this? I have not stopped! I will not stop! I will continue pursuing the truth! I will force justice's hand… But… do not torture me for my heart… Please…

Killian paused at the door to his Command Hall. He was only going to glance back to watch Ambrosja walk, but his hand tightened on the handle when he saw her feet frozen in place, while her hand rubbed the arm he had touched.

"*Ambrosja…*" he whispered to himself, pulling away from his door and walking right back to her. "Ambrosja," he said with a calm tone, despite it being spoken through gritted teeth, "there is something I wish to discuss."

Without leaving room for argument, he placed his hand on the middle of her back and pulled her away from the spot where everyone could see she was most vulnerable.

The Commander pulled only one side of the curtains to his office closed, just so the afternoon glow could still light the room up. His eyes kept moving to Ambrosja's spot, where she sat on the chair near his desk. Her eyes seemed vacant, and her fingers kept playing with a lock of her hair.

Killian walked back and took a seat beside her, not across from her. "Are you alright?" His voice was softer now. "You looked frozen out there, and you look frozen now, just in a different manner."

Ambrosja nodded, eyes meeting Killian's. "I am fine, I was just—"

"You're lying."

"I am not." Ambrosja's brows furrowed as she leaned closer. "Do not speak for me."

"I'm not speaking for you," Killian clarified, "I'm pointing out that you are lying, and you were about to provide a pretty little lie attached to that one just so you could get out of sharing what's wrong… Or so you can spare me. So, what is it?" He leaned forward just as she did, elbows resting heavily on his knees. "Did my touch bother you? I won't do it again if that's the case."

The Empress was silent for a moment. Her eyes simply traced every bit of Killian. Then she looked away and sighed heavily. "No, it was not your touch… Or… maybe it was. I just know that… as much as I liked it… I couldn't help but feel happy, then feel guilt over my happiness. Over guilt about Mora." She turned her head away. "But I do not want you to part from me, to increase your distance once more. It will only make me feel worse."

Killian nodded. He leaned closer, shoulders lowered. "Tell me about Mora, Empress." His hand reached out, gently grabbing hers.

Ambrosja's gaze shifted to Killian's immediately. Her body tensed for

a moment — then relaxed. "I... I do not know anything about Mora... except she..." Ambrosja smiled. "She liked carrots. Every time I saw her... she had a carrot." Her eyes began to water. "She had a carrot in her pocket when I found her body!"

The Commander immediately reached over, big and rough hands found Ambrosja's body, and without a question, he brought her to rest onto his lap, letting her press her face into his shirt. He let her shake, let her soak the fabrics and his skin. He simply ran a hand down her back, trying to soothe the guilt that had so deeply embedded into her bones and wrecked her body.

"Just a little girl," Killian whispered. "She didn't deserve that. None of them did, Ambrosja, but especially little Mora." He took a deep breath. "But you also don't deserve to feel chained to the very hells you think you should be. You didn't know about the attack. You did what you could."

"Did I?!" Ambrosja looked up at him, grasping at his shirt. "Did I do everything I could?! Because all I remember is trying to hide a little girl, save a little boy, and fight! And fight! Until darkness took my vision and I awoke alone! Surrounded by the bodies of those I should have protected!!"

The Commander didn't raise his voice; he wouldn't. He continued speaking softly, but his tone was firmer, more sure, "But you were one woman, Ambrosja. A single woman cannot defend an entire hamlet."

"Why not?!"

"Because you can't."

"But why?!"

"Because it is impossible," Killian squeezed her now, "because no one has done it! Not even Skeldr, not even Brynhjora! But you fought! You fought, and that is what matters! And as long as you continue to fight, that is all that will matter!"

Ambrosja stared at Killian, then looked down, just sobbing harder. "I am what my people call me... An amber... Nothing less, nothing more." She shut her eyes tightly. "The greatest thing I had ever done was take out a naval fleet to protect my home... But even then... it was vengeance for my father's death. It was never about protection..."

"So?" Killian shrugged.

"So?" Ambrosja was startled. She met his gaze again. "So, it was selfish!"

"Everyone is selfish," the Commander said without hesitating, "and that doesn't make us less. They call you an amber for what? Because amber doesn't mean selfish."

Ambrosja looked away, shame coming over her expression. "They call me the Amber of the North because I have been deemed as delicate."

Killian tilted his head, one hand leaving to rub his chin. "Yet... Even then... an amber comes from the old Norr word *ambyr*— to carry the sun..." Killian leaned back then, bringing Ambrosja closer. "It is a gorgeous word, and when those tiny orange gems were found throughout your country... They called it *amber,* not because it was so easily breakable, but because it was so beautiful, like sunlight captured within a stone."

The Empress rolled her eyes. "Stop that!" She crossed her arms, but she was no longer crying. "I hate it when you speak of *my* country like you know so much more than I do."

"Ah, you didn't know this piece of history, did you?"

"I was not taught about gems! I was taught about customs, politics, languages, and combat."

"Let me ask you a question, Ambrosja..." He paused, waiting for her to look at him, and when she did, he continued, "Who gave you the title?"

The Empress paused. Not because she didn't know... But from hesitation. "The Elders did, they feel a connection to the stone, to the people, and that is the name they felt within the mountain."

"And the Elders are?"

Ambrosja swallowed. "The Elders are my advisors... They are my link to the stone, and to my gods."

"Do you think that is what the mountain meant? That you are weak? Even after knowing all that you have gone through?" Killian leaned forward, just a breath away from Ambrosja, still cradling her on his lap. "Do you think they are calling you delicate because you can break? Or because you are willing to break to do what must be done? That you are willing to carry the sun even after so much darkness has plagued you?"

The Empress was stunned. The words, the proximity... it was... intimate in a way Ambrosja could never have imagined, or felt, in a way that seemed to peel her flesh apart to reveal sins that she, herself, had carved into her very bones. "I suppose not..."

AMBER, AMBYR

The word Ambyr is one of the oldest in the Norr tongue, translating roughly to "to carry the sun." From this ancient word came Amber — the name given to the small golden gems found deep within Nordorn's mountains. The Nordorners named them not for what they were, but for what they meant: light preserved within darkness, warmth carried through the cold.

Though ambers are mined in caverns where sunlight has never reached, they are regarded as symbols of joy and endurance. To hold one is to be reminded that even in the deepest dark, the sun endures — and that its light can be carried by mortal hands.

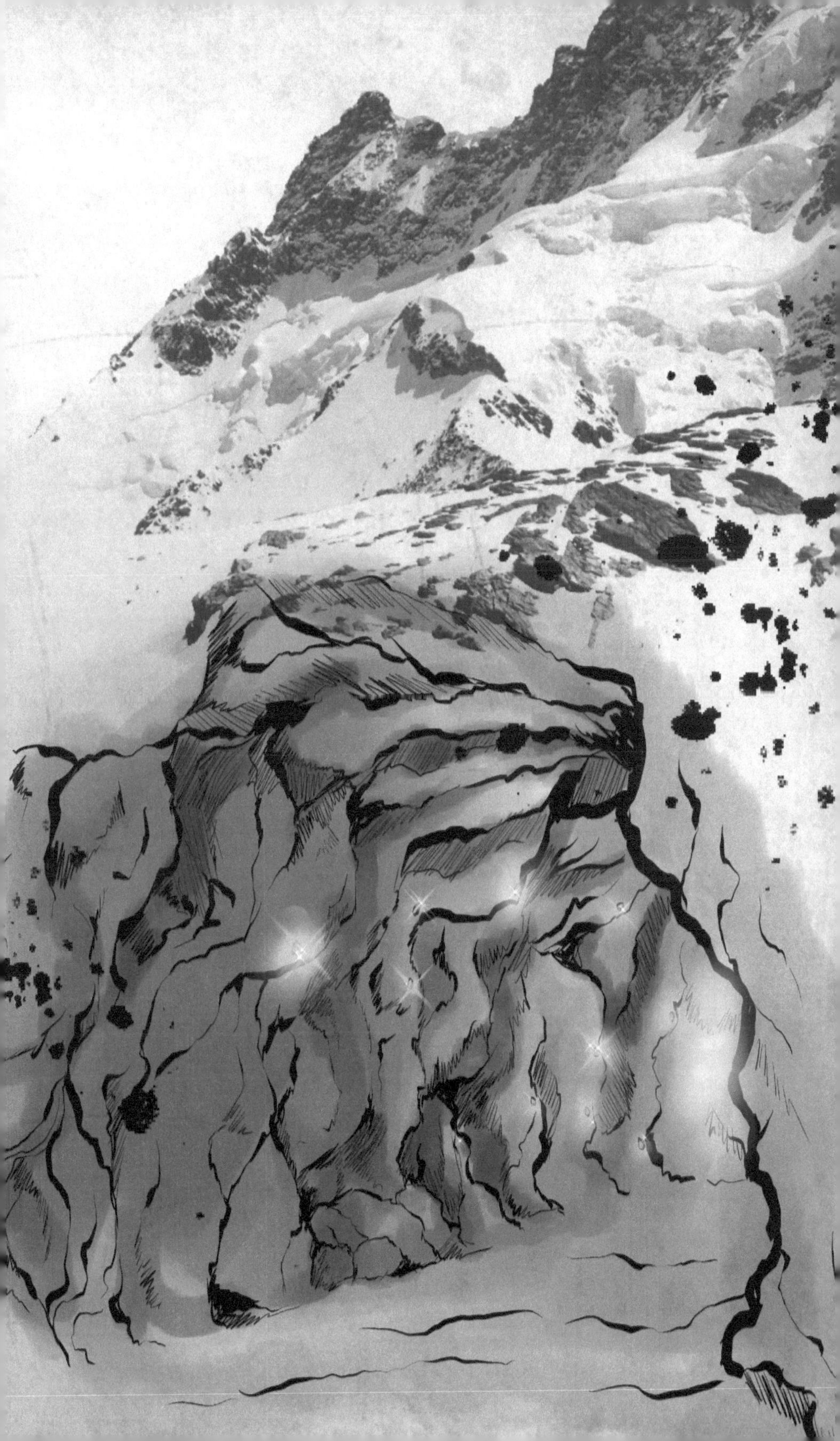

OF DARK HORSES

Jareth's papers were scattered across the breakfast table. His fingers were tight around his coffee mug. His blue eyes were sharp as he read through drafts upon drafts. Until finally a sharp whack of a rolled Stone's Gazette hit the table beside Jareth's hand.

"What is this?" Isolde's piercing blue eyes met her son's. She unrolled the Gazette, letting Jareth see it in full view.

The Diplomat looked down. And there it was. A sketch of his image, not staring back at him, but staring into the eyes of a nameless woman. While he was surrounded by four others at a gentleman's private salon, the *Gilded Aerie*. His legs were spread, his coat undone, a woman's hand drifting across the fabric adorning his ribs, another touched his chin while her breasts pressed into his side, a cheek resting against his knee, a chin resting against the other, while another rested atop his shoulder from behind.

"So much for private," Jareth muttered, taking another sip of his coffee.

"Do you think this is funny, my son?" Isolde narrowed her eyes at him. "A Thorn being swarmed by easy women?"

"I didn't laugh, mother," The Diplomat said, leaning back in his chair, "I thought you wanted to have breakfast together. I didn't realize that an interrogation would have been part of it. I would have come up with a white lie to get out of this."

Isolde sighed. She walked around the table and took her seat.

"If your father sees this—"

"Oh, I saw it," Aaric emerged from the archways that led down the halls, "I also saw rumors of apparently... *Lord Jareth Thorn rekindling old flame with Lady Mira Harte,*" Aaric paused for dramatic effect, "'*Will Stonehaven's most eligible bachelor finally settle and break the hearts of Stonehaven... or will he just break one?*'" He took his own seat and tapped the Gazette before Jareth. "Page three."

Steps were heard. Unhurried but cheerful. From the doorway emerged Lyra, wearing a long, dark blue gown with sheer sleeves that were puffed. Her long black hair swayed with every step, her blue eyes fixed on Jareth.

"Disgusting," Lyra said as she took her seat beside her mother. "If you are truly with Mira once more, I will request that Father disowns you."

Jareth was already flipping through the pages. Then he saw it, a sketch of him getting in a carriage with Mira. He stared at it as if it had offended his bloodline. He was silent. Just reading the words. Cold eyes sliding across the paper before him, tracing the sketches. "Yes, well... I suppose it is what it is."

Aaric's hands laced together, elbows resting on the table, "It is what it is?" Aaric repeated. One brow arched, "So, which one is true? The one with Mira or the five women in one night?"

Jareth's tongue pressed to the inside of his cheek. He didn't answer. "It's best if we discuss matters of importance. Not rumors."

"Yes," Lyra immediately agreed, "I prefer to hear about Wintersong and the future of our hamlets instead of where my brother... *buries* himself."

"Maybe if you didn't romance books, you'd have your own business to tend to, Lyra," he gestured vaguely in the air, "like possibly giving our parents grandchildren?"

Lyra snapped her head to Jareth as if he had just suggested she mate with a dragon. "Disgusting! I will not be the one responsible for supplying our parents with another set of kids for them to dote on! That's why mother has her garden!"

Isolde stared between her children. "Lovely," she took a sip of her tea, "I love that all of my children have decided they have no desire to continue the Thorn bloodline."

Jareth raised a hand. "I didn't say that—"

"Yes, mother," Lyra interjected, "worry not, I'm sure all five of those women are already carrying your grandchildren."

Now it was Jareth's turn to twist his head towards Lyra as if she had accused him of impregnating a dragon. "That is not even funny."

Isolde lowered her head; her black, gray, and white locks fell over her

shoulders. "The closest I ever came to seeing my children have a family of their own was Killian and Capricia, I swear," Isolde sighed wistfully, "those two were just right. He was… well, *him*—"

"Brutal?" Jareth interjected.

"Loyal to a fault?" Lyra suggested, scowling at her brother.

"At war with himself," Isolde said firmly, "while Capricia always grounded him. She was bright, offered games to relax, so polite, such a lovely girl."

Lyra smirked. "She would have definitely made a better sister-in-law than Mira."

Jareth gave a false smile, leaning forward as he stared at his sister. "Well, I suppose it's a good thing Mira was going to marry me, and I called it off, so I could *spare you the terror*, dear sister."

"Children…" Aaric raised a brow, staring at his children from over his own coffee cup. He sighed. "Let us move on from this," he leaned back, relaxing in his chair, "Dragonrise is weeks away. We have plenty of things to do before then, requisitions, orders of Dragonflares, food for the banquets, invitations to the people of Stonehaven must be sent out!" He looked at his family. "As Thorns, we need to be more presentable than we have ever been. The Gazette's writers will be watching us, and we already have too much on our plates."

"Speaking of…" Jareth slid a letter to his father. "Greybarrow responded. They've sent a portion of their soldiers off to Wintersong…" The Diplomat sighed heavily. "Everything was destroyed. Every home was burnt. And they're currently gathering the bodies. So far from what they've counted… The entire hamlet might be dead… But they've also noticed some people who didn't belong."

Aaric was reading the letter, but his ears perked up when Jareth said that. "Didn't belong?" he echoed, "You mean to say… that those responsible might very well be among the wreckage?"

Jareth nodded. Aaric exhaled sharply, his fingers let the letter slip from his hands so he could brush his dark hair with threads of gray back, like a weight being dropped.

"But they've yet to do a proper inspection of the bodies… Within a week, we might actually learn if Nordorn is behind the attacks, father."

Those dark cloaks were snapping against the wind once more. Hair beneath black helms knotted in the air. The snow on the ground became less and less as the riders headed southwest. Now, it was mostly snowflakes that fell through the air like a silent witness to the Black Hand's approach.

"Sister-Hand Serana!" Cressida called out. "Let us take a break! The horses have been pushed further than they should have!"

"You think we have time to stop?!" Serana called back, still blazing ahead. "If the Empress is dead, then *everything* we have worked for will be in ruins! We have already wasted enough time waiting for those damned Vaestorian soldiers to get far enough ahead!"

"We won't have horses to take us the rest of the way if we keep going like this!"

Silence. The hooves kept moving.

"Serana!" Cressida finally shouted, her call piercing through the sharp, cold winds.

The hooves of Serana's horse came to a stop. The beast's nostrils flared as it took heavy breaths. Everyone followed suit, hooves slamming in the damp ground to come to a stop. The riders looked back as Serana slid off the saddle. She walked, crunching branches and leftover snow beneath her boots. She adjusted the leather of her gloved hands like a nervous tic.

"We're close," she muttered. "We might make it to Greenfield in two days."

Cressida made her way to Serana. She stood back, not too far, but definitely not too close. "Serana," her voice was low, eyes fixed on her, "Are you mad? Pushing our horses like that?"

Serana's head snapped to the side, scowling at the woman from within the slits of her helm. "You answer to me. You listen to me. You do not question me. You do not judge me. We are given orders by Grand Marshal Gaspard, and we *will* follow them."

"And your plan is to, what? Let our horses ride to their deaths so we can march after an Empress—an Empress that we don't even know for certain is in Vaestoria? And then march back on foot to Greymire?"

"If she is here, and we lose her?" Serana tilted her head, a bitter smile crossing her lips. "The horses will be the lucky ones. Now, do your little fancy Nature Magic and tend to them. I plan to ride out as soon as the sun graces us."

*From the journal of Guinyldr Thorn,
Dreknfell, 17, 997*

DRAGONRISE

Dragonrise is the most radiant of Vaestoria's festivals, held each year in the month of Elandruxx to honor the dragons that once soared above the realm. For two days and nights, parades fill the streets, feasts are prepared, and the gates of every great city stand open to all — lord and laborer alike. The celebrations are funded by the regency's stewards and nobles, a gesture of gratitude and unity that bridges every station.

At the heart of each city stands a great table set beneath banners of dragonkind, where the people gather to share in food, story, and song.
Space is never promised, yet none are turned away; even those who stand beyond the circle are considered part of it. As the feasting begins, the regents rise to speak words of promise and remembrance, vowing to lead with the wisdom and strength of the dragons who came before.

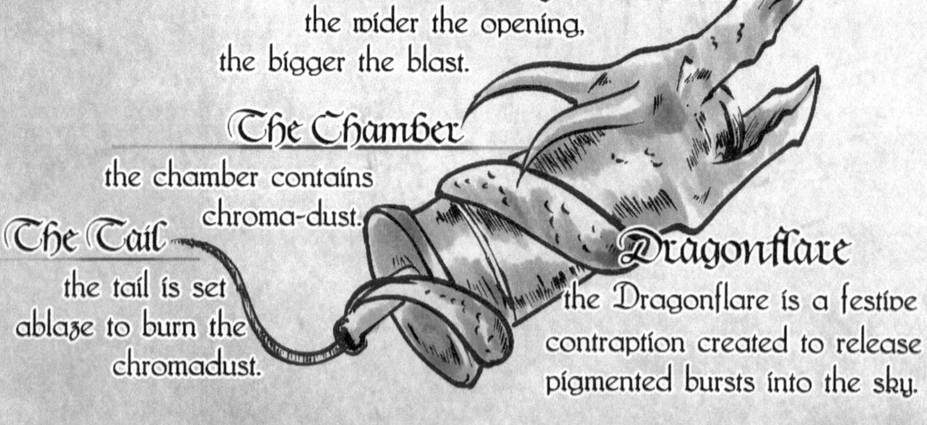

CHAPTER TWENTY-FIVE
SWEET-ROT

Ambrosja and Killian were walking side by side. Her hand rested on his thick forearm, which he couldn't help but flex, as if trying to impress her whilst pretending not to. Her smile was like the sun, bright and warm. Killian's free hand was holding a book, reading from it, his voice low like a lover whispering secrets.

Cinder watched this from half-closed eyes. "Disgusting," she muttered with a smile, taking another bite of her sandwich that was poorly put together by the Black Hand's cook.

Then she flinched—the bow and quiver hit the ground at her feet, spattering her boots with dirt.

"Good," Berric had grunted. "You can be disgusted out in the woods then."

She stared at the bow for a moment longer, then looked up at Berric. "Aw, what's this?" She taunted, "Are you kicking me out already? I thought we were just getting used to each other. You know, after you slapped me."

Berric crossed his arms. "Funny, you're going hunting. We're low on meat, and you've been chosen to go out there and hunt since your two old friends are busy with other matters."

"What makes you think I won't just run away as soon as I pass those gates?"

"Because you're going with him," Berric gestured to Donathan with a jerk of his chin. "And we can track him, so if you two *do* decide anything funny, you'll no longer be hunters—you'll be the hunted."

"Ooooh!" Cinder mock-shivered. "So scary!"

Berric leaned forward, his face inches from Cinder's. "Get to it," he growled, then straightened, looking at Donathan, who was hunched over at the other end of the table. "Hey, you, traitor! You're going hunting with her! So, finish up, now!"

Donathan looked around, then looked at Cinder. His eyebrows shot up, hazel eyes wide. He pointed at himself, and Cinder nodded. He picked up his tray and moved closer to her, sitting right beside her and setting his tray beside the bow and quiver that Cinder had placed onto the long table.

Donathan cleared his throat. "So, we're both going out into the woods, huh?"

"Yeah, and I'm using you as bait."

"O-okay," a pause, then Donathan whipped his head to Cinder again, "Wait! What?!"

Cinder laughed, leaning into Donathan, "I'm teasing!" She swung the quiver over her shoulder, sliding it to wrap across her chest, then the bow went onto her other shoulder. "Let's get going, I really don't want to be out in the Bramble at night."

"Yeah, that wouldn't be a good idea." Donathan fixed his cloak. "And maybe we should stay near, right? We wouldn't want to venture too far off, and also get a search party after us."

"Except you can be tracked," Cinder grinned, reminding him.

"Oh—yeah, you're right."

"Let's go, Flame-Boy." Cinder grabbed Donathan's hand and began to lead him towards the gates. She raised her voice with a dramatic flair. "Let us head off into the Bramble, hunt for these *oh-so-powerful* Black Hand guards, while possibly being hunted by a Mourntalon!"

Berric watched this display with heavy brows and a frown. "Commander Thorn killed it! It'll be weeks before it's grown again, so go on, do your job and stop complaining!"

Cinder rolled her eyes, but she didn't say anything else. She picked up her pace with Donathan, heading out the gates and stepping into the woods immediately. She kept close to the camp, but not too close. Her eyes immediately darted to the ground, intent on tracking hooves. Occasionally, she looked up at the branches of the trees, eyes narrowing to find birds.

"We're going to need something big for the camp," Cinder muttered, stepping over a thick tree root. "Maybe a buck, maybe a boar. Just something to satisfy the fat bastards in that camp."

"I'm surprised they're not just doing some trading with Greenfield," Donathan replied, dodging the same root that Cinder had stepped over. "But maybe they're trying to save coin for other operations. I don't think the Black Hand freely has funds to spare. Or things to trade. They need all the materials they can get."

Cinder looked over at Donathan, her steps slowing to a stop. "Hey, do you know if the Black Hand ever targeted Marrowind?"

He tilted his head in thought. Then gave a slight shake. "Honestly? I don't know, Cinder." With that, Cinder began walking, and a low sigh escaped her lips that Donathan caught. "Why are you asking?"

"I lived in the regency of Marrowind," she explained. "The hunting and horse training village of Deepwood. At least half of it was burnt down, and my family's home was part of that half. Marrowind didn't bother putting the resources back into it. Kids were sent to orphanages, adults sent to infirmaries made out of twigs and tents…" Her brows furrowed as she recalled it all. Then softened when she looked at Donathan, "Just wondering if maybe the Black Hand had something to do with that."

His nod was gentle, not even noticeable. "I'm sorry, Cinder—I wouldn't know."

"Eh," Cinder shrugged, moving forward at a faster pace. "I figured you wouldn't. It happened years ago, but I thought I would ask, just in case."

"It makes sense."

They pressed forward, now in silence as Cinder moved her head at different angles to listen to the wilderness around her. The forest was vibrant with songs of birds and foliage that beamed in a green glow in the woods. The sounds of the mining camp had faded behind them.

"Alright," Cinder whispered. "Now that we're further away from that camp, there's bound to be something out here to hunt."

Donathan followed behind, his eyes on Cinder's feet. He was doing his best to move like her. Then he looked at *her*. Stealing a glimpse of her face when she turned. "Is this why you're so good at hunting?" He moved to walk beside her. "Because you're from a hunting village?"

"Yeah—my dad taught me." Cinder smiled, a genuine, kind smile, and Donathan couldn't stop staring when she did. "He said it doesn't matter if you're a girl or a boy, everyone needs to learn how to hunt, because the wild is unforgiving and it doesn't care who or what you are."

"Wise man," Donathan said with a gentle voice.

"Yeah, the best." Cinder smiled. "Now I have a new dad and an uncle who is tired of everything and everyone."

Donathan chuckled. "Well, clearly you got your good looks from your mom."

Cinder didn't stop walking, but her eyes widened for a fleeting moment—too brief for Donathan to notice. "Oh, look at you! I didn't realize you could flirt."

Donathan's cheeks tinted a pink hue. He pulled on his collar. "Y-yeah, just… Giving it a try. I guess." He cleared his throat. "Not often I get to go on a hunt with a pretty girl."

"You're laying that sweet-rot on really thick, Donathan."

"S-sorry, never flirted…" He chuckled nervously.

"So, you *are* trying to flirt?" Cinder looked at him now, her steps slowing.

"I guess so…" Donathan rubbed the back of his neck. "If you want, I can stop. I know I'm not the best at it. I'd hate for you to feel the need to dig a grave— you know, after you kill me for all this sweet-rot."

Cinder barked out a laugh. She quickly covered her mouth, letting soft chuckles escape her. "And you're funny, who knew?"

The two smiled, but walked in silence. They stepped over a small creek where frogs hopped from one rock to another. Cinder's eyes searched for disturbed patches of grass or prints within the earth. She kneeled occasionally, brushing away fallen leaves to find anything that could point her in the direction of a wild animal.

"Just small animals…" Cinder scratched her head. "Small isn't going to cut it. We're going to have to go further out into the woods, the big ones probably realized they're too close to people."

"You're pretty fearless, huh?"

Cinder was silent for a moment. She chewed on her bottom lip, her eyes still downcast, still trying to find evidence of anything that would lead her to a large game. "I wouldn't say fearless… I'm just—smart, I guess. I know where or how to hunt. I know how to be silent… Doesn't mean I'm not scared." She looked at Donathan now. She felt her vulnerability creep in, so she smirked instead, "Though I do rarely get scared." Donathan chuckled at that. Cinder continued, "How about you? You don't seem like you often went out into the wild. Like a scholar or something."

"Scholar?" Donathan grinned softly, tilting his head with a smile as he looked at Cinder. "No, most definitely not a scholar. I was a miner, actually. My family and I worked together in the biggest mine at Stonecreek Hill." He scratched his neck. "Didn't do much, too shy or scared. My big brother often *tried* to get me to court a girl, but—" he waved his hand, shaking off

the thought. "Eh, you don't want to hear that. Basically, yeah, I guess I had a scholarly social life, but not the job."

"Too shy, huh?" Cinder bumped her shoulder into Donathan's. "So, no kiss?"

His cheeks became pink, a vibrant shade against his olive skin. "N-no—no kiss, no entanglements or… anything."

"Anything?" Cinder cocked a brow. "So, no placing your sword within a sheath?" Donathan's eyes widened at that, but Cinder went on, "No polishing the knob? How about dipping your wand into a pool of magic?"

"Cinder!" Donathan choked. "N-no! None of that! I'm a virgin!"

Cinder slowed her steps, then stopped. She just stared at him for a moment, watched how his cheeks had gone from pink to red, how his neck was flushed, how he couldn't meet her eyes. She took a deep breath, then took a step forward. "Do you want to be?"

"W-what…?"

"Do you want to be a virgin?" She shrugged now. "If you want," she gestured to the woods. "It's just us, I could teach you a thing or two—if you want."

Donathan's eyes had nearly bulged out of his skull with how wide they had opened. He stuttered on nothing. He took a few steps back, nearly staggering. He felt awkward. Unsure. He looked away immediately, rubbing his neck aggressively. "I—you—you're just messing with me… Right?"

"Not at all…" She shook her head gently. "So, do you want to?"

Donthan's chest was heaving. His voice could barely escape his throat. And when it did, it cracked, "Y-yes…"

Cinder walked forward, her hands grabbing at his shoulders, firmly, not unkindly, and she pushed him until his back met bark. Her lips met his. There were no words shared. Nothing needed to be said, just an understanding between two people. Cinder dragged her lips down from Donathan's, treading to his chin, to his jaw, then to his neck. Her hands moved lower, undoing the buttons of his cloak to open it further. Donathan's hands were awkward. He simply held her waist tightly, fingers gripping into her leather tunic, gently tugging on it with unsure but needy hands.

Donathan's cloak was tugged open. Cinder's hands were now on his woolen pants, undoing the buttons. His breath was shaking, then he jolted when he felt Cinder plunge her hand into his nethercloths without warning. He nearly choked on air, his breathing had gone ragged when he felt Cinder's hand moved.

"C-Cinder…" His voice was shaky. "By Dragon's Breath…"

Cinder looked up at him, a smile on her face as she watched his expression. "Huh, you trim…"

"Y-yeah… I trim… You don't — you don't have to point it out."

"Why? It's not like you're getting any softer."

Cinder pulled her hand away, undoing the laces on her tunic, one by one, letting Donathan watch as she peeled open the leathers so he could see every inch of her. When her breasts spilled free, Donathan's eyes went wide, immediately set on the sight before him. Without a word, Cinder had guided his hands onto her, letting him cup the weight.

"Donathan…" Cinder whispered against his lips. "Only one part of you needs to be stiff. So, just relax, okay?"

Donathan nodded. His hands gave a firm squeeze, they moved slowly but more confidently every time Cinder's lips parted to give in to a whimper. He peeled one hand away, moving down her ribs, to her waist, giving another squeeze there, then to her pants. His fingers trailed until he reached the leather tie of it, giving it a firm tug until it loosened. Then his other hand cupping her moved to join the other, both gripped her pants, giving slow, gentle pulls. His eyes watched hers, waiting for any hesitation or any sign of her discomfort. But there wasn't a single one—in fact—it looked as if Cinder was praising him through her eyes.

She touched his chest, now guiding him to a patch of grass where no rock was found. She pushed him down onto it, and when he settled a thud of his body, her hands moved fast, tugging quick at his pants, pulling them down with his nethercloths *just* enough. Cinder sat atop of him now. Her heat so close to his, but not just there yet. She kissed him again, deeper. Biting on his lip and giving it a tug before moving along his jaw, up his cheek, until she met his ear.

"Grab my hips, Donathan," she warned him, her voice dropping to a sensual tone. "Because I am going to ride you now."

Donathan didn't hesitate. He grabbed Cinder's hips as she lifted up, squatting above him. Her descent was slow. Donathan groaned when he felt her heat beginning to wrap around him. His head tilted back but snapped forward again, his eyes on Cinder's. Every nerve of his was on fire, then she sank all the way down and he released a gasp, just as Cinder did. Her hands pressed into Donathan's chest. Her hips rolled, grinding back and forth. Her hips swayed atop of him, pressing down hard until she felt that swollen head reach her deepest parts. Cinder's moans echoed in the space between them. She grabbed his tunic like a woman in heat as her legs shifted for her to bounce on him now. Donathan was breathless—he was staring at Cinder like he was lost in the pure pleasure she was giving him. He moved one hand to her waist, squeezing her tight while he groaned. His hips bucked up without meaning to, meeting her halfway.

"Just like that, Donathan..." Cinder whispered against his cheek. "Keep meeting me."

At first, Donathan's movements were clumsy, eager, which made it fun for Cinder; her grin was wide, holding onto Donathan's shoulders now as they slowly moved in-sync, then slowly turned feral. Her voice against his skin was getting louder, whimpers intertwined with moans so soft, so needy, that Donathan never imagined it could have left her lips, not like this. His eyes locked on hers, they were going wide, wide with realization, wide with pride. He didn't think about what he was doing, he was just following instinct now, following *her*. He sat up, his hands moved until his arms wrapped tight around her, bringing her chest to chest with him. She gasped, a sound of surprise and pleasure. His right hand slammed into the grass beside him, putting his strength into it while he bucked his hips up, faster. Harder.

"D-Donathan," Cinder whimpered. Then a breathy laugh left her. "Fuck—look at you!"

"I can't help it—" Donathan groaned against Cinder's neck. "You're driving me mad, Cinder."

"Ooh—oh fuck," she moaned, her sounds turning breathless. "Don't—don't stop, I'm almost there."

"Tell me what you need," his eyes met hers, searching for answers in every pinched brow or pouted lip.

"Just keep doing this," she moaned, "just this!"

So he did. Even as his muscles ached, Donathan didn't stop. He sought to wring out every bit of pleasure from Cinder. His hips followed her moans, never faltering. When he felt her tighten, he groaned, feeling himself being strangled and nearly forced to the edge with her. Then Cinder hugged him tight, moaning against him, and he felt it—the sudden tightness, the sudden warmth surrounding him, the way she trembled. Donathan fell backwards onto the grass, bringing Cinder down with him as he bucked up until he felt his own pleasure erupt, thrusting his hips upwards one last time until both he and Cinder were off the ground.

Their breathing had gone into ragged pants, beating against the other's skin as they calmed down from the high. Donathan lowered his hips then. His chest was heaving, his breathing far more ragged than Cinder's, and his eyes were blown wide, as if he couldn't believe that *he* was the one who just did that. Cinder laughed against his chest, a soft sound, contentment laced

with ecstasy.

Then *snap*. A twig broke. Cinder sat up, she didn't get off of Donathan, but her hands gripped her bow, stealing an arrow from the tossed quiver and aimed it. Then released.

Donathan barely had time to understand what had happened. His eyes were now wide with shock. He looked in the direction of where Cinder had shot her arrow—a boar. Collapsed now, the arrow was embedded deep into the creature's eye. Donathan twitched within Cinder. Cinder? Oh, of course she felt it. Her own eyes went wide, also with shock. She looked down at him, staring at his flushed face.

"Are you—are you getting hard again?"

"Listen," Donathan cleared his throat. "What you just did," he pointed at the boar, "while like *that*," he gestured to all of her, bare and still on him, "that was…" he sighed, unsure how to explain himself. "I like strong women, okay? It's — it's a turn on." He looked away now, red and bashful.

Cinder stared. Then laughed. But it wasn't a mocking one. It was disbelief, but also something close to… flusteredness at Donathan's admission. She cleared her throat. "Wow—well, I am happy to know that… that does it for you."

"Now you're poking fun at me."

"No! No!" Cinder dropped her bow, her hands now on his shoulders, "No, I am being genuine." She continued to let the vulnerability creep in, "It's nice to know that you don't mind me as I am, that you genuinely like *this*," she gestured to herself. "And you weren't just… eager to get a quick fuck."

Before Donathan could respond, Cinder was already getting up. He groaned when he felt her slide off, his head tilting back into the grass. He laid there for a few seconds, just hearing the rustling of fabric as Cinder dressed herself again. He eventually sat up, reluctantly so, but he pulled up his pants and nethercloths.

He watched Cinder move, walking towards the dead boar and pulling out the arrow, looking over the arrowhead, the tip was steel, barely damaged, just covered in blood and soft tissue from within the skull. She tilted her head in praise.

"Well, that was a clean kill," Donathan called out, just finishing buttoning his pants. "I bet your dad taught you that, huh?"

"Sort of," Cinder shrugged. "I mean, he taught me how to shoot, but it took years past his death to actually aim so damn well I could get an arrow through the eye."

"Did your mom teach you any hunting?"

"Oh, by Dragon's Breath, no!" She laughed at the thought, grinning and shaking her head while she tied the boar's limbs together. "My mother was a teacher, and she was often trying to teach me to be a lady. Told me that I should marry rich, so I have opportunities. Travel, studies, whatever it is that a rich man could provide for me."

"Ah, so, she was the kind of mother that wanted you to be a lady, whereas your father wanted you to just… survive."

"Pretty much." Cinder's smile was wide, then slowly it faded into something smaller. "But, she had my little sister. My little sister *loved* tea parties, reading, and writing. She was the one that loved doing lady-like things." She then hoisted the boar over her shoulders. "And how about you? What was your mother like? Did she also tell you to marry rich or chase after greatness?" She looked at his hands then. "Maybe see about pursuing magic?"

Donathan rubbed his neck. "My mom?" He gave a half-smile as he thought about it. "Nah, my mom was the kind of woman who was really strong, probably more hard working than most men I've seen."

"Is that right?" Cinder's voice was teasing now. "Did your father ever feel emasculated by her?"

Donathan saw the hoisted boar over Cinder's shoulders finally and took a few steps forward. "Hey, let me carry that." He took the boar from her and quickly put it over his shoulders, his muscles flexing as he worked. "And emasculated? I don't think so, maybe threatened, because she was much younger and had far more energy than him. Probably bigger muscles, too, at some point."

"How much younger?"

"Twenty years."

Cinder stopped in her tracks. "Woah! Your mom was twenty years younger than your dad? Okay, totally not weird, Donny-boy."

"It's — it's not like that!" Donathan stammered. "She pursued him, he tried running away, he couldn't get away, he gave in, and yeah."

"What do you mean he couldn't get away?!"

Donathan sighed, rolling his shoulders as he kept the boar over him. They were both walking back to camp now. "She moved to Stonecreek Hill at the age of fifteen, she had nothing, no coin, no clothes but those she wore… So, she joined the mines. She had energy, and she was strong, so, she went to work. My father was the one that approved her—and he also mentored her, but… She proved to be pretty capable, so, he only stood around for a few days, and he went off to mine in his own section."

Cinder walked close, listening intently, not once interrupting Donathan.

He continued. "So, my mom developed a crush on my dad. Not for his looks. Not for his age. But for his work ethic. She admired how hard working he was, how he never stopped until it was breakfast, lunch, dinner, or time to sleep." Donathan's smile was awkward now, but proud. "So, she pursued that. And she didn't stop."

"Uh huh…" Cinder squinted at Donathan. Donathan paid no mind, he found it amusing if anything.

"Anyway, at first my dad thought she just wanted to learn some more, and he's the kind of guy who likes to show off, all men like to show off for a pretty woman. But then over time—my dad realized that my mom wasn't being so innocent, she was *hunting* him." Cinder laughed at that. "She followed him, stalked him, honestly. She would check which section he was mining and told the Foreman she was going there. And my dad? Oh, he noticed. And he started to get paranoid. Stubborn little thing chasing after him, young enough to be his daughter."

They were approaching that same creek now, their steps slower. Donathan kept his pace steady with the boar he carried.

"He tried setting boundaries." Donathan smirked, as if he believed his father didn't try hard enough. "She didn't listen, yeah, she wasn't really the, uh– respectful kind. So, that didn't work, he spoke to the Foreman, but the Foreman didn't do anything because my mom was a better miner than half of the men there. So, my dad kind of just dealt with this for years."

"For years?!" Cinder was aghast. "Years?!"

"Well, yeah. My mom had nowhere to go, and Stonecreek Hill was my dad's home," Donathan explained. "He was born and raised there. But, anyway… He tried entangling himself in romantic ties, but it was really hard because a lot of the women felt intimidated by mom, *but not only that*," he gave Cinder a look, "apparently, my dad often looked for my mom, he wouldn't say if it was because he actually did like the attention or because he was trying to distance himself," he let out a low chuckle at that. "Finally, she's twenty. She has had enough of my dad evading her. So, she challenges him. She says they'll arm wrestle, and if she wins, he *has* to court her. If he wins, then whatever he says goes."

"Did she win?"

"Oh yeah, she won. She slammed his arm down so hard he actually couldn't mine for a week."

"Damn."

"Anyway, guess it worked out, because not too long after, my mom

was pregnant with my older brother, and right after that, I came along, then another two boys."

"All boys?"

"Mhm," Donathan smiled, though his smile faded fast. "Yeah," he sighed. "And of course, of all the children to survive, it had to be me."

"Donathan—"

"Don't," he shook his head. "I'm not trying to start some sort of pity-fest, Cinder. I just find it ironic. All of my brothers, even the little ones, were brave. Strong. But me? I don't know why I ended up so different. But, I hope I can make it up to them. Live up to the Wren men."

"Wren?"

"Oh, yeah," Donathan looked at her with a soft smile. "My last name is Wren."

"That's a nice name," Cinder admitted, brushing her arm against Donathan's. "Wouldn't mind passing it down to my future children."

Donathan nearly tripped from that. His heart pounded in his ribs. "Don't—don't tease me like that, Cinder, or I'll—" he stopped speaking when Cinder turned to face him with that sultry smile. He took a deep breath, gathering his courage. "Or I'll make sure you do."

"Oh?" She was already unbuttoning her clothes.

Donathan dropped the boar immediately. "Oh."

Cinder walked up to Donathan, her breath mingling with his, her head tilted up so she could meet his eyes. "I'll hold you to it, Fire-Hands."

"Fire-Hands?" Donathan's voice trembled with eagerness and bashfulness.

"Mhm, think of it as being promoted from Flame-Boy."

Her hands then met his chest again, pushing him against a tree like she did before, but this time she lifted her leg up high, pressing her knee to his side. Donthan didn't resist. His arm hooked under her leg, his other arm wrapping around her waist to bring her flush to him as their lips met once more. Heated and filled with promises of something long-lasting.

STONECREEK HILL

Stonecreek Hill rests high among the northwestern ridges of Stonehaven's regency, a humble yet vital hamlet carved into the mountainside.

Its homes climb the rocky slopes in uneven tiers, each path winding toward the mouths of the mines that have long sustained the region. Known as the heart of Stonehaven's mining trade, the hamlet once gleamed with the light of forges and lanterns deep within the stone.

When Stonecreek Hill fell under attack, the blow was felt across the regency. Its loss marked not only the ruin of mines and livelihood, but the dimming of Stonehaven's proudest flame. In the time since, both the hamlet and its people have labored to rise again—stone by stone, breath by breath—carving resilience from the very mountain that bore them.

From the journal of Guinylar Thorn,
Dreknfell, 36, 997

DEEPWOOD

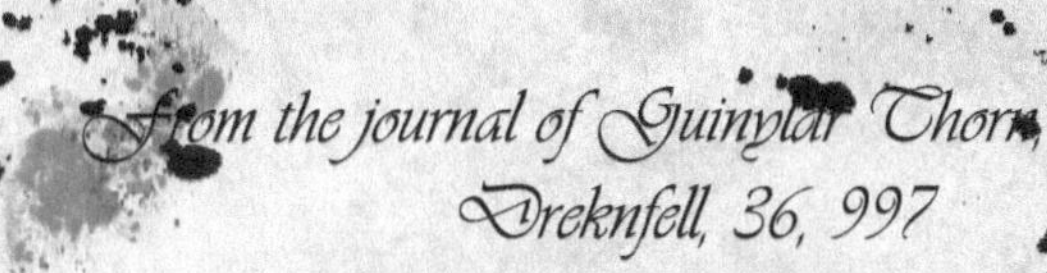

Deepwood once stood where the grasslands of Marrowind met the shadow of its forests – a village known for its hunters and for the proud horses bred upon its open fields. The people lived by balance: the riders tending the plains while the hunters vanished into the trees.

When Deepwood was attacked, years before the fall of Stonecreek Hill, the village burned in halves – one side scorched, the other spared. Yet Marrowind did not rebuild. Whether from loss, fear, or the pull of newer lands, its people drifted away, and Deepwood was left to the forest's slow reclamation. Now only foundations and overgrown fences remain, markers of a place the maps still name but the living no longer remember.

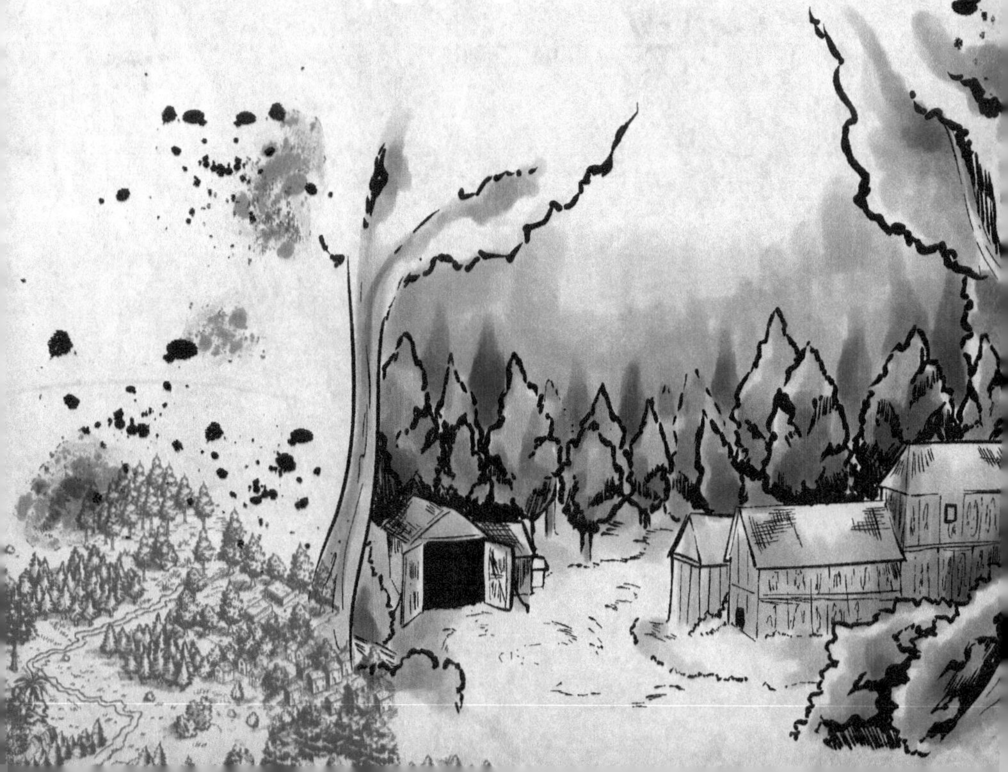

CHAPTER TWENTY-SIX

DRAGON OF STONE

The camp's night was lively with chatter. Donathan and Cinder had returned hours prior with a heavy and thick boar. The excitement that the crew, miners and Black Hand alike, showed through the lingering stares and tales of the great spit-roast they would have that night. And what a feast it was. The cook for the Black Hand actually brought out his most expensive spices and his best knives. Others were already moving to clear the camp and gather coals.

For hours, all eyes were on that spit-roast, the many pieces that had been buttered up with salt, crushed garlic and onions. How a glaze of honey mead and apple was applied every so often to keep the roast from drying out. Caramel and woodsmoke thickened the air, clinging to every cloak and tent even in the open night. Not a single soul could focus properly. And for tonight… That seemed to be okay.

Tankards of mead—mead that had been *acquired* by desperate and young Black Hand soldiers—were passed around. Drinks were tipped back, men daring each other to drink themselves stupid, while women made bets on which man would drop their trousers the fastest if asked. One soldier, drunk like a bee feasting upon a fermented fruit, had pulled an unused pot onto his lap and began to tap onto it with a surprisingly steady rhythm. The lute—the one meant to bring morale to miners, but hardly ever touched—had finally been grasped, and song fell from fingers like ink pouring down a quill.

For once, it felt the night was well-earned. Miners, paid or otherwise, had a smile on their face as they dug into pieces of the meat and the grilled vegetables on their plates. Cinder and Donathan bumped into each other, leaning close like whispers being passed from one lover to the next. Gunnar had patted—more like slammed—Johann's back so hard that Johann nearly choked on his piece, prompting Gunnar to actually slam this time. Ambrosja sat across from them, a wide smile on her face. She hadn't taken her own plate yet. She was waiting, excited. And delighted to simply watch her friends revel.

"Lass," Gunnar grunted while chewing on his slab of boar meat, "If you don't grab your damn share soon, someone else will."

Cinder pushed Gunnar's shoulder. "Leave her be—most of these fucks are getting stuffed from mead anyway. The size of that boar should last us *at least* three days." She cut him a sly glance. "As long as you don't keep going back for seconds."

Johann ignored the bickering between Cinder and Gunnar. He gestured to Ambrosja and the empty space in front of her. "Why haven't you gone and gotten your share?"

Ambrosja smiled softly. "I am waiting for Killian."

Donathan smiled at that, his voice dropped to a whisper as he tilted his head to just behind Ambrosja. "You won't have to wait for long."

Sure enough, Killian was a few steps behind, carrying a single plate that had a gorgeous piece of a boar's leg, not the entire thing, but a hefty one. Its color was of darkened reds and browns, glistening from the honey glaze, small baked potatoes decorated the sides, with greens scattered about. Killian stopped just behind Ambrosja, his body just grazing her back. He set the plate down for her, hunching over just enough where his chest touched the crown of her head.

She tilted her face up to meet his gaze. "Are we not eating together?"

Killian lowered himself, bending until his lips touched her forehead and his hand cupped the side of her face, his fingers encompassing her chin. "Afraid not," he murmured against her skin. "I have some plans to go over with my Lieutenant and Captains." His thumb brushed her cheekbone "But I will come find you, right after."

Cinder and Gunnar had stopped whatever bickering they were in to watch this exchange. How the Commander had so freely kissed Ambrosja's forehead in front of anyone. How, as if, he wasn't ashamed of this *affair*—or whatever it was.

"Enjoy yourself and your dinner with your friends, my Sóleygr." He kissed her again, his lips lingering on her forehead for a moment longer be-

fore pulling away with a smile and walking away.

Ambrosja's cheeks were red, not that bashfulness, not embarrassment, it was contentment, simple happiness. Her chin was now resting in the palm of her hand, her free hand absentmindedly played with her potatoes. She turned slightly, watching Killian walk to the raised platform where Berric waited. She hadn't noticed how Berric looked impatient, his jaw was rolling as he stared at Killian, brows furrowed, his lips pointed downward enough to express disgust.

Cinder hadn't really focused on Berric; she was too busy smirking at how hopelessly lovestruck Ambrosja looked. Leaning forward, she flicked the Empress's nose. "Aw, *high in the tree where sweethearts hide, trading kisses, side by side! First the wooing, then the band! Then comes a babe in mother's hand!*"

Ambrosja whipped her head to Cinder, panic flashing in her eyes. "What! No! I am not — he has not — he has not presented a ring! I am not pregnant, Cinder! There is no babe! We have not done anything like that!"

Donathan snorted into his hand, laughing. Gunnar let out a low chuckle, while Johann only sighed and gave Cinder a look before turning to Ambrosja. "It's just a childish song," he said pointedly—his glance flicking back to Cinder—"meant to make a fool of a friend who's clearly smitten."

Cinder opened her mouth to retort—but a potato was stuffed into it before she could speak. Ambrosja's eyes were wide, her hand pressed against Cinder's flushed face. But the huntress only squinted, chewing slowly… deliberately… like a predator proving a point.

Then Cinder's hand shot forward, jamming a potato into Ambrosja's mouth.

Donathan blinked, voice dropping to a whisper. "…I don't even know what I'm looking at anymore."

But Ambrosja and Cinder broke their stares with laughter. Their hands eased off of each other as they ate their potatoes, giggling like girls who had shared an unspoken secret between food.

Killian passed Berric, sitting down at the center of the table, overlooking the camp. He grabbed his tankard, and took a slow, steady sip of his mead. Berric cursed under his breath and moved to sit beside Killian so he could also oversee the camp.

"That display of affection was disrespectful, Killian," Berric muttered while he grabbed a thick piece of bread and ripped it in half. "We're the Black Hand, not some godsdamn camp for lovers, and you are meant to be Commander of this outpost. You should act like it—"

"Are you done?" Killian was staring daggers into the side of Berric's head. "I will do as a please, if it doesn't reflect poorly on my work, then I suggest you keep your mouth shut, *Lieutenant*." He continued, "There is a reason that *I am* Commander, and you work *for* me. You'd do well to remember that."

Berric's jaw clenched hard. Shifting from side to side. "Very well, Commander Thorn."

Killian leaned back into his chair, rolling his broad shoulders to relax. He turned to look at a Captain that sat not too far from him. "Well, how much Nythralt have we found, Wex?"

Wex rubbed his chin in thought. His dark eyes looked at the entrance to the mine, then to Killian. "Not enough for what the Grand Marshal wants. We had a lucky break when that big guy found another vein of Nythralt, we might be able to fill a third cart."

Berric raised a brow, but didn't look at anyone. "We'd be able to fill it faster if he hadn't been removed from mining-duty."

Killian ignored that. He remained seated, his legs spread wide, his hand relaxed around the tankard atop the table while his frame took up more space than the average man. "We have two cases of Nythralt ready for the delivery to Mistvale Crossing, but we need two more." Killian dragged his tongue across his teeth. His voice dropped to a growl. "I will not send a half-filled wagon of Nythralt out."

Another captain, a woman with a long blonde ponytail and tanned skin, Lilian, leaned forward. "We could expand or gather more miners to focus on the new vein," she said carefully. "But ever since that beam was nearly destroyed by our prisoner, the roof has looked unstable."

Killian shook his head, his lips twisted to the side as he considered it. "No," he finally said, exhaling sharply. "Last thing we need is losing the miners to falling rocks, and now we're responsible for their deaths, we'll be explaining to the families in Greenfield why what happened happened, and then we have to put coin forward to ease their troubles." He took a heavy sip of his drink, his throat bobbed with his swallows. Finally, he set the cup down, heavily so. "The Black Hand is already trying to keep all the resources it has, Lilian. Let's fix that beam, even if it sets us back, then we'll see about gathering more miners at that vein."

Berric scoffed. "Well, ain't this just sweet?" he leaned back, giving a slight swirl of the mead within his tankard. "First, you go easy on the pale girl—you don't kill her friends for eavesdropping. You don't kill the traitor for being a traitor." Killian exhaled sharply, his face slowly turned towards Berric, but Berric didn't care. He continued, "Next thing we know, you're off playing *Fleet-Touch*, and cuddling by rivers, you have that girl in your chambers, spending nights with you—"

Lilian interrupted, fixing her throat. "But she has been working the mines—"

"I'm not done, Lilian!" Berric growled, slamming his mug onto the table. He looked at Killian, meeting his stare head-on. "She wears your clothes, you two cuddle, you two walk hand in hand while you read her stories, give her kisses, and now here you are—concerned with the lives of miners."

Berric didn't see Killian move. One second, he was seated. The next, a hand closed on the back of his skull and shoved him face-first through his plate. Meat and potatoes skittered across the table; the crack of bone against wood swallowed the camp's chatter. Blood beaded along the grain, and every head turned. Ambrosja rose, but Johann's hand clamped her elbow and shook his head — a silent demand to stay.

Killian hauled Berric upright until their faces were inches apart. "You mistake my restraint for weakness," the Commander growled, low enough to vibrate the air. "You know what I do to men who question me. Do you wish to join them?"

Berric didn't respond. He snarled. He tried to swing, twisting his body to turn around so a fist could properly meet Killian's side, but Killian kicked the chair beneath Berric, making his knees fall hard onto the ground, as his jaw caught on the table. He grimaced. A tooth had broken. He spat the blood out along with the shards of bone. Killian grabbed Berric's head once more, lifting him up and slamming his face back into the table again.

"Commander!" Lilian cried, halfway sitting up but stopping short when Killian's stone-cold gray eyes snapped to hers.

Killian looked back down at Berric. "I am Commander of this camp because I understand the brutality that comes with leadership. Ever doubt me again, and I will do far worse." He pulled Berric back up again. "And if you ever..." Another slam into the table. "...speak of *her*—whether it has to do with me or not—I will crush your bones so terribly that you will merge with the very ground itself."

Killian kept Berric there, unbothered by the silence that was now across the camp. He looked over it, spotting Ambrosja, and immediately he softened, not physically, just within. He could feel the heat of his anger starting to simmer now. Eventually fading. He released Berric completely, letting him fall to the floor with a bloodied face.

Killian looked down at Berric's slumped form. There was no regret in his eyes, nothing that spoke of him being sorry. His eyes were cold, brows relaxed, as was his face. His lips only parted to speak, "You've soured dinner, and you've gotten your blood all over my food." He grabbed his plate, dumping the boar meat and potatoes onto Berric. "Disgusting." He then tossed the plate to the side, unbothered about where it went. He sat once more. "Go on then," he waved his hand in the direction of Wex and Lilian. "Let's finish our discussion."

Everyone in the camp shifted now, completely turning away. Johann tugged at Ambrosja's elbow, getting her to sit down. The music had shifted; the fingers beating on pans or tugging on strings were quieter now. Chatter was barely holding itself together anymore — too many shoulders were wound tight.

Wex shifted in his seat, his eyes lingered on Berric's fallen form for a moment before speaking. He cleared his throat as if that could take the edge off. "Perhaps we can invest in stronger beams. I'm certain there's someone in Greenfield who can accomplish that in a short time. We'll start with one to replace the damaged support and take it from there."

Lilian looked at Killian, nervously so. "What are your thoughts, Commander?"

Killian leaned forward, elbows resting on the table. He thought for a moment, it was obvious by the pinch in his brows and the way his fingers drummed against his bloodied fists. "Sounds like the best course of action, we don't want a risk of repeat, hells, the beams all probably need replacing soon, the last Commander that was overseeing this outpost was sloppy."

The Commander's expression shifted once more when his eyes landed on Ambrosja, who was sneaking glances at him. His lips almost twitched into a smile. He nodded then. He took another sip of his mead, then wiped his mouth with the back of his hand.

"Seems we have our answer. Replace the beam, then dig into that new vein. For now, let us try to enjoy the rest of the night." His eyes slid to Berric's form, then away. "However much we can."

The two captains at the table followed Killian's figure as he moved to sit with Ambrosja. Ambrosja looked surprised. Her face was beaming. When Killian had sat completely down, she moved hesitantly closer, until he wrapped a strong arm around her and dragged her so close that her side was nearly crushing against his. Cinder observed this through squinted eyes. Johann looked cautious, while Donathan was curious. But Gunnar was hunched over, his eyes were the same as Cinder's, suspicion, but mixed with a wariness.

Killian didn't say a thing. He started picking at Ambrosja's plate. His shoulders seemed to immediately relax once Ambrosja was beside him. Ambrosja, herself, didn't say much, too busy trying to calmly eat and not look like a swooning lover beside Killian's massive frame. But Cinder wasn't letting it slide.

"By all the Gods looking down upon us," Cinder scoffed, rolling her eyes. "Ambrosja, you're as red as a little girl who received her first flower on Oathbound Day."

"No—" Ambrosja only lit up harder. "...I do not even know what that is."

"It is a day for romance," Killian explained with a smooth voice, deep and thundering, as he looked down at Ambrosja, now refilling her tankard with mead. "Oathbound Day is the day when lovers exchange perfumed letters, words, and meals. Poetry, gifts, and flowers are to be expected."

"Sounds... Romantic."

"I would hope so," Killian chuckled. "If it didn't, then I would say Vaestoria is doing its lovers injustice." Ambrosja bit her bottom lip—Cinder gagged—but before she could make a remark on Ambrosja's flustered state, Killian looked at Cinder, and set a heavy and comforting hand on Ambrosja's arm, bringing her closer to him. "You did well on your hunt, Cinder. The miners and soldiers here haven't had quite a feast like this in some time."

Cinder was momentarily taken aback by Killian's praise. She squinted her eyes again. "Yeah—none of us are ignoring what you just did to your Lieutenant. However much he deserved it."

"Cindeeerrrr..." Ambrosja harshly whispered, eyes wide, brows knit together.

"Ambrosjaaaa,"Cinder mocked. "I don't even understand how you are all giddy now. *He,*" Cinder gestured to Killian with both hands, "is covered in blood!"

"I am not shy of blood or battle!" Ambrosja was firm in her voice. "Where I come from, we settle our problems with words, but if we must escalate it to fists, we shall. Killian reacted to a man provoking his honor, I am sure."

"And you're in love, *I'm sure,*" Cinder mocked again, this time rolling her eyes, and Ambrosja went an angry shade of red, both flustered and annoyed.

Donathan nudged Cinder with his elbow. "How about we just eat, *please?*"

Gunnar nodded, biting into his food like a starved soldier. "Yes, let's just savor this. Tomorrow you all go back to the mines, and I go back to sweating over." He continued, not even bothering to swallow first, "This meal is the finest fucking thing I've eaten since that barmaid in Greenfield."

Johann choked now. Donathan's eyes went wide while his cheeks burned. Cinder looked like she was ready to throw up. Ambrosja's hand was covering her face partially. But Killian? His mug froze in the air. Just nearly touching his lips. Then he slammed it down. His laughter shook in his chest. His shoulders were shaking, rising like a quake running through a mountain. Everyone was staring as Commander Thorn was losing himself. Gunnar had paused, but after a moment, he, too, was laughing. Both giants of the camp were letting out these sounds that resembled thunder and joy put together. Ambrosja's eyes were locked onto Killian's face, the unrestrained laughter that seemed to vibrate in his body, so much so that his own face had reddened, she looked as if the stars were in her eyes, her heart full at his reaction.

Killian reached across the table and clapped Gunnar's shoulder. "Women — the best thing a man can have in his mouth if it isn't food."

"The fucking truth!" Gunnar raised his drink in a toast. "To women and the way they taste on my tongue!"

Killian slammed his drink into Gunnar's. Laughter, first cautious — then bright — rang out through the camp now. Men raised their mugs in unison, as did some women on the side, while they nudged their more shy partners. But Ambrosja? Her smile had faltered slightly at *that*. Her hands pulled on the black top she wore. The one she accidentally stole from Killian. Her fingers fidgeted with the buttons. Killian noticed her shift immediately.

"What's wrong?" His knuckles almost reached out, but he stopped. "Ugh," he groaned, looking at his hand. "Let me wash my hands before I touch you with blood that isn't mine." He stood up, but bent down to kiss her cheek. "I will return."

Ambrosja nodded, forcing a smile while her eyes turned glassy. She held back the burning within her eyes the best she could—but she couldn't hold back the memories.

She stood in the chamber of her bedroom, in a red gown with a deep cut that exposed her inner breasts, the freckles trailing down from chest to stomach, golden embroidery along the hem. She wore a white fur cloak that decorated her shoulders; her ashen locks were brushed, with sections braided into her crown. And before her… stood Hådvard, tall, strong, imposing, and commanding. The most fit to lead the military of Nordorn. His long blond hair was in a ponytail. His blue eyes were burning into hers.

"*I can smell the envy off of you, Ambrosja,*" Hådvard's voice was low, each word dripping with bitterness. "We had an agreement, an understanding. Since we were forced into this promise, I could bed any woman I wanted, and now here you are—" he gestured to her with dismissive waves of his hand, from her face to her chest, "—staring at me like I've been a treacherous dog! But you are the one who suggested this!"

Ambrosja was silent. She stared at Hådvard with golden eyes that were ablaze. Hådvard didn't like that.

"Say something, woman!"

She clenched her fists. Then she stepped forward. "We had an agreement, yes! But that doesn't mean fuck the women in front of me!"

Hådvard chuckled, rolling his eyes, rubbing his face roughly and pacing away from her, then back to her. "I can fuck them, just don't do it in front of you," he echoed, nearly mocking her. "So, this is what it's about. Fucking them in front of you."

"Yes! It's embarrassing!" Ambrosja shouted. "You do it right in front of me! You grab your shield-maidens, pull up their skirts and fuck them, Hådvard!"

"What did you expect would happen?!" Hådvard shouted back. "Do you know what it's like to be promised to a thirteen-year-old girl when you're twenty-two?! You don't! I do! Waiting twelve years to touch a woman again would be maddening."

"Oh—don't give me that! It's not my fault! You think I wanted to hear about a husband when I was still a child?!" She stepped forward, standing close. "I gave you the freedom to be with whoever you want until we marry—you could at least give me the decency of not fucking the women in front of me. It hurts. It hurts to see them getting what I should be getting," she gestured to herself, her eyes glassy, her palm pressing to the center of her chest. "How I should be treated, like you want me, need me, love me!"

Hådvard shook his head, rubbing a hand down his face and scratching his beard. "*I can't deal with this right now, Ambrosja. We had an agreement, that's that.*" He then walked away, pushing past her and leaving her there.

Ambrosja didn't even notice Killian's return when he sat beside her on the bench. His hand touched her cheek—and that's when she blinked, meeting his gaze. He stared at her for a few moments, just silent. His thumb was brushing her cheekbone, then he leaned in, just enough for it to be intimate. Just enough so his whisper would only reach her.

"You are stunning." his lips brushed her cheek, trailing along her skin until he met her ear. "I want to take you to my room, and praise you, Ambrosja, every inch of you." He noticed her lips part, the way they always did when his words affected her. But she was silent, no bashful smile, no burning in her cheeks. Just her eyes on his. And that's when he saw the slightest sheen.

Killian didn't say another word. His arms wrapped around her. One around her waist, the other scooping beneath her legs. He picked her up, holding her close to his chest. Ambrosja's body curled in shock at the sudden movement.

"Grab your plate."

She nodded. Ambrosja reached down, grabbing her plate and her tankard. Once those were in her hands, Killian turned, leaving the table and camp behind as he made his way to the Command Hall. Cinder didn't make a remark, Gunnar was silent — but he gave Johann a look that made him groan. And Donathan simply looked at Cinder.

Killian climbed each step, carrying Ambrosja like she weighed nothing, yet everything to him. When he reached the top floor, he kicked his bedroom door open with the tip of his boot and closed it with the heel once he passed the threshold.

Upon reaching the bed, he set her down. But he didn't climb over. He didn't devour her. He got on his knees and looked up at her. His hand was resting on her thigh, his thumb drawing slow circles against the fabric.

"Why is there sadness in your eyes?" he asked, his voice softer than it had ever been.

"Why do you care?" Ambrosja's tone wasn't defensive. It was genuine curiosity.

Killian tilted his head. His brows pinched. He was caught off guard. "Why do I care?" He echoed, almost in disbelief. "Why wouldn't I care about you, my Empress?" Both hands were on her thighs now. "You are mine. *My Sóleygr.*"

"But you could have any woman."

Killian froze at that. He stood up slowly, still staring at her, as if he was trying to undress her very skin to peer into her heart. "I don't want *or* need any woman." He walked to the curtains of the bedroom, closing them one by one, a means to give her physical space, but not emotionally. Not when he knew how much she loved being chased. "Tell me, Ambrosja, what

has happened?"

At the last curtain, he left it open. He turned to face her, bracing his hands against the sill as he leaned into it. The twin moons outlined his frame as he waited—silent, patient—for her to spill every wound and stitch from the cages of her heart.

"You're going to think I'm stupid—or childish." A tear slipped down Ambrosja's cheek as she said it. She looked away, unable to bear the weight of his stare, afraid she'd see Hådvard all over again.

Killian's gray eyes widened at that tear—so small, yet so devastating. He stepped closer. "Ambrosja, if you're crying, then it isn't stupid or childish." He closed the distance carefully—not abruptly, not with hunger, but with care. His hand cupped her face; the other rubbed her arm. "Look at me. Don't look away."

Ambrosja hesitated, then met his gaze. She took a shaky breath. "Hådvard and I… had an agreement. An understanding. I told you this before—remember?" Killian nodded, silent, waiting. "We agreed that he could bed any woman he wanted, since he couldn't touch me…" Killian braced himself then—waiting for her to confess guilt, or regret, or that she loved Hådvard, that maybe being with him had made her realize where her heart truly lay.

But those words never came.

Instead, her voice cracked. "It hurt. It hurt to see him touch other women. And when you and Gunnar… when you two cheered about women—about how they taste…" The Empress squeezed her eyes shut, another tear slipping free. "I wondered if maybe you would do the same. Be with me and still seek heat from other women. I fear that I am not enough, Killian, since you—you will not lie with me to respect my crown." She curled in on herself, softly crying.

Killian was silent for a bit. Then he exhaled sharply. "I've done things I hated, Ambrosja, but there was always something I've taken great pride in… My belief, my worship of dragons. I've strived to be just like them. Noble. Loyal. Strong in mind and body." His hand moved from her cheek, now resting on her other arm. He softly pushed her onto her back. "And—*Sóleygr*, a dragon does not abandon his hoard." When her back met the bed, he leaned in, whispering against her lips, "And you… You are mine. And you are *most* wanted."

He pulled her into a kiss. His lips met hers with need, passion. His tongue pressed against hers, seeking every bit of her. Then he leaned back, strands of their passion connected their lips. Ambrosja's eyes were heavy-lidded as were his.

"Tell me something, Ambrosja..." Killian whispered against her lips, taking his time to speak as he looked into her eyes. "When Brynhjora became the Empress Eternal, was it decreed she could not bed anyone?"

"N-no..." Ambrosja was still trying to catch her breath. Her chest heaved from the proximity, from how close he was; this was the closest they had ever been since he kissed her against the wall days ago, and now... they were on the bed, something softer, far more intimate than a wall. "It was written in stone that Brynhjora did not even wed until she was well past one-hundred..." Despite the heat that was making Ambrosja shiver, her mind was steady, but her voice was not. "F-For she could not find a man worthy of her love until then... The rule of twenty-five comes from Brynhjora finally touching the heart of Chaos at the age of twenty-five, and letting it rest within her womb... Only for her to pass it from herself, to her firstborn daughter, where it shall rest within her womb next, only to be freely given once she reaches twenty-five, and so goes the cycle..."

Killian dragged his lips down Ambrosja's neck. "So... The true rule is that... You cannot *bed* until twenty-five..." He leaned back, supporting himself on his knees. "But... can you be feasted upon?" The Commander licked his bottom lip then.

"Feasted upon?"

"Yes," Killian growled. He lowered himself, bracing his hands and knees on the empty space of the bed each side of her. "I may not be able to bed you, but allow me to feast upon you, so you may know just *how much* I desire you."

Ambrosja was biting on her forefinger, eyes heavily-lidded. "Please, Killian... I want you to touch me..."

"As you command, my Empress."

The Commander's body met hers again, pressing the Empress into the mattress as his hands slid down her waist, fingers digging into her soft flesh as he pulled the black blouse out from her fitted pants with the hunger of a man trying not to ruin silk, pulling it over her head, leaving her breathless and adorned in the leather of her bustier. Killian's lips found Ambrosja's neck next, dragging across her soft skin and down her collarbone. Then lower, pausing in the dip between her breasts. His hands now found her pants, undoing the belt, then the strings, then the pants. Removing them slowly, carefully. Killian's hands now lingered on her wide hips, fingers hooking into her soft linens.

"Last chance, Ambrosja," Killian warned her.

"Chances be damned," Ambrosja breathed out, her voice shaking

with heat and need.

Then she gasped—Killian's thick fingers dragged along the damp spot. Her eyes widened, her hands holding tightly onto him. Knees already shaking.

"You're soaked..." Killian growled, burying his face in the curve of her neck.

Killian trailed lower, slow at first—then with a hunger that wouldn't wait. His lips brought heat across her body, from where her leather bustier kissed her breasts, until he met the softness beneath her navel. His lips lingered there as his fingers now tugged the fabric of her linens down. Slowly baring her to him.

His lips met Ambrosja's heat. Damp, soft, and raw. He pressed a slow, heated kiss, his hands firm on her hips like he could hold her unraveling together. His tongue darted out to taste her—a growl erupted from his throat. He pressed his tongue further in, parting her for him.

"You taste like *mine*," Killian said, dragging her further down so he could press his tongue more firmly and deeper into her.

"K—Killian!" Ambrosja gasped. Her fingers entangled in his long, dark hair. She now found herself arching her back as she trembled, unable to stop the way her body responded.

The Empress's breaths came in broken gasps. She clung to the Commander, desperate to hold on to something—anything—while he unraveled her beneath his tongue. Every time he dragged his tongue across her slit, she would recoil from the feel of it all. Then she felt it—the thick tongue hit her sensitiveness. She jolted, her mind blanking at the rush of heat that threatened to undo her. No warning. No mercy.

She looked down at Killian, her brows knit, an expression half-wild, half-begging. He looked up but didn't stop his tongue from moving. Instead, when they locked eyes, he moved to her entrance, swirling against it, before pushing his tongue inside her. Her hips bucked. Her hands fell to her sides, softly slamming into the mattress as her body squirmed. She gripped the sheets, toes curling. Her head fell backwards, eyes closing tightly as her entire body shook, barely held down by Killian's massive hands that held her hips so firmly.

Killian slowed his movements, then eased his tongue out of her. He slowly parted, his eyes heavy and locked onto hers. They were both breathless. Chests rising and falling. His hands reached for the laces on her bustier, ready to undo them. Her hands instinctively covered her chest.

"Ambrosja?"

"Sorry—I just... feel prettier with my clothes on..."

Killian's eyes found hers, more sincere, more unguarded. "Ambrosja," he let out a soft but genuine chuckle. "You're mostly naked."

"I know..." She bit her bottom lip nervously, shyly. "I just—don't want you to see my scars..."

Killian paused. He nodded once. Then leaned down, one hand bracing beside her body, the other holding her waist firmly. "Your scars," he said softly, "are one of the most beautiful things about you."

The Empress's eyes tracked his, as if trying to study him. Trying to find any lies—she found none. "You do not mean that..."

He leaned in closer, his nose nuzzling hers, "I do. I meant it as much as I meant it when I said you are perfect." He breathed her in, kissing her neck before parting to look at her once more, "I find so much of you beautiful. You are... The most beautiful woman I have ever seen, Ambrosja. And your scars?" His hand dragged over those black markings, the roots within her pale skin, fingers tracing each one. "They are a part of you, and if you allow me... I will kiss each scar you have."

Her breath caught again, stuck in her throat like she might drown. Her eyes were glassy, peering into his. "Would you really?"

"Gods—yes," he whispered, his own breath nearly gone. He kissed her cheek, lips dragging until he met her neck. "I swear on Vorthunal—you are the most stunning creature I have seen, and I want *all* of you, Ambrosja."

Ambrosja's back arched as a gasp escaped her. Her hands were greedy, traveling across Killian's strong and scarred torso until she reached his pants, fingers shaking as she sought to undo the strings holding them up. His own hands moved along her bustier, pulling at the laces on the side to loosen it up.

When she was completely bare before him, Killian was frozen. His eyes traced every inch and every freckle, committing her to memory like a painting he feared he'd never see again. The Commander's breath had left him. The dark roots adorned her body like vines beneath flesh — from neck and shoulder to rib, to the curve beneath her breast. His fingers slowly reached her skin, tracing softly. Every bit of her was memorized with reverent hands.

"You are stunning, Ambrosja," Killian whispered, "Absolutely divine." He started to inch backwards, his lips kissing her breasts, greedy lips on sensitive peaks until he reached beneath her navel again. Then his voice turned commanding, "Eyes on me," he whispered. "I want you to *see* how much I *choose you*, Empress."

Ambrosja met his eyes again, as heat crept across her cheeks, like a stain that showed him just how much she needed and wanted him.

But even as her knees rocked and her body trembled just right, she relaxed beneath him. Trusting him.

"Do—do you promise?"

Killian paused. "I swear it, beneath Vorthunal, beneath the moons, and before you."

His tongue found her once more, and another growl erupted. He dove in, like he couldn't get enough of her. His rough hands needed the soft and strong flesh of her thighs, crawling up to her hips, then her waist, dragging her closer to his face again, as if his tongue could reach her heart in a way that words couldn't just yet.

The Empress was a whimpering mess. Hands curled above her breasts, one forefinger pressing into her lips as she watched him through pale lashes. The pink of her cheeks only spread down to the rise of her breasts. When she felt Killian give a little bite on her sensitiveness, she had arched her back so sharply it was like a bow being drawn taut.

The Commander's hands found her breasts, softly kneading them while rolling the peaks between his fingers. Her own hands had found his, holding him there and pressing down as she cried with a pleasure so intense her body could barely catch its breath.

Killian could feel it—hear it. Ambrosja was close, and he wouldn't stop until she felt the pleasure he had desired to give her for so long. He pressed his tongue more firmly against that spot that was making her shake, lapping at it, rougher and without mercy as he heard her cries pick up.

"K-Killian! I—I—" she couldn't finish her sentence before she dug her nails into his skin and her hips started to buck against his face, a foreign pleasure was crashing over her, something intense and hot pulling at her from deep within.

The Commander growled as he felt that thick wetness rush out of her to coat his lips. He guided her through, softly squeezing with his hands as his tongue adjusted to her cries, to her shivers.

The Empress looked down at him while she was still going through the waves of a pleasure so intense she felt as if her entire body was going numb, from her heels to her shoulders, and she found him staring right at her, which only made her knees shake harder. His eyes, those silver ones, had been locked onto her golden gaze while his lips delivered a forbidden whisper against her skin.

From the journal of Guinyldr Thorn,
Rodvrmane, 01, 997

THE WOMB OF THE EMPRESS

It is written in stone that when Brynhjora, the Empress Eternal, first touched the force of Chaos, she did not just wield it — she bore it. In that moment, the wild current of creation anchored itself within her womb, granting her immortality until the birth of her first daughter. Thus was forged the bond between Chaos and the bloodline of Nordorn, ensuring that its thread would never be severed from the mortal world.

From Brynhjora's firstborn, the thread of Chaos passed from mother to daughter, generation to generation — an eternal inheritance that binds each Empress to the very fabric of existence. The power grants life unending until the moment of succession, when the next vessel draws her first breath and the mantle of divinity shifts.

SINS CARVED INTO BONE

Empress Ambrosja Nordravn always had high expectations set on her since she had lost her mother at the tender age of five. Her father left shortly after the death of his wife, unable to bear the loss, and abandoned his daughter. Ambrosja was raised beneath her grandmother's rule, and at the age of nine, the crown was placed upon Ambrosja's head, ruling her as the youngest to ever ascend the throne. Carrying a burden no child should.

When she was thirteen, she was told a suitor had been chosen for her, Hådvard, the only man who could rival her father's prowess, and weeks later, her father, Vidar, returned. He knew it was time for her to learn war, strategy, to think and fight like a warrior.

Lessons and lessons had been forced upon her. A childhood stripped, a family strained, and something that should have been love had been turned to resentment. But even with all of the damage and unfair *or* unfortunate hands dealt to Ambrosja... Yrsa stood in the grand stone hall of the castle's courts and admired the painted portrait of her granddaughter with pride.

Yrsa, Empress Mother, the Winter Rose, stood before the wall that had been decorated with each Empress, a portrait crafted for their rule. She adjusted the gray fur coat that hugged her, taking a deep breath as her golden eyes drifted over the portrait of her beloved granddaughter.

"Staring at that painting won't make her come back any sooner,

Empress Mother," Hådvard muttered as he passed the older woman.

Yrsa sighed wistfully. She tilted her head, her white hair falling down her shoulder, with the pale roses that were braided into the locks. "I miss my granddaughter… Isn't she just gorgeous, Hådvard?"

Hådvard turned. He looked at Ambrosja, from her eyes down to where the painting ended near her ribs. "Yeah," he said simply, turning once more.

"You could use more enthusiasm when talking about your future wife," Yrsa scoffed, scowling at Hådvard. "You use more enthusiasm in the way you stare at your shieldmaidens."

Hådvard crossed his arms. "Pardon me for being too preoccupied with having to deal with Ambrosja's affairs."

"Ah," Yrsa hummed, taking a step forward, fingers interlacing in front of her. "I hadn't realized that taking eight women to your bed the night prior would put you in such a sour mood in the morning, Hådvard. Clearly, juggling eight women at once must have taken a toll on your sleep."

"Don't give me that sass, woman."

"I will give you whatever sass I choose to, I am Empress Mother, and you have yet to become Hrafwarden," Yrsa warned him, "just because Ambrosja trusted you enough to take care of Nordorn does not put you above me."

The Empress Mother strode down the length of the long wooden table, where snowbears, ravens, and the story of Brynhjora had been engraved. Her fingers met every groove and grain.

"And let me warn you now, Hådvard, if I ever find out you have cheated on Ambrosja as her husband…" Yrsa looked at him. "I will feed your balls to my Snowbear, and she will devour anything…" Her eyes looked him up and down now. "No matter how disgusting it is."

The Empress Mother walked away then, adjusting the thick fur cloak that kept her warm, heading out of the chambers and striding through the open wooden doors.

Hådvard watched Yrsa leave. Then shifted his gaze back to Ambrosja's painting. "Blasted Nordravn women, if only your stubbornness could be as small as your height."

Ambrosja's foot had slipped off the bed at some point in the night. Her fingers pressed into her face as she stretched. Her back arched, she smiled like

a heavy weight had been lifted from her hips. Her toes curled, then stretched. She hadn't opened her eyes, not yet. She only did so after her hands had settled down onto the red blanket and she felt her body bare beneath it.

Her golden gaze went wide. She lifted the blanket enough, and there she was, nude and with Killian's arm lying across her waist. Her eyes followed the length of his tanned, scarred arm. It rested beneath the barrier he had made for her. The barrier was still there, but he had breached it from beneath so he could hold her through the night.

Everything hit her at once. And she melted into the sheets like molten gold dripping into a delicate rose-patterned mold. Ambrosja bit her bottom lip as she remembered the Commander's tongue on her, moving fervently across her heat with strength and desire. She smiled with that plush lip still caught between her teeth. She curled inwards, like a young girl feeling butterflies for the first time. Her feet kicked in the air beneath the blanket, and she smiled, beaming like a ray of sun.

The Empress's hands found Killian's arm, and her nails gently caressed his skin in soft drags, feeling the bump of every scar and vein. She thought of his words, how he would not consume her, but feast upon her. How he showed her that he would choose her again and again, even with a crown upon her head.

Her eyes met the barrier again. And without a second thought, she wiggled closer to it, sneaking under it until she was on the other side—then planted herself firmly beside Killian. The Commander's grip around her waist tightened in his sleep. He shifted from sleeping on his stomach to sleeping on his side, where he curled around her, forcing her body to mold with him as he buried his face into her hair in the haze of his sleep.

"Sóleygr," Killian whispered against her moonlit strands, "you're so perfect."

His hands roamed over her, tenderly squeezing her sensitive flesh. Ambrosja gasped, backing into the Commander with need. But that gasp woke Killian immediately. His hands let go, and he propped himself up on his arm, creating distance between them. He dragged his hand down his face, fingers pressing into his eyes as if he sought immediate clarity.

"Ambrosja," he rumbled, now looking down at her. "What are you doing? Why are you on this side?"

"I just… wanted to be close," she confessed, now lying on her back to look up at him.

Killian sighed and rested his forehead against Ambrosja's, his dark strands threading into her pale ones. "Very well…" He reached over with his hand and grabbed a pillow from the barrier, deliberately placing it between them, creating a wall between their most intimate areas.

Ambrosja scowled at that. "Are you serious?"

"You are naked, Ambrosja," Killian reminded her, nuzzling into her cheek to soothe her. "What would you have me do?"

"Oh, I do not know… Hold me regardless of nudity?"

The Commander wrapped his big arms around Ambrosja, pulling her in tightly and letting her back meet his chest as he pampered her with soft kisses along her shoulder and neck.

"Like this?" He kissed her again and again, squeezing her more tightly against him. He lifted his heavy leg over hers, wrapping himself around her, now kissing her fervently. "How about this? Is this better, my Empress?"

Ambrosja began to giggle, wriggling in his grasp, feeling her skin being brushed and tickled by his stubble. And Killian didn't let up. His lips touched every surface he could, across her chest, her shoulders, her neck, and all over her face. Her laughs escaped her, breathless and wild, feet trying to kick into the air but unable to as he restrained her with love.

Then finally, he slowed, kisses becoming softer. He hovered over her, staring down at her, despite the fact that she was bare… his gaze didn't linger on what a weaker man might have stared at. His eyes focused on her—and her scars.

Lips soft and rough touched the dark roots that decorated the Empress's pale skin. Killian traced the lines down from her shoulder to her rib to beneath her right breast. Ambrosja trembled ever so slightly from the contact, curling inward with a fluttering softness. Eyes heavy-lidded, not with heat, but as if she felt like treasure beneath a dragon's gaze.

Then a heavy weight crushed her heart.

"I am sorry," Ambrosja immediately rolled away, grabbing the blanket and covering herself, knocking the barrier there.

Killian watched as Ambrosja scrambled, blanket wrapped tight around her while her hand clenched her heart. Her eyes closed tightly.

"You did not do anything wrong," she reassured him, "it is just that… these scars are — are a reminder of when everything went wrong, and… I feel they do not deserve the praise you are giving them."

She turned to look at him then. Eyes with a slight sheen.

"Gods," she laughed, the sound was bitter and weak, as if mocking herself, "I have done nothing but cry these last two days…" She wiped her eyes. "You must think I am a crying babe."

Killian didn't rush as he got up from the bed. His strides were slow

and purposeful, hands finding Ambrosja's arms through the fabric of the blanket.

"Not at all, I think the fact that you're willing to cry is beautiful," he whispered against her hair, "not everyone will do it, especially when they're expected to be strong." His arms came around her. "My sister used to cry a lot. She was… sensitive. She struggled growing up because she was smarter than most kids her age, and they hated that. And most who weren't her age, those much older with the smarts more like hers… didn't want to play with a girl her age." He turned Ambrosja to face him, and a calloused thumb caught her tear. "I cannot tell you how many times she has cried in my arms. And if you must cry, if you *want* to cry, you can, Ambrosja."

He pulled the Empress closer to him, hugging her with all the tenderness a man like him could muster.

"Do you wish to talk about it, Ambrosja?" Killian whispered against her hair, his thumb brushing against her cheekbone, pushing the hair aside so he could kiss her.

Ambrosja pulled away, not from Killian; it was just as if her mind had simply called to pull her away. She closed her eyes, and all she could see was fire—fire spreading from the hearth, encasing her, then turning as dark as night as it crept upon her body. Then her mother's cries. It hurt. The weight of her heart seemed to plummet down into her stomach, but it didn't stop; it kept falling, as if a bottomless pit were within her, and her heart kept hitting countless thorns as it fell.

The Empress pressed her hand to her forehead, looking away as tears pooled in her eyes again. "I—I killed my mother…"

Killian immediately crouched. His hands dragged down her arms to steady her, but he rested his massive body into a squat, lowering himself for her. He cupped her face, guiding her to look at him. "It's okay, I am not here to judge. I am here for you, and I will listen. To every word." He found her hands, pulling them together and kissing her knuckles. "Tell me, Ambrosja, if you're ready."

Her shoulders trembled. She squeezed his hands, shaking, eyes closing tightly as the tears fell down her cheeks. "I was… I was five. I cannot remember all of it. But I remember — I remember being upset… I was playing by the hearth. I think I got scared? And… my powers of chaos… they moved the flames to crawl across the ground, burning everything in its path. I started to cry and scream…" Ambrosja opened her eyes as she stared at the ground, tears dropping onto the wood beneath her feet. "My mother rushed in. She shielded me from the fire — but it grew too large…"

The Empress squeezed her eyes tightly again. Her whole body trembled. She bent at her waist, curling inwards while she squeezed Killian's hands so tightly she left indents on his skin.

Ambrosja lifted her gaze to meet Killian's. "I awoke, and she was burnt to death, while I was protected, raven feathers were found all around me… And I made it out with this scar…" She lowered the blanket to show the scar once again, her eyes closed, the burn of keeping them open pained her too much. "A result of my loss… The loss of control. Loss of power… and the loss of my mother…" A choked sound escaped her. "I always looked at it as if it were a symbol of the end of my life, because… after my mother's death — I never had another happy moment again." Her eyes met Killian's once more. "Until you…"

Killian raised himself so he could hunch over her, caging her like a man who could carry her world and pain. His hands cupped her face again. "Ambrosja, you couldn't have known. You were only five."

Ambrosja pulled away sharply. Furious, enraged. "I know!" She cried. "But I killed my mother! I killed my mother all because Brynhjora had to pass her damned Chaos through the blood of women, and here I am!" She punched the wall, then her knees gave out, falling into it as a silent sob left her. "I have always been told that I am the creator of my own path — I am the goddess of my inner world, but I have set myself onto a path of ruin since before I could even comprehend the meaning of the word *loss*."

The Commander didn't hesitate. He reached her in few steps, dropping himself to wrap his arms around her.

"Why did *I* have to be the firstborn?" Ambrosja turned to hug Killian's broad shoulders. "Why could I have not been second or third?! Why did I have to inherit this godsawful power that has brought nothing but ruin and loss into my life?! Why — why did Brynhjora feel the need to save the world?!" She hugged Killian more tightly, her tears dampening the skin of his chest. "If humanity was on the brink of extinction through no faults other than their own — did they deserve to be saved?!"

Killian cupped Ambrosja's face, bringing her to look into his eyes once more.

"You may have felt like you doomed your path, Ambrosja, but only you have the power to choose which steps to take, when, and where." His voice was firm, but warm against her skin. "Just because you started off with ruin—does not mean you will end in such a way." He got onto his knees again, fingers threading into the pale locks at her nape. "You are an Empress, the descendant of Brynhjora… and the Amber of the North."

From the journal of Guinyldr Thora,
Rodvrmane, 04, 997

BRYNHJORA, THE EMPRESS ETERNAL

Brynhjora, the Empress Eternal, stands at the dawn of Nordorn's history — the first to claim the mountain's crown, and the first to bear its name. Legends tell that she ascended the peak of Nordravn, the tallest mountain in the world. There, she wielded the power of Chaos Magic to rend the realm of Vaeldorwynn in two, shaping the land that would become her empire.

Under her reign, Nordorn rose to unmatched might. She forged the cruelest of armies, yet ruled the kindest of hearts, binding her people not through fear, but through reverence. To her, strength and compassion were not opposites but twin blades — and with both, she carved an age that would not be forgotten.

It is said Brynhjora was the first human to transcend mortality, her spirit bound eternally to the mountain she conquered. From her name came the Nordravn line, and from her will, an empire that endures — feared, honored, and ever unbroken.

THE **FRACTURE**

The Fracture marks the end of one world and the birth of another. It was wrought by the forces of Chaos Magic—a power vast enough to cleave the realm of Vaeldorwynn in two.

From its sundering rose the twin lands of Aldorwyn and Eldorwyn, forever divided by the wound that saved them. Though the act brought ruin to countless lives—beasts, forests, and cities alike—it was deemed a necessary sacrifice, the only means to preserve what remained of humanity. From that moment onward, time itself was reborn, the first year counted as 0 AF — After Fracture. The scholars of both realms agree on little, yet all concede this truth: the Fracture did not merely split the world's land, but its soul.

CHAPTER TWENTY-EIGHT
To Burn For

Day and night had come and gone. The mining camp of the Black Hand, just beyond Greenfield, stank of oil, wet leather, and ash. Fog clung to the ground like old breath. Boots sank in slop. Carts got stuck. Tempers were shorter than the days. The only relief came from the meat of the boar that Cinder and Donathan managed to capture days prior. But even that was at risk of rot.

Gunnar leaned forward, elbows firm on the table, his boar-meat stew forgotten. "Ambrosja has been laying it on thick with the Commander." He shook his head with a grunt, brows low, his face a frown as he watched Ambroja running away from Killian, trying to dodge him while his stance was wide and powerful, always jerking forward in a threat to capture her. "Almost makes me think she's forgotten this whole seducing him wasn't meant to be serious. I fear she's falling for him, Johann."

Johann grunted in agreement. Thoughtful for a moment before letting out a heavy sigh. "Yeah, I think she has, Gunnar… I think she has."

His friend grunted, muttering *damn it*.

Johann, instead, tried shifting the conversation as he spotted a familiar duo not too far. "Cinder and Donathan have been getting along well." Gunnar simply huffed a *hm?* In response. Johann gestured with a jerk of his chin in the direction of the couple.

Gunnar looked, squinting, seeing the two through the fog,

gathering their bowls together, smiling and talking—leaning too close to one another for his liking. An aggravated exhale that sounded awfully like a growl escaped him. "…She is looking at him… But… It's as if she has no desire to punch him. She's standing too close…"

Johann laughed, head falling forward, shoulders shaking. "Is that right? You just noticed that?"

"What do you mean *just* noticed that?"

"They've been close since that day in the mine—you know, when she comforted him." Johann shrugged, "They've only gotten closer in recent days. Could be because they're close in age, could be they got along well on the hunt… Or could be because the lass has finally developed a romantic interest in something that isn't her bow."

That made Gunnar's head slowly turn to Johann, "Don't speak such nonsense."

Gunnar grunted, but quieted as soon as Cinder and Donathan got closer. His eyes were focused on Donathan entirely. Studying him, like a predator sizing up prey, weighing the consequences of what would happen should he decide to remove this particular prey from the food chain.

Johann noticed. And decided not to give his friend a reason to get burned today. Instead, he looked at Cinder, who was now approaching with Donathan. "So, what's your opinion about Ambrosja and the Commander?"

"What opinion should I have? We already agreed she's gone for him." Cinder plopped down beside Gunnar. Donathan joined her. "I practically shoved her onto his lap, and he took hold of her hips and said *mine* like some rabid wolf."

"I'm worried she'll hurt herself," Johann sighed, fingers dragging through his beard. "She's too young… This is temporary. Or at least it's meant to be."

Cinder paused her eating. Her eyes looked off to see Ambrosja currently being carried around by Killian, hoisted over his shoulder, while she laughed in the distance. How they had chosen playful moments instead of eating. The huntress sighed deeply.

"Well," she spoke, "it's too late to worry if she'll hurt herself. She's entangled with him, probably fucking him, or ready to."

"Gods, Cinder," Johann scowled, "have some decorum."

The huntress simply blew a raspberry and returned to eating.

Gunnar sighed heavily. Burying his face in his hands. "Why?" He muttered. "Why are all of you sinning?"

Cinder paused. She turned her neck, eyes on Gunnar, "Who is *all*,

Gunnar?"

Gunnar peeked up at her through his fingers, then slowly lifted his head up. "Oh, don't play dumb with me, Cinder!" He pointed at her and Donathan, "I see the way you're looking at him! You two are walking around like lovebirds exchanging perfumed letters on Oathbound Day!"

Cinder rolled her eyes, "Gunnar, please! And even then, so what?! You're not my dad!"

Gunnar gasped, offended, his broad frame leaning back, hand clutching his heart. "After I took care of you? Raised you since you were a wee lass?!"

"I was grown when we met!"

"And you were just born into the world! You had never left home before then!"

"I used to go hunting in the woods with my father, Gunnar! What do you mean?!" Cinder waved her hands dramatically, shaking her head, then she snapped, waving a finger in Gunnar's face. "You know what?! Why don't you go lecture Ambrosja?! She's the one bedding the enemy!"

Gunnar's brows lowered into a furious scowl. He stared hard at Cinder, then jabbed his finger in her direction, "You're not off the hook, Cinder."

"What hook?!"

Donathan was furiously blushing this entire time, eyes wide and staring down at the table. He fixed his throat, "Uh… Maybe we should lower our voices? Everyone is staring…"

And sure enough, when Cinder and Gunnar looked around, they saw it. Miners had scooted away from them, but stared, leaning in to listen. Black Hand guards even had their heads cocked with interest, as if this were the most fascinating gossip they had ever heard while working in the camp.

Cinder waved dismissively but not unkindly. "Well—if Gunnar wasn't always so dramatic… We wouldn't have an audience."

Gunnar scoffed, "Dramatic?" He was staring at Cinder, then he caught Donathan's eyes. Donathan immediately recoiled and looked away. "Oh no, boy, look at me." Donathan did so, hesitantly. "You—" Gunnar pointed at him, "You're also not off the hook. I see you. I bet you're enamored with Cinder because she's older than you. You think she can show you new moves." Cinder nearly choked on her soup, but Gunnar paid no mind as he continued looking at Donathan from over Cinder's head. "But guess what? She's been with me since she lost her family. I've watched over her. I've protected her. You try to fiddle with her linens with ulterior motives, and I'll make sure you can never cast your fancy little spells again."

There was an audible gulp from Donathan's side. Donathan went to scoot away from Cinder, but the huntress's hand came hard onto his thigh, holding him in place. The poor boy wanted to shrink and hide. Gunnar noticed Cinder's hand. And now, both Gunnar and Cinder were staring at each other, like a daughter challenging her father's rule.

Johann sat up straighter. "Both of you, stop this. As Donathan has pointed out, everyone is staring. Do you want to continue making a spectacle of yourselves?" Johann looked at Gunnar now, "And you—stop it. Cinder is twenty-five, Gunnar. She is a *grown* woman. Let her be. She's been with us for years; we can trust her to make her own damn decisions."

Gunnar grumbled but dropped the subject. He looked away from Cinder and went back to tending to his now-cold soup. While Donathan's cheeks never dropped that reddened hue, his eyes darted down to see Cinder's hand still on his thigh, then he pointedly looked at his soup, as if it held answers to whether or not Gunnar was actually going to break his hands later. Cinder was silent now, side-eyeing Gunnar occasionally, and most definitely slurping her soup a little too loudly to provoke him. Some of the miners fixed their posture, but still glanced at the group, waiting to hear the next piece of drama.

"If you all cared as much about the coming war as you do each other's beds, we'd already be home," Johann muttered.

Cinder stood abruptly. "You know what?" She grabbed Donathan's hand. "We're going hunting! Again!"

Donathan stumbled off the bench as Cinder yanked him, but he didn't resist. The tips of his ears were red, and his eyes were wide, doing his best to not look back as he heard the low rumbling of Gunnar's growl—like a dragon protecting its hoard deep within a cave.

"Cinder—" Donathan whispered as he allowed her to lead him towards a Black Hand. "Do you actually want to go hunting, or are you trying to get me killed by your not-actual-father?"

Cinder didn't reply. She stopped before the Black Hand armorer. "Can't do any pushing or pulling of carts with weather like this. And that meat—" she jerked her thumb to the boar on the spit. "—that'll spoil soon."

The armorer stared down at her, then, with a casual shrug, he stepped aside, giving way to the racks of weapons. Cinder grabbed the bow and the quiver of arrows. She tilted her head towards the open gates that led to the woods of the Bramble.

"Let's go, Fire-Hands."

Donathan sighed, but once again, he didn't resist. He followed her every move.

Killian leaned down, kissing Ambrosja's cheek while he held her chin. "I must return to the Command Hall," he said, placing another kiss on her cheek, "I have matters to tend to. Enjoy the day of rest, we're all useless under this weather."

Ambrosja smiled. She leaned up onto the tips of her toes and looped her arms around him. "Okay," she whispered against his neck, "thank you… for — for being so good to me, Killian."

The Commander gave Ambrosja half smile as they parted. The kind only meant for her. His thumb brushed her chin a few times. "That is not something you ever need to thank me for. You are my treasure, my Sóleygr, I will never treat you as anything less."

He started walking backwards, still smiling, until he turned and made his way to the Command Hall and disappeared through the doors. Ambrosja watched him until he had left her vision. Now shifting her focus to where she saw Johann and Gunnar sitting together.

The Empress approached her friends and took a seat on the bench with them.

"Why do you look so upset, Gunnar?" She looked over the older man's face, the hunched shoulders, the frown, and the low-set eyebrows that nearly hid his eyes.

Gunnar craned his neck to the side and down to look at her. "Because every girl I have adopted has decided to remove her linens and play with instruments they know nothing about."

Ambrosja tilted her head. "What?"

Johann immediately interjected, "Do not ask him to—"

But Gunnar explained anyway, "Cinder is with Donathan," then he pointed at Ambrosja, "and you are lying with the Commander."

Ambrosja gasped. "How dare you!" She pointed back at him, standing now. "And you are bedding every woman here!"

"I—" Gunnar went to retort, then shook his head. "That's not the point!"

"Cinder taught me about this!" Ambrosja snapped, hands clenched, searching for the word as her frustration spilled over. "There is a phrase for it—uneven measure!" She jabbed a finger at him. "You weigh me by a scale you would never place upon yourself."

"OH! Cinder is just teaching everyone everything now!" Gunnar groaned, standing to his full height. "She's teaching Donathan how to *hunt*, she's teaching you new words! I bet she'll be teaching Johann a new religion soon!"

Johann immediately scooted away. "I have no desire to be included in this."

Cinder held Donathan's hand tightly. She kicked at rocks and twigs that stood in her path. The bow was slouched over one shoulder. Donathan just stared at the back of Cinder's head. *She's so headstrong,* he thought to himself, a smile forming on his face.

She stopped abruptly and turned. The quiver slid from her shoulder, and the bow was tossed to the side. Her hands moved to the sturdy strings of her leather tunic. Fingers confident and fast as they undid the brown laces. Donathan's eyes widened, and his brows shot up to his hairline once the realization of what was happening hit him square in the chest.

"O-oh?" His voice shook with surprise. "Are you sure?"

Cinder looked away from her laces to glare at him. "Why? Are you *not* sure?"

"N-no! I mean—yes! I'm sure!" Donathan buried his face in his hands. "Third time, just nervous, because—" he gestured to her, his eyes raked over her in admiration. "It's you! You're–perfect!" His hands fell to his sides.

Cinder's lips twitched into what nearly was a bashful smile. "You're ridiculous, Donathan."

"Yeah, for you…"

She groaned, rolled her eyes, and then pushed him into a tree. "Don't make this into sweet-rot, Donathan." Her lips found his, and his hands found her hips, firm and sure. Her fingers trailed down, tugging at the openings of his cloak and tugging it off his shoulders—only to stop suddenly and pull her lips away.

Donathan's breath had left him; his hands were still on her hips. He pulled her against him until he noticed her looking off to the side. "What is it?"

"Shh…" she shushed him. She inclined her head ever so slightly.

The sound was distant, but Cinder's keen ears picked up on it. The heavy huff of breath and the jingle of metal seemed to have a rhythmic pattern. Something heavy was stepping into mud. She stared into the trees, eyes scanning the distance. She saw nothing that looked odd at first glance, just brush, bark, and rock.

"We're close to the road…" Cinder whispered.

"Yeah?" Donathan kept his voice low as well, already following Cinder's lead. "Pretty sure we're near the road that leads from Greenfield to Mirewatch."

She bit her bottom lip, smirking. "Let's go spy." She tugged Donathan's hand again. Once more, he didn't resist, but he did look down at himself, mourning the half-standing soldier.

Killian's quill moved across the paper with an unnatural grace. He didn't rush his usual writing. This time… he was patient. Weighing every word he wrote. His fingers only pressed harder into his forehead as he tried to search the words he needed… or maybe the words he didn't know how to write.

'Brother,'

That was the introduction. Something short and simple. That was easy.

'I'll have no use for riddles this time. I am sending something your way.'

But that's where his quill faltered. He buried his face into his hands, unbothered by how the ink dripped onto the edges of the parchment. He growled, frustrated and tired. He dragged his head back up, his eyes finding the carved dragons he had made for his sister. He exhaled sharply, letting his eyes close. Then flexed his fingers and picked the quill up again.

Brother,

I'll have no use for riddles this time. I am sending something your way. Something most precious to me—

The rapid opening of his bedroom door made his gaze snap up, his shoulders tensed, but upon seeing Ambrosja, he softened.

"O-oh!" Ambrosja looked slightly surprised as she stared at Killian. "I apologize, I thought you would be in your office."

"Ambrosja," Killian said, standing up and sliding the letter he was working on to rest beneath another, "is something wrong?"

"No, not at all." She smiled, approaching Killian. "Gunnar just… annoyed me. So, instead of breaking *another* nose out of habit, I figured I would retreat here."

Killian smirked, his finger finding the bridge of his nose. "Ah, saving those for me, are you?"

Ambrosja looked down, a little bit bashful and a little bit shameful. "I still feel quite awful about that."

"Don't be," the Commander grinned. "Frankly, it was a bit of a turn on. No one has ever dared try to reach my nose as you have. And… you actually surprised me. Which was impressive." He took a step closer. "So, what did Gunnar do?"

"He insinuated that you and I would entangle our bodies at night!" Ambrosja groaned, raising her hands to let them fall heavily at her sides. Then she muttered, "If only." Then, once realizing what she had said without thinking, her face burned a soft pink.

Killian's breath caught. His jaw clenched, tongue pressing into his cheek. "You are… maddening," he whispered softly, far too soft for the heat coiling in him. "You will break me one day, Ambrosja."

The Empress looked up at Killian. She thought about what he said, that she could take any step, she could shape her future. And the heat stirring in her was something she wanted to pursue.

"Is that right…?" she leaned into the table, letting the fabric on her shoulder shift down her skin, naturally, this time. "Do I drive you mad… Commander?"

She lifted her foot, and the leather of her boot met the fabric of his pants. Killian's jaw was tight, his hands coming to rest behind his back as he kept his posture. A sharp breath of air left his nostrils.

"Empress… You are pushing me," he warned her, "I am just a man, and you — you have your own promises."

Ambrosja lowered her foot then.

"And I am just a woman," she reminded him, "starving beneath you, again." She took a step closer. "I want you, Killian, I want you…" She took a deep breath, "… I want you to be the one to take me," she confessed.

"I can't…" Killian took a step back, eyes closing once. His fingers flexed, itching to touch her skin in ways he hadn't yet.

"You cannot…" Ambrosja whispered, "But it is because you won't, because you — you fear I will regret it, but Killian…" She followed his step, getting closer to him. "I fear I will regret it if you are not the one."

Killian's chest heaved. A tightening feeling crossed all over him as his gray eyes tracked every movement. He didn't back up this time. He couldn't. He didn't want to.

"You don't know what you're saying, you're young—"

"Yes," Ambrosja interjected, "I am young, but I also know that when I look at you, my heart hurts…" she titled her head, cheek pressing into her

shoulder as she gave him the softest smile she had ever given, "And I love the way it hurts, because… my ribs feel too tight to hold all that I feel for you."

The Commander's breathing had faltered at her words. He looked down at her, *trying* so desperately to contain himself. But those sweet, soft words had coiled around his ribs, making the space feel just as constricted for him as it did for her.

Killian's eyes glanced once at where the letter was, then back at Ambrosja.

"Say you want it then," the Commander growled, hunching his back so his breath could caress Ambrosja's cheek, "say you want me."

"…I want you," she whispered breathlessly, "I want you so much, Killian."

Killian didn't waste another second. His hands found her waist, and he hoisted her up until her breasts crushed against his chest. Ambrosja gasped, wrapping her legs around him as he carried her to the bed and dropped himself onto it with her on top. His hand squeezed her thigh, the other threaded into the locks at her nape to pull her close, closing her lips down onto his as he kissed her with a hunger he had tried so hard to hold back.

"You're mine," he whispered, his hands traveling with reverence, "not Hådvard's, not some other candidate to your hand. Mine." His hands then gripped her blouse, the one that once belonged to him, and he tore it open; the buttons scattered, and the laces came undone.

Ambrosja arched her back, pressing herself down onto Killian, gasping as his hands now gripped the flesh of her breasts above the leather bustier.

"I am yours, Killian," Ambrosja proclaimed. "All yours."

The Commander's hands drifted to the sides of the bustier, undoing the laces and then pulling it up over her head along with the blouse.

"You are so stunning, body and mind," Killian growled. "You drive me mad."

He rolled them, and he was now on top. The laces of her pants came undone. His massive hands tugged them down, and when they reached her knees, Ambrosja was kicking her legs to get them off of her completely. She was far too impatient. Her own hands were undoing the buttons to his blouse, messy and hurried, then she began pulling as well, causing his own buttons to scatter onto the bed.

Their hands roamed, roamed until they were both bare. Killian was on his knees on the bed. His shoulders were wound tight. Fingers flexing as he stared down at her. Ambrosja stared up at him, trembling with want and need. Her own eyes drifted over him, from the scars across his chest, to the hardened shape of his torso, to the lines that led along his pelvis, then to the heavy and thick length of him. She was biting on her finger as she looked at it.

Killian's hands pressed into Ambrosja's thighs, spreading her softly, keeping his eyes on hers, always looking for hesitation, or regret, or uncertainty. He moved slowly, and when her legs were spread, his knuckles ran along her inner thighs. Making her shiver and inch closer. And when she didn't pull away… That's when he lowered himself to brace a forearm beside her shape.

"If we do this…" He began to speak, voice warm and husky, "…you will be betraying the tradition placed upon your crown."

"I do not care," Ambrosja confessed, "not when you are the one I would betray it for."

He kissed her again, deeper this time. His hand moved down her body, fingers curling around her thick thigh. His own leg moved to push under hers, forcing her leg to hook around his, spreading her wider for him. He guided himself to her, thick and heavy in his hand, eyes never leaving hers. His hand left to grip her waist, holding her firmly, anchoring her in this moment.

"I will be gentle," he whispered against her lips. "As gentle as I can be."

Then he moved his hips forward, pushed into her heat slowly as he felt the slightest resistance. Ambrosja's eyes widened, unfocused as the heat now crept low in her stomach. She was gasping, breathless. Her hands gripped Killian's broad shoulders, her entire body trembling from the stretch. Killian's own breathing was ragged as he eased himself inside her, feeling her heat tighten around him and pull him in. He pressed in until he reached her deepest parts, unable to move any further.

His hand left her waist, now gripping her jaw, something tender and possessive. "Look at me, Ambrosja," he murmured to her, nose brushing her cheek. "Are you alright?"

Ambrosja's lips parted, but words barely escaped, only the slightest little cracked sound left her as she nodded. Killian gave a crooked smile, breathless himself. He began moving slowly, testing. Pulling himself out, then pushing in. Ambrosja's eyes only widened, lips parted further to let out the gentlest of sounds and breaths. Killian kept moving his hips, slowly picking up the pace.

"Godsdamn—" he growled, voice dark and husky. "You're perfect."

Ambrosja's hands moved down, drifting to Killian's chest, fingers threading through the dark hairs there. Her breaths came out heavy, another one tumbling out right after the other.

"Killian," she gasped, her voice trembling with want. "Gods—it's so deep… I can feel you everywhere. I can't even catch my breath, but I don't want to. I just—want more." Her eyes squeezed shut as a moan slipped past her lips, her back arching hard beneath his touch. "You're so thick… so big…" Her words dissolved into a shuddering exhale, hips pressing closer. "I want all of you—*every inch.*"

Her breathing became heavier, the air thicker. Her head tilted back, her eyes closed, relaxed, taking in every sensation that Killian delivered while entangled in her body. He buried his face into the curve of her neck, teeth scraping against the soft skin.

"You—gods—" He couldn't help himself. He picked up the pace ever so slightly, thrusting into her like a man seeking to touch her heart. His breath was hot against her skin, lips lingering on every inch of her. "Every inch of you is making me mad, Ambrosja, and I love it."

"Killian…" Ambrosja began whimpering, her moans tumbled out like vibrations as he moved more wildly with every thrust. "…Fuck—"

He groaned against her skin. "Ambrosja," he growled, his control wavering, "Do you think if you keep sounding like that—feeling like sin wrapped in silk, I'll be able to hold back?" His lips pressed into her neck once more, sucking the flesh, then dragging his tongue over it to soothe the spot.

"I—I can't help myself, Killian, I'm—I'm—" She couldn't finish it. Her heat had tightened, walls that had wrapped around him and grasped at the hard length within her. Her eyes had widened from the foreign sensation. Killian was now hitting a deep spot. Again and again. "Killian—!" She gasped, her breathing turning fervent as were her moans, tangled with whimpers, helpless and real. Her fingertips dug into his chest, her curves bouncing in time with his thrusts.

Their feet were light; Donathan did his best to mirror Cinder's movements. She was like a graceful cat, while his steps belonged to a lazy hound—regardless, he was still quiet. The two of them tread up a mound, their step deliberate as they dug the tips of their shoes into the mud and steadied themselves with their heels. Cinder grabbed at branches and trunks of trees to ease the climb. Donathan fell forwards, hands falling straight into the mud.

He groaned with annoyance. Cinder bit her lip to not giggle, instead she crouched and helped him up.

At the top, the sounds were now clear to Donathan. "Horses…" he whispered, his eyes on Cinder's. She nodded and lifted her finger to her lips, urging him to remain silent as they walked ahead, following the sound of hooves stepping onto patches of mud along the dirt road.

Trees began to space out now, and from a distance, they saw a ruined fence line. And just beyond it, they saw the sleek figures of dark horses. Riders adorned in cloaks of black. Donathan instinctively took a step back, but Cinder halted him. She watched them. The playful mood she once had was replaced by something edged with caution.

Cinder took a few steps closer, crouching low to peek through the openings that the trees provided. She saw them. Six riders in dark cloaks that were torn and faded at the edges. Helms hid their faces; their appearance was unmistakable. *Black Hand…* She took his hand without another thought and began to rush down the mound they had just climbed up, letting low-hanging branches and leaves hit at them.

Cressida, ever poised atop her horse, immediately looked to the sound of the brush shifting in quick and fading movements. Her eyes narrowed at the sound.

"Ignore it, Cressida," Serana said. "Probably a simple beast, keep moving. All of you." Serana inhaled deeply as her horse carried her. "I can smell Greenfield. We are near."

Killian felt it. Her heat clenched tightly, her walls pulsing, and a sudden rush of warmth surrounding him. Thick and needy. "Gods—" Killian grit his teeth, body shaking as he felt her climax wrap around him. His movements faltered, "Ambrosja, you're choking me." Another growl escaped him. He moved into her, guiding her through her climax while holding his own back.

"Don't—don't stop!" Ambrosja begged, her accent thicker, her words messy, eyes wide and locked onto his. Her thighs were shaking, "Harder! Harder! Please!" Her hands found his ribs, gliding around so her arms held him close, and her nails now grasped at his shoulder blades.

Killian took a deep breath. He moved for her, following every sound she released, following every tremble her body gave him, even as the bed groaned in protest. His eyes locked on hers, which only made his own need stronger. More wild. More persistent. He watched her intently, studying her

like holy scripture as he saw every flicker of emotion in her face, in her eyes. He was swelling within her, thickening with need. With pure pleasure.

"Ambrosja," he called out softly to her, voice still husky with need, "I can't hold back anymore—I need to give you everything."

Ambrosja didn't protest, and Killian moved for his own needs while still studying her body. He found himself burying inside her again and again until his vision blurred. Groans escaped him, breathing against her lips, never tearing his gaze from her once.

Then one last thrust, burying himself to the hilt. His hips were flush against hers, keeping himself there. She felt him throb within her, the sensation made her back arch sharply, head tilting back onto the pillows, as if his release was her release, as if each rope of his need that poured into her heat belonged to her alone.

Their breathing was ragged, mingling like forbidden love. Killian eased himself down, his hands pressed into the mattress, forearms bracing on either side of Ambrosja as he settled his weight atop of her, caging her but not crushing her. His hand met her face, thumb brushing along her jaw and cheek. Their eyes were locked; no words were needed. Killian kissed her—soft at first, then hungrier. Like he was starving, and she was the only thing that could feed him.

When he pulled away… The Empress pushed him, rolling them over until she was on top. Killian growled, already feeling himself burn for her once more.

The scrape of a crate being dragged through the mud was all that Johann stared at as he watched his giant of a friend release his anxiety on the innocent wooden box filled with ores. The Black Hand guards paid no mind as they patrolled the vicinity of the camp. Miners who had approached Gunnar to help were shooed away with a growl. Johann rubbed a heavy hand over his face and stepped beside his friend.

"I'm going to say it," Johann said as he moved to stand in front of Gunnar's vision. "You're acting like a seventy-year-old brat."

"Me?" Gunnar stopped pushing the crate now. "The brat is the one who ran off with the damn boy to defy me."

Johann rubbed his temples. "So what? What are you so afraid of?" He stared at Gunnar. "That one day she won't rely on you but instead on Donathan?"

Gunnar didn't answer immediately, so Johan continued. "One day, Cinder will have her own life. Possibly a husband, possibly a wife, possibly kids. Maybe a house. Or maybe she will keep traveling the country with us, fighting bandits, exploring ruins… But one day—we'll be gone… And Cinder? She will be alone, because *you*—" he jabbed his finger in Gunnar's chest, "—you were too scared to let her go."

Gunnar's brows lowered, and his eyes softened. His fists clenched as he stood there. He looked away with shame.

"Damn it, I hate that you're right…" He sighed heavily, as if he were trying to shrug off the weight of his worries. "You're right," he repeated. "It was nice being needed, being looked up to. I see myself in that girl… I see what I could have had if I stayed in one place. If I pursued love instead of adventure. She's like a daughter to me, Johann. And *even though* I met her when she was nearly grown, she still looked like a sad little girl who just needed *someone* to hold onto."

Johann's hand reached Gunnar's shoulder. "Friend, she will always need you. She will always *want* to need you. You just have to let her be, because shoving her away?" He shook his head. "Old friend, that will teach her not to need you."

"Gunnar!" Cinder's voice cracked through the air.

Gunnar's head snapped toward the entrance of the camp where Cinder was coming from. Her brown hair bounced with every step, the half-undone laces of her tunic whipping in the wind. Donathan trailed behind, already out of breath.

Gunnar moved immediately, meeting her halfway while the Black Hand guards only watched — eyes following the pair before glancing toward the path they'd come from.

"Lass, what happened—" Gunnar's voice faltered as he took in the state of her clothes. His gaze shot to Donathan. "What did you do, boy?!"

Cinder pressed both hands against his chest. "Hey! He didn't do anything!"

"I'll say!" Gunnar gestured sharply at her tunic. "Then what's this, eh? And why were you running from him?"

Cinder scowled. "I wasn't running from him! He's just *slow*, Gunnar!"

Donathan opened his mouth to protest, then thought better of it and stayed quiet.

The Black Hand guards stepped forward now. A bigger one called out, "Hey! Keep it down! Unless someone is dying, we don't need a godsdamn parade that you four are so keen on throwing."

Cinder shot that guard a glare, but didn't mind him for an extra second. She grabbed Gunnar and Johann's hands, urging them to a quieter corner of camp. "Donathan and I—we spotted more of the Black Hand."

Ambrosja moved atop of Killian. Inexperienced but passionate. Her whimpers touched his lips as his hands guided her hips in the heat of their passion.

"I love you, Killian…" Ambrosja whispered softly, eyes glassy from the intensity of everything coming down onto her.

Killian released a breath that was more like a growl. His hands tightened on her hips, and he sat up, now moving her body completely with his strength.

"And I love you, Ambrosja," he whispered right back, gazing into her eyes, "I was doomed the moment I saw you."

Hooves stopped at the western edges of Greenfield, just touching the outskirts. Eyes of the Black Hand roamed over the people, who were now frozen in place. Kids who were playing nearby suddenly stopped, just for a moment before darting away to their mothers. Serana's eyes watched everything, but only for one purpose: to spot the woman with pale hair and pale skin. The trot of the horses was soft now, eerily calm as their nostrils flared with fierce exhales, mist escaping them in the gentle cold of the outskirts of Greenfield.

THORN, THE LEGENDARY DRAGON - RIDER

The Thorn Lineage begins with a man known only as Thorn — a Nordorner by birth, yet Vaestorian by fate. Of his early life, little is recorded save that his hair was as black as midnight, a rare mark among his people, earning him the name the Black-Veiled One.

He crossed into Vaestoria not as conqueror but as survivor, carving his place through blood, honor, and unrelenting endurance. Those who met him claimed that his presence was both grace and wound — a man whose words could bind like silk and cut like steel.

When Thorn reached his thirtieth year, the dragon Vorthunal, the Spine of Stone, descended from the high peaks in search of a mortal soul to match his own. It was said that among all men, only Thorn's spirit mirrored the dragon's patience and resolve. Their bond was immediate, forged in recognition rather than ritual, and from that day onward, Thorn became the first mortal to ride the dragon's back.

What followed became legend. The descendants of Thorn were said to inherit not only his courage but Vorthunal's favor. Through centuries, the dragon returned to the same bloodline, choosing again and again from among Thorn's kin — a bond unbroken by time or death. Thus the Thorn family rose to prominence in Stonehaven, bearing the mark of dragons in their hearts and a legacy that whispered of both pride and burden.

"Keep your eyes open," Serana warned. "The woman *is* our priority, but should we not find her, then we look for the boy. See what he knows and why he's here instead of being within the ranks of Evander's Hand."

As the riders grew closer and closer, mothers gathered their children and headed inside. Men halted their work, whether that was hauling lumber or tending to cattle; they stopped and watched with wary eyes. One man who stood near the main road leading into Greenfield turned on his heel, not walking too fast, but heading in a clear direction.

"Sister-Hand Serana," Cressida, the Black Hand soldier with a dark-feathered hawk, spoke. Her voice was low but clear enough for those nearby, "I believe that gentleman is heading in the direction of a Watchstead."

Serana, for once, looked amused beneath her helm. "Is that right, Cressida?" she asked smoothly, "Well, you've got such a sharp eye, perhaps you should keep a close watch on him, hm?"

Cressida smiled. "It would be my pleasure." The reins whipped once, and she moved ahead, following the man who was moving further into the village.

Serana gestured to the two to her left, "I want you two to go ahead and scout through the village." She then looked to her right, "And you two follow me." She whipped her reins and trotted ahead,

"We'll be checking the inn."

Villagers stepped aside without question, their feet carrying them faster than they realized as they touched the grass-covered sides of the main road, eagerly heading away and paying no mind to the sudden arrival of the dark riders in their midst. It didn't take long before they spotted the Goose's Nest.

Serana moved from her saddle, leaving the other two riders behind. Her hands moved to her helm as she kicked the doors open. Everyone within the inn paused their tasks, whether that was eating or sweeping. Serana moved to the bar, she gave an assessing glance over the man who tended to it, he was tall, thick in the waist, with blond hair brushed back.

"Tell me," Serana leaned forward, elbow resting firmly into the wood of the bar's counter. "Did you happen to have a Nordorner within your inn?"

The barkeep stared at Serana for a moment before giving a grunt of amusement. "A Nordorner? Here? *Right.*"

"Oh," She tilted her head, mock-cooing. "Do you think a Nordorner is capable of respecting boundaries? *Country* boundaries? They've never been known to ask for permission to step on soil that isn't theirs." When the barkeep didn't answer—Serana's hand reached out fast, grabbing at the man's collar and dragging him close to her. "Let me rephrase my question… Have you had a woman with pale skin and pale hair within this inn?"

He trembled, his hands braced against the wooden counter, eyes focused down at Serana's hand. "Wait!" A woman called out, stepping forward with a broom in her hand.

Serana turned to face the woman, studying her olive skin and dark hair, "What?"

"We had someone like that here many days ago," the barmaid admitted. "But we don't know where she went…"

Serana let go of the bartkeep, now completely facing the young woman before her. "Was she with anyone?"

The barmaid nodded. "I believe four others. She arrived with three at first, but on the last day here she left with four…"

"Did you see where they went?"

The barmaid shook her head, knuckles whitening from how tightly her shaky hands clenched the broom. "No, I don't know… I'm sorry."

Serana cocked her head to the side, glancing briefly at the trembling man before looking back at the barmaid once more. "No need to apologize," she said coolly. "You've just saved this man's life." With that, she walked out, putting her helmet back on.

Outside the Watchstead, in the thicket beyond the road, Cressida lingered. Her gaze lifted as the upper window eased open with a faint creak. A man stepped into view, a pigeon perched on his wrist, a small scrap of parchment tied to its leg. One nudge of his arm sent the bird fluttering skyward.

Her lips curved in something between a smirk and a snarl. Her gloved fingers stroked the dark-feathered hawk still perched like a shadow on her shoulder.

"Intercept," she murmured.

The hawk leapt, claws tearing from the leather, and cut into the winter air in a violent surge of wings. Its cry split the quiet as it rose to meet the pigeon's path — and end it.

Killian adjusted Ambrosja in his hold, centering her better on his chest, his arms wrapped around her completely. His cheek rested against the crown of her head, and every time she shifted in her sleep he pulled her closer. His own body exhausted from the entanglements of their coupling. Everything felt right…

Only for a knock to interrupt.

The Commander's eyes opened, narrowing in an instant as he growled. Then softened when he felt Ambrosja stir. But he only soothed her, running a rough hand along her spine. He carefully rolled to the side, placing Ambrosja to rest flat on her back. He grabbed the blankets, pulling them up to cover her completely. He kissed her cheek before parting.

His hands found his towel thrown over the folding screen; he wrapped it around his hips as he made his way to the door. When the Commander opened the door he saw his Captain standing there, nervous and awkward with brows furrowed.

"Wex?" Killian narrowed his eyes onto the man, reading him. "What is it?"

"Sister-Hand Serana," Wex whispered, "she's in the camp."

Killian stilled completely. *Gaspard's personal scout*… He thought to himself. His jaw rolled, then he spoke, "I'll be down in a moment. Leave."

The Captain turned on his heel and left, and Killian closed the door soon after. Gently so as not to rouse Ambrosja. His jaw clenched. His hand grabbed at his own face, fingers digging into his flesh as he leaned into the door like a man coming undone.

They know… he thought to himself.

His eyes found Ambrosja's sleeping form, then drifted to the forgotten letter on the table.

The Commander wasted no time. He strode to it, unbothered by the towel slipping from his hips as he sat at his table once again, quill in hand, and this time… His writing was not gentle or careful. It was messy.

Serana walked in the center of the mining camp. Her heavy boots parted the fog on the ground like a dragon pacing through its dominion. Her hands laced behind her back, her posture easy — the sort worn by someone who knew no one would make it within a foot of her before a blade met their ribs. The rest of her riders stood near the entrance to the camp. Their eyes were studying the structures, the tools, the exits, the miners—even the Black Hand guards within the area, as if trust wouldn't be found even from those in the same uniform.

Cinder's arms were crossed tight against her chest. She stood beside Gunnar, her own eyes fixed on Serana. "That's half of them." Her voice was low, but dropped to a dangerous edge, like a wolf ready to pounce upon feeling cornered. "How fucked are we, Gunnar?"

"Let's not assume the worst just yet, lass," Gunnar muttered. His eyes followed the riders atop of the horses. "It's safe to say they didn't come here for the scenery. They want something."

"Maybe they're here to pick up a shipment of Nythralt," Johann whispered. He glanced at Donathan who stood beside him. He leaned in close, "Anyone you recognize?"

Donathan shook his head. "No… I've never seen her." His eyes studied Serana, then the riders. "No, they're not here for Nythralt—unless they have some cart nearby I haven't noticed. But their horses don't have the equipment to pull a cart, not to mention—too few of them." He gestured with a jerk of his chin towards the sealed crates of Nythralt and then back to the riders. "Nythralt's too valuable to be guarded by so few."

"Maybe they've got more riders…" Gunnar whispered.

Cinder shook her head. "No, I only saw six on the road." Her hand subtly moved towards Donathan, giving a gentle yet firm squeeze of reassurance. Her voice dropped to a whisper for him only, "I'm not letting them take you back."

Donathan gave a wide-eyed side glance to Cinder. His cheeks had bloomed to a softly sweet red. "Th–thanks, Cinder…"

Killian finished buckling the shoulderplates of his armor. Everything was set in motion. He had done it all silently, not waking Ambrosja once.

He took a deep breath, nostrils flaring as he did so, then exhaled sharply. He looked once at the sleeping form of his lover.

"To preserve humanity…" Killian whispered in her direction, "…you must be willing to abandon it."

Killian pushed open the doors to his Command Hall and stepped outside. The fog parted for him as it did for Serana. The Sister-Hand turned. Her gaze fixed on Killian's broad frame as he approached — and stopped, just short of striking distance.

"Sister-Hand Serana," Killian's ever-commanding voice rang out without needing to be loud. "I trust your journey has been well. To what do I owe the pleasure?"

Serana's lips cracked into a smirk, her posture was still infuriatingly relaxed, but her hands had unlaced from each other. "Well, you could say I'm on a bit of a hunt, Commander Killian Thorn." Serana turned, her eyes scanned the miners that were off to the side along the walls, the tables, near their tents. Their card and dice games paused. Mugs untouched. Serana's brow arched. *No blondes…* She thought, lips curled in annoyance.

"A hunt?" Killian followed her gaze. "A hunt for what? The next shipment is ready to be sent out by nightfall, if that is what you are here for."

"That is good to hear, Commander," Serana nodded. Then tilted her head back as she took a wide step to the side, "But no. You could say a pale whelp has escaped the Grand Marshal's claws." She took a step closer. "Tell me, Commander Thorn, by any chance do you have a woman working in the mines, or maybe just lingering nearby with pale skin and pale hair? She most likely sounds like she's from Nordorn."

Killian's hands moved to rest behind him, though they didn't rest; his knuckles cracked, fingers pressing into his palms as he urged to control the storm brewing within him. "Can't say that I do, Sister-Hand Serana."

Berric stood off to the side, leaning against a wooden beam, his arms crossed tight. One side of his face was scarred and still bruised; a damp cloth, laced with healing herbs, covered the gash where his face had met the sharp shards of porcelain—courtesy of Killian. He watched the exchange, his expression twisted somewhere between irritation and calculation.

Serana didn't speak for a moment. Her brown eyes simply studied Killian's face. But that led to her eyes flicking briefly to the bruise on his neck. And she noticed the clench of his jaw. Her gaze met him once more. "Huh, the Grand Marshal must have forgotten to mention you were a romantic, Commander." She gestured to the blooming bruise. "Was she a means to warm your bed for the night or is she still upstairs?"

Berric called out then, "Isn't that girl in your chambers a pale sort? Want me to rouse her?"

Killian's eyes snapped to the Lieutenant. His glare spoke volumes of warning without uttering a single word. His hands now clenching behind his back. He took a step forward, eyes meeting Serana's. "This Nordorner of yours is not here, Sister-Hand Serana."

Cinder and Gunnar watched with eyes that spoke of wary and fury. Cinder's hand squeezed Donathan's tightly. Her voice was low, "She's talking about Ambrosja…"

Gunnar nodded, "Aye, she is."

Johann looked up towards the window, "If we don't say a thing she's safe in there."

Donathan even chimed in, "…Killian is protecting her."

Serana, still facing Killian and none the wiser about the whispers of Ambrosja, simply smiled. She took a step back and looked around. Her eyes roamed over the miners once more. She walked in a semi-circle, hand lacing behind her back again. "If any of you have encountered a woman with pale hair and skin, now would be the time to speak, as we have reason to believe she's made her way to Greenfield." Serana waited, but she caught the way a miner shivered, clenching their mug too tightly, the way eyes had drifted far too nervously to the Command Hall, to Killian — then away.

She turned to Killian, her voice rising once more, "This woman arrived on a royal rowboat from Nordorn. We believe she may be a part of the royal family, or possibly the Empress of Nordorn herself." Serana's smile widened, but the warmth of such a smile never arrived. "As you can all imagine," she looked over everyone again, "we're quite worried, as if she dies on Vaestorian soil… Nordorn will come with the fury of a storm and leave nothing untouched."

Everyone froze and yet gasped at that moment. Cinder's eyes widened, lips parted in disbelief, her own hand shook in Donathan's. Gunnar muttered *Impossible,* Johann gripped his holy symbol and Donathan's head simply shook in something close to fear. His other hand latched onto Cinder's, cupping hers in something that sought comfort and reassurance. Serana reveled in their reactions, and waited.

Berric was walking forward now, hands clenched tightly. His shoulders were hunched. Killian immediately snapped his head in his direction, causing his black locks to fall over those harsh, stormy eyes. But Berric paid no mind.

"He's got a girl he keeps up in his chambers," Berric spat. "Pale skin, paler hair. Her R's are rougher—rolled, nothing like a Vaestorian."

"Is that right, Commander Thorn?" Serana cocked a brow. "Naughty, naughty." She leaned forward, bending at her hips, looking at Killian as if he were a child. "Now, you should know better than to lie to me…"

Killian smirked, gesturing toward Berric. "This man suffered a blow to his godsdamn head. You think he's thinking straight? Fine—investigate the camp if you want. But right now…" He stepped forward, his broad frame casting a shadow over her. "I have a mine to run, and you're disrupting the short-lived peace of my workers. And we both know the Grand Marshal values results, so I suggest you leave—and come back at dawn. Perform your little investigation then."

Serana stared. Then tilted her head back as she laughed. She paced in a circle once before stopping before Killian. "You think you can tell me what to do, Commander?" Her voice dropped, low and deadly, "I am on a mission from the Grand Marshal himself. I suggest you either give her up and let us walk away without burning something down… Or we can brand you as a traitor for interfering with clear orders."

The Commander crossed his arms. He stared at her. Then with the smallest shake of his head… "No."

The Sister-Hand's eyebrow twitched. "No?"

"As I've said, I have a mine to run, I have a shipment to be delivered, and while you are in my camp… You are under my Command," Killian gestured to her with one hand, "you may think you stand above me for being the personal scout… But you are *nothing* once you step into my rule."

His arms uncrossed. He took a step forward.

"Now, I suggest you leave… Before I send you back to the Grand Marshal with a warning attached to your skull."

Serana smiled coldly. "I always did enjoy a good hunt, Commander. And worry not… I will grab that girl." She then looked at her riders. "Let's head out, I am craving something bloody… And burnt."

THE BLACK HAND

The Hand's cruelty is matched only by its structure. Captured prisoners are bound in iron and marched far from roads and memory, taken to isolated outposts where the world itself seems to conspire in their breaking. There, discipline is not taught—it is extracted, through endless toil, regulated hunger, and punishment delivered without emotion or spectacle. Pain is not inflicted in bursts of rage, but administered with patience, as one would shape stone.

Those who endure are not rewarded with mercy. Instead, they are reshaped. Their names are stripped, their pasts rendered irrelevant, until labor becomes instinct and obedience replaces thought. Survival itself is made conditional upon submission. In time, many cease to resist—not because they believe, but because resistance no longer occurs to them.

To outsiders, they are little more than marauders: faceless riders, fire in their wake, brutality mistaken for chaos. Yet those who have seen their camps know better. The camps are orderly. The violence is regulated. Every movement serves purpose. Tents stand aligned, schedules are enforced with ruthless precision, and even suffering follows structure.

The Black Hand is not bound by loyalty, nor sustained by belief. It does not ask to be loved. It requires only compliance. In this, it is far colder than any horde or kingdom—it is an empire of silence, built not on devotion, but on fear so complete it no longer needs to announce itself.

OF SECRETS UNSAID

Pale fingers reached across the bed.

"Killian?" Ambrosja called softly, eyes blinking as she looked to his side of the bed. "Killian?" She called again when she noticed he wasn't there.

The Empress dragged herself to his side, resting atop his pillows. She bit her bottom lip, her body was sore, her hand fell onto his bedside table, hitting it hard. She felt the top shift, the sound was hollow. Her head turned, and she rolled to lay on her stomach, a soft whimper escaping her as her body still recovered from the newfound experience of earlier.

Ambrosja's hand reached out, grabbing at the top of the bedside table again. Shifting it around.

"Is this… a false lid?" She whispered to herself, brows pinched, eyes narrowed.

She lifted the lid up, revealing a thin space of letters, documents, and orders. Her eyes widened when she spotted a map and markers, and the word *Nythralt* on one of them. Ambrosja immediately sat up, grabbing the contents and bringing them to her lap while she held the blanket tight to her chest.

"You have one hour left! After that—get back to work! I don't care if the carts are getting stuck in the mud! Manage it!" Killian then walked, not back inside the Command Hall. He walked towards Gunnar and stopped short of him, but didn't face him, didn't look at him. "Are you still friends with my father?"

Gunnar's brows lowered, his eyes steady on Killian. "I better be!" He huffed. "I fought beside him against riots and bandits in the outskirts of Marrowind and Drevrath. And fought alongside him against invading forces on the shores of Greymire. Attended his wedding to Lady Isolde."

Killian turned his head slightly, eyes on Gunnar's. His voice dropped to a whisper, one of calm urgency, "I need you to leave to Stonehaven. Tonight. Take Ambrosja with you."

Gunnar tilted his head slightly, "So it's true…"

Cinder watched, hands shaking, but she couldn't even understand why they were. They had never shaken this badly. She chimed in. "Fuck–she's— that's why she's been so secretive. Isn't it?" Johann immediately shushed her but not coldly.

Killian continued, "It doesn't matter whether it's true or not. She's not safe here. I need your group to take the shipments of Nythralt out of here, along with Ambrosja. But most importantly, take Ambrosja." He turned to face them, "I am lifting your sentence. I will have papers prepared saying you are to deliver the shipment. I will sneak Ambrosja out." He exhaled sharply. "Do what you want with the shipment, I don't care, not about the Nythralt. Just make sure Ambrosja gets to Stonehaven." His eyes moved from Gunnar all the way to Donathan, assessing the group. "Don't fail." But his hand reached for Gunnar's arm. "Can I trust you to be near Nythralt this time? To conquer your wounds and keep going?"

Gunnar was silent for just a moment. Then with a sharp nod. "Aye, you can."

"Around dinner time, when Serana's riders are distracted, you'll leave with her." Killian turned, he called out to his own guards, "These four will deliver the next shipment to Mistvale Crossing! Gather the wagon and the crates! We have a schedule to keep!" His legs carried him to the Command Hall, already moving back to Ambrosja.

"Are we seriously doing this?" Cinder hissed. "Are we grabbing a fucking wagon filled with illegal ore and one *Empress of fucking Nordorn*, Gunnar?!"

Gunnar's head snapped down and to the side, eyes settling on Cinder. "Keep your voice down."

Cinder retorted, "It is down!"

Gunnar continued, "This is what we wanted. A reason, proof. And we're being given the chance to escape to Stonehaven. We keep Ambrosja a secret, let her decide what she wants to do when we get there, but the Nythralt? Lass, that might be the physical proof we need that there's a force in Vaestoria that *must* be dealt with."

Donathan's hands trembled slightly, though he clenched his fists to control himself. "Am I joining you?" He looked at each of them, desperate and hopeful.

Cinder immediately responded, "Of course!"

Johann nodded, "You're one of us." Donathan released a shaky exhale.

Gunnar gave a firm pat on Donathan's shoulder and gestured to the others, "Come on, let's get this shipment ready by dinner."

Killian reached the double doors of his chamber, hands urging to softly grab at the handles, but his body betrayed him as his grip created a sound of metal cranking beneath the strength of his palms. He opened the doors slowly, but never wide. Not anymore. Not while she was in the room. Killian's eyes were downcast only until he closed the door behind him. When he looked up, his cold gray eyes took in the scene. He saw Ambrosja sitting on his side of the bed, a blanket wrapped tightly around her while her hands shook around the papers in her hand. His papers.

Ambrosja lifted her gaze, now staring back, "Killian..." Her voice was soft and trembling, as if a dagger had been wedged into her ribs and she wasn't quite sure how to take it out. "...You're the one who has been siphoning Nythralt..." She moved, now standing, holding the papers in her hand. "You have been organizing routes, drop-offs... You beat a poor miner for something *you* were doing..."

Killian stood at the far side of the room near the doors. His body coiled tight, his face now a scowl as he looked at her and the papers in her hand. His boots hit the wooden floors of his chamber, moving until he stopped right before Ambrosja. "...You're leaving."

The Empress's eyes went wide, her whole body froze up. "...What?" Her voice cracked. "Killian," she shook her head, "You are—pushing me away for this?"

"No," The Commander said simply, "you and I were never going to work. We both knew this was going to be fleeting. And now... It is done.

We're done."

Ambrosja walked forward, quick, without a thought. Her body collided into his, arms wrapping around him, "Please, Killian!" She tilted her head up to look at him through her tears. "Why? Why must we be done? We could leave together!"

Killian's hands rose fast, he grabbed her shoulders and forced her back. "Stop this, Empress. You are leaving tonight. I don't care where you go. But you're not staying here. The plan has failed."

Ambrosja's heart sank fast when he forced her away. "P-plan? What plan, Killian?"

He stared down at her. His face was perfectly neutral, and his voice was a cold rumble that could freeze the air between them into the thinnest shards of ice. "I was using you." Killian straightened further, his hands moved to lace behind his back. "I hoped to gain your trust, combine my soldiers with yours, expand the strength of the Black Hand, and use your Nythralt in the process, eventually placing the Black Hand under my complete control. But your cover has been blown. Everyone outside knows exactly who you are, Empress. And now? Now others from the Black Hand chase after you."

Ambrosja was shaking as she listened to every word that Killian's cold voice spoke. Her fingers were flexing hard. Her knees wobbled. Her shoulders were trembling so hard it looked as if they could displace themselves out of their sockets. "K-Killian? This — this is not funny…"

"This is not a joke."

"But you said I was your hoard…" Her voice trembled. "You are my dragon — and I am your hoard…" Her voice faded—then shouted, "You lied to me! You lied to me!" She stepped hard, her foot hitting into the wooden floor with a ferocity that mirrored the first time she charged at him. "I let you have me! I let you take every inch of me, Killian! I said I loved you!" She pushed him then. "And now—now you are treating me like a pawn! Like—like I am just a scrap of parchment filled with messy lines and smudged ink that you can toss about however you desire!"

She grabbed the papers, the ones filled with lies, and trickery. She threw them at him, tears now falling like a scorching touch against her cheeks. She moved to push past him to grab her clothes but Killian grabbed her by the waist.

"I said tonight, not now."

"Let go! You have lied! You lied to me!" She cried, squirming to pull herself away. "Unhand me, you kjötskalle!" She pushed at his hands, every movement messy and desperate behind a fury of emotions.

The Commander held her against him still, regardless of her thrashing or her Nordorner insult. "I know listening to me is not your best skill set, and regardless of how this ends…" He paused, adjusting her against him as he chose his next words, "…Your life doesn't have to end here because your heart is being torn to pieces by a few moments of heat."

That made Ambrosja still. *A few moments of heat*, he had said. She finally pulled away, stared at him with anger, rage, *heartache*.

"You think this was heat?!" Ambrosja's voice trembled, fury aching in every inch of her bones and burning through her flesh. "I broke my vows, my faith, my *customs* for you! An Empress does not give herself before marriage—but I did! I did, because I thought—"

Killian interjected, "You shouldn't have given it up so easily."

The words slashed through her, cutting deeper than any blade ever could. Her hand struck him before she could think; the sound of her palm meeting his cheek snapped through the air. Killian's head was to the side. Then straightened. Slow. His nostrils flared and his shoulders rolled.

Ambrosja stared at him. Her eyes spoke of regret, but her hurt was stronger. Her fists were clenched tight, one still holding the blanket around her, shaking. Then, as she moved to leave, his arm caught hers—rough, desperate. He drove her back toward the bed, forcing her down onto it, pinning her wrists to stop her struggle.

"Stop," he growled. "You can't go out there."

"Let me go!" She thrashed. Lifting her head up to scream at him. "Let me go! You — monster!"

Killian didn't budge. His hands moved fast to her arms, holding against the red silks. "Not until you calm yourself. Not until it's safe."

Their breaths tangled—hers sharp with anger, his steady with effort. The silence that followed was deafening. They stared at each other. Then finally — Ambrosja broke again. Tears slipped from her eyes, tracing the ache, hurt, and loss she felt. Her body shook so hard that it felt as if her ribs may shatter, as if her heart might burst from the ache echoing within her. Ambrosja's cries were raw, hiccups that nearly sounded like chokes. As if she couldn't get a single breath in.

Killian's grip switched from loosening to tightening. He simply stared at her, those stormy gray eyes peering down into her face that was reddened, not with the usual bashfulness she felt near him — but from the utter heartbreak he caused her. He lowered his head, his forehead touching her collarbone as he refused to let her go. And refused to take back any of what he said.

Ambrosja hadn't moved much. But when she did… her body felt sore for reasons that were no longer of love. She had cried herself to sleep beneath Killian. And now… She was only awake because he had told her it was time.

Those golden eyes of hers, so bright within the last few days… had gone vacant. Her gaze was downcast as she felt Killian wrap a black cloak around her, one similar to that of the Black Hand. She barely registered to his touch, even as he twisted her moonlit locks into a tight coil to place beneath her cloak.

"Let's go," Killian finally said, "your allies are ready by now."

She gave a cautious look up, her eyes looked up from beneath her cloak, finding his face. The stoic expression, the scar across his cheek, how his cold gray eyes didn't seem to shift, until he risked glancing at her and their eyes locked. But he said nothing. He looked ahead again, still wearing that neutral expression that gave nothing away. As if this were the very first day they had ever met.

When they reached the double doors that led out of the Command Hall, Killian paused for only a moment. He took a deep breath, palm bracing against the wood. His breathing steadied as he began to push it open, but carefully so to avoid unwanted eyes settling on them. Ambrosja swore she saw some hesitance in him, but still, his expression gave nothing away.

The long tables beneath a canopy in a corner of the camp were filled with workers, they ate the same boar-meat stew from earlier, slapping their knees as they told jokes. Some of the men laid it thick on the women, some giggled and some groaned. The guards had their own tables scattered throughout, none giving Killian much of a second glance… Beside the familiar shape of Berric.

A guard and a miner were helping set up the last of the crate of Nythralt onto the wagon. Cinder was tending to the horses along with Donathan. Gunnar tightened the latches of each crate while Johann had already begun climbing up to sit at the front. When Killian approached them, the guard and miner straightened up.

"Are we ready?" Killian asked, looking over everything. The miner and the guard simply nodded and took a step aside. They hadn't noticed Ambrosja, not with how Killian's presence was looming over them. "Good, everything is according to schedule." Killian moved, his hand still resting against Ambrosja's back. Cinder watched everything with a wariness while Donathan watched with nervousness he had felt since first arriving at the camp.

"Let's get going," Cinder muttered, climbing up and grabbing the reins. Donathan followed after her. Gunnar gave a look to Killian and Ambrosja before nodding and climbing up to sit in the back with the crates of Nythralt.

Killian guided Ambrosja to the back where she could hop in. His hand lingered on her, sliding down to her waist and betraying him, giving a final squeeze. Like a goodbye he couldn't afford to say. Ambrosja felt it. His hands, his presence. She almost cried again, but reined in her emotions by closing her eyes tightly. And slapping away Killian's hand. She refused a tear-drop now that others were nearby. And she refused his touch.

Killian didn't fight back. He accepted it and straightened. "When you get to Stonehaven, meet with the Diplomat," he whispered, "tell him I sent you. He will understand. And he will provide a means for you to return to Nordorn on a proper vessel. And…" Killian reached beneath his own cloak, behind his back, and pull out a box. "Deliver this to him, he will know what it means."

Ambrosja reluctantly took the box. She wanted to slap that as well, but she forced herself not to. She set the container down onto her lap.

The Commander looked at all of them now. "Complete this task, and consider your sentence paid off." Killian remained still with cool authority. "And trust me," his voice dropped to a dangerous tone, whether it was for show or a true threat was uncertain, "I will know." Then he stepped back once more, his cold eyes following every move.

Gunnar grunted, "Yeah, we know," his own tone dripped with disdain. "We'll get your precious cargo delivered." Then he slapped the side of the wagon, "Let's get going!" With that, Cinder whipped the reins.

The horses pulled the wagon away. Unbothered by most eyes… But…

Cressida was crouched on a thick branch. Her dark feathered hawk rested on her shoulder. Her pupils were glowing as she tracked the wagon. "Scout," she whispered to her hawk, which dropped down, flying towards the wagon, and low enough to look at the faces of each figure within the bounds of it. Everything the hawk saw? She saw. "Well then…" Cressida whispered as she looked through the eyes of her hawk and saw the faintest glimpse of pale blonde hair beneath a cloak. "…Found you."

Once the horses pulled onto a more steady path, Cinder whipped the reins again, the horses immediately picked up their pace, hooves pounding into the dirt as their muscles flexed and worked to pull the heavy wagon behind them. The air had been thick, not with just the musty fog of the land, but with tension and questions that were buried beneath their skin.

Cinder's leg was furiously bouncing in place as her eyes scanned the path through the trees and every corner around it. Her knuckles were white. Donathan noticed and so did Johann. Donathan's hand tentatively reached out to touch hers, trying to steady her. Cinder's eyes flicked down, but Donathan's touch only made her burst.

"What the fuck!" Cinder called out, not too loud, but definitely not low. She turned in her seat, eyes boring onto Ambrosja's hooded figure. "What the fuck, Ambrosja?!" Ambrosja's head jerked in Cinder's direction.

Johann immediately tried to shush Cinder, "Please! Not so loud!"

"No–No! I have to!" Cinder handed the reins to Donathan. His hands clumsily caught it, eyes going wide as he tried to command the horses now. Cinder turned completely, knees planting into the wood of her seat. "You're the fucking Empress of Nordorn?!"

Ambrosja froze. Her lips parted and whenever she tried to speak only weak and broken sounds came out. She swallowed then, steadying herself. "I did not realize you also knew that — I thought it was just the Black Hand."

Gunnar interjected at this moment. "A woman came to the camp— Serana, or something like that." He shrugged heavily, taking a moment to gather his words. "She came here, asking about a woman with pale skin and hair, a Nordorner. When no one gave anything up—she announced to the entire camp that this woman might be the Empress."

Ambrosja's grip tightened on the wooden edge of the crate, "Killian said they were after me—" her voice cracked on his name. "I fail to understand how they know I am here."

Gunnar shrugged, "We can't bother trying to figure out that part, lass. The Black Hand woman said that if anything happened to you on Vaestorian soil—we'd be fucked. And she's right. Nordorn would come for blood if their Empress fell by the hands of some sorry sod here."

Cinder shook her head, "We should be getting her back to her fucking country!" She hissed. "Not taking her further into ours!"

Johann sighed heavily, "Cinder, please…"

"No!" She looked at all of them now. "This is fucking insane! If something happens to her while she's here? We're all fucked! Nordorn has been the conquering force for years! I've heard whispers of how they fight! Like beasts that have been cornered and have nothing yet everything to live for! How dying in battle is glorious to them, so they never shy from death!"

She looked at Ambrosja once more, "We're getting ourselves into deeper shit for you, Ambrosja. Oh, sorry—Empress." Then Cinder turned, sitting once more and taking the reins from Donathan.

Serana's ungloved hands held onto a slab of meat tightly. Teeth sinking in like a woman starved for blood and food. The patrons of the inn had kept away from her table which was right in the center of the entire establishment. The air within the candlelit rooms of the inn was thick with tension and fear. A man's hands trembled as he saw his pigeon laying dead beside Serana's plate. The note that was once attached to it was now unfurled with a knife piercing the parchment straight into the wood it lay upon. Grease smudged alongside the urgent scribbles.

Everyone drank and ate slowly; fearing that just by breathing too loud would be enough of a reason for them to not wake up beside their loved ones in the morning. The only movement anyone made was a sudden flinch as three Black Hand guards shoved open the door, Cressida at the center. Her hawk wasn't with her.

Serana's sharp brown eyes raked over Cressida, noting the absence of her dark-feathered companion. "Well?" She wiped her lips with the back of her hand. "You're not here with the woman. What happened? Is Killian still being a stubborn fool?"

Cressida stepped forward. "Killian is trying to play games with us. He smuggled the Empress onto a wagon with four others — they ride southwest. With a shipment of Nythralt."

Serana stretched, her hands lifted high for a moment, then came down to rest behind her head, fingers laced together. "I always did love a good chase. I take it your winged companion is flying over them?" Cressida nodded with a smirk. Serana continued, "Excellent."

She stood up now, grabbing her knife and unwedging it from the table. She paused for a moment, grabbing the note and looking over it once, then sighed, a mocking sound.

"Your precious Stonehaven won't come. They never have before." The note was crumpled into a ball and tossed into the fire of the hearth at the far side of the room.

The Black Hand stepped in beside Serana and followed her lead; leaving the Goose's Nest, one thundering footstep at a time. The patrons of the inn were still, even for a few moments after the Black Hand left. The door

slowly creaked behind them and shut with something that echoed a finality. One man, the man who had tried releasing his pigeon earlier, stood up, moving to the dead creature laying on the table that Serana once sat at. His fingers twitched as he scooped the gentle bird up and held it close for a moment.

Serana led her riders back to the horses. Boots swung over saddles, postures adjusted, and reins were whipped. Men, women, and children watched in silence as the dark riders left the village, following the roads that led southwest, all listening to the heavy beating of hooves against the ground echoed in the distance.

MISTVALE CROSSING

Mistvale Crossing stands as Stonehaven's final threshold — a bustling village perched along the eastern road that leads to the capital's great gates. Though modest in size, it thrives on constant motion: merchants bartering over wares, travelers trading stories, and swords for hire waiting on coin or cause. Its name comes from the morning mists that roll down from the highlands, veiling the bridge at its heart.

The village is divided in two by this great stone bridge, which spans the river and connects the outer markets to the road that climbs toward Stonehaven.

Unique among the settlements of the regency, Mistvale Crossing bears its own wall and gate — a fortification born of both necessity and pride. Its people are vigilant yet welcoming, accustomed to the rhythm of arrivals and farewells. To pass through Mistvale Crossing is to feel the pulse of Stonehaven itself, just before its echo meets the city walls.

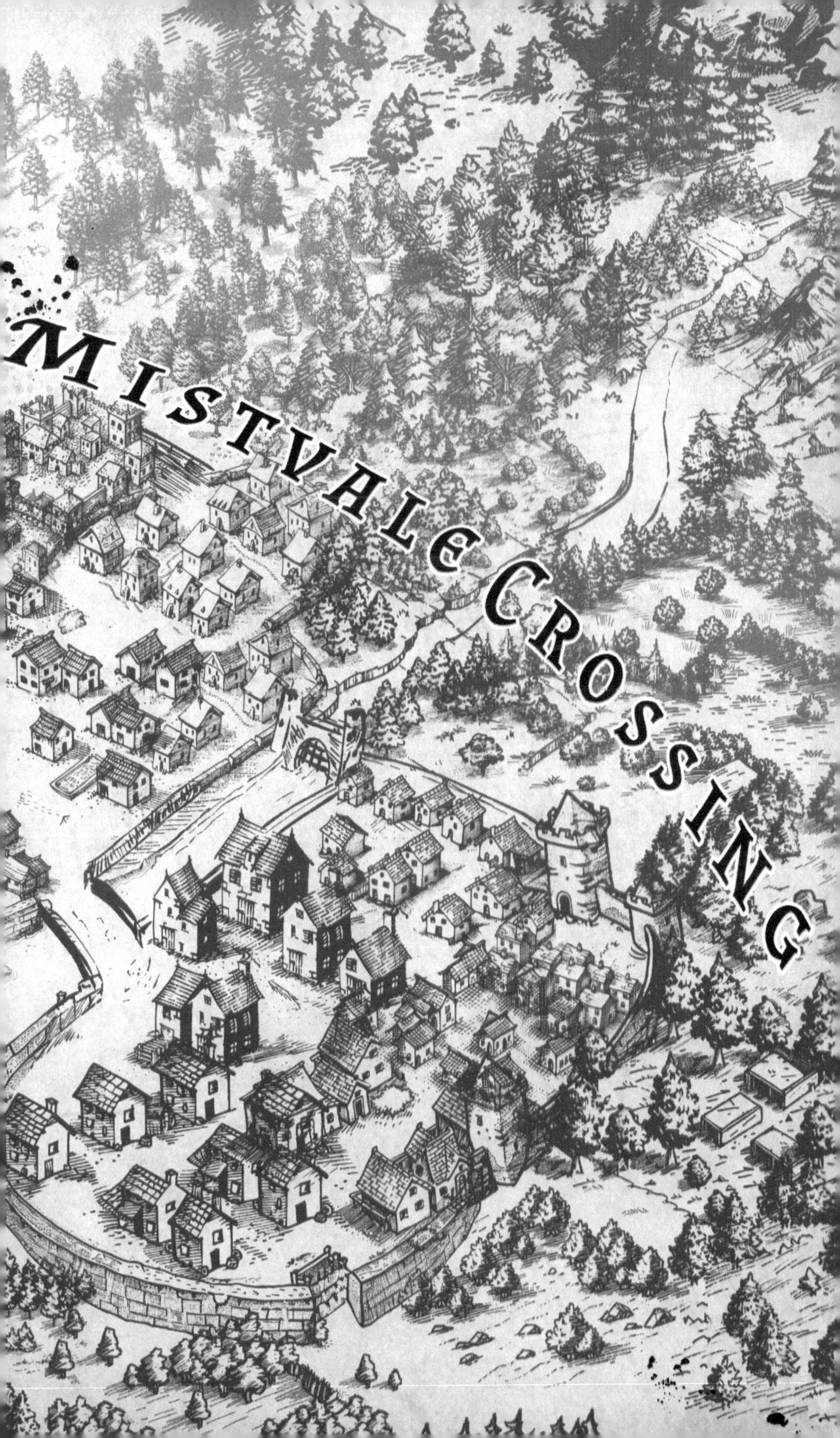

MISTVALE CROSSING

CHAPTER THIRTY-ONE

AND BLOOD SHED

 mbrosja's fingers were tightly gripping the hilt of her sword.

Their weapons, the ones they had to give up upon entry to the mining camp, were returned — given when the papers for the shipment were handed to Gunnar. But now, Gunnar was sharpening his axe with a whetstone in silence. After Cinder's words earlier? There could only be silence. And the silence? It was deafening. Only the quick gallops of the horses, the creaking of the cart, and the occasional singing of bugs and hoots of owls surrounded them.

None of them looked at each other. Ambrosja stared at the box in her lap, not paying mind to anything else. Her gaze was so vacant it was as though she was no longer there in the wagon with them. Gunnar saw this; he had seen this look on so many girls throughout his years. The look of heartbreak and loss. The sudden feeling of your world getting pulled out from under you. Johann kept to himself; he was always the quiet man, only speaking during such times when it was absolutely necessary. He knew that silence could sometimes be the best answer to the hardest questions. But silence was never Cinder's strong suit. Her leg kept bouncing. Impatience, annoyance, both very likely. Donathan tried to ease her; his hand was on her knee, thumb brushing her fabric, and it helped. Her knuckles were no longer white against the reins.

"It's so fucking dark," Cinder muttered, her eyes squinting, trying to adjust to the path of the road.

Johann glanced to the side, "There should be a lantern hooked already."

Cinder cocked her head to the side, "Shit, you're right!" She nudged Donathan with her elbow, "Can you light that up?"

Donathan gave a single nod and stammered, "S-sure!" He turned sideways and snapped his fingers until flames grew from his skin. Donathan moved his hand close enough for the flame to catch.

Cinder excitedly slapped a hand on Donathan's shoulder, "Yes! I can see!"

Gunnar gave one last swipe at the blade of his axe with the whetstone, then looked straight ahead at Ambrosja. "So, Empress of Nordorn, huh?" Ambrosja's eyes immediately flicked to his, as if she were waiting for some sort of lecture about honesty. Gunnar continued, "Now, what in the dragon's bones are you doing here?"

Ambrosja sighed and leaned back against the wagon wall, drawing her sheathed sword close. "I told you the truth—I came for Wintersong. The people there... they left Nordorn centuries ago. Couldn't stomach the brutality." Her cheek rested on the sword's pommel. "It was during Empress Solvieg's reign. She waged war, and some Nordorners fled south, into Vaestoria. Built Wintersong from the snow up." She exhaled, almost laughing. "Years later, Vaestorian soldiers stumbled across the hamlet—totally baffled. And the villagers?" She laughed softly. "They convinced them they had *always* been there." She sighed then, her tone softening further. "At least that is what Wintersong's Elder told me."

"Soldiers must have been drinking not to question it further," Gunnar smirked, but not widely. It quickly died as he weighed his next words. "Lass, focus on that. Focus on why you were here to begin with. Don't let love—or heartbreak—get in the way of your goals. You sought justice for Wintersong." Gunnar leaned forward. "Then do that. Go to Stonehaven, get a ship to return home." His voice became steadier than, more resolute, "Or... tell the council of Stonehaven what the fuck happened. Tell them everything, but don't let one single man crack the ground on which you walk." He leaned back, his tone softening, "You're stronger than that, lass."

"*Strong*," Cinder scoffed, her voice, her tone? It was all still bitter, "You know what I don't get? How you're the *only* person alive, Ambrosja. All of Wintersong is dead, but here you are. You survived. How?"

Ambrosja's gaze settled onto Cinder's figure, from the tightness in her shoulders to the way her hands gripped the reins. Ambrosja looked down, hands clenching in shame, gloved fingers flexing. "I cannot recall it—not exactly. I remember screaming, fighting, the people were too inexperienced in battle… They could not fight. Then fire… Then nothing. After that?" Ambrosja was silent, flinching as her eyes shut tight with a sudden headache. "I — I do not know." But when she thought harder… she could only see eyes, black like ink, staring back at her. She shook her head, rubbing her temple.

"Don't give me that. Whole hamlet burns, and you can't remember a thing? Either you're lying to us, or the gods are protecting you."

"Stop it," Johann interjected, his voice louder than usual; that calm he usually wore was gone. "We're all tired. Everything in the last two or three weeks, who knows how long now, has been a lot to deal with." Johann shook his head, his hand running down his face. "We're exhausted, we are days away from Mistvale Crossing." He twisted his body to look at everyone, from Gunnar to Donathan. "We finally have evidence to spring Stonehaven into action. And the most important part of it all?" Johann let the silence stretch for a moment. "We have a clear objective: save lives, as many as we can. No matter what."

Gunnar nodded, he slumped back slightly, "Johann is right. It doesn't really matter where we come from, not now, not when there is a threat that doesn't care about that either." Gunnar lifted his feet up to rest against the crate of Nythralt, "Cinder, wake me up in one hour, I'll take the reins from you so you can rest."

"I'll make sure the lantern stays lit," Donathan whispered, leaning his shoulder into Cinder to comfort her with his presence.

Serana huffed. An air of frustration left her lips. The horses had come to a halt as Serana lifted her hand to signal. They soon came to a full stop, their heads shaking from side to side as they sought to gather their breath once more.

"How far ahead are they?" Serana turned to look at Cressida.

Cressida sighed, her own frustration leaving her, "Maybe three hours. Maybe less."

Serana growled, "Damn it." She eased off her saddle, her boots hitting the damp ground harder than necessary. One hand found her hip, the other rubbed harshly across her lips. "We'll let the horses rest. We'll catch up to them. It's clear where they're going," Serana muttered, looking at the ground and the curve the road created moving from south to southwest.

One Black Hand spoke up, "Their horses are most likely work horses, made for endurance, not speed…" He rubbed his chin in thought. "We'll catch up. Sooner or later."

"Sooner is better than later. That pale whelp gets to Stonehaven, or any city in Vaestoria? Who knows what happens? How far will we get set back?" She undid her gloves, fingers tugging at the fabric. Eyes set on the road ahead. "No matter, we rest, the horses rest, then we continue. We have to stop, but so do they."

The skies were a dull blue; the sun was blocked by dark grey clouds. Donathan stood beside a horse, his hand moving across its body as it drank. Cinder emerged from the woods, two pheasants in one hand, her bow over her shoulder, and arrows in her quiver. No one spoke, not much. It wasn't until the pheasants were cooked that Cinder approached Ambrosja, who was sitting down on a rock with the box as her only company. Cinder was holding two big leaves that held a leg quarter of a pheasant.

"This is for you…" Cinder said, Ambrosja looked up, but didn't reach for the offer just yet. "I was a damn ass last night," Cinder growled. "And I'm sorry…" She sat down beside Ambrosja. "I think I was just—feeling a little betrayed. I knew you were a Nordorner, but not the damn Empress. Next thing I know, you'll tell me you're a damn dragon."

Ambrosja smiled, but it was faint. She dipped her chin, eyes fixing on the rock's surface beneath her legs. "Yes, I know, and I am sorry. Truly. I only hid that part of myself because a Nordorner is not meant to step foot onto Vaestorian soil, or really any soil that isn't Mercinari's, I figured presenting myself as the Empress would just make it worse."

"Is that why you speak all proper?" Cinder squinted. "Because you're nobility?"

Ambrosja shook her head with a smile, "No," she admitted. "I speak like this because I was told that this is how Vaestorians speak…"

"Huh." Cinder smirked, then started laughing, "Wow. Must have been a shock for you when you met me."

"It was, actually." Ambrosja teased, "I genuinely felt lied to."

"Do you think you're going to drop that little proper way of speaking?"

"Hm," The Empress hummed, thinking. "I do not think so. I have grown used to it, and just maybe one day this will work in my favor." She nudged her shoulder with Cinder's. "After all, we still have Stonehaven to get

to."

Ambrosja looked down at the box when Stonehaven came to mind. Her fingers traced the edges. There weren't any intricate designs, but the box had been built with care. She gently opened it without thinking… and found herself frozen as she looked into it.

"This is… for his sister," she murmured to herself, looking over every dragon figurine he had carved.

Cinder leaned in, looking inside. "Wow, he carved these? Damn, if this is what his fingers could do, then no wonder you were so smitten with him."

"Cinder!" Ambrosja snapped, but Cinder only cackled, holding her belly and falling to the side.

From a distance, the men watched. Donathan released a sigh of relief, "Well, that makes me feel better."

Gunnar nodded, "Aye, same here."

Johann lifted his waterskin, mock-toasting, "Let's pray it stays this way."

Clouds drifted past, and the dull skies only turned darker as the day went on. The rumbling of the wagon carrying the crates of ores and the weight of five friends was the loudest thing on the road. The horses trotted on, pulling the weight of everything behind them as if it didn't bother them one bit. Cinder was in the back of the cart, Donathan beside her. The two of them were whispering, playfully so, that made Gunnar's brows rest so low that it seemed his eyes had disappeared; he just did his best and tried to ignore the two lovebirds in the back.

Gunnar spoke low to Johann, "We've been through a lot, never quite imagined we'd be escorting the Empress of Nordorn to Stonehaven."

At that, Johann looked over his shoulder. Ambrosja was seated at the back of the wagon, her feet dangling off the edge. Johann looked at Gunnar, "…She fell in love with that Commander, huh?"

"Yeah," Gunnar sighed, "but did he love her back?" He shook his head, frustrated, "Damn it, do you think we should ask her about it? See how she's feeling?"

"I mean—we should check on her," Johann nodded, then looked at Ambrosja once more. "We don't need her to spill her heart if that's not what she wants, but– she looks like she's holding more than she should."

"Girl's an Empress, she looks too young for love, too young for a crown, too young to be leaving her country and prancing through one she probably knows nothing about." Gunnar sighed, his shoulders sunk heavily. "She's holding onto way more than just that, I'm sure."

"Hey," Cinder called out, not loud but not low, "tell me I'm not the only one who has noticed this hawk following us," she jerked her chin towards the dark-feathered hawk that was flying nearby and maintaining the same pace as their wagon. "Swore I saw it last night, too."

Ambrosja looked up, following the hawk's movements. "Maybe we have something it wants?"

"Like what?" Cinder scoffed. "That thing is too small to fly away with our horses, and too smart to wait for us to get it food. That's a predator through and through."

"What," Donathan looked at Cinder, "do you think it's following us deliberately?"

"Kind of, yeah."

Gunnar looked up, he scowled, then whipped the reins harder. The horses sped up. "I don't like that," he muttered. "I don't like that one bit."

Cinder remained quiet. Donathan glanced at her, his eyes studying her face, "Cinder? What's wrong?"

Cinder looked down, watching the trembling of the cart. She pressed her palm to it; she felt the usual rumbling a wagon would give, *and* more. Her face whipped to the northern parts of the road, "Riders are approaching!" She grabbed her bow and arrows, already moving to crouch behind a crate.

Everyone else reacted accordingly. Donathan was shaky ever so slightly, but he got behind another crate, his veins already glowing an orange tone beneath his skin. Gunnar handed the reins to Johann, reaching over and grabbing his axe, while Ambrosja rolled backwards deeper into the wagon and unsheathed her sword. Johann gripped the reins tightly, and for as old as he is, as many adventures he had gone on, his hands still shook as he looked ahead.

They were watching, waiting. Then, around the bend, from the cover of trees, they spotted Serana and five riders following her. Their horses were moving fast, inching closer and closer with every hoof that beat against the ground.

"Shit! The Black Hand!" Cinder hissed, already nocking an arrow and pulling the string of her bow and releasing.

The arrow flew, sharp and fast, but as it approached Serana, her arms moved, outstretched and waving in front of her; a brief yet undeniable

wave of flame quickly moved through the air, knocking the arrow off course and burning it. Cinder's eyes went wide. She faced Johann, "Faster!" Johann whipped the reins a few more times, harder. The horses began to gallop, the wagon swayed from the weight, the road, and the speed of it all.

Ambrosja moved to step out, but Gunnar grabbed her by her shoulder and pulled her back until her form was flush against the wooden sides of the wagon. "Are you insane, lass?! They're here for you! And we're on a moving wagon! What are you going to do?! Jump off and fight them alone?!"

Ambrosja's brows furrowed, she took a few heavy breaths, "I have to! As you said, they are here for me! Not you!"

"Doesn't matter," Gunnar protested, making sure Ambrosja didn't move, "they *know* we're here with you, as soon as they get you, they'll kill us, whether or not we're defending you."

"Then what do you propose?!"

"We just try to keep our distance! We're heading to Mistvale Crossing, it's a larger village, they wouldn't dare follow us into the gates without facing a decent-sized militia."

"Mistvale Crossing is still far!" Donathan's voice was laced with desperate urgency. "How are we going to keep that distance?! Our horses are pulling a wagon with two crates of ore and five people!"

Gunnar snapped his head towards Donathan, "Lad! Use your brain! Running away has always been your go-to! What would you do to make sure you could keep running away and make the enemy falter?"

Donathan's head shook side to side as he desperately searched his mind. Then he stood; he didn't say anything. His veins continued to pulse that orange-gold hue, and steam rose from his skin. He cautiously made his way to the edge of the wagon, his arms outstretched, angled towards the ground. He shouted, "Let's hope this holds!" Flame shot through his fingertip and spread outwards to cover his hands. Then, with a rapid flick, he raised his hands up, creating a six-foot wall of fire that rose from the trail, barely touching beyond the pathway and sure not to touch the foliage. Serana's horse abruptly stopped. Neighing as they stood on their hind legs, snouts desperately pulling away from the heat.

"Yes! Yes!" Cinder cried, standing up and wrapping her arms around Donathan, "You've gotten so much better!"

Donathan was bashful; he let out a low chuckle and cleared his throat, "Well, that's thanks to you, Cinder, you've really been helping me with my focus."

Gunnar whipped his head in their direction, already glaring. "Oh?

When have you been teaching him *focus*, Cinder?"

Johann immediately interjected, "Right now is *not* the time!!"

Ambrosja released a shaky breath, "Johann is right, this is temporary. It may have bought us a bit of time, but who knows how long?" She looked at Donathan, "What you did was brilliant, you *did* buy us time, and that is what matters now." She looked back at where the wall of fire was, then sighed once more, slumping against the wagon.

"Godsdamn it!" Gunnar growled.

Everyone followed his line of sight, even Johann looked over his shoulder, only to see Serana parting the flames and then killing it. They just watched as she remained seated atop her horse, unmoving except for her shoulders rolling. Then she whipped her reins once more, and the chase was on again.

Johann's short but broad stature stood up from his seat, whipping the reins faster. The work horses galloped fiercely now, nostrils flaring with every sharp breath they exhaled as they pushed harder. One Black Hand raised their hand, the leather glove exposing palm and fingertips, leaving flesh for flame to gather. Light began to emit from their fingertips, then centered around their palm.

"Fuck!" Donathan cried, "They're going to set the wagon ablaze!" The blast left the Black Hand's palm, striking straight forward, embers sparking and lighting the darkened path.

Everyone ducked behind a crate or lowered themselves just enough as the flames struck across the wood, the glow glided through the wooden grains, and scorched it. The wagon began to catch fire. "Shit!" Cinder shouted, and Ambrosja recoiled, her hands trembling as she saw the fire rise and nearly touch her feet. Gunnar was already reaching over for the cloak that Ambrosja once wore. He wedged himself between the crates and slapped down the fabric onto the rising fire. His rough hands repeatedly patted down the spots.

"No…" Donathan whispered as he looked ahead, a second Black Hand was already raising their hand to do the same, "No, no, no!"

Cinder watched, nocking another arrow and firing it without a second thought. The second Black Hand's eyes widened as suddenly the arrow pierced right through their palm and out the other side of their leather glove, and blood flew past the riders as they galloped ahead. A pained shout was heard, a momentary breath of relief escaped Cinder, until she saw a third Black Hand lift their hand to do the same.

"Fuck!" Cinder growled. She looked to Donathan, "Do something!"

Donathan panicked, hands clenched against his cheeks, "I'm trying not to piss myself! Does that count?!"

Gunnar looked to the side as he noticed Ambrosja was still lying low, hands trembling as her eyes remained fixed on the cloak that was singed and tattered now. Gunnar crawled backwards, his hand found her shoulder. "Lass! Snap out of it!" Ambrosja didn't; her golden eyes were still locked onto the cloak. "Ambrosja!" Gunnar barked, yanking her towards him by her shoulder-plate. Her eyes finally met his. "What's gotten into you, girl?!"

Ambrosja swallowed thickly, voice trembling and hands fighting to be steady, "I am sorry—I have never handled fire well…"

Cinder stared at Ambrosja, lips parted in disbelief. "You—you've never handled fire well?!" Cinder had echoed her words, but with desperation and annoyance. "Well, that's just lovely because we have an enemy that only deals with fire!"

Johann shouted, "Like I said before! Now is not the time!" He looked over his shoulder, "They're catching up, and these horses can't go any faster!"

Cinder looked at Gunnar, "We have to kick off the crates of Nythralt!"

Gunnar's eyes widened, "What?! No! We do that, then we'll be responsible for whoever comes across it!"

"It's too much weight, Gunnar!"

They gasped as another bolt was fired at them — but Donathan stole it, controlling the flame with all of his strength and focus even as his legs shook atop the moving wagon. "No!" he shouted, shooting the fire outwards, fingers splayed wide as he thrust his hands toward the sky. A second wall of fire erupted—taller, hotter, roaring like a living thing that singed tufts of grass on the road to ash.

Donathan blinked, breathless. "Oh, shit…" he whispered. "I… did that."

Gunnar chuckled, slapping Donathan on the shoulder. "That's it, lad! You're getting promoted from Flame-Boy to Flame-Spitter!"

"Donathan—" Cinder was breathless. "I am going to drag you to a chapel and marry you beneath Sylaera."

Donathan blushed heavily, red crossed from ear to ear. "Cinder—I—sure?"

Thwick!

Droplets of red sputtered across Cinder's vision, coating her left cheek in crimson. It suddenly felt as if everything had slowed down. Ambrosja was rising to her knees, Gunnar was reaching forward, and Johann was looking over his shoulder as he felt a droplet hit his right hand.

Donathan's hand grasped at the bolt piercing the flesh between his heart and his shoulder. The young fire mage staggered backwards, almost falling, but caught by Gunnar's arms. A groan of pain escaped him, his eyes fighting back tears with every blink.

"Donathan!" Cinder cried as she fell to her knees beside his cradled form. She tugged at the fabric around the wound, one hand gripping it, the other reaching for her dagger and cutting it open. "M–move your hand away!" Her voice was trembling with desperation. "I have to see the damage – I have to see!"

Gunnar held Donathan steady, trying to ease the young man's hand off the bolt. "Ease up, lad," Gunnar whispered, his voice rough from emotion, but calm enough to keep others from panic.

"Ambrosja…" Cinder called, her voice now breaking as her hands moved across the bloodied fabrics, "Help me with this." Ambrosja immediately scrambled to Cinder's side. "You–you can heal, right?"

Ambrosja nodded, "Yes, yes, I can heal."

Cinder cried, "Heal him—please…"

Ambrosja removed her gloves; her motions were nervous, quick, but resolute. When the leather was gone, her hands touched Donathan's bare skin, her pale fingertips sinking into the pool of blood that was gathering. Her irises began to glow faintly, her fingertips turned a glowing gold. "I—I can't…!" She cried, her brows furrowing as she tried to focus harder. "I can't heal him! Why can't I heal him?!"

"Don't you dare say it's too late—you said you could heal him! Do it!" Cinder cried, now cradling Donathan.

"I know! But something is blocking my connection!"

"What's going on back there?!" Johann called out, still holding the reins in his hands.

Gunnar called out, "Donathan has been shot!" He then looked at Ambrosja, "Switch places with Johann, hold the reins, and let him heal!"

Ambrosja didn't protest; she nodded and rose to her full height and quickly stepped over to sit in the box seat of the wagon. The swap of reins was fast. Johann was already moving with the practiced motions of a healer who had seen and been through too much. He quickly took his place at Gunnar's side, his hands helping Cinder spread open the fabric further.

Johann wiped most of the blood away with his own sleeve, desperate take a look at the wound. "Dragons preserve us…" His eyes betrayed whatever calm he tried to maintain. He traced the dark veins form-

ing from the wound, turning a bit of the blood that was pooling into a blackened shade. "...That's Veil Magic."

From the journal of Gunyldr Thorn,
Rodvrmane 23, 997

VEIL MAGIC

Veil Magic is often called the forbidden child of magic—a power both coveted and condemned. It is outlawed throughout nearly all of Eldorwyn, save for Nordorn, where a measured use of it is permitted for communion with the spirits beyond. Scholars believe the Veil to be the boundary between life and death, a shroud where the souls of the departed linger and the world's rawest magic pools. To touch it is to draw upon that untamed current, potent enough to slay with a whisper or unmake flesh with a thought.

The practice is perilous. Even the most skilled channelers speak of losing pieces of themselves to the dark between worlds—of hearing voices that are not their own, or feeling the pull of something eager to return in their stead. Punishment for its use ranges from lifelong imprisonment to death, depending on the depth of transgression.

It is said that Veil Magic is the twin sister of Chaos Magic— born of the same source, but tempered by the quiet of the grave. Where Chaos Magic rends the world apart, Veil Magic threads its unseen seams. To master it is to court divinity, yet those who try are often left hollow, no longer fully of this world.

CHAPTER THIRTY-TWO
STORM OF MINE

Johann pressed his fingers into the thick, black ink-like ooze that poured from Donathan's wound. The bolt was still embedded into it. Cinder held Donathan's hand tightly, tears mingling with the rain.

"T-this…" the young fire mage took a sharp inhale, "this is it for me, isn't it?"

"I don't know, lad!" Johann admitted, grief crossing a face usually so composed, "But I am going to try all that I can!" His hands began to glow entirely, a pale tone that seemed to sparkle and light his surroundings.

Donathan gasped, eyes widening as he felt a rush of relief, fresh and warm, run through him. Only to wince when the pain reme-merged, not as sharp as before, but there. "I–I don't think it worked!"

Cinder's teeth were clenched, her brows lowered into some-thing grief-stricken. She looked back at the road, the hooves of hors-es could be heard in the distance. "Damn it! They're on their way already!"

Thunder could be heard in the distance, and suddenly, rain hit atop their skin with heavy drops. The only thing they could hear now was the rain that surrounded them. Ambrosja's eyes widened at that. She felt the cold hit her. The water graced her skin. The sound of thunder echoed in her mind. She felt as if she was back on a moun-tain. Bracing the storm with her father at her side. Her brows then lowered, her face shifted that into clear focus.

Ambrosja shouted, "How close are they?!"

"Close enough!" Gunnar called back, his voice rising over the rain and thunder.

Ambrosja looked up, watching the storm. The reins in her hands were clenched tightly; she closed her eyes just as tight. Then she stood up. "Someone! Take the reins!"

Gunnar immediately took her place, their hands swapping the reins as Ambrosja hobbled over onto the wagon, searching for her sword. Once she found the black grip of it, she pulled it up, raising the dark steel to the skies. The groove within the blade began to light up an azurite blue, starting from the hilt and crackling like lightning through the groove in the center.

"Do not abandon me father," Ambrosja pleaded in a whisper, her voice lost in the heavy rain, only meant for herself and the man long gone. "Not this time."

The storm began to center above them, swirling like a tempest searching for a conduit. Then lightning came, from above and from below — seeking her. They hit the tip of her sword, and the cobalt blue lines glowed like a winter fury. Ambrosja yelled, then aimed her sword at a line of trees. Lightning poured from her blade and hit along the thick trunks; a sickening sound of wood ripping and tearing echoed in the storm. They toppled and were set ablaze with embers of blue.

Ambrosja fell backwards, her spine hitting the crate of Nythralt. Her hand was wrapped tightly around the grip of her sword. Her fingertips were ashened as if singed, her eyes wide and unfocused. Cinder's own eyes had gone wide as she witnessed this. Johann was unable to speak. Donathan simply held tightly to Cinder's hands, and Gunnar could only hear what was going on as he focused his own vision onto the road ahead, blinking as he fought off the heavy rain that beat down against his face.

"Can someone tell me what in the Dragon's Breath I just heard?!" Gunnar shouted sharply.

Cinder was unable to speak, so Johann did it for her. "Ambrosja just—she knocked a few trees down!"

"What?!"

Johann didn't answer; he turned to Ambrosja, who seemed as if she were in a different realm. He watched her singed fingertips return to normal as if nothing had touched her, how her golden gaze glowed faintly against her pale skin beneath the stormy skies above. "She's fine…" He whispered to himself before returning to Donathan, who was still awake, still alive, and

his eyes set only on Cinder's.

"Scazza!" Serana's voice was filled with rage as she stared at the trees that blocked her path. She turned her horse, guiding it to the side, "We'll go around! I don't give a damn which direction any of you take, just get the Empress!"

Horses neighed as they were pulled in different directions, hands whipping reins with urgency, heels digging into their flesh to get them to move. The horses were damp, the lightning in the sky reflected off the glistening fur and armor, and the Black Hands moved like a blur through dark trees and brush.

"Cressida!" Serana barked, "Can you see through your hawk's eyes?"

Cressida shook her head violently, "Not clearly! Not with this rain! But they're still on the same path!"

"Good enough," Serana growled, digging her heels into her horse to speed ahead.

"When I pass, this sword will be yours, Ambrosja." Vidar's voice was deep, like the sound of a boulder rolling down a mountain, and each hit echoed off the walls. Ambrosja's body may have been on that wagon, but her mind was elsewhere. Deep in the rock-carved walls of the Nordravn mountain. *"Storms do not answer to this sword, but the sword does answer to the storm. You cannot bend what the Gods gift us, but you can embrace it—and one day, I will take you to the top of Nordravn, and I will show you how, my daughter."*

Ambrosja blinked as she felt the heavy drops of rain hit her cheeks, and Johann's hand waved in front of her face, his voice calling to her like a distant echo that slowly got closer and closer, until— "Ambrosja!" Johann yelled over the rain and thunder, "Get yourself together, girl!"

The Empress shook her head, and her hand came to wipe away the soaked locks from her face. She got onto her knees and moved closer to where Cinder and Donathan were. The two of them were looking at each other. Donathan's hand was gripped tightly in Cinder's. Cinder was leaning in close so she could hear every word Donathan had to say.

"H–Hey…" Donathan whispered, his broken voice barely audible over the pouring. "Are you ever going to tell me your real name?"

"Gods no," Cinder laughed through her tears, "no one wants to hear that. Cinder keeps it mysterious. Keeps *you* coming back."

Donathan chuckled, then winced as he felt the pain creep up his chest. His eyes closed tightly for a moment, then he looked at Cinder again. "You know, I'm sure–sure you're often told a lot that–girls shouldn't speak with vulgarity… But—I always thought it was kind of attractive." He looked away briefly, but returned to meet her eyes, his own cheeks red against his paling skin, but now he was bold. "There's something really admirable and amazing about a woman who isn't afraid to speak how she wants, or say whatever she thinks…"

"Shut up, Donathan!" Cinder's own cheeks were red, a tear escaped her eye, and none noticed through the rain, but Donathan did.

His hand came up, warm from the lingering power beneath his skin, his thumb brushed it away, mingling it with the raindrops, but his thumb lingered there. His *hand* lingered against her, now cupping her cheek.

Donathan scoffed, but not cruelly, "Why are you crying over me?"

"Because!" Cinder hunched over, her forehead pressing to Donathan's. "…Remember when we first met, and you said you were a nobody and I was an utter bitch and agreed?" Donathan nodded, and Cinder shook her head violently, "I didn't mean it! I don't mean it! You're not a nobody, you're Donathan! And—" Cinder didn't hesitate next. She leaned in, wrapped her arms around Donathan's shoulder, and pulled him into a kiss that didn't need heat to be deep.

Ambrosja and Johann remained quiet, letting Cinder and Donathan have their moment before everything came tumbling down again. Ambrosja stared down at the ground now, her silence palpable as she thought of Killian and the twists and turns of everything that had taken place in the last week.

When Cinder and Donathan parted, his hand grabbed her shoulder, not bruising but firm. "Cinder—"

Cinder interrupted him, "Clarissa," she whispered. "My real name is Clarissa Fairchild."

"Clarissa… Clarissa Fairchild…" Donathan smiled, repeating the name to himself with reverence, as if he sought to engrave it into his very bones. "That's gorgeous. Like you." He saw the pink rising in her cheeks, and he smiled again, wider. "You know, I would love to see where this wagon goes. I would love to see where *we* end up." Cinder went to interject, but Donathan shushed her, "Sh," he shook his head, "we both know I'm not going to make it, Clarissa. Not with Veil Magic poisoning my veins."

"Donathan…" Ambrosja interjected, "We–we can do something

about it. We can!"

"Can we?" Donathan sighed, each breath laced with pain. "Even if we do, how long will it take? How much healing must Johann sacrifice to ensure that I live *just* long enough to get to someone who can figure this out and remove this poison?" He shook his head again, this time with conviction, "No—no. It's only a matter of time before the Black Hand is upon us again, and when they are… I will sacrifice myself."

"Donathan!" Cinder cried, "Don't – don't say that!"

"Clarissa—" Donathan tried to push himself upwards. He grimaced from the pain once more, his elbow almost giving out. "It makes no sense! I'm just added weight. I couldn't have the gall to stay and save my family when the Black Hand attacked, but hells—I'll fucking stay this time, and I'll set them ablaze no matter what." His hand reached for Cinder's chin, making her look into his eyes. "I can do it. Knowing that you'll be safe? Knowing that my sacrifice will give you a chance of escaping this? I'll do it."

Johann grasped at Donathan's shoulder, "And how do you plan this? Huh? With this rain pouring down on us as if it were the very tears of the dragon Marezora?! Let's focus on trying to get *all* alive out of here."

Cinder eagerly nodded, looking down at Donathan, "Johann is right!"

"I know Johann is right!" Donathan barked. "I know! And that's why I have to do this! The rain is too heavy for them to use their fire properly, so if I use my entire body—if I sacrifice myself—it will work. I'll create a wall of fire using all of me, and they won't be able to stop it without risking themselves."

Ambrosja shook her head, "No—there must be another way."

"There is no other way!"

"All of you shut up!" Gunnar bellowed. "Let's cross that bridge when we get to it! Our main focus is getting through this damn weather! It's raining, it's nighttime, and we've got the Black Hand on our asses! We're in a shit situation, with shit choices! Just stay huddled together, and stay safe."

Cinder nodded weakly, curling up against Donathan, laying her cheek against his shoulder, and hugging him tight. Johann leaned back, and Ambrosja moved to sit near the edge of the wagon, her eyes looking at the road they were leaving behind them, just waiting for the dark riders to catch up.

The thunder had long gone, but the rain remained into the early hours. The sun wasn't even up. The wagon was stopped, and the horses now lay on

patches of wet grass and mud to recover the energy they had spent. Ambrosja tended to the horses, her hands moving over each one, seeking to repair what may have been damaged with whatever magic she could muster. Cinder was close to Donathan and Johann. Cinder was keeping him upright and helping him sip water while Johann sought to heal him and slow the poison coursing through Donathan. Gunnar had been fastening the crates of Nythralt more securely.

Everything had been tense. Ambrosja could barely look at anyone without feeling like *she* was the added weight, not Donathan. Guilt gnawed at her with every glance and whisper. Constantly echoing in her head the thought that—if she had never joined them—they'd be safe. Donathan would be well.

Ambrosja turned her head to look at Gunnar. "The horses cannot keep going like this," she called out. "They need more rest. If we push, they could collapse and die."

Gunnar ran a hand down his face, pausing at his beard. He nodded as he thought. "We'll rest. I'm sure their horses had to stop as well. They won't risk killing their horses to chase us on foot. We'll stay here and rest, but as soon as those horses are ready to go? We leave. Donathan needs a healer, and *you*, Ambrosja, you have to get to Stonehaven."

The rain had let up ever so slightly. Everyone was moving again. The horses were guided back to the wagon, while Cinder and Johann helped Donathan back to it as well. The bolt in his body was long gone, replaced by stitching only a healer with years of experience could create, despite it holding together a wound that refused to heal.

Cinder settled Donathan into the back corner of the wagon, using whatever fabrics she could to prop him up. Her movements stopped when she spotted a familiar dark figure flying above them.

Like clockwork—they all moved once Cinder called out, "It's that damned hawk again!"

Gunnar strapped the wagon back onto the horses, and everyone climbed in. The sound of reins whipping and wheels rumbling across rock and mud was heard once more through the ever-persistent drizzle of rain. But the Black Hand was gaining ground. Serana was leaning forward in her seat, the damp braided locks of her horse whipped in the air, hooves snapping against the mud.

Cressida was mounting her crossbow, the bolt already loaded, and her hands were steady despite the gallops of her horse. She looked, her eyes focusing on who to target. Then she noticed the young woman with the bow in her hand. Without needing an excuse, she fired the bolt.

Cinder's eyes widened as she felt herself suddenly pulled back, and found Donathan's form swapped with hers. The bolt had pierced closer to his heart this time.

"Donathan!" Cinder cried, "What are you doing?!"

Donathan only stood for a second longer than he thought possible before he collapsed to his knees, his eyes locked onto the bolt in his chest. "There's — there's no point in you getting hurt as well, Clarissa." He looked over his shoulder, his eyes locking up onto hers, "It hasn't been long—but I love you." He let out the weakest of chuckles, "Especially when you bossed me around in the mines."

"Donathan?" Cinder lunged forward as she saw Donathan's hand press into the wagon to roll himself off of it, "Donathan—" she moved to reach him, only for Johann to hold her back, "No! Let me go! Noo! Donathan!! Please!"

Ambrosja had been frozen, the ooze of black scattered across her face when the second bolt hit Donathan. When she touched the dark liquid, she felt herself elsewhere again. Facing those dark eyes once more… Only to come to and witness Donathan just falling off the wagon.

Donathan hit the mud hard but dragged himself upright, soaked and panting. The pounding of hooves grew louder—closer—but he was already steaming. He turned back toward Cinder, lifted two fingers to his lips, and blew her a kiss. A crooked, soft smile curved his face—one meant only for her. Then his fingers sparked to life. Flame danced across his arm, his chest, his legs—until he was ablaze, head to toe. His eyes never left hers.

A roaring wall of fire erupted around him, towering high, casting wild, golden light across the darkened road. Serana screamed, her fury shaking the air. The hunt had been interrupted again. Her voice echoed through the mist like a curse.

Cinder's eyes flooded. Rage and grief warred across her face. She ripped herself free from Johann's grip and spun toward him and Ambrosja, jaw set and fists trembling.

"Why?!" she shouted. "Why did you stop me?!" She was staring right at Johann, "It was foolish! We could have healed him!"

"Healed him?!" Johann echoed, his own frustration palpable. "He had taken two bolts! The second one was likely touched with Veil Magic just as the first! They were seeking to weaken us, Cinder! If they shot you, we'd be down two able bodies! Donathan understood there was no coming back from that second bolt."

"I loved him!" Cinder yelled, "I loved him and you *both*—" she pointed at Ambrosja now, "—let him light himself ablaze for us! For what?!" Ambrosja was just frozen in shock, too many emotions at once. Cinder couldn't handle it. "You're a shit Empress! You just stand there while men and women plunge to their deaths, don't you?! Have you ever seen a battle?! *Real* battle?! This is *your* fault, Ambrosja!"

"I am sorry!" Ambrosja called out, desperation laced in every letter of every word. "I did not know how to react! I was frozen in place! And I am sorry!"

"Yeah! You're always frozen in place! When the wagon catches fire, when Donathan throws himself off the wagon! You're unreliable! Nordorn is doomed beneath your rule! No wonder people in Wintersong died! You probably froze up there, too; that's why your excuse is that you blacked out!"

That made Ambrosja still. The memories of Wintersong. Mora. The Elder. The flames of it came flooding back in like an avalanche. Her heart pounded as every scream flooded her memories, and how she was the only capable person of fighting. How she tried so hard to fight off every Black Hand that was lighting the homes aflame. How she turned—met dark eyes, pale skin, dark hair—a touch against her forehead. Cold and familiar. Then nothing.

Ambrosja stepped forward, her hands shaking with rage. "I fought for them!" she shouted, her golden eyes now lit with fury. "I will not lie and say I fought bravely, or that I did my best, because truth be told? I have no idea what in the icy hells happened in Wintersong! Because I cannot remember! I may have frozen up, I may have fallen, but I know I tried! I know I tried because I have always tried! I would shed my own blood before letting someone shed theirs for me!" Ambrosja's scream turned into a sob. She curled in on herself, like a flower wilting. "I am so sorry about Donathan… Truly. I wish I could have healed him."

She turned away, moving to a corner of the wagon and slumping into it, arms crossed above her knees, her head lowered into her arms. Her shoulders shook with silent cries. Gunnar had remained silent through all of this, and it pained him. Pained him because no words could fix this. Only silence. And time.

"Cinder," Gunnar's voice was low. He lifted his arm. "Come here," he looked over his shoulder and gestured with a dip of his chin, "don't leave your old man waiting now."

Cinder's eyes were brimming with tears. She climbed over to sit beside Gunnar, where she tucked herself into his side, her fingers digging into the fabric of his fur coat as she cried. He lowered his arm and gave her a squeeze, holding her close to him, letting her find whatever comfort she could in a world so cold and cruel.

From the journal of Guinyldr Thorn,
Blodhvargr, 04, 997

THE STORMCALLER'S SWORD

The Sword of Vidar, commonly named Storm Caller, is regarded as one of Nordorn's most sacred relics, though its forging lies within recent memory rather than distant antiquity. Vidar himself is said to have shaped the blade atop Mount Nordravn, working Nythralt drawn from the mountain's veins while storms gathered relentlessly overhead. Those present spoke of thunder rolling so close it shook the anvil beneath their feet.

When lightning struck mid-forging—splitting sky and stone alike—the blade did not shatter. Instead, the strike was taken, absorbed into the Nythralt core as though steel itself had learned to breathe.

It is often said that Vidar could call the storm with the blade in hand, that lightning bent to his will and thunder answered his voice. This is a convenient telling, but an imprecise one.

Storm Caller does not summon
the storm. It does not create thunder
where none exists. Rather, it
binds—linking steel to sky, allowing
lightning to be drawn
into the blade and
contained without destroying the
wielder outright. When released,
that stored force is reflected outward
with terrifying clarity, turning the
heavens' violence back upon those
who stand in its path.

This distinction matters. The blade
does not obey command; it responds
to alignment. Vidar wielded it not
because he ruled the storm, but
because he could endure it. He
did not force the lightning—he held it.

Following his death,
Storm Caller passed to Ambrosja.

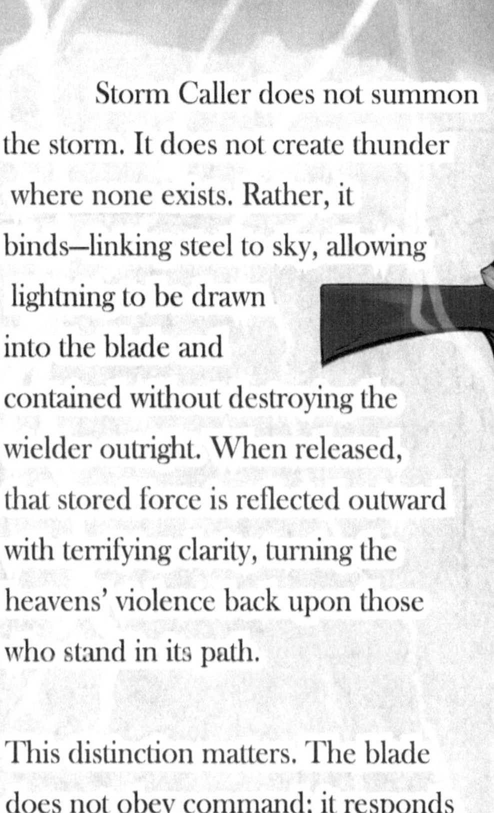

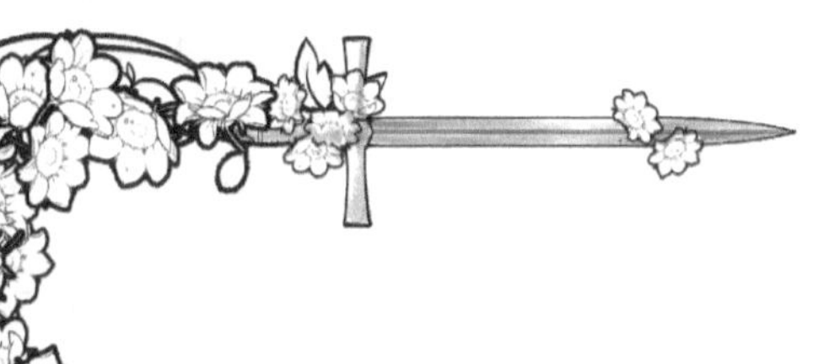

CHAPTER THIRTY-THREE
THE WOMAN WHO SPLIT THE GROUND

The wagon moved slowly now. Cinder had passed out against Gunnar's side, tucked beneath the damp fabric of his cloak. Ambrosja's leg was subtly bouncing in place, her hands gripping each other so hard that her skin had turned a mixture of pale and pink from the pressure. Johann stared at the skies that no longer hung heavy with rain, just grief.

They hadn't said a thing. Not since Cinder and Ambrosja's fall out. Not since Donathan's sacrifice. Ambrosja took a deep breath, then looked up at the sky along with Johann. And that's when she saw it. The dark-feathered hawk. Ambrosja turned to Johann immediately, a low *pst* sound escaped her lips.

"Hm?" Johann looked at Ambrosja now.

"Are you any good with a bow?"

"I'm afraid not."

Ambrosja turned towards Gunnar, "What about you?"

Gunnar looked over his shoulder, still making sure his arm remained gentle yet firm around Cinder. "Up close and personal has always been my thing, lass." He squinted at Ambrosja now, "Why?"

Ambrosja subtly nodded towards the sky, "The hawk that Cinder noticed earlier is still following us."

Gunnar grunted. "Shit, I bet that's how they're tracking us."

Johann didn't even bother risking a look in the hawk's direction. "Do you think one of the riders is looking through its eyes?"

Ambrosja immediately nodded. "I think so," she looked between Gunnar and Johann. "The Vardvölur back in Nordorn have the magical means to see through the eyes of their familiars. I think they are doing the same thing here, they're using Nature Magic."

"That makes sense," Gunnar looked at the muddied ground of the road, "we've passed at least one crossroads and two forks, and they're still on our tail."

"Hawk or no, that doesn't matter now," Johann muttered. He grabbed Ambrosja's shoulder and nudged her to turn around.

The gallop of hooves was heard once more, and soon the riders of ash came into view yet again. Some of the horses had been burnt, the fur gone along their legs, and reddened scars across their snouts. Ambrosja's hand immediately reached for her sword.

No… Ambrosja thought. Her hands clenched around the grip of her sword. "I cannot keep doing this anymore." She grabbed the box that Killian instructed her to hold, the one she now knew was meant for his sister, and tied a rope around it, ensuring it was tight and safe before tightening it around her waist and hips.

Johann looked up at Ambrosja, watching her stand, "Girl, what are you doing?"

"They are after me… So I am going to get off this wagon, and I want you guys to go wherever you see fit." She swallowed, hands now trembling with rage. "None of you deserve this—Donathan didn't deserve this—and it is all my fault we are here now."

Gunnar immediately turned around the best he could, shifting Cinder just enough where her eyes fluttered. "Ambrosja," Gunnar warned, "don't you dare get off this wagon."

Cinder rubbed her eyes. "What's going on?" One eye cracked open, she turned her head just enough to see the blurry vision of Ambrosja standing, her sword ready. She turned further now, and she saw a dark blur approaching. Immediately, she snapped awake, reaching over the wooden wall and grabbing her bow. "These Black Hand fucks—" she growled, already readying an arrow.

"Cinder," Ambrosja turned her face just enough to look down at her, "shoot the hawk."

"The hawk?" Cinder squinted, then realization dawned on her. Her sharp eyes moved towards the sky, and just like a huntress, she spotted the dark, feathered creature. There was no hesitation. Only understanding. She pulled the string back and released it with a snap. The arrow went flying fast, and there was a shriek that soon died as feathers fell and the hawk hit the muddied ground.

"No, Valor!" Cressida shouted, urging her horse to move faster as she put her crossbow away.

"Fall back, Cressida!" Serana ordered, glaring at the desperate form of the woman trying to ride ahead.

Ambrosja took a deep breath. *I have to do this. I must.* She turned to the others. "This is it… I will head to Stonehaven—eventually, but you three—go wherever you must," She glanced down in shame, then her eyes met theirs—she had to face them. "I can't undo what has been done, and I am still so sorry about all of this. But godsdamn it! You've all bled enough for me! For Wintersong!" She cried, "And I will bleed for you now!"

"Ambrosja!" Gunnar shouted. He moved to stand, but the reins were yanked, making the horses falter. He had to sit back down—helpless. "Ambrosja!!"

Ambrosja rushed forward and leapt into the air. Then she screamed. Her golden gaze set ablaze with power as her voice pierced not only the skies, but the earth. The ground came up into jagged edges, splitting apart and tearing open. Swallowing at least two of the Black Hand riders along with their horses. Crying neighs were all that was heard as the ground swallowed them. The wagon that Gunnar fought so hard to control tumbled slightly as the earth quaked from Ambrosja's scream. Cracks surrounded the earth around them.

Cinder's eyes tracked each one. She slapped Gunnar's arm with desperation. "We need to go! Now!" Cinder then rushed to the edge of the wagon and called out, "Ambrosja! You'd better make it out! Because Donathan sacrificed himself for you, too! And when you do make it out—just keep running straight! Mistvale Crossing is straight ahead!"

Johann's knuckles were white from how hard he was holding his holy symbol, whispering a prayer under his breath as he watched Ambrosja stand just ahead, waiting for the Black Hand upon their dark steeds.

"Vorthunal, give her the strength to stand. Nymera, lend her your skin. Marezora—guide her back to us." He had to look away, chest rising and falling out of fear, helplessness, and grief.

Gunnar kept muttering *godsdamn it* beneath his breath, trying to steady the horses as they bucked and cried from the sudden fractures that cracked into the road.

Ambrosja's hands were tight around the grip of her sword, legs parted as her feet planted firm into the ground, not once backing up or trying to flee. *Not this time*, she thought to herself.

One Black Hand rider rushed forward, his wrist twirling as

he moved his sword, his eyes set on Ambrosja's still frame. Too still. The rider narrowed his eyes, trying to study Ambrosja's form from atop his horse—only for their vision to blur when a raven embedded itself into the side of his neck. Blood gushed from his lips; his head tilted back. The raven wedged itself deep, wriggling out through flesh and blood until it burst out on the other side. Its wings outstretched and flew once more. The rider slumped forward on their horse, and the creature galloped past Ambrosja and away.

Serana growled beneath her helm, now looking to her other rider, who had just fallen off their horse—and witnessing a raven bursting from the rider's eye. Serana yelled, a fierce war cry as she reached for her blade and whipped the reins of her horse once, dodging every crack and jagged edge as she charged ahead at Ambrosja. Ambrosja moved in front of the horse and crouched just as the beast moved closer, forcing it to jump over Ambrosja's form, where she raised her hands, guiding the earth around her to pierce through the horse, impaling it.

Serana leapt from her bloodied beast, falling into a rolling tumble, her helmet tossed off as she rolled. "You—you wretched bitch!" Serana's hands met the ground, and she pushed herself upwards, reaching for her blade and quickly spinning on her heel. "You are nothing but a child! A child who has brought me more trouble than an entire army."

"And you've brought nothing but death." Ambrosja raised her sword. The hilt nearly touched her face as her eyes stayed centered on Serana. "But something tells me you don't care, so neither will I."

The ravens joined Ambrosja, each one moving to fly beside her and then shift. Their forms turned from feathers to tall, broad figures in armor that was as black as night. Feathers adorned their plated shoulders, cloaks and silver masks hiding their faces. Serana took a step back, her eyes darting from one dark figure to the other.

Ambrosja raised her hand, halting them in place. A clear signal that this fight? Was hers. Ambrosja surged forward, chaos and vengeance in her blood. Her sword swept low—so low it scraped sparks from the earth—before she twisted and arched the blade up toward Serana's ribs. Steel met steel with a shriek. Serana blocked, her parry clean and practiced, but Ambrosja was relentless. Another swing. Another block. The rhythm of their blades became a deadly drumbeat.

Clang—clang—CLANG!

Sparks danced with each blow as they circled one another in the mud, veils of breath visible in the cold air. Serana pivoted sharply, dodging a sweeping strike and slamming the flat of her boot into Ambrosja's chest. The impact knocked the breath from her lungs. Ambrosja stumbled back, and in that instant, Serana lunged forward with a feral grin, blade slicing through the air. Steel bit into flesh. A line of crimson opened across Ambrosja's cheekbone, painting her pale skin with blood. Her head snapped to the side from the force, a spray of red trailing behind her like a comet's tail. She staggered, boots skidding in the wet dirt—but didn't fall. The dark figures watched, unflinching and waiting.

Serana's smirk was cruel, victorious. Until it wasn't. Ambrosja lifted her head, slow and steady. The gash along her face was already sealing, her blood retreating as if called back beneath her skin. Flesh knit together in unnatural silence, as if the wound had never been. Her golden eyes locked onto Serana's—unflinching, glowing with fury. Serana's smirk faltered

"What the fuck—" Serana had whispered. She took a step forward—only to stop once a flash of steel drifted past her. A crossbow bolt pierced into the side of Ambrosja's neck.

Ambrosja's hands flew to the bolt. Her veins were darkening. Blood began pouring out from between her lips.

"No!" Serana yelled, her gaze now turning to follow where the bolt had come from and finding Cressida. "What did you do?! We need her alive!"

Cressida didn't answer. The body of her dead hawk was now tied to her belt. She put her crossbow away and walked over to Ambrosja's form that could barely stand now. Ambrosja's hand clenched tightly around one side of the bolt—then she ripped it out, falling to the ground as her blood poured onto the dirt beneath her. The figures in feathers of black were nearly forgotten in the chaos of the moment. They simply watched Ambrosja's body with an eerie calm.

Serana's eyes were wide with fury and shock. She looked at Ambrosja, then at Cressida, "You've doomed us, Cressida."

Cressida's eyes met Serana's, unflinching and unforgiving. "They killed *Valor*."

"Valor…? Your hawk?!" Serana hissed, her fists clenched tight, her sword nearly ready to be plunged into Cressida's ribs. "And you killed the godsdamn Empress of Nordorn! *The Empress of Nordorn!*" Serana was now marching forward until she met Cressida, "You will answer to Grand Marshal Gaspard Devereux for this."

"You don't understand the bond one has with their companion!" Cressida shouted back. "Valor was a part of the Black Hand just as much as I am." Cressida leaned down slightly, meeting Serana's gaze evenly. "You knew this when you recruited me — my companion, my hawk, Valor, was not *just* a hawk."

Serana looked ready to growl, to shout, to beat Cressida's face into a bloody mess. Then she paused. She looked at the dark figures that were just staring at Ambrosja. Serana followed their gaze. Ambrosja's eyes opened slowly, heavy-lidded with exhaustion. The gold of her iris turned to watch the two women hovering over her, glowing faintly as the taint of Veil Magic was forced out of her neck, like liquid obsidian being expelled from her flesh.

The following was like a blur; Serana could barely react in time from when Ambrosja gripped the bolt tightly in her hand, then quickly sat up to stab it into the ribs of Cressida. Cressida let out a sharp cry, her body shaking as she looked down; her eyes met the vision of Ambrosja, pale and bloodied, and very much alive. Serana took a step back, already readying her sword again as she watched Ambrosja stand to her feet, using Cressida's body as support while she plunged and twisted the bolt in deeper.

"May the Veil take you—" Ambrosja whispered sharply, "—and may it *devour* you." She then pulled the bolt out and swung her arm up to drive it deep down into the chest of Cressida.

The body of the Black Hand woman fell in a slow but devastating slump. Knees buckling and folding first, then falling to the side with a finality that rippled through the pools of water in the muddied ground that gathered with blood.

"So it's true," Serana hissed. "Every Empress of Nordorn is immortal."

Ambrosja's gaze met Serana's, and her entire body turned to face her. "And this is how you know you won't win. Not without an army. And even if you do bring an army…" Ambrosja took a step forward, "…I will tear the ground open and swallow them whole."

Serana rolled her wrist, twirling her sword in her hand. "You may be immortal, you may be able to survive even the darkest of magic, but I doubt you can grow back your legs once I cut them off."

Ambrosja twirled her own sword, mirroring Serana's challenge. "You'll have to try."

Serana charged. A war cry escaped her lips—cut off abruptly as the ground tore open. A sickening crunch echoed from below her—then it closed, crushing her calves and driving the metal of her boots into her flesh.

She let out another scream as she felt it crush even further.

Ambrosja walked until she was behind Serana. She reached down, hands tangling into the dark hair, and yanked Serana back until Serana's spine met her chestplate.

"You've killed the people of Wintersong, *my* people. Burnt them all

to ash…" Ambrosja whispered against Serana's ear, "And for that you will pay." She lifted her sword but stopped when Serana called out.

"It wasn't me!"

Ambrosja paused, not in realization, but calculation. "Oh? Then who?" Her fingers tightened in Serana's hair, pulling at her scalp. "Who?!" Serana didn't answer; maybe it was the pain, or maybe it was hesitation. Ambrosja was at her limit. "Are they worth your life?" She growled.

"Evander Kingsley," the name tumbled out of Serana's lips like a lifeline, "he's a general in the Black Hand. Last I saw him, he was near Greymire." Ambrosja was silent. Then she nodded. Her hand rose with her sword, the edge touching Serana's neck. Serana panicked, "I told you! I gave you his name—" she winced as she felt the faintest cut against her skin.

Ambrosja pulled her sword away and shoved Serana's head forward. "I should kill you…" She stood now. "But instead, I'll leave you alive. So you can go to your precious Grand Marshal *Gaspard Deverux*—" Serana's eyes widened as she looked up at Ambrosja, "—and tell him that I know his name. And I will come for him. And I will come for Evander Kingsley."

She tilted her head then, then. She never smiled once — too much anger, rage, and frustration gnawed at her bones. She just stared at Serana's trapped form.

"Let us hope you can get out of there before wolves — or starvation takes you."

Ambrosja turned to the dark figures. "Ravensworn, return to Hådvard. Let him know what has happened—but warn him to take no action."

The dark figures—the Ravensworn—nodded in unison and shifted into smoke, feathers growing from it as ravens appeared once more, flying high and heading north.

Ambrosja watched them for a moment longer, then looked down the road. Not the road that the wagon had taken. But back from where the wagon had come from. She walked past Serana, past the shouts and demands, and Ambrosja paid her no mind. Her sword was sheathed now, she touched the box once, ensuring it was still there, then grabbed the reins of the horse that once belonged to Cressida, and she mounted onto it. She looked once at Serana, then back again. Back to where she knew Donathan's body had to be.

And so, she gave chase.

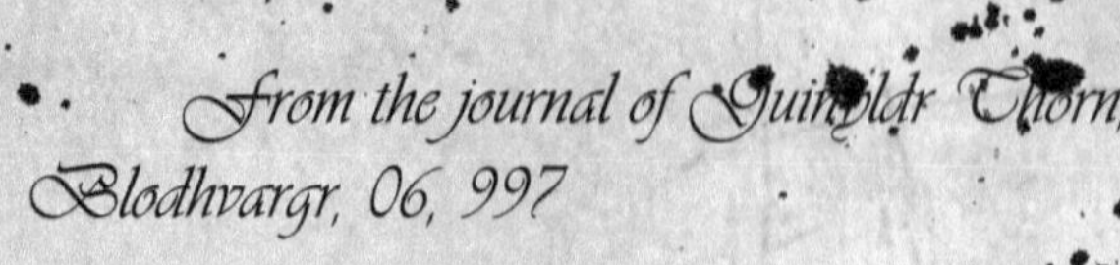

CHAOS MAGIC

Chaos Magic is the eldest and most ruinous of all
known magicks — the current from which creation
itself once sprang, and the force that unmade
it in turn. It is said that even mastery offers
no safety from its reach; every casting
ripples through the world like a stone cast
into the sea, its echoes birthing storms,
quakes, and calamities far beyond the
caster's intent.

For this reason, Chaos Magic is forbidden
across all of Eldorwyn. Only in Nordorn
is its use permitted, and even then, solely
by the hand of the Empress, whose
divine lineage is believed to anchor its
wild design.

Of all the arts, none inspire such fear.
Few dare to study it, and fewer still to wield it,
for the price of Chaos is never measured
in the moment — only in what it
leaves behind.

THE RAVENSWORN

The Ravensworn are said to be born of Chaos itself — sentinels from beyond the Veil, shaped first as ravens   before taking the form of men. They are beings of both shadow and purpose, descending upon the mortal realm with knowledge of warfare already etched into their spirits. Bound not by oath but by origin, they serve a singular charge: to guard the Empress of Nordorn.

In their avian guise, they haunt the skies above her palace and city, silent watchers whose black wings catch no light. In human form, they are imposing and wordless, their loyalty unquestioned yet curiously detached.

The Ravensworn do not serve the crown, nor the woman who bears it—they serve only her existence. What she does, whom she loves, what wars she wages—none of it concerns them.

So long as the Empress draws breath, their purpose endures.

AMBROSIA'S THORNS
BLOODBOUND

She carries a greater weight with her into the
south — the last weight she ever wanted, and one
she refuses to abandon.

Stonehaven rises ahead: a city of stone walls and
sharper tongues, where allies coil like hidden vipers
and whispers cut as clean as blades.

But she will not flinch.
She will not falter.
She will stand, draped in red — the hue of
her crown, her wrath, and every truth that must
be bled out in the days to come.

Ambrosja: (AM-broh-syah), a flower that only blooms in Nordorn and only on the first day of the new year.

Snjorhald: (SNYOR-hald) — Snow Hold, the third month in the Nordorn calendar.

Bjarnvakt: (BYARN-vahkt) — Bear's Vigil, the fourth month in the Nordorn calendar.

Nordorn: (NORR-dorn), the northernmost country in Eldorwyn. // **Nordorner**: (NORR-dor-ner) — Northern // Northerner, someone born in Nordorn. // **Norr**: (NORR) — language of the Nordorners.

Vaestoria: (VAY-stor-ee-uh), a country in the middle of Eldorwyn. // **Vaestorian**: (VAY-stor-ee-uhn), someone born in Vaestoria. // **Vaestorian**: (VAY-stor-ee-uhn) — language of the Vaestorians.

Drakesmoke, a rolled smoking leaf commonly enjoyed by Vaestorian nobles, officers, and scholars, prized for both its ritual significance and its distinctive scent.

Braxia: (brahk-SEE-ah), the northernmost country in Aldorwyn. // **Braxis**: (brahk-SIS), someone born in Braxia.

Hådvard: (HOHD-vahrd)

Nyhralt: (nith-RAU-lt)

Killian: (KILL-ee-uhn), veiled one; protector.

Nattbær: (NAHT-bair) — night berry.

Nordravn: (NORD-rah-vin) — North Raven // Raven of the North

Eldorwyn: (ELL-dor-wen), the continent on the right-hand side of the map.

Vorthunal: (VORR-thu-NAHL), one of the largest dragons of Vaestoria.

Vorthenday: (VORR-then-day), first day of the week in Vaestoria's calendar.

Solgraen: (SOHL-green) — Sun-Green, the fifth month in the Nordorn calendar.

Olyr: (OH-leer), the wisest of dragons of Vaestoria.

Marezora: (Mare-ZOR-ah), the "Mother" dragon of Vaestoria.

Sylaera: (sil-LAY-ruh), the dragon of spring and nature of Vaestoria.

Caeldryss: (KA-elle-driss), the dragon of wit and charm, the most charismatic of Vaestoria.

Nymera: (nee-MEH-rah), the second-toughest dragon, with lava for its blood, the scariest dragon of Vaestoria.

Tharnyx: (thar-NIX), the dragon that is said to bring dreams and bring the sun back into the sky.

Ziraxia: (zee-RAY-ksee-ah), dark essence.

Skeldr: (SKYEL-der)

Olyr's Watch, the Vaestorian name for the fifth day of the week.

Elyra: (ELLE-lie-ruh), the name Vaestoria gives the smaller moon.

Arkenna: (ar-KEN-nuh), the name Vaestoria gives the bigger moon.

Vardmara: (VARD-mah-rah) —Veil Soul // Soul of the Veil, the name Nordorn gives the smaller moon.

Skjoldna: (skee-UHLD-nuh) — Shield Mother, the name Nordorn gives the bigger moon.

Sóleygr: (SOH-lay-grr) — Sun-Eyed, a Nordorner's term of endearment for a loved one.

Ja: (Ya) — Yes // Yeah, in Norr.

So-er: (so)-(ERR) — so, it is // it is, in Norr.

Brynhjora: (BRIN-hyor-ah), the name of the first Empress of Nordorn.

Vaeldorwynn: (VALE-dor-winn), the name of the realm.

Aldorwyn: (ALL-dor-wen), the name of the continent on the left-hand side of the map.

Mercinari: (MUR-see-NAH-ree) the southernmost country of Eldorwyn. // **Mercinaris**: (MUR-see-NAH-rees), someone born in Mercinari. // **Merci**: (MUR-see) — language of the Mercinaris.

Dreknfell: (DRE-kin-fell) — Drake's Crag, the sixth month in Nordorn's calendar.

Sweet-Rot, a Vaestorian term for corny or cliche.

The Veil, where the dead reside—feeding the magical threads of Vaeldorwynn.

Hush and Seek, a game where a selected player must count to an agreed number while others must hide and be quiet to avoid being caught.

Fleet-Touch, a game where a selected player must chase after others, and whoever is touched next, must now chase.

Stonegame, traditional Nordorn games characterized by the use of carved stone pieces as playing tokens atop a flat slate of stone.

Rodvrmane: (RODV-ur-mayn) — Blood Moon, the seventh month in Nordorn's calendar.

Watchstead, A watchstead is a compact outpost of civic authority — part constable's office, part holding block, part administrative nook.

Kjötskalle: (kyut-SKAHL-leh) — Meat skull, idiot. A Nordorn insult.

Scazza: (SKA-zah) — Shit, damn it. A vulgar and offensive word in Mercinari.

Vardvölur: (VARD-vuh-lur) — Veil Witch/Seer, Nordorn's term for someone who is practiced in the magic of the realm.

Dramtis Personae

<table>
<tr><td>NAME</td><td>|</td><td>PRONUNCIATION</td><td>|</td><td>REFERENCE</td></tr>
</table>

Ambrosja: (AM-broh-syah), the Empress, the pale-haired woman

Gunnar: (GUN-nar), the taller man, the old warrior

Cinder: (SIN-der), the huntress

Johann: (yo-HAHN), the older man

Donathan: (DON-uh-thin), the young mage, the young man, the fire mage

Hådvard: (HOHD-vahrd), the warrior

Killian: (KILL-ee-uhn), the Commander, the Black Hand Commander

Berric: (BEHR-ik), the Lieutenant

Jareth: (JAIR-eth), the Diplomat

Varian: (VAIR-ee-an), the Marshal

Oswin: (OZ-win), the Reeve

Rosalind: (ROZ-uh-lind), the Treasurer

Emeric: (EM-er-ik), the Cultural Steward, the Steward

Mira: (MEE-ruh), the Court Advocate, the Advocate

Aaric: (AIR-ik), the High Regent

Lyra: (LIE-ruh), the young sorceress, the sorceress

Isolde: (IH-sold)

Evander: (eh-VAN-der), the General, the Black Hand General

Ziraxia: (zee-RAY-ksee-ah), the dark sorceress, the sorceress

Gaspard: (gas-PAR), the Grand Marshal

Serana: (seh-RAH-nuh), the Sister-Hand

Cressida: (KRESS-ih-duh)

Yrsa: (EER-sah), the Empress Mother

Vidar: (VEE-dar)

Brynhjora: (BRIN-hyor-ah), the Empress Eternal

Thora: (THOR-uh)

ACKNOWLEDGMENTS

Thank you to those who let me ramble about my worlds, my characters, and every idea that kept me awake at night. Thank you to those who kept believing in me, even when I felt like giving up.

Along this journey, I learned that there truly is power in every word. So, to everyone who offered honesty and kindness as you read through the rougher versions of this story... thank you, your words shaped me and in turn shaped my story.

Thank you to David,
You supported me through so much while I chased after every dream I had. I wouldn't be where I am without you.

And thank you, Papai — my Dad,
You believed in me since I was a little girl, through every wrong turn, every doubt, and every moment I thought I couldn't do it. Your faith in me was never shaken, and because of that... I found my way back.

Born in the United States and raised in Brazil, Alisbeth Vale taught herself English at eleven simply so she could read the stories she loved. Writing followed naturally after that—and never really stopped. She fills notebooks with imagined worlds and stubborn characters, often as a way to make sense of the real one. When life grows loud, she returns to the page, where characters come to life again.

Ambrosja's Thorns: Ashbound is Alisbeth's debut novel, her invitaiton to adventure, and her series, Ambrosja's Thorns is her love letter to readers who crave deep journeys and deeper character journeys; from messy humanity to slow-burning danger.

Alisbeth is endlessly grateful for every reader who steps into her world.

THE AUTHOR'S PERSONAL NOTE, *the meal*

If you've reached this section before beginning the story—or if you are returning to it—I would like to offer a simple suggestion.
Ambrosja's Thorns: Ashbound is a tale meant to be read warm and full. If you are able, I recommend a bowl of corned beef and cabbage with potatoes—something hearty, humble, and grounding.
Should that not be available, a thick beef stew will serve just as well, heavy with carrots and potatoes, the sort of meal you might eat beside a campfire while snow drifts quietly beyond the light.

THE AUTHOR'S PERSONAL NOTE, *the music*

If you have reached this note before finishing the book, I gently urge you turn back, adventurer.
But if you have come to this page having completed Ashbound, there is one song I hold close to this story. One that speaks to it so intimately that it aches in my bones in a way I cannot fully explain.
Please listen to **"I'm Not Calling You a Liar"** by *Florence & The Machine* — the *Dragon Age* remix.

Published works and updates:
@alisbethvale
alisbethvale.com